THANK YOU

A donation has been made on your behalf for purchasing a new copy of *The Choice: Death Is Just The Beginning* to help alleviate the suffering of abused children all across the globe.

Together, we can make a difference.

—Slade Combs

THE CHOICE

THE CHOICE
DEATH IS JUST THE BEGINNING

A NOVEL BY SLADE COMBS

THE NEW YORK
STANDARD PRESS

Published by The New York Standard Press, Inc.

This is a work of fiction. The characters, incidents, and dialogue are products of the author's imagination and not to be construed as real. Any resemblance to actual persons, living or dead, is entirely coincidental.

Criteria for Dissociative Identity Disorder reprinted with permission from the Diagnostic and Statistical Manual of Mental Disorders, Fifth Edition, (Copyright 2013). American Psychiatric Association.

Scripture quotations are taken from the King James version of the Bible. Public domain.
"On Another's Sorrow" by William Blake, 1789. Public domain.
"The Anathemas Against Origen," Fifth Ecumenical Council, 553. Public domain.

Edited by NY Book Editors nybookeditors.com. Jesse Coleman.
Copyedited by Martha Cameron and David Coen.
Cover art by Ivo Horvat.

ISBN: 978-1-942224-89-1

Printed in the United States of America

FIRST PAPERBACK EDITION

1 2 3 4 5 6 7 8 9 0

For Andrea:
my best friend, wife, and guardian angel.

Sad task and hard, for how shall I relate
To human sense the invisible exploits
Of warring spirits . . .

—Milton, *Paradise Lost*

NOTES

INVISIBLE MATTER & HIDDEN DIMENSIONS

On July 4, 2012, the existence of the Higgs boson was detected at the Large Hadron Collider (LHC) at CERN—an event marking the dawn of what some have called a new era in physics. Hypothesized to exist in 1964, this previously held theoretical particle was under particular scrutiny because it was said to be hidden in an invisible field of energy with a physical composition unlike anything known to science.

The LHC has since undergone extensive upgrades in hopes of finding more hidden particles, especially those fundamental to leading theoretical frameworks such as string theory. If found, these particles would not only peel back yet another invisible layer of reality, but also uncover the existence of unseen dimensions hidden all around us.

In short, if there is something science has to say about our universe, it is perhaps that there is far more out there than we have ever previously imagined.

THE ANATHEMAS AGAINST ORIGEN
FIFTH ECUMENICAL COUNCIL–CONSTANTINOPLE, 553 A.D.

I.

If anyone asserts the fabulous [feigned] pre-existence of souls . . . : let him be anathema.

VI.

If anyone shall say that there is a twofold race of demons, of which the one includes the souls of men and the other the superior spirits who fell . . . : let him be anathema.

DISSOCIATIVE IDENTITY DISORDER
DIAGNOSTIC AND STATISTICAL MANUAL OF MENTAL DISORDERS,
FIFTH EDITION (DSM-5). AMERICAN PSYCHIATRIC ASSOCIATION.

Dissociative identity disorder is associated with overwhelming experiences, traumatic events, and/or abuse occurring in childhood. The full disorder may first manifest at almost any age (from earliest childhood to late life).

Individuals with dissociative identity disorder may report the feeling that they have suddenly become depersonalized observers of their own speech and actions, which they may feel powerless to stop. Such individuals may also report perceptions of voices. In some cases, voices are experienced as multiple, perplexing, independent thought streams over which the individual experiences no control.

The dissociative amnesia of individuals with dissociative identity disorder manifests in three primary ways: as 1) gaps in remote memory of personal life events; 2) lapses in dependable memory; and 3) discovery of evidence of their everyday actions and tasks that they do not recollect doing.

Many individuals with dissociative identity disorder report dissociative flashbacks during which they undergo a sensory reliving of a previous event as though it were occurring in the present, often with a change of identity, a partial or complete loss of contact with or disorientation to current reality during the flashback, and a subsequent amnesia for the content of the flashback. Individuals with the disorder typically report multiple types of interpersonal maltreatment during childhood and adulthood.

Interpersonal physical and sexual abuse is associated with an increased risk of dissociative identity disorder. Prevalence of childhood abuse and neglect in the United States, Canada, and Europe among those with the disorder is about 90%.

AUTHOR'S NOTE

All works of art, artifacts, descriptive plaques, museums, and historical figures referenced in this novel are real.

PROLOGUE

THE DARK-HAIRED MAN WALKED OVER TO HIM, HOLDING a black plastic garbage bag in one hand. He stooped down, placed the bag by his side, and looked at the boy of five.

"We're going to play a game."

The child nodded in hesitant agreement. The man pointed at the door behind him.

"She's going to come out here and get into this bag."

He lifted the bag and opened it to show the small empty space inside.

"When she gets in, you're going to help me tie a knot in the top, and then I want you to hold it like this."

The man gathered the top of the bag in one hand and held it tight in his fist, his knuckles turning white.

"And then I'm going to see how long it takes you to get her to go to sleep."

A look of fear suddenly appeared in the boy's eyes.

"Don't worry, she's not going to get hurt," the man said. "We just need her to forget a few things. If you help me to get her to go to sleep, she won't have to worry about remembering anymore. You understand, right?"

Staring at the man in silence, the boy suddenly began to whimper.

The man grabbed the boy forcefully, yanking his arm. Realizing that he may have frightened the child, after a moment or two, he loosened up on his grip.

"Sorry, I didn't mean to grab you like that," he said, "but you need to calm down. You're going to hurt yourself again if you can't calm down."

He paused, making sure the boy was still listening.

"Are you okay?"

The boy sniffed, trying hard to control his watery eyes.

"We're buddies, right?"

The child nodded.

"You don't want them to take me away, do you?"

The boy looked up, the fear of loss suddenly on his face.

"If you play this game with me, you won't have to worry about that. We can be together forever."

The man leaned in to wipe a few tears from the child's eyes.

"Don't worry, everything will be okay," he explained. "I just need your help. It won't take long."

The man lifted the boy's chin.

"Can you do this for me? Can you be brave?"

The boy sat staring, unresponsive.

"It's the only way we can all stay together. That's what you want, right?"

The boy nodded.

"That's what I want too," the man said with a smile. "Don't worry, I won't let anything bad happen to you. I love you."

He gently squeezed the child in a fatherly embrace. Kissing him on the head, the man then loosened his grip and pulled back to look at him.

The child's tear-soaked eyes glanced from the man down to the plastic bag.

A wicked smile slowly grew on the man's face. He turned to the doorway behind him and shouted.

"Lily, come here. Charlie has a game he wants to play."

———

An alarm rang out. The young man shot up in his bed. The sheets were soaked with sweat. His breathing was erratic, and his head started to spin with a sudden nauseating jolt.

"It was a dream," he said to himself frantically, darting his eyes around the dark room to see what had woken him up.

The only reply was the sound of his alarm, piercing the silence.

Beeeep.

Beeeep.

Beeeep.

He felt his body trembling.

Beeeep.

Beeeep.

"Please, God . . . oh, God, please . . ."

His stomach suddenly lurched and vomit came spewing from his mouth.

1

THE SAND WAS AS BLACK AS MIDNIGHT. EACH DARK
crystal clung to the feet of the two young men as they approached
the shore.

"Beautiful," Chris mused, looking into the distance at the powerful crashing waves.

"Mhmm," Jonas replied while looking around, somewhat taken in
by the luster of the green coconut trees that flanked the beach. His
eyes followed their coarse brown trunks to the black volcanic sand.
Placing his surfboard carefully on the ground, he sat down.

Looking at his feet, Jonas noticed how the crystals of sand stuck
to his skin, a fragmented mosaic set against a canvas of pale flesh.
Each particle looked clean, smooth, shaped by the constant erosion
of the tides. He picked up a handful and rubbed it between his fingers, observing the dark contrast against his white skin. His fingers
were whiter than usual today. His blood was running thin with the
thought of the waves they were about to ride—waves that were
much larger than any he had attempted before, waves that silently
terrified him.

"Whaddaya say?" Chris smiled as he looked at a wave crashing on
the razor-sharp coral reef below.

"There's a first for everything, I guess," Jonas said.

While looking up to observe the waves in the distance, Jonas tried
hard to hide his fear from his companion. Learning to surf had been
a passion of his ever since his family began visiting Maui when he
was a child, but he couldn't forget the time when, at the age of
twelve, he had tried to surf alone. The experience left him with two
scraping reef scars on his back. He flinched as he remembered the
tumbling, relentless motion when the wave overcame him that day.

His lanky, prepubescent body was thrown from the safety of his surf-board into the plunging depths below. He had once heard a statistic about waves having as much as six thousand pounds of pressure per square foot. Looking at the waves today, he wished that he had never learned that bit of information.

"It's going to be awesome," Jonas said halfheartedly in an attempt to convince himself. As always, he waited for his companion to make the first move.

"Looks like we should be safer over there." Chris pointed, speaking confidently for his friend's sake.

As much as Jonas had tried in the past to mask his fear of surfing, Chris had surfed with him too many times to be unaware of Jonas's shaky hands when it came time to put on their ankle straps. Strapping on the leash was the final act before walking into the water, so Chris would usually say something encouraging at this point to put Jonas's mind at ease—how safe they would be if they took a certain route or how warm the water felt even when the initial icy sting was enough to take their breath away. But Chris knew his courage was easily gained, since he had no permanent scars on his back.

The two stood up with their surfboards under their arms and began walking to the water's edge. Their footsteps left imprints on the sand as they made their way together.

Jonas could feel his heart beating in his chest as he listened to the crushing waves in the distance. He was always ashamed that he still felt nervous every time they reached this point. He had once tried to get rid of his fear at a tropical "Surf Camp" he took with Chris and a group of their buddies in Costa Rica; but somehow the camp only taught him to ride bigger, stronger, fiercer waves.

"The water's perfect," Chris announced.

Jonas had heard a comment like that many times before, but this time when he felt the glassy sheet of liquid rush over his feet, he agreed. Taking courage, he walked cautiously into the dark blue water and slapped his board down onto the surface.

Taking in a breath, he lunged facedown onto the board and began paddling out into the ocean.

The water was warmer than usual today, but still cool to the touch. He stroked on either side of his board, propelling himself forward. He could feel the wind now whipping at his neck in uneven swells as the heat of the sun relaxed the muscles in his back. The tension he had carried while walking into the water was now beginning to vanish as his muscle memory began to take over. As athletes in college, both he and Chris experienced subtle mnemonic effects similar to this while running hurdles together. That's actually how they had met. They were paired together as training partners and spent countless hours on drills in the dry heat of the noonday sun. In the afternoon, they would head to the weight room for an hour or so of weightlifting. While the work was hard, and often tedious, it all paid off when it came time to race. Their conditioning had a way of kicking in the minute the gun fired, and they were able to let their bodies take over, doing most of the work. In fact, the effects of conditioning were so instinctual that Jonas actually had a hard time remembering most of his races. He could remember the gun firing, a moment or two if he bumped a hurdle with his leg or if he received an elbow from a competitor, and then the finish line. Not much else. But, for whatever reason, he couldn't quite get to that place on a surfboard.

A salty splash suddenly hit Jonas in the face, bringing him back to the present. He lifted his head a bit and spat the swill back into the water. The strong taste of the ocean still took him by surprise. On occasion, it had filled his nasal cavities to overflowing as he had been tossed into what surfers call the "washing machine," the violent chamber created when the peak of the wave crashes down on itself. Any surfer caught in it soon finds himself holding his breath against the clock as his body is tossed about.

Be strong! he thought to himself, increasing the speed and depth of each stroke. He pushed harder now, lifting his feet so they wouldn't drag behind him, preparing himself for the set of waves that he would have to break through in order to clear his way into the open area where he could safely wait to catch a wave.

He looked up. A small yet menacing-looking wave was coming

his way. Instinctively, he grabbed the front of his board and pushed himself under the water so as to pass safely beneath its tumultuous grip.

Whooosh! A clear rushing sound became an echo chamber of deep vibrations as his head plunged under the wave and into the water. Jonas could feel the strength of the wave rush over the top of his back as it passed. Feeling the pull of the water at his feet, he raised his head and popped back up safely to the surface.

Three more waves to go, he thought to himself with a new determination. Since waves come to the shore in multiple sets, Jonas knew he wasn't out of danger quite yet.

It wasn't the fear of the wave that frightened Jonas; it was being tethered to the surfboard. After his accident as a boy, he had determined to face his fear by ditching the board and learning how to bodysurf. He was somewhat surprised to discover that when he was not connected to a large piece of floating fiberglass, he had more freedom to move about. He could swim deeper under the waves, avoiding their neck-breaking strength. He also felt more agile, because he wasn't trying to move what felt like a ball and chain across the water's surface. His legs had always been much stronger than his arms, and when swimming, he could use them to propel his body through the treacherous watery terrain. He felt surprisingly at home in the ocean as long as he wasn't tied to a cumbersome board. But right now he happened to have one strapped around his ankle.

Kaboom!

This time the wave hit with much more force, pulling Jonas back and interrupting his progress. He had been so busy thinking about how much he wanted to ditch his board that he was caught off guard by the impending wave, failing to dive deep enough to escape its frothy strength.

C'mon! Jonas chided himself while being jostled about under the wave.

He popped up again, this time taking precise note of his surroundings. Getting back on his board, he began pumping his arms faster so as to catch up to Chris a few body lengths away. Jonas usually struggled when they paddled out together; his arms were more slender than Chris's. There were times when he had to give up completely and turn around because he had expended all his energy fruitlessly trying to get past the breaking waves. He couldn't think of a time when he hadn't been out of breath from the ordeal. Even though he was still in great shape, the endurance he once had in his college days had been diminished by long hours in an office on Madison Avenue.

Listening to the rumbling in the distance, Jonas looked ahead and saw another white wall coming his way. His shoulders strained as he tried to build up speed so he wouldn't be forced backward if he collided with the wave.

Smaaash!

The wall hit him head-on, tossing his board from underneath him and setting him back several body lengths of hard-earned progress.

He was now a good twenty feet behind Chris, with another wave headed his way. He was going to have to sprint to avoid being pushed back again.

Getting back on his board, he took a deep breath and began paddling faster. He could see the wave building in the distance, which triggered him to exert even more force. But with every stroke, he felt his muscles strain. His mind was quick, but his body was having a hard time keeping up.

"Hurry!" Chris yelled from somewhere in the distance.

Jonas's muscles burned as he began paddling with a new sense of determination. He wasn't going to get caught in the wave no matter how bad it hurt. It was just a question of mind over matter, and he was going to force his body to listen to the logic of his mind.

Faster and faster he paddled, with the burning sensation in his shoulders slowly moving into his back. His body was reluctant, but the thought of being tossed around in the washing machine was frightening enough to keep him churning. As the burning began to turn into sharp pinpoint stings, his lungs started to grow heavy with each breath. He knew all he had to do was pass this wave and rest would be waiting on the other side. Looking up, he drew an imaginary finish line floating safely in the distance beyond the impending danger and pushed toward it.

Feverishly paddling against the strain, Jonas saw the wave begin to break. The rays of the sun shining through its peak made it look like a translucent skyscraper about to collapse. Taking two more excruciating strokes, Jonas held his breath and dove down into the safety of the water below.

He heard a thunderous roar overhead. He could feel the pull of the wave on his legs, the suction of the water tugging at the leash strapped to his ankle. But he had spent his energy wisely, escaping the wave's grip at the very last moment. Passing safely beneath it, he took a second to enjoy his small victory before pointing his head back toward the surface.

He felt the warmth of the sun kiss his back again, a reassurance that everything would be calm, at least for a bit. He took note of his arms. Straining to get to safety had taken its toll. He could feel a mixture of dull and sharp pains in his muscles. He would need the next few minutes to rest while they waited for another set of waves to come in.

"Not bad, huh!" Chris smiled as he sat upright on his board.

Jonas coughed. "That was close back there."

"Yeah, I thought you were going to get smacked by that last one."

Chris looked up as a black-necked stilt flew overhead.

"Man, it's beautiful out here," he said.

Jonas sat upright, wiping away the water that stung his eyes as he looked around.

The sky was clear blue, with only a few tufts of clouds coming from the east. The sun sparkled as it hit the water, dancing about like a thousand fragments in a prism. Jonas looked back to where they had been sitting on the beach, where silky black sand met enormous towering cliffs. Their still-visible footprints led toward a set of tall coconut trees swaying in the wind. Their rhythmic rocking brought him a sense of peace that was a welcome respite from his thumping heart. All around them was tranquility and ease. Jonas's pulse slowed as he watched the water slowly wash up onto the black shore.

Heaven, he whispered to himself. The beauty of this island had a way of transforming him. He loved coming back to this place, his home away from home.

"When do you think your parents are going to get here?" Chris asked, no doubt as an attempt to keep Jonas's thoughts off the waves that would inevitably come.

"I think they fly in around three."

"Are your brothers and sisters coming?"

"Unless they miss their flight again."

Jonas smiled at the thought of his brothers and sisters coming to meet them. Even though Jonas felt more himself with Chris, he had to admit that having everyone around was more fun. In some ways Chris was more of a brother to him than any of his siblings, but that didn't stem from any kind of resentment or rivalry. It was just that Jonas's personality was very different from his brothers' and sisters'. His parents tried to convince him that it was simply because he was more "introspective" or "contemplative" than they were, but he knew the truth to the difference was in his eyes. His eyes were blue; everyone else in his family had brown eyes.

"What about Sarah?"

Jonas's countenance lit up, but he contained his impulse to smile overtly. "She'll be with them," he said.

"You gonna pop the question?" Chris chuckled, half serious.

Jonas shrugged his shoulders to keep Chris's attention away from his blushing face.

"That ring I've got in my suitcase is going to be a big waste if I don't," he replied.

"Serious?"

Jonas looked ahead and grinned without saying a word.

"Wow," Chris said, "and to think that I made out with her just last week . . ."

Jonas turned and began to splash Chris in the face as his friend burst out laughing and fell off his board.

"All right, all right!" Chris laughed as his head bobbed in and out of the water.

Jonas gave him a few more sprays before helping him back up.
"You're really serious though?" Chris asked again.

"It's not like she's said yes yet," Jonas replied. "She could say no."

"You gotta be kidding me," Chris chuckled. "If you guys don't get married, there's definitely no hope for the rest of us."

Jonas smiled as he listened to the confidence in his friend's voice. It was true though. At times it seemed like he and Sarah were meant for each other, but Jonas sometimes wondered if he was good enough for her. She was just so honest, so cheerful and kind. Of course, he never actually expressed his doubts to her for fear of reprimand, but she just had an uncanny way of bringing out the best in him. And while he was still not the man he felt she deserved, he hoped that she might give him a chance to spend the rest of his life trying, with a ring around her finger.

Jonas felt a splash of water in his face, bringing him back from his thoughts.

"Hey! You can pick out your wedding colors later," Chris said before pointing into the distance. "Right now, you better get to focusing on that."

Jonas turned to look. A wave was approaching in the distance that set his heart racing once again. He took in a deep breath and drew a mental line to his destination. Shifting his weight to the back of his board, he lay with his chest flat against it.

No worries, he whispered to himself as he tried to visualize Sarah's soft red hair. He loved her hair—how it flowed over her shoulders in just such a way that made her look like a model in one of those catalogs people never seem to throw away. He would tell her that from time to time, especially when he got caught staring at her from across the room. But of course, that would only make her blush, which Jonas loved even more.

"Hey!" Chris yelled. "Wake up."

Chris had already paddled two body lengths ahead of Jonas in preparation for the next wave. Getting in the right position was half the art of surfing, as Jonas well knew. Gathering his thoughts again, Jonas obeyed his friend. Plunging his hands into the surface of the dark reflective liquid, he pulled himself along. He wasn't going to get caught this time.

The two paddled themselves into position. A set of four waves began to form, with the closest one coming fast.

"You want this one?" Chris yelled.

Jonas looked back at the wave. It was growing, mounting in the distance.

"Yeah," he shot back.

While the wave evoked a genuine sense of fear, Jonas had learned from experience that the first wave of any set is generally the smallest. Armed with that information, he usually tried to go first.

Maneuvering into position, he began to feel the strain of his paddle out, realizing he was more out of breath than he should be. His shortness of breath could have been from fear, exhaustion, or just plain anticipation: he couldn't tell. But he knew he wouldn't last very long if he got caught inside the washing machine.

"Go! Go!" Chris shouted as he grabbed Jonas's board, pointing it toward the beach. Surprised by the sudden movement, Jonas slipped a bit but steadied himself and thrust the board forward with everything he had. Faster and faster he plunged his hands into the water. His muscles strained and his heart pounded. In the midst of his thrashing he felt the back of his board lift, his cue to stand up. He put his hands directly beneath his chest, ready to pop up into full stance—but suddenly he felt the board beneath his feet begin to tip back down again as the giant swell passed underneath him.

He had missed it.

"Get back! Get back!" he heard Chris yell. He turned to look as an even larger swell was beginning to form. Spurred by panic, he rotated his board back toward the wave and began to paddle. If he could get to it before it broke, he would be close enough to go over it. If not, this wave could very well throw him backward onto the coral reef below, holding him down for the next two waves to smother him.

He pounded the water harder, his muscles tensing with each stroke. The water felt nearly solid as he slapped it fiercely with nothing but his pelvis and thighs still touching the board. Looking up, he saw Chris turning his board around to catch the wave.

Fighting for his life as he moved toward the wave, Jonas felt the entire board suddenly lift to a near vertical position, forcing his eyes heavenward and his feet straight down. The wave was cresting, and the momentum he had built was the only thing that would stop him from flipping backward and getting caught in the violent turbulence that would inevitably ensue. He reached desperately with an outstretched hand and grabbed the very top edge of the wave, ripping through it in a last-ditch effort to pull himself over. Spray went flying in his face as he saw a thin sheet of water come over the top of his board, forcing him to shut his eyes. Then he felt himself fall forward, carried by his momentum up and over the top of the wave.

As he clung to his board, his fall ended with a loud *slap* against the water. His chest rammed hard against the fiberglass board—it felt like belly flopping onto solid concrete. But he had shot himself over the top of the wave, out of its dangerous reach. Although momentarily relieved, he looked back up only to see the next wave coming his way. He wouldn't have much time to celebrate his feat if he was going to avoid disaster.

Taking a breath, he gritted his teeth. *Strong!* he said in his mind as a new surge of adrenaline rushed though his veins. The next wave was already coming in quickly, building in speed and force. He shot his hands back into the water, doing his best to ignore the shooting pains in his shoulders and back. As he paddled closer to the wave, he felt the nose of his board being lifted again by its rapidly approaching base. He rose with it, higher this time, but not as vertical as the last wave. He was clearing it, but not by much.

As the wave crested, he found himself directly on top of it, looking fifteen feet down in all directions. To the side he could see the length of the swell running parallel with the beach. In front he could see the surprisingly low level of the ocean beneath, almost as if he were peering off the edge of a cliff. Behind, he caught a glimpse of Chris riding his wave to shore.

As Jonas continued to paddle, he felt the momentum of the swell being sucked away beneath his board. The next wave was approaching, but he knew he would be safe. The distance he had made up was enough to keep himself from being hit, but that didn't hide the pain he now felt in his muscles. He began to wonder if he should just call it a day.

Passing safely up and over the last swell, he took a moment to catch his breath. He pushed himself up to sit on his board while wincing at the pain. Looking back, he saw Chris's fist raised in triumph. Jonas couldn't help but be a little envious of how easy surfing was for his friend. Chris was built broader across the chest and had much more muscle definition in his arms, which made every one of his strokes count for two of Jonas's. But most of all, there was a certain confidence that followed Chris wherever he went; a belief that he could overcome any obstacle that came his way.

Jonas felt ashamed of his thoughts, though he had felt this way many times before. Usually this feeling of envy came over him in social situations. When they both went to a party, Jonas would inevitably end up sitting on the couch while Chris told engaging stories that would keep the whole room entertained. As much as Jonas loved his friend, he couldn't help but be a little jealous. People loved Chris. He had an innate charisma that drew people to him. From time to time, Jonas tried to mimic his personality, but it never really worked. Charisma wasn't something you could train like a muscle.

If Jonas was really honest with himself, though, he knew it wasn't his friend's charm that upset him. Rather, it was Chris's family situation that made Jonas envious. He told himself over and over that it didn't matter, but he couldn't get over the fact that Chris's parents were his biological ones—which meant that no one had ever wanted to give him up. Jonas was adopted, and although he knew the thought was silly, he couldn't seem to get over the fact that someone somewhere apparently didn't love him enough to keep him. Chris never had to think about anything like that, which is why Jonas knew this was the real reason for his envy.

"That was nuts, right?" Jonas heard Chris yell.

Jonas couldn't help but smile as he watched his friend paddle back, excited to share the experience. That was the other thing about Chris. Even when he did something that made Jonas envious, he had a way of making Jonas feel like he was a part of it. That's why he could never really be mad at his friend. Put simply, Chris was a good person, and Jonas realized that the contention in their relationship, if there was any, was mostly in his own head.

"Nice job!"

While Chris paddled toward him, Jonas took another moment to look around again at the beauty that surrounded them. The clear sky. The birds soaring through the air. The smooth cliffs that seemed to tower over the beach. It was the perfect place for two people to be alone. Too bad he was enjoying it with Chris instead of Sarah. He could hardly wait for her to arrive. He knew Chris would understand, making himself scarce for an hour or two while he spent some alone time with her. His friend would, of course, start a rousing game with the rest of Jonas's family to divert their attention from his and Sarah's absence. Envious as Jonas was of Chris's talents, they did come in handy every so often.

"You almost had that one!" Chris yelled, paddling closer.

"Yeah, I just . . ." Jonas looked at his hands as if there were something mechanically wrong with them.

"Seriously, you almost had it," Chris said again, now just a few yards away. "You just needed an extra push, and you would have been over that thing."

"I'm just glad I missed the one you caught," Jonas replied.

"That was huge, right?" Chris said with a smile. "I saw you going straight up out of the corner of my eye. I wanted to look, but I would have fallen off my board. Did you fly off the other side?"

"Big time—it hurt like a mother when I landed."

Chris clapped his hands together loudly as if to illustrate what it must have felt like to hit the water after falling from such a height. They both laughed.

"That was an awesome wave you caught though," Jonas said.

"Oh, yeah. That was pretty crazy. I'm glad I popped up right. I was a little off balance."

"You got up, though. Almost made it look easy."

Chris chuckled, "Yeah." He pointed behind Jonas's head. "We got to get you up on this one, though."

Jonas followed Chris's finger to a new set of waves beginning to form in the distance.

"You've got this one," Chris said encouragingly. "I know it."

Turning his board to look at the new set of waves, Jonas felt the same sinking sensation in his stomach. His swelling heartbeat began to close off his throat with each *tha-thump* in his chest. But he wasn't going to give in to it, he told himself. He was going to face his fear, even if it killed him.

2

JONAS BEGAN PADDLING TOWARD THE WAVES IN THE distance. He stroked the water slowly at first, deliberately, calculating the best angle at which to approach.

"You got it!" he heard Chris yell.

Paddling faster, he began to focus on a point in front of him where he would be in the best position to catch the first wave. Reaching the spot, he took in a breath and then spun his board around to face the shore in preparation for what was to come.

"You got this one!" Chris yelled, as he paddled beside Jonas into position.

You can do this, Jonas whispered to himself. He looked back, seeing the wave grow behind him. Glancing toward the beach, he began to stroke his hands into the water. A rush of adrenaline spread through his system, igniting his muscles to react with surprising strength. Plunging his hands into the water, he gritted his teeth with every painful stroke. He looked back. The swell was preparing to peak.

Staring back down at his board, Jonas focused all his attention and energy on his arms. He paddled faster, becoming more afraid with each stroke that his shoulders would give out if he had to go much farther. The sharp pains were replaced by a deep burning sensation that told him he only had a few moments left before his upper body would be rendered completely useless. He wheezed as he tried breathing deeper in an attempt to get oxygen to his starving muscles, but it had little effect. He pushed harder with his hands in preparation for the moment when he needed to stand up on his board. But when that moment came, he felt the wave beginning to pass beneath him. Desperately he struggled, punching through the surface of the water, straining every muscle to make himself go faster.

Then, from behind, he felt a sudden push on his board, just enough to get him in front of the wave where he could stand up. Instinctively he popped up in position, caught his balance, and, almost in disbelief, saw himself rushing toward the bottom of the wave.

It was then that he felt it—the adrenaline and exhilaration that can only be experienced while gliding smoothly across the surface of the water. The wind against his face, the shimmering smoothness of the sun's rays as they reflected across the glassy liquid. He looked at the water and noticed how quickly it ran underneath his board, almost as if he were the one standing still, a blue highway whizzing beneath his feet.

He leaned slightly to the left at first, feeling the board's agreeable reaction. He then leaned a little to the right, confident in his control. The small push Chris had given him was all that he had needed to experience the joy he felt. Looking up at the beach, he saw the beautiful black sand and the trees swaying sweetly in the breeze. His pains were all but forgotten as a surge of pleasure spread across his entire body. He would have pinched himself to make sure he wasn't dreaming, if doing so wouldn't have caused him to lose his balance. But there was no need for that. He was awake, and alive— never more so than at this moment. Every sensation in his body was singing together in harmony, lifting him higher, pushing him farther along the blissful blue water.

Then, in that moment, he thought of Sarah. How he wished that she could be there, watching from the beach, clapping her hands in excitement. Her smile, her happiness, would make this experience complete.

Jonas felt himself slow up a bit. The wave was reducing in size as it moved closer to shore. Pulled from his thoughts, he concentrated on staying balanced so he could squeeze every last ounce of pleasure from the ride.

"Yeahhhh!" he heard Chris yell from behind him.

Riding a few more yards, Jonas saw that it was time to come to a stop. He either had to turn around or jump off his board. Too tired to paddle back yet, he leapt, landing safely in the shallow water. Feeling full of accomplishment, he took a moment to catch his breath. He was winded, but his lungs felt stronger. His heart was pounding, but pounding in joy. His arms, though—they just plain hurt. It was going to take a while before they were up to the task of going back out.

Yes! he whispered to himself.

Excited to see his friend catch his next wave, Jonas turned back toward the open ocean. As he did, he saw Chris waving enthusiastically. But as Jonas raised his own hand to wave back, he noticed a huge swell growing behind Chris's back. It was moving rapidly, with his friend oblivious to the fact that it was almost upon him.

"Chris!"

The monstrous wave was closing in. Chris, still unaware, continued waving.

"Turn around!" Jonas yelled.

Still not able to hear over the sound of the ocean, Chris gave him a thumbs-up.

"No! *Behind you!*"

Jonas was no longer yelling though—he was now on the verge of screaming as he frantically waved his arms toward the monstrous wave. Chris still couldn't hear him. Instead he looked as if he were trying to figure out why Jonas had become so animated all of a sudden.

But then, something must have clicked, because Chris turned to look behind him. The wave was too close. There was no way he could escape it.

In desperation, Chris began to paddle furiously on his board in the direction of the beach, but the wave's suction had already begun to counteract his efforts. Even though he was paddling frantically with every bit of strength he had, he was making no progress. He was quickly being pulled into the wave's unrelenting grasp.

"PUSH!" Jonas screamed. His every muscle was tense. He was completely focused on watching what was happening to his friend. Chris was being sucked up into a wave larger than either of them had ever surfed before, and Jonas could do nothing but watch his friend's frenzied movements as they both realized what was about to happen.

The wave crested, a white translucent peak forming just at the top. Chris had now been pulled so far back he was nearly vertical, halfway up the wave with his head pointing straight toward the bottom. The force of the water was so strong, there was nothing he could do at this point but to hold on to his board and prepare for the wave to crash.

Jonas watched in horror as the wave broke and flipped his friend—board and all—upside down into the air. It happened in an instant, but watching him drop twenty feet seemed to take an eternity.

Thick foam erupted with an explosive *BOOM* as the wave collapsed into itself, leaving a frothy mound in its place. Jonas knew that Chris was being tossed in the washing machine—his body hurled in every conceivable direction, each limb feeling as if it were being torn from his frame. Jonas silently hoped that his friend would be able to keep a safe distance from his board, so as not to get hit in the head and drown.

Searching the foam for a sign of what to do next, Jonas saw a board shoot halfway out of the water in the distance. But just when he thought he should see Chris's body popping up after it, the board was pulled unnaturally back into the water.

He gasped as he watched the tip of the board bob up and down in the water like a cork, a phenomenon surfers often called "tombstoning." Something was pulling on the board from below, and Jonas knew it was Chris. For some reason, his friend wasn't coming to the surface. A surfboard of that size, as buoyant as it was, could easily pull both of them upward. But there was something down there, something that was keeping Chris from coming up.

Without thinking, Jonas dove into the water. He knew he only had a minute or two before Chris's lungs would burn so deeply that they would give out. He only got a few feet, before he felt a sudden tug on his ankle from behind. He screamed bubbles of frustration under the water as he realized that he was still tethered to his board. He knew he had to untie himself from the cumbersome object if there was any chance at getting out to Chris in time.

He scrambled underwater, feeling for his own foot, ripping at the Velcro that held him. He tore the strap from his ankle, freeing him from the board. He popped his head back up for a quick breath of air as he searched frantically for where Chris's surfboard was bobbing in the distance.

GO! Jonas screamed to himself as he dove back into the water. His legs kicked feverishly against the current. His arms, although spent, found a burst of strength. Interestingly, his mind became suddenly still, as if he were working out of pure instinct, if it could be called that. Time seemed intangible. He wasn't sure if everything was happening in a single instant or if the seconds were pouring out slowly like honey from a jar. A sense of being, of existence, was all he could feel as he moved quickly across the water. The roaring of the waves was nothing more than silent whispers in his ears. His body shut out any sensation that didn't affect his mission to save his drowning friend.

Resurfacing for air, Jonas saw the bobbing surfboard only a few feet in front of him. He looked below the water for any sign of Chris. Seeing the faint, blurry outline of a figure below, he grabbed on to the leash connected to the back of the board, took a breath, and dove headfirst into the abyss.

The salt water stung as he opened his eyes. He pulled himself down with the aid of the leash toward his friend, and the water grew colder and colder. This was a circumstance he had never been in before; instinct and muscle memory weren't going to get him out of this situation. He was going to have to think quickly, rationally.

He continued to pull himself downward feeling the pressure of the water push painfully against his ears. The liquid around him became dark against the black sand below. Then, the image of a ghostly white body came into focus. It seemed to be caught under the ledge of a massive black rock.

Fear surged through Jonas's veins, causing his heart to throb a painful beat. He wasn't sure what he had expected to find. A thrashing body? Someone tearing at his own ankle? But not this. Not a floating corpse undulating in the flow of the chilling underwater current. Ignoring these distracting thoughts, Jonas grabbed Chris's hand.

At first he thought it was just his imagination, but Jonas felt a gentle squeeze from the limp hand, assuring him that, at least for the moment, Chris was still alive. A newfound sense of determination rose from within, and Jonas began looking for the place where the leash was attached to his friend's ankle.

His fingers found the strap, and without skipping a beat, he ripped it from Chris's leg. Then, grabbing his friend's thighs, Jonas placed his own feet on the black rock for leverage and pushed straight up.

At first the jump rocketed both of them upward, but as they rose, Jonas felt their progress slow as the density of the water worked against them. Understanding that every second wasted could mean the difference between life and death, Jonas pushed Chris's body up with every bit of energy he had left.

He watched Chris rise toward the surface as he felt himself forced downward by the motion. He had done everything he could possibly do, but he was still awaiting a sign that would confirm Chris was okay.

Suddenly, Jonas saw Chris's legs kick. He could imagine his friend gasping for breath as he breached the surface of the water, lungs on fire as he inhaled life into his body. The thought of it brought a sense of peace to Jonas's mind, even as he felt himself sinking deeper and deeper. The thought of Chris being alive was such a relief in fact, that he would have gladly sunk all the way to the bottom of the ocean and rested there a while.

But Jonas couldn't stay underwater forever, and as he started to feel his lungs burn, he realized how his current situation could quickly become dire if he didn't do something fast. Paddling on the surfboard had strained his muscles, missing the wave had burned up a good deal of energy, and the swim out to save his friend had taken more of a toll on him than he could have imagined.

Still sinking slowly downward, he took note of his body and realized that he could barely move his arms. It wasn't so much that they were tired, or even that they hurt at this point; they just wouldn't move. His legs weren't much better, but he began to kick them none-theless, feeling a sharp stinging sensation on the bottom of his soles. He looked down, and saw a cloud of dark red around the white flesh of his ankles. He had cut the bottom of his feet on the razor-sharp lava rock when he had pushed up to the surface. Working against the pain, he began to slowly rise.

Higher and higher he went, the burning sensation in his lungs becoming more and more acute. As Jonas kicked, he noticed how his arms dangled helplessly to his sides. Looking toward the surface, he saw Chris's legs treading water. He smiled at the thought of his friend alive; spitting, coughing, and wheezing perhaps, but still alive.

While lost in that happy thought, Jonas suddenly felt an intense pressure building in his ears. At first it didn't make any sense to him, because pressure was only supposed to build the deeper one went under water. His legs were kicking, and he could definitely feel his body rising. For a moment, he thought that he might have vertigo, a condition that had caused more than one surfer to swim toward the bottom of the ocean, all the while thinking that they were swimming toward the surface. But there was light above him. He could see the outline of the sun glimmering in the watery ceiling. But the pressure in his ears was now beginning to cause a ringing in his head.

Then, a terrifying thought came into his mind, more terrifying perhaps than even seeing his friend floating helplessly at the bottom of the ocean. While Jonas wasn't sinking, the water was in actuality becoming deeper—a condition that could only be caused by one thing: a giant wave forming overhead.

Too tired to kick or struggle any further, Jonas found the sky darkening as a massive wall of water moved in to obstruct his view of the sun. With no energy left, he decided to hold perfectly still, using as little oxygen as possible. Flashes of the scar on his back shot into his mind as he floated helplessly. Trying to push those images away, he began to think of the one thing that could bring him happiness in a situation as desperate as this. He could almost hear himself calling out her name as her face began to form in his mind.

Sarah . . .

It was a wonderful thought. A beautiful thought.

Jonas then felt all the pressure of a thousand-ton wave crushing in on his chest, forcing all the precious air out of his lungs. It drove him onto the razor sharp reef below, shredding his back like a cheese grater, scraping the very vertebra of his spine. He began to panic. The thought of giving up became a realistic option. He could give in, take a breath, and wait for the darkness to take him. Or he could hold on and fight to the very last second for the hope of seeing her again.

Making his decision, he focused on what he could control as his body was tossed in the washing machine. If he gave in to the urge to breath, he would surely drown, so he clenched his teeth as tight as he could. He had to *not* breathe. He had to fight the very urge to give in to what his body wanted most.

He could feel his lungs on fire, burning up inside of him. The lack of oxygen created an excruciating, toxic sensation that climbed from his lungs to his chest and then up his neck, surging quickly into his head. He felt the poison spread its tentacles around his skull as if it were gripping it in a crushing vice. His head began to swoon with the sheer volume of pain attacking all of his senses. But just at the moment when he thought he couldn't bear it anymore, when the pain in his body would overcome his will, his head suddenly broke through the surface of the water.

With a gasp, his lungs quickly filled with air. A blanket of white sea foam had covered the water's surface, making it nearly impossible to see. He was going to have to swim upward in order to get his body above the foam. His arms flailed helplessly at his sides. He kicked from underneath, but it only allowed him a few foam-choked breaths. He was buying time, but there was another wave right behind him, which he realized when he heard his friend yell.

"Jonas!"

He looked toward the voice and saw Chris, about thirty feet away. His friend looked terrified as he struggled to keep himself afloat. But as Jonas looked into Chris's eyes, his mind became strangely quiet. Somehow, seeing Chris alive and fighting in the water quelled the horror that he himself was experiencing. For a split second he didn't even think about the foam scorching his windpipe. He only saw his friend. Swimming. Alive.

And then Jonas felt something bump the back of his head, and all he saw was black. At first he wondered if he had just shut his eyes, but then he became conscious of a sensation near the back of his skull. It was warm, not cold like the ocean water. It enveloped his head with relief. He relaxed his body to welcome the peaceful feeling, giving himself over to a picture that was slowly forming in his mind.

At first it was like looking through dark spectacles, but as he focused, the picture became brighter. There was also a feeling of motion, like he was flying through the air. He could even feel the wind in his face. As he turned his head right and left, he saw golden trees appear from nowhere, shimmering in the brightness of the sun. Mesmerized by the beauty of their dazzling color, he took a moment to feel the reflection of their light on his face. It was warm. He turned his head skyward to feel the warmth of the bright sun kissing his skin. There was no darkness here, no bone-chilling cold closing in on him. Only warmth and beauty.

He switched his focus onto something he saw moving in the air alongside him. There, floating with him, was an angel. She wore a robe and had wings like eagle's feathers flowing in the wind. She carried flowers in her hand, lilies, pure and white. He watched her float toward the earth, her bare feet alighting on a fountain of water, holding out her hand to something below.

Looking at where the angel was reaching, Jonas then saw something even more beautiful, even more wonderful.

Sarah.

Her beautiful red hair was flowing in the breeze. Jonas drew near to her, noticing a tear in her eye as she suddenly became aware of his presence. Her skin glistened in the sun as he watched her look back at him, reaching out to touch him. She was longing for him, as he longed for her. And as he saw her lift a hand to touch his face, Jonas felt himself free from all worry and every care. He loved her, and he knew she loved him, and in that moment nothing else mattered.

Chris . . . the waves . . . the water . . .

Confused, Jonas looked back at Sarah. She was still right there in front of him. He reached out to touch her, but his arm was too heavy to move. Darkness began to obscure his vision as he felt himself floating above and away from her. Blackness began to fill the picture around him, clouding his vision even more. He felt himself rising higher and higher, with darkness filling everything below.

As he turned to look above him, he saw shafts of light penetrating the void that surrounded his body. He wanted more than anything to reach that light, and so, stretching for it, he lifted his arm until he saw his hand disappear through an invisible ceiling.

Frightened, he pulled his hand back, turning it slowly in the light. He waved it in front of him a few times, but when he did so, he saw that the air around him wasn't air at all. The air around him looked much more like . . . water.

Shocked, he quickly looked below him and saw the sandy black ocean floor. Glancing above, he saw the shimmering light for what it really was—the sun. Taking stock of his body, he noticed that he was still clenching his jaw. Relaxing it a bit, he thought next of his lungs. Surprisingly, they felt fine. The air he sucked in with the foam must have been enough.

He began to kick his legs, realizing that he had no idea how long he had been underwater. He didn't feel the burning in his lungs anymore, or anywhere else for that matter.

Moving upward, it was easy to understand now why his hand had disappeared when he reached past the water's surface: he had lifted it out into the open air. But as his head rose past the reflective barrier that opened to the sky, he still had to wonder why his body didn't hurt. He had been thrown around at the bottom of the ocean. Thinking about it, he realized he must be in shock.

For all he knew, he could have a broken leg or fractured a rib. He knew he had hit that rock on the bottom of the ocean hard enough to break his back in two, but he couldn't feel any pain. In fact, the more he thought about his body, the better he felt. He began to make his way toward shore.

As he did so, he took a moment to look around. The sea was now quite still. There were no more waves behind him. As he looked in all directions, he realized he had drifted a far distance from where they had been surfing. Glancing up at the sky, he saw the same birds, flying toward their nests in the tropical trees on the beach. And there on the beach in the distance he saw Chris, bent over on his hands and knees, wheezing for breath.

"Chris!"

There was no reply. Chris must have been in shock as well. Jonas felt that maybe he should wave to let his friend know where he was, but not wanting to aggravate any unknown injuries, he decided to first make his way to shore to check himself.

Slowly, Jonas made his way to the sandy beach a few hundred yards from where Chris knelt in pain. As he did so, he was careful not to make any jarring movements. Turning over to lie down in silence, he glanced toward Chris, still on all fours, throwing up. He thought to himself how his friend must have swallowed quite a bit of seawater on his way back. The waves that had come for them must have hit him pretty hard too.

Turning his attention back to himself, Jonas felt his ribs. Nothing seemed unpleasant as he poked around. No sharp pains or dull aches. He turned his hands over, opening and closing them to see if some hidden pain would emerge. None did. He felt his arms, and all seemed fine. He looked at his legs next, pushing against his thighs to make sure nothing was broken. Either shock took a while to wear off or Jonas had escaped his treacherous fate unscathed. Grateful for this, he decided to close his eyes and rest for a few minutes before going over to check on Chris.

Listening to the calming sound of the breeze blowing through the trees, he tried to visualize her face again. Sarah. Her beautiful, bright face and those stunning green eyes. Smiling, he gave himself over to his drifting thoughts.

"Jonas," came a female voice.

Jonas was surprised to hear his name called out. Wondering if this was the beginning of another blissful dream, he decided to open his eyes, perhaps to find himself surrounded by the golden shimmering trees again, with the girl he loved right in front of him.

Slowly opening his eyes, he squinted instinctively at the brightness of the blue sky overhead.

"Jonas, over here."

There it was again. The voice that called to him. It was strangely familiar, but not Sarah's. He couldn't place it exactly, though he was sure he had heard that voice many times before.

"I'll come over, you stay right where you are," the voice instructed.

Jonas turned his head to look in the direction of the voice. He saw a middle-aged woman walking toward him on the black sand. She was tall and slender, with long, sandy brown hair. She had a way of walking that was also familiar.

He rubbed his eyes and sat up, trying to focus.

"Beautiful day," the woman commented as she came closer. She looked him over.

"How do you feel, dear?"

Jonas was silent.

"Are you surprised to see me?"

He stared back in disbelief.

"Aunt Claire?" Jonas whispered, almost more to himself than to the woman beside him.

She smiled, reaching for his hand.

"I'm so glad you made it. It's been so long."

Jonas thought to wake himself from this dream, but he was transfixed by the sight of his aunt right in front of him. He couldn't take his eyes off her. He was afraid to blink.

"It's impossible," he said out loud.

Aunt Claire smiled, a look of empathy in her expression.

"I know how it seems . . ."

"But . . ." Jonas began to stutter.

"It's okay, Jonas."

He looked at her with trepidation in his eyes, shaking his head as he felt the words fall instinctively from his lips.

"It's impossible—you're dead."

3

THE BOY HELD THE GARBAGE BAG TIGHTLY ABOVE WHERE
the dark-haired man had made the knot.

Holding out the watch, the man continued to count off the seconds.

"Forty-five, forty-six, forty-seven . . ."

Suddenly, the little boy heard a high-pitched cry from within the bag.

"Keep holding it," the man said. "Fifty-three, fifty-four, fifty-five . . ."

The little boy's heart pounded. He looked from the dark-haired man
to the garbage bag. The screams grew louder, and he felt himself turning
stiff with fear.

"Daddy?" the little boy whispered, as he began to shake.

The dark-haired man grabbed the little boy's hand and squeezed it
even more.

"Damn it, Charlie! Hold it tighter or she's going to get hurt."

The boy watched as the dark-haired man began to shake with rage.

"A minute ten, eleven, twelve . . ." he kept counting.

Suddenly, the little boy noticed how the screams turned to whimpers.
There was less movement in the bag now.

"She's not hurt, is she, Daddy?" the little boy pleaded.

The man grabbed the boy by the collar, and pulled him into his fierce
gaze.

"What do you think I am?" the man said with trembling fury. "Do
you think I'm some sort of murderer? Keep your hand on the goddamned
bag until this watch beeps!"

The man threw the watch on the floor next to the boy.

"When you hear it, untie the knot and come and get me."

The little boy looked up as the dark-haired man released his grip.

"If you let go too soon, she's going to get hurt," the man said as he
walked toward the door.

The little boy glanced back at the bag and then at the watch. He held the bag tightly as he had been told, watching the numbers tick by.

"Don't you dare let go of that bag," the man shouted from the open doorway with a final glance, just before leaving. "If you do, I'll kill you myself."

With that, the door slammed shut as the boy was left alone, holding the bag, with the watch ticking at his side, his pants now wet with fear.

Time passed, each minute longer than the last. The little boy could feel his hand cramping as he tried to hold the bag as he had been told. His hand was starting to throb. Just when he thought he couldn't hold on any longer, the watch beeped.

Hurriedly, he let go and tried to untie the knot. It was very tight, and no matter how hard the little boy pulled at it, it wouldn't loosen.

He ran to open the door, only to find it locked from the outside. He tried to turn the knob, but it wouldn't budge. He looked back at the motionless bag and began to scream.

"Daddy! Help! Please! I can't do it!"

The little boy ran over to the bag and tugged at the knot again. It wouldn't budge.

"Daddy, it's too tight!"

Running back to the door, he began to pound on it as hard as he could. Suddenly the door opened.

"What the hell are you doing?" the older man yelled.

Tears streaming down his face, the little boy ran to the bag.

"It won't open. It's too tight!"

The man stood in the doorway, watching the boy pull at the knot in the bag.

"I told you to untie it, Charlie! What the hell have you done?"

"Please, Daddy. It won't move."

The man pushed the little boy to the ground as he slowly untied the knot, taking much more time than was necessary. He peered inside, then turning, he looked at the boy on the ground.

"What have you done?"

"Is she okay, Daddy?" the boy said, frozen with fear. "Did she forget?"

The man looked at him with a fierce gaze.

"You killed her . . ."

The little boy's face went blank.

"I don't know how you did it, but you killed her."

The little boy watched as the man peered back inside before slowly tying the bag back up. Standing to his feet, he began to walk toward the door, but suddenly looked back at the boy he was leaving behind.

"No one can know about this, you understand," he began. "If anyone finds out what you've done, they'll kill you and send me to prison."

He stared into the boy's eyes.

"Is that what you want?"

The little boy was too scared to move. Noticing this, the man turned and walked back. He knelt down so as to be eye level with the boy.

"I'm going to get rid of this, but you can't say anything to anyone, okay?" he cautioned. "Not even Mommy."

The little boy's face was still blank, overwhelmed with fear and confusion.

"Don't worry, Charlie. I won't let anything happen to you. I love you. I won't tell anyone that you did this."

Then, in a practiced manner, the man began to unbutton the little boy's pants.

"Lay back, Charlie, you need to calm down."

4

"EVERYTHING'S GOING TO BE OKAY, JONAS."

Sitting there on the black sand beach, Jonas was staring at the impossible. The aunt he hadn't seen in over twelve years was kneeling right beside him, holding his hand, as if a single day hadn't passed since that dark day long ago . . .

"How?" Jonas said, feeling the words emanate from his mouth, almost against his will.

"I'll explain," said Aunt Claire, as she gave Jonas a gentle squeeze.

Looking down at her hand, Jonas had an instinct to recoil. But feeling the tender stroke of her fingers, he found himself mesmerized. This was no middle-aged woman's skin making contact with his. This was skin as soft as a baby's. There was a feeling like subtle electricity flowing through her fingers too. It was a sensation Jonas had never felt before, and it caused him to scoot back a little, afraid at what was happening.

"It's okay, Jonas. Everything's going to be okay," Aunt Claire reassured him.

It was difficult for Jonas to find comfort in her words, as the last time he heard her speak, she looked nothing like the way she did now. Instead of having well-set hair and beautiful skin, his aunt had been gaunt, sickly, only eighty-five pounds, struggling for her life with every single breath. All of the youthful exuberance that had come to define her adulthood had seeped away, until she could barely smile without an accompanying wince of pain.

It had been a terrible thing to see his aunt sick like that. Jonas never understood why someone with so much zest for life had been taken that way. It didn't seem fair. At the time, she was raising two girls and taking care of a household, all while serving at a local organization that helped children struggling with autism. She was the type of person who always said hello, offering a helping hand to nearly everyone she met. Which is why Jonas found the truth of her illness so hard to understand those many years ago.

He was only fifteen years old when it had happened. His father came home early from work, asking all the children to gather together in the living room for a family meeting. There were already tears in his mother's eyes. As he waited for his father to speak, Jonas quickly felt a terrible sinking sensation that he and his siblings were about to be given horrible news. Were his parents going to get a divorce? It almost seemed that way, but they were holding hands much tighter than they ever had before. If the news wasn't about them, then who, or what, could possibly be causing so much distress?

"Kids," his father finally began, "your mother and I have something to tell you."

Immediately upon hearing his father speak, all Jonas wanted to do was throw up. It didn't make sense of course. He didn't even know what was wrong, but he had never seen his parents so distraught, his mother so sad, and his father so visibly shaken. It was as if they were preparing themselves to relay the kind of news that leaves an indelible mark on the minds of those unfortunate enough to hear it. The kind of news that forces children to grow older, and adults to long for more innocent years gone by.

"You know how Aunt Claire hasn't been feeling very well over the past few months . . ."

Of course they knew. But they also knew it wasn't anything to worry about. It was just a really bad flu or something like that. Quite a bit of time had passed since they last visited her house for dinner, but it wasn't anything to get upset about, right? Just a bug? Just something that was going around that could be cured with some strong medication and a few weeks' rest?

"She's been very sick kids," Jonas's father continued. "There was a hope that she might be getting better, but it doesn't look like that's going to happen."

Jonas knew exactly what his father was really saying. Vague as it might sound to his younger siblings, he knew all too well the finality those words implied. Jonas didn't want to believe it, but he knew by the look on his father's face that there was no way of escaping it.

"Is she hurting?" asked Jonas's younger sibling Peter, a little boy of six.

"She was," he said slowly, "but the doctor gave her a special kind of medicine to make her feel not so sick all the time."

"So she's better?" asked Chloe, an eight-year-old who wore a smile that rarely vanished.

Jonas watched his father pause while his mother fought back tears.

"She's feeling better, yes," he replied, "but Aunt Claire has a sickness that's become quite serious. She's probably not going to be coming over to our house anymore. From now on, we need to go visit her."

"Is she at a hospital?" Jonas's younger brother Mark asked.

"She was at the hospital for quite a while, but the doctors decided to let her come home where they thought she would be more comfortable."

Jonas observed the innocent confusion in his siblings' eyes. They looked at one another as if what they were hearing was actually good news; she was well enough to come home from the hospital. But Jonas knew the kind of homecoming being discussed wasn't the kind that families wanted to have. There would be no more doctor visits after this homecoming. No more scans or x-rays or whatever else she must have been through. There would just be home, and after home, something else more terrifying than Jonas wanted to imagine.

Glancing once again at his father, Jonas could tell there was more to come for him—more disturbing details to be shared away from the small ears and impressionable minds of his younger siblings. And only a few minutes after the family council concluded, that's exactly what happened. Jonas was escorted to the master bedroom and told the truth of his aunt's condition. There was information his mother and father most likely withheld from him even at that moment, but considering the circumstances, Jonas didn't want to learn more than he already had to know.

"Jonas, I wish I didn't have to tell you this," his mother said, with the residue of tears still glistening on her cheeks, "but Aunt Claire has been battling cancer for quite some time now."

There was a pause as she gathered herself together before speaking again.

"She's fought so hard, but it's just not going away."

Jonas didn't know what to say. All he could do was nod and try his best to hold it together.

"We didn't want to tell the other kids just yet," she said. "It will take a bit more time to help them understand, but the doctors are telling us she only has a few weeks."

A few weeks? A few weeks till what? Jonas thought to himself, though he knew the answer deep down inside. His mother had stopped herself before actually saying the words. Was it simply too painful? Was she still holding out for some sort of miracle? Jonas wasn't sure, but he knew it would take a lot longer than a couple of weeks for him to grapple with the situation in his own head.

He thought for a moment. Aunt Claire was sick. That he could handle. She couldn't leave her house. That was okay. Things might change as he had just been told, but until then, Jonas would do what he could in the moment. His aunt was sick. She needed a visit. Maybe some chicken soup. That would be good. Some chicken soup would make things better.

Jonas didn't want to hear any more. He had been told what was wrong with his aunt, and now he had thought of something he could do. After all, it was his aunt who had taught him the joy of losing oneself in the kitchen. She had instructed him many times on how to toss a strip steak salad in champagne dressing and how to grill asparagus over an open flame. Perhaps he felt the instinct to help her in this way because of the stories she told while they cooked together, humorous stories that gave Jonas a glimpse of what life was like for his aunt and his mother before everything changed into the familiar backdrop of his childhood memories.

But later that afternoon, when Jonas brought his aunt the most meticulously prepared chicken soup he had ever attempted, he saw that things were much worse than he wanted to believe. Walking into her bedroom with a hot bowl between his hands, he was met with the sight of his aunt strapped to her bed—tubes and wires running like shackles around her delicate frame—holding down a body that had been robbed of every trace of familiarity. She was frail, breaking, sunken, and still. Yet Jonas saw an unexpected gleam in her eye as he entered the room.

"Jonas," came his aunt's voice. He could see her mouthing the words from her position on the bed, but the words he was hearing were not coming from his memory. They were coming from the woman on the beach. The one who looked exactly like his aunt. At least the way she looked before the illness took its toll.

"Jonas," she said again, bringing him somewhat to the current state of things. "Just lean on me. I'll help you up."

Without thinking, Jonas felt his aunt take his hand, placing it around her shoulder, and lifting him with surprising ease to his feet. He had no idea how she did this, as he weighed far more than she did.

"Jonas, walk with me."

He heard her voice in the present, but his mind took him back to his memories of her, back to when she could barely move her own hand as she lay helplessly in bed. Weeks after visiting his aunt with the chicken soup he had spent so much time making, Jonas found himself sitting at her bedside again, listening.

"Jonas, I want to thank you," she said in a whisper, the kind of painful, strained whisper that aches with every syllable.

Jonas fought back the tears as he realized the purpose of this conversation—one to express her feelings of love, no doubt, but also a message laced with urgency, as if the sands in the hourglass were slipping faster than either of them thought possible.

"Thank you for always being so kind to my little girls—you've been just like a big brother to them."

Jonas felt the weight of the compliment as he watched his aunt struggle to smile. He had always thought of Aunt Claire's two children as his sisters, but he never imagined they would have to face this kind of future at such a young age.

After a few slow, controlled breaths, Aunt Claire continued.

"Watch out for them, would you? They look up to you so much."

Jonas nodded in reply, wishing to do what she asked, but silently hoping she would talk about something else. As much as he wanted to be by her side, helping her in any way he could, he didn't know how much more of this finality he could possibly take.

"And be kind to your mother," she added. "I know you are—but just tell her that you love her every once in a while. It would mean so much to her."

Jonas nodded again, willing to do anything asked of him to ease her pain. In fact, as he agreed to fulfill these small, seemingly insignificant wishes, he thought he began to see a relief in his aunt's eyes. It made him believe for a moment that she might actually be getting better. Perhaps there were certain diseases that couldn't be cured by medicines or therapies. Perhaps it took something stronger, like the faith of a loved one, to chase the illness away.

"One more thing," she whispered, straining to lean in as close to Jonas as her frail body would allow. "There is something that I want you to remember . . ."

Jonas held his breath as he leaned in as well to listen.

"I want you to know that I love you very much," she said, "and no matter what happens, that's never going to change."

Jonas held her gaze and then nodded to show he understood. As he watched her staring up at him, straining with every bit of effort she had left, he wanted to say something too, something that would let her know how much he loved her as well. But as the tears came and his voice began to choke, all he could do was hold her head in a gentle embrace.

"It's okay, Jonas," she said quietly. "You don't have to say anything."

She leaned her head back slowly, painfully, trying to catch her breath after the ordeal of reaching out to him. But as Jonas heard her say that, he realized that he did, in fact, want to say something—something that would let her know how much she meant to him, how special she had been to him all these years. But he just didn't know how to do it. She was like a mother to him, but the only words he could possibly think of to say seemed to be a disservice to what he felt inside. There were no words that could possibly reflect the complexity of emotions that he barely understood himself. And so, he watched her as she closed her eyes, trying his best to take comfort in the idea that perhaps she was right—perhaps some things don't need to be said aloud in order to be understood.

That was the last time Jonas saw his aunt. She passed away peacefully the following day. Her husband and daughters had gathered together at her bedside before it happened, but Jonas and his family didn't learn about it until after. Jonas's mother and father received the call telling them of the news, but when they asked Jonas to come along with them, he declined. It wasn't that he didn't want to come—he wanted desperately to see his aunt again—but he couldn't bring himself to see only the *thought* of her. He couldn't believe that the aunt he had known his entire life could actually be gone. He wanted to keep thinking of her as still alive, still smiling, still happy—still waiting for the chance to teach him something new and brilliant in the kitchen. If she had indeed gone somewhere, like everyone was saying, he would think of it as somewhere good, somewhere far away, but nevertheless, somewhere real and tangible that would allow her to return when she decided it was time to come back. Right or wrong, that's how young Jonas saw it. He didn't allow himself to believe his aunt had passed. She would be back, he reassured himself, and all this talk of funerals and death, of heaven and rainbows, would be seen for what it really was—a simple misunderstanding. Then, every tear and painful memory brought about by the viewing of old photographs and the retelling of melancholy stories would be replaced by the simple knowledge that she had never actually left in the first place. Everyone would then see how meaningless it was to cry, how strange it was to speak her name in the past tense, or how offensive it was—yes, offensive—to assume that the only way in which she would live on would be in "the quiet whisperings of their hearts." Aunt Claire was a person after all, a real live person—not a thought or an idea or a wisp of smoke. His aunt was out there somewhere, he knew, and one day he would be allowed the opportunity to once again pick up the conversation he never had the chance to finish with her. Yes, some things might not need to be said aloud to be understood, but not when the person you love with all your heart leaves before giving you the chance to decide that for yourself.

"Jonas. Walk with me."

Hearing his aunt's voice, Jonas found himself doing exactly as he was told. He began to follow his aunt's orders because after all these years—after all the years of waiting and wondering—the aunt he knew and loved had finally come back. It might not have made sense to anybody else, but to Jonas it made perfect sense. She left, but had come back, and that's all that really mattered. Everything else would work itself out over time as he learned the story of how she had come to meet him on the beach this day. But until then, he would be happy to follow her lead, to take her hand once more and do whatever it is that she needed him to do.

"Okay," he replied, easing up on the amount of weight he had placed on her shoulder after having been picked up.

"How are you feeling?" she asked, glancing at him every so often as they made their way toward the top of the beach.

Jonas took a moment to reply.

"I'm okay," he said, pausing when he realized who they were leaving behind.

Turning to look back in the direction of the water's edge, Jonas felt the instinct to call out to Chris, whom he last saw kneeling all alone.

But his friend wasn't alone now. As Chris was heaving the last bit of seawater from his oxygen-starved lungs, Jonas saw two other people kneeling right beside him—a young couple who seemed to be offering words of comfort and encouragement to help him regain control of his body once more.

"Who are they?" Jonas found himself asking, having never seen the young, rather handsome-looking couple anywhere on the beach before. Glancing around, there were no visible footprints that might have offered evidence of the direction they had come from.

Aunt Claire looked back, pausing for a moment herself before replying.

"Don't worry, they're here to help."

Still feeling a bit confused about it all, Jonas looked back into the eyes of his aunt.

"We're going to get Chris more help too," she said, glancing once more at Jonas's friend and the two people near his side. "There aren't many people on this side of the island, but Chris is going to need some special attention over the next few hours to help him get through this."

Still feeling a bit hazy, Jonas looked back, but acquiesced quietly as he followed his aunt's lead again toward the main road at the top of the beach.

When they got to the narrow strip of asphalt that separated the beach from a dense jungle on the opposite side, he saw his aunt glance at something down the road before turning to look at him.

"Jonas, do you remember playing hide-and-seek as a child?"

Jonas looked at her questioningly.

"What . . . ?"

Aunt Claire smiled.

"Hide-and-seek," she said again. "I hope you don't mind, but I need to play a little game with you. I know it might seem odd given the circumstances, but I need you to close your eyes and count to ten while I go and run a quick errand."

She paused to look at him.

"Do you think you can do that for me?"

Jonas wasn't exactly sure what to say. His head was still so fuzzy.

"Count to ten?" he asked.

"I know it's a strange request, but if you would, Jonas—for me," she consoled. "I promise, I'll explain everything later, but right now we need to get Chris some help."

Feeling quite out of place, but seeing the sincere look in his aunt's eyes, Jonas decided to close his own. He stood there quietly, but after a short moment he felt the instinct to open his eyes a bit, if for no other reason than to see what was going on.

"Jonas, please," his aunt said the moment he had done so. "I know this doesn't make a lot of sense, but I need your help—we don't have time to waste."

Glancing back at his friend once more, wanting to help however he could, Jonas slowly closed his eyes once more.

"Thank you, Jonas," Aunt Claire said. "Just count to ten. Everything will be all right, I promise."

Listening to the sound of his own breathing for a few moments, Jonas began to count off the numbers as he had been told.

"One, two . . ."

"Perfect, Jonas," he heard his aunt say. "Just count each number, *slowly*."

Taking the correction, Jonas began counting again, this time, enunciating the numbers with greater deliberation.

"One . . . two . . . three . . . four . . ."

He heard little else but the hushed breeze of the wind flowing through the coconut trees that swayed in the distance.

"Five . . . six . . ."

There was a faint rumbling of a car engine down the road.

"Seven . . . eight . . ."

The car was coming closer now.

"Nine . . . ten."

Jonas opened his eyes. He was still standing near the road, but his aunt was now nowhere to be seen. He looked to his right and saw the car he had heard moving in his direction. Instinctively, he backed himself off the shoulder of the road as he watched the automobile come to a stop right beside him.

A well-groomed, mature-looking couple peered out the driver's side window. The driver himself was tanned, with a distinguished air about him. His wife, in the passenger seat, seemed to be craning her neck over his shoulder to get a better view of the beach.

Ignoring the fact that he was standing right in front of them, the couple discussed how the beach made the perfect spot for an afternoon picnic. As they began to pull into an empty parking spot, Jonas could have sworn that he saw something in the backseat that he couldn't quite explain.

"Aunt Claire?" he whispered to himself, taking a step toward the car to see if he had actually seen her sitting in the backseat. He didn't get very far before he heard his name called from behind.

"Jonas, over here," he heard her familiar voice say.

Jonas turned around and saw his aunt standing just a few yards away. Confused, he looked back at the car that had just passed him, seeing the couple exit after having parked it. There didn't seem to be anyone in the backseat now.

"How?" Jonas whispered to himself, looking back at his aunt as he felt his pulse begin to race.

"That's Dr. Baltimore and his wife," Aunt Claire said. "They're here in the islands celebrating their thirtieth anniversary. Lucky for us, they were driving by this very spot when the idea to stop suddenly came to them."

Jonas looked back at the couple as they stood in front of an open trunk, pulling out a basket full of cheese, bread, and fruit.

"You know them?" Jonas asked, turning to stare at his aunt more intently.

"In a way," Aunt Claire replied with a slight hesitation in her candor. "Dr. Baltimore is a cardiologist, which is fortunate for us—he's probably the most capable person to help Chris right now."

Hearing his friend's name mentioned simultaneously with the word "doctor," Jonas looked back toward the beach.

"Is Chris okay?" he asked, suddenly concerned that his friend's condition might be worse than he had assumed. Unfortunately, he was unable to see Chris from his vantage point.

"He's okay," Aunt Claire replied. "Physically, I mean. But he's going to need some help processing what happened here today."

Jonas saw his aunt glance at the couple as they closed the trunk.

"Dr. Baltimore has seen this kind of thing before, so he'll know just what to do."

Turning to look at the couple, Jonas saw them clasp hands as they made their way down the beach. Just when he was about to follow them, he felt a hand on his shoulder.

"How are you, Jonas?" Aunt Claire asked, looking deep into his eyes. "You went through a lot back there—how are you feeling?"

Looking from his aunt back to the doctor and his wife, it took Jonas a few seconds to register the question. Glancing down once more at his body, he poked a few ribs with his fingers to make sure he was intact.

"I . . . I feel fine," he said.

Aunt Claire nodded in response, though she seemed to take her time reacting to his informal diagnosis. Seeing her hesitate, Jonas poked around even more to give evidence of his truthfulness. While Chris may have needed the assistance of a doctor, the last thing Jonas wanted to do was get stuck in a hospital when Sarah would be waiting for him at the airport.

"Really, I'm fine," Jonas reiterated, just to make the point.

"Okay," Aunt Claire said, somewhat content with his reply for the moment. "Would you mind following me though? There's something I want to show you that I think you should see."

Looking back in Chris's direction, Jonas wavered for a moment.

"We're going to see Chris again, don't worry," Aunt Claire said. "He'll be fine for now."

Jonas watched the couple make their way down the beach.

"Are you sure?" he asked, feeling a little uncomfortable with the thought of leaving his best friend behind in such bad shape. "I should probably tell him where we're going."

"Chris is in capable hands, Jonas," Aunt Claire stated matter-of-factly, "and so, might I add, are you. I've come to show you something though—something very special. But you need to leave Chris behind for a moment and follow me in order to see it."

Jonas looked back at his aunt, mesmerized again by her healthy glow.

"Do you really think it's best?" he asked once more.

"I do, Jonas. But don't worry. I think you're going to like what you see."

After registering the excitement in his aunt's voice, Jonas paused, and then held out his hand. He wasn't sure where she intended to take him, but he thought he'd at least follow her for a bit to see the mystery behind all the intrigue.

As they walked side by side, he followed her lead toward a familiar dirt path that cut into the jungle on the opposite side of the road. The path led to a cave-like opening of twisting tropical trees and long, python-sized vines. The shadows cast by this dense, overarching vegetation gave their surroundings a dark and rather ominous feel. Everything around them became oddly still. Only a few strange animal sounds could be heard in the distance.

Following behind his aunt along the dark corridor, Jonas's attention was soon diverted by the noises, which seemed to intensify as they made their way farther into the jungle. Though he had walked this path a number of times before, he never remembered hearing such a commotion. Squawks and squeals, tickings and rustlings: it was as if every living creature hidden in the shadows had suddenly been disturbed by their presence. As Jonas and his aunt kept on walking, the sounds grew louder and stronger, with large branches breaking in the distance and strange hooting and howling noises echoing through the air. But just when he thought to glance at his aunt to see if she was having the same unnerved reaction that he was, an opening came into view, a shaft of light cutting through the darkness.

Picking up the pace, partly out of an eagerness to leave this strange bit of jungle behind but also to keep up with his aunt's quickening strides, Jonas soon found himself emerging from the cave of vegetation, out onto an open meadow of beautiful green grass.

"Jonas," Aunt Claire said pointing, "this is what I've brought you here to see."

As he came from behind her, looking in the direction she pointed, he felt himself stop short. There in the middle of the tranquil meadow was something he had never seen before: a white, wood-planked building gleaming in the sunlight.

As he looked closer, Jonas decided it resembled something more akin to a small, nineteenth-century colonial church. It had a peaked roof and large double doors on the front. A white picket fence surrounded the entire structure. But there were no religious signs or iconography anywhere on it. No steeple, no crosses, no stained-glass windows.

"Where . . . ," he began, somewhat in disbelief, "where did this come from? I've never seen this before."

"I know," she replied, turning to look at him with excitement in her voice, "but it's been here since before you were born."

Glancing at his aunt, then back at the building, Jonas was sure she must be mistaken. He'd traveled in this area hundreds of times, but either he had never paid much attention or his aunt had somehow taken an undisclosed turn while they were in the depths of the jungle.

"Jonas, I know you've been wondering where I've been all these years," she said as she reached for his hand and gave it a gentle squeeze.

Jonas looked down, feeling the same sudden rushing sensation of soft electricity flowing between them.

"Well," she continued, "I think it's time you learned."

Looking back up, Jonas saw his aunt turn toward him.

"Come, follow me."

5

A YOUNG WOMAN WITH SOFT, FLOWING RED HAIR
made her way out of the airplane. She checked her watch, making
sure that she wouldn't be late for the connecting flight to her final
destination. In doing so, she noticed the absence of any ring on the
fourth finger of her left hand. She wondered if things would be different at the end of this trip. She had been given a free ticket to one
of the most beautiful places in the world. It was difficult not to smile
at the implications.

"Hawaiian Airlines flight 206 to Kahului now boarding," came a
voice over the intercom.

Shouldering her bag, the girl with red hair walked quickly through
the airport terminal. She had no idea what would happen once she
arrived at her final destination. It was exciting to think about the
possibilities, but whatever they were, she had a feeling something
was about to change her life forever.

6

JONAS WALKED WITH HIS AUNT TOWARD THE WHITE building gleaming in the distance. It was beautiful yet simple, set against the lush green forest that surrounded it. As intriguing as it was, Jonas just couldn't stop thinking about how out of place it seemed. Of all the times he had visited this location in the past, he had never seen more than a walking trail anywhere in the vicinity.

"Here we are," Aunt Claire said as they passed through the white gate and approached the steps that led to the front doors.

Jonas looked again at the building, noticing how beautiful it was up close; so white and clean. For a structure as old as this was, he imagined there should have been at least a few signs of wear on it, but there were none to be seen. If his aunt hadn't said anything to the contrary, Jonas would have guessed this building had just been constructed in the last day or two. But even though the building looked brand-new, there was something that did appear quite old—ancient, in fact—as he approached the front doors.

There seemed to be some sort of carving inscribed on the façade, the indention of which was inlaid with gold. At first Jonas thought it might be a picture of some kind, but it soon became apparent that it was more like an ideogram: assorted characters written in a strange foreign language. As he took a step closer to inspect it, he saw it was most definitely a language, but one that he neither understood nor recognized. Whatever it was, it seemed to be quite out of place, as he would have expected to see writings like that on the interior of an ancient tomb, not on the doorway of a nineteenth-century church.

"What is that?" Jonas asked, pointing to the inscription.

"It's a marker," she said. "It explains the kind of building this is."

Jonas took a step back, trying to figure out just what kind of building it really was. As he took a second look at each of the mini-malist yet impressive architectural details, he began to notice a sub-tle magnificence about it all.

"It says TRUTH."

Jonas looked from the building's façade to his aunt.

"The inscription—it says TRUTH," she repeated.

Jonas looked back at the golden writing.

"Although," she elaborated, "it's written in an extremely ancient language, one I've yet to learn myself, actually."

Taking in the intricate details of the inscription, Jonas began to wonder where a language like this could have originated. Having never seen anything like it before, he didn't even know in which di-rection it was written—or for that matter, if it was written at all, and not illustrated. As intrigued as he may have been about its history, though, his attention was soon diverted as his aunt approached the door and opened it.

Turning the simple brass knob, Aunt Claire cracked the door slightly, just enough to peek inside. The second she did so, Jonas suddenly felt a breeze blow from within that seemed to carry with it a smell he could only describe as fresh spring grass mixed with the sweet scent of honeysuckle. But this smell, refreshing as it was, paled in comparison to the sounds he could hear emanating from inside.

Initially, Jonas thought the sound he heard was a soft melody, one that reminded him of a children's lullaby. But the whispering music flowing delicately through the air was so light and gentle, he wasn't actually sure if it was music he was listening to or something else altogether.

"Before we go in, there is one thing I need to tell you," Aunt Claire warned.

Nodding to show his compliance, Jonas took a step closer in an attempt to look through the crack she had made in the doorway.

"If you see anything that seems to be out of place," she cautioned, "anything at all, feel free to ask me, but do so in private. You may feel the urge to ask me things that, if said out loud, could make some here feel quite uncomfortable."

Jonas hadn't expected his aunt to say this, though he realized she knew more about this incredible place than he did. He agreed to her condition. More than anything, he just wanted to look inside, to see where all the sweet smells and sounds were coming from.

Aunt Claire smiled in recognition. And with a look of giddy anticipation, she opened the door.

———

Jonas couldn't believe it. There was no way, he thought, an interior of this size could possibly fit into a building that appeared so small from the outside. Looking up at the ceiling, he felt this assumption confirmed, as its volume seemed more like that of a grand cathedral, designed with the same vaulted ceilings one might find in a structure of that kind. But, unlike any cathedral he had ever visited, there was no darkness here whatsoever; no shadowed outcroppings to be illuminated with flickering prayer candles. In fact, he felt the instinct to squint as he looked upward because of the intensity of the light, which, somehow, brought with it a warm feeling. There was an intimacy he would not have expected in a space this large.

As he looked at the light, he noticed that it seemed to be concentrated at the apex. He assumed that the ceiling must have been made from some sort of transparent material, which let the sun's light shine directly through it.

As his eyes adjusted to the intensity of the light, Jonas noticed something that took him by surprise. There, high in the room, reflecting off each of the walls, was an awe-inspiring display of—*color*.

His mouth fell open as he looked upon thousands and thousands of colors. And they were no ordinary colors. They were shimmering, twinkling, *living* colors. They reminded him of a lesson from his high school science class wherein he learned there are colors in nature that humans cannot see because they exist on a wavelength outside the visible human spectrum.

But this—this was exactly opposite. In this room, Jonas was almost overwhelmed by the number of colors he could see, and by their incredible intensity. At first it was the stronger, more basic colors that he recognized: reds, blues, greens, and yellows. But with each passing second, as his senses became more attuned to his surroundings, he saw every color in between—some he knew he had never experienced before. He saw iridescent pinks, electric turquoises, radiant blues, and vibrant shades of royal purple. But the more he looked at them, the more he realized he had no appropriate names he could possibly give them. The names he tried to invent for them seemed more like emotional descriptors than anything else. Bright. Happy. Intense. Mesmerizing.

After a few moments of this bliss, he saw the source of all the colors: seven enormous chandeliers floating high in the air. Whether they were hanging from something hidden by the brightness above or attached in such a way as to make them appear to levitate, Jonas couldn't tell; but they shimmered as the brightness of the light above reflected through them.

As he looked farther down from the ceiling, Jonas saw that the reflective bits of color began to disappear and the natural colors of the room took shape. The pillars, for instance, appeared like translucent glass above but turned slowly into white marble and then into the color of living redwood. He also kept thinking of the word "living" for the fact that he swore he could feel the building breathing.

At eye level, Jonas then noticed how the dancing colors began to coalesce, giving a warm, peaceful glow to the surroundings. Looking from left to right, he also noticed that while the pillars had turned into a magnificent shade of deep redwood, the walls themselves remained a luminescent white all the way to the floor. And at the base of each of these walls, recessed beautifully in the lustrous white stone, there were wooden bookshelves, made from the same kind of redwood as the pillars.

But the thousands of books held within these shelves were not at all like those one might find in a stuffy academic library. These books were far more colorful—and they were arranged by color, so as to give the impression of a rainbow stretching across each wall and leading toward a set of enormous, arching, double brass doors at the other end of the chamber.

Holding his breath in astonishment, Jonas took a few unconscious steps farther into the voluminous nave, wondering just where his aunt had taken him.

"What is this place?" he asked.

"It's what we like to call the Reading Room," Aunt Claire remarked as she gently closed the door behind them. "It's a special place where we can read and spend time with those who are under our care."

It was then that Jonas turned his attention to all the people in the space. Amid what looked like a very comfortable living room—or rather, sets of living rooms—there were children and adults interacting with one another. To his right, there was a small group of children, sitting on a soft rug, listening attentively to an adult who was reading to them. Across the room from them, there were other children sitting on the laps of a few adults, sounding out words from books held in front of them. Others still looked as if they weren't reading at all, but acting out the stories they must have been reading just minutes before.

"What do you mean, those who are under your care?"

Aunt Claire turned toward him.

"Believe it or not, Jonas, you're in a hospital."

Jonas looked around him in astonishment.

"A hospital?" he echoed, rather loudly, drawing the attention of a few people in the room.

Jonas apologized and retreated a few steps to be nearer his aunt. But as he continued to look around, he became convinced that this couldn't be a hospital. There were no nurses, no doctors, no hospital beds—nothing like the sterile interiors he had come to associate with hospitals.

"You're kidding, right?" he said offhandedly, sure his aunt was making some sort of joke.

Aunt Claire smiled as she took his hand again, leading him a few more steps into the roomy interior.

"You may want to think of it as a children's hospital for now," she remarked, "though we don't exactly refer to it that way. It's simply a place where each of these young ones can come and get the special care and attention they need."

Glancing at his aunt, Jonas was taken aback by the fact that she was actually serious. But looking once again at his surroundings, he decided he didn't care much; he just wanted to see more of what this place had to offer.

While surveying the marvelous space that surrounded him, Jonas suddenly noticed a little girl dancing alongside a beautiful brunette, just at the moment the little girl turned to wave in his aunt's direction.

Aunt Claire smiled back.

"Claire! Claire!" the little girl shouted gleefully as she turned to run toward them. "Look! I've got new legs!"

Jonas watched as the small child ran straight into his aunt's arms, wrapping her tiny hands around her neck in a big bear hug.

"I see! I see!" Aunt Claire said excitedly, holding the little girl out in front of her as if observing a new discovery.

"Look, I can twirl like a ballerina and everything now," the little girl said as she took a few steps back and spun around.

Aunt Claire clapped her hands and smiled.

"I'm so proud of you, Karen," she said as the little girl continued to spin. "And you look like a ballerina too!"

Jonas watched as his aunt scooped the little girl up into her arms for a few twirls of her own. Seeing their spirited enthusiasm together, he began to think this must be some sort of game they all play here, perhaps something originating from one of the books stacked neatly in the shelves.

"Jonas," Aunt Claire introduced, "this is my friend Karen."

Jonas smiled at the little girl in his aunt's arms.

"Hello, Karen," he stuttered as he tried to focus on the conversation at hand.

"And, Karen," Aunt Claire pointed, "this is my nephew Jonas. He's just arrived."

"You'll love it here," the little girl exclaimed. "They have all kinds of toys and people to play with—and the birds are right down the hall . . ."

Jonas nodded as if he was following along, but he had to admit he was doing nothing of the sort.

"I've got to show Jonas around for a bit, Karen," Aunt Claire said, placing her back down on the floor, "but perhaps when I get back, we can dance together?"

"Or race!" said the little girl eagerly as she bent down in a sprinter's position.

"Yes, we could do that too," Aunt Claire replied with an encouraging smile.

"Jonas," the little girl said while crouching for an imaginary competition, "do you want to see me race with my new legs?"

Jonas looked from Karen to his aunt, who was giving him a nod as if to say yes.

"Sure. I'd love to," he said.

"Stand back!" the little girl ordered.

"Yes, of course," Aunt Claire said. "Jonas, we better watch out."

Jonas mimicked his aunt's posture as they both took a step backward, deliberately appearing cautious while doing so.

"One, two," Karen said with great anticipation. "*Go!*"

They both watched as the little girl ran as fast as she could back to the arms of the strikingly beautiful woman she had been dancing with earlier.

"So you guys play a lot of games like that around here?" Jonas asked quietly as he watched the duo smiling and giggling in the distance.

"Racing games?" his aunt replied.

"No," Jonas turned, using his fingers as quotations marks, "'I just got my new legs' type games."

"Oh, I see," Aunt Claire said, "that would seem rather out of place, wouldn't it."

Pointing to a set of couches in a private corner of the room, Aunt Claire offered Jonas a seat.

"Please, I'd like to explain a little bit about that for a moment if you wouldn't mind."

Confused by the remark, Jonas nevertheless made his way toward one of the sofas, and soon found himself sitting on the most comfortable couch his bare skin had ever touched. The texture of the fabric beneath his fingers was so soft and silky, he couldn't help but run his hand over it again and again.

Meanwhile, Aunt Claire took a small detour toward the bookshelf against the far wall, where she paused to select a particular volume from the yellow section of the rainbow. Pulling it out and flipping through it, she returned to sit on an adjacent couch kitty-corner from where Jonas sat.

"Jonas, does this book look familiar?" she asked as she leaned forward to hand him the volume.

Taking the tall, thin book from her hands, Jonas recognized instantly what it was.

"*Babar?*" he said, enthusiastically, remembering that he had read this book nearly every day as a child. "Where'd you get this?"

Smiling, Aunt Claire made a slight gesture to the children surrounding them.

"This is a children's reading room, after all."

Nodding with a smile of his own, Jonas returned his attention to the book in his hands, flipping it over a few times to make sure it was indeed the one he remembered. Thumbing through a few of the pages, he recognized several illustrations that made him grin.

"Jonas, I don't suppose you remember the story, do you?" his aunt asked.

Jonas paused for a moment, recollecting how the plot of this particular book followed an elephant named Babar who had been invited to be a guest of the president of the United States and all of the adventures he had while visiting various locations during his trip.

"Sure," he said.

"So you remember the story of how Babar came to America from his homeland overseas?"

Jonas nodded, looking once more at the book in his hands.

"Good," Aunt Claire acknowledged. "Then I assume you can tell me the means of travel by which he arrived at his destination."

Flipping through the pages of the book, Jonas paused, realizing that he was being asked a very specific question.

"Sorry?"

He looked up at his aunt.

"How he arrived," Aunt Claire repeated. "Do you remember how Babar traveled from his homeland to visit with the president of the United States?"

Thinking for a moment, Jonas flipped a few pages of the book toward the front until he landed on a cartoonish depiction of an airplane flying high over the city of Paris.

"He flew?" he guessed, wondering if this was what his aunt wanted to hear.

"Precisely," his aunt said with genuine enthusiasm. "Isn't that interesting?"

Looking up at her once again, Jonas wasn't sure what exactly she meant, or for that matter, what kind of a discussion she was trying to start.

"I don't think I understand," he said politely.

Aunt Claire grinned as she pointed toward the book.

"The plane," she gestured with an open hand. "Have you ever stopped to think about how rare that is?"

Jonas looked back down.

"An elephant riding on a plane?" he attempted.

Aunt Claire began to laugh.

"Well, yes, an elephant on a plane would be a rather interesting thing to see," she agreed. "But how about the simple idea of a person riding on a plane? Do you know how rare that type of travel is in relation to the history of the world? It's a fascinating idea when you think about it."

Still having no idea what she was getting at, Jonas just looked back up and shrugged his shoulders.

"I guess it's kind of interesting," he offered.

"Oh, it might sound trivial, I know," Aunt Claire added, "but not many people take the time to stop and think about the many miracles that surround them—the impossible things that have become quite ordinary because of one simple thing . . ."

She held up her finger as if to identify the singular importance of her thought.

"Truth, Jonas," she said. "The concept of truth. For thousands of years, humankind gazed heavenward, staring longingly out into the open sky. Yet, in all that time looking up at the birds flying high overhead, it was only recently that the principles necessary to attain the same kind of freedom were actually discovered."

Remembering the inscription on the front of the door, Jonas began to listen a bit more intently.

"The principle of lift," she continued, using her hand to help illustrate, "when combined with the right amount of thrust—it's a very powerful idea when you think about it. It allowed people like you and me to travel to foreign countries, to see the world beyond our own corner, to experience life from another's point of view. Quite brilliant, really."

Hearing it put to him this way did make the idea slightly more interesting, though Jonas still had a hard time understanding just what, if anything, it had to do with the little girl and her "new pair of legs."

"I'm sorry—weren't we talking about Karen?" Jonas reminded his aunt, gesturing politely toward the little girl dancing with her companion in the distance.

"Yes, exactly, and her new legs," Aunt Claire confirmed.

Jonas turned back to his aunt.

"Yeah, but that's just a game you play here, right?" he said.

Aunt Claire raised an eyebrow.

"Is it?" she challenged.

Jonas shook his head as he held back a grin, sure she was kidding again.

"Jonas," Aunt Claire said slowly, "what would you say if I told you we can do things here that might seem impossible—not unlike the idea of human-engineered flight to someone who lived in the fourteenth century?"

"What do you mean, impossible?"

"I mean, what would you say if I told you we could do things here that you couldn't do back there," she said, pointing toward the door through which they had entered. "Things you might even have a hard time believing yourself."

"Like what?" Jonas challenged.

Smiling as if this were the very thing she had wished he would ask, Aunt Claire moved from her seat to be closer to her nephew.

"Would you really like to know?" she asked enthusiastically.

Jonas glanced once more at the little girl before looking back at his aunt.

"Sure," he said with slight hesitation.

"Wonderful," Aunt Claire replied, "though I think we should start with one of the basics—I don't want to overwhelm you with too much on your first day."

Jonas leaned back a few inches in his seat after hearing this.

"Don't worry, it's nothing too frightening," Aunt Claire reassured him as she leaned forward, making up the space in between. "All I need you to do is look into my eyes and think of a number, any number, and I'll tell you what it is."

Jonas had to suppress a smile once more. He hadn't quite anticipated the performance of a magic trick.

"Think of a number," he repeated with a slight grin, relaxing now in his seat, "and you'll tell me what it is?"

"Precisely," his aunt replied. "Any number. But make sure not to say it out loud—that would defeat the purpose."

"Of course," he said, smiling openly now.

Looking around, Jonas began to wonder if anyone else was witnessing this.

"Are you ready?" Aunt Claire asked.

Focusing back on the situation at hand, Jonas took a few seconds to make his selection before nodding.

"Okay, then," Aunt Claire replied. "Here we go."

She cleared her throat while shifting in her seat a bit.

"You're number is—thirty-six."

There was a pause, and then complete silence, just before Jonas leaned in toward her.

"Wait," he said, sure he had missed something. "What did you just say?"

"Thirty-six," Aunt Claire repeated. "That's your number, isn't it?"

Jonas shook his head in disbelief. He wasn't exactly sure what just happened. He asked her to do it again.

"Okay," Aunt Claire said. "But think of a more difficult number this time, just to make sure."

Ever more confused but intrigued now, Jonas began to think of another number, one he was sure no one would ever be able to guess.

"Make sure it's a good one," Aunt Claire requested.

Adding a few integers at the end of his selection, Jonas nodded when he had made his choice.

"Okay," she said, "listen closely."

Jonas leaned forward in his seat once more, just to make sure he wouldn't miss anything this time.

"Your number is—four million, seven hundred, sixty-eight thousand, five hundred and twenty-three."

Jonas's posture became eerily erect as his aunt read off the numbers in his mind. He couldn't believe that she had actually done it. It was impossible, he thought. But after she had fallen silent, he began to feel a small sense of triumph, as there was still more of his number to be guessed.

That was, until she finished it off.

"And don't forget to add to the end of all that, a quarter," Aunt Claire said, apparently amused that her nephew had attached a fraction to the end of his number in an effort to make it more difficult to guess.

Jonas was stunned, silent, and unnerved. As he sat there, staring at his aunt, he began to wonder exactly what was going on. Sure, he had seen similar tricks performed on the street and in bars before, but each of those magicians had to ask a few questions in order to narrow the range. But this—Jonas thought to himself as he stared at his aunt—this was nothing like that. His aunt had just said what he was thinking without the slightest hesitation, almost as if she could truly read his mind.

"How . . . ?" Jonas began to say.

"I told you," Aunt Claire said, "it's this place—everything's different now."

"But . . . ," Jonas said, shaking his head.

"It's okay, Jonas," his aunt reassured. "You probably had no idea when you walked in that door, but you can do some pretty amazing things now that you're with us. You just have to give it a try."

Try? Jonas thought to himself. *Trying* wasn't the issue, he was sure. Breaking the laws of physics was the real challenge.

"It's impossible," he stammered once again.

Aunt Claire shook her head.

"You may want to be careful how you use that term in this place. You'd be amazed at what is considered ordinary here."

"No," Jonas stated, "I mean—there must be some sort of logical explanation—no one can read someone else's mind."

"You're correct," Aunt Claire replied, "if you don't want your mind to be read, and you have the mental discipline to keep it that way. But for all other situations, reading minds is very much a reality in this place."

Jonas simply shook his head.

"Jonas, I know how odd it may seem—it was quite a bit for me to take in when I first arrived here too. But let me reassure you: there are no magic tricks here, only the lack of understanding. Get over that hurdle, and you'll soon come to learn how useful things like reading minds can actually be."

Looking at his aunt, Jonas hadn't yet thought about the *usefulness* of being able to read other people's thoughts. He was still grappling with the concept of it even being a *possibility*.

"It's quite simple, really," she said. "Would you like to give it a try?"

Jonas shook his head once more.

"Really, it's not as difficult as you might think," Aunt Claire prodded. "All you need to do is look into my eyes and clear your mind. I'll take care of the rest."

Somewhat intrigued with the offer, Jonas nevertheless began to feel a growing discomfort with this strange place he had been brought to. It was beautiful, yes, but now there was something that was making him feel quite out of place. Wishing to learn the secret behind the trick, though, he agreed to follow her instructions, if for no other reason than to put himself at ease.

"Maybe just for a minute," he conceded.

"Wonderful," Aunt Claire replied. "Just look into my eyes then. Nothing to it."

Jonas looked uncomfortably at his aunt and shifted in his seat slightly.

"Ready?" she asked.

After a moment or two, Jonas nodded.

"All right, here we go . . ."

Aunt Claire nudged a bit closer to him in preparation for what was about to happen.

"My number is—three."

Jonas's expression went somewhat blank, and his head tilted slightly to one side. He looked confused, and seemed for a moment to be unimpressed by what he had heard.

"You said three," he stated rather frankly.

"Yes, exactly," Aunt Claire replied with a smile. "Well done!"

Jonas scratched his head.

"Yeah, but you said it out loud," he clarified, feeling for a moment as if he were helping the magician perform her own trick.

Aunt Claire's smile became even more pronounced.

"Did I?" she countered.

Jonas nodded once more, though he began to wonder.

"I'm pretty sure," he said.

"Well, then," Aunt Claire replied, "perhaps we should do it again. Maybe this time you should try looking at my lips."

Still slightly confused, Jonas looked at his aunt's lips and then glanced toward the front door. This whole experience was beginning to feel a bit strained—like the kind of dream that starts out pleasantly enough but leaves you pinching your own arm in an effort to wake up. Sure, it was intriguing to think about the possibility of telepathy, but the impact of even the best magic tricks begins to wane when compared to the more important responsibilities of everyday life. Chris, for example, was most likely in need of an extra hand back at the beach. And Sarah—she would soon be waiting for someone to pick her up at the airport. As much as Jonas wanted to learn more about this strange and amazing place his aunt had brought him to, there were pressing matters outside that required his attention. This tour would be far more intriguing anyway if he had his best friends with him.

"Jonas, I'm serious," Aunt Claire said sternly, interrupting his thoughts. "You might think this is some sort of game, but I came to pick you up at the beach to help you understand something very important. It's not easy to fully comprehend what you've been through as fast as it all happened, but you need to at least try to understand your situation before you end up in a place you really don't want to be."

Jonas looked up, shocked by his sudden feelings.

"I'm serious, Jonas. You need to listen to me."

Jonas couldn't believe what was happening. His aunt's words traveled like waves of energy, unlike anything he had ever experienced before, hitting him with physical force and causing his very frame to shudder. This feeling radiated from her being—an emotional shockwave that struck him with sudden awe and amazement. Staring at her lips, Jonas realized that his aunt was not speaking with her mouth; instead, she was transferring her emotion in some sort of metaphysical way he couldn't fully comprehend. It was as if his aunt's empathy, her compassion, even her acute concern for his welfare became momentarily tangible, allowing Jonas to feel the thoughts and intents of her heart. Stunned with the sudden phenomenon, Jonas began to realize that his aunt seemed to possess some sort of otherworldly power that filled him with her own un-

derstanding—her own reality, as it were—to the point of near trans-
ference. For a few short moments, he even swore her view suddenly
became his: he literally saw himself as if he were gazing into a mirror.
He could see a terrified young man cowering in his seat as a wave of
light began to pulsate toward him. But just as quickly as this vision
opened, it closed, leaving him breathless in the aftermath.

Jonas staggered backward.

"As I told you," Aunt Claire explained, but this time with the use
of her mouth, "we can do special things here."

Still searching for some explanation, Jonas began to calculate the
improbability of it all.

"How can I . . . ?" he stuttered, still trying to regain control. "How
did you . . . ?"

He looked at her, trepidation in his eyes.

"I'm sorry to shock you like that, Jonas," Aunt Claire apologized,
"but you need to begin to understand your situation. What happened
at the beach back there has far more implications than you know."

Jonas stared at her with overwhelming confusion in his eyes.

"Now that you're here, with us," Aunt Claire gestured, "you can
do some amazing things, but you need to stop and think about it
before I can teach you any more."

Jonas's eyes widened.

"More?"

"Of course," Aunt Claire replied. "There's much more—speech,
travel, enhanced physical sensation; there's a whole new host of abilities within you waiting to be tapped. But none of it will be of any
significance unless you come to understand that one simple principle I told you about earlier—"

Jonas watched as his aunt gestured toward the door.

"Truth," she said again. "You must understand the fundamental
nature of truth. It might sound rudimentary, I know, but truth is the
means by which we are able to enjoy all of this, the means by which
we will one day reach perfection."

Jonas leaned forward in his seat.

"Perfection?" he asked, troubled by the onslaught of information coming at him all at once.

"Yes, perfection," Aunt Claire repeated. "It's really quite a simple principle when you think about it: truth begets knowledge and knowledge begets power—whether that power comes in the form of understanding how airplanes fly or how to speak with one's thoughts. It's all one and the same: eternal truth that eventually leads one along the path of perfection—or to the place called heaven."

Jonas shook his head, completely overwhelmed now.

"Surely you've stopped to think about what heaven must be like?" Aunt Claire said, noticing her nephew's response.

Jonas paused. He really had no idea what to say.

"Think about it," she said. "Heaven is a perfect place, isn't it? A place of perfect peace, perfect joy, perfect beauty? Why should we expect to live up to any lesser standard if we want to enjoy the weight of that kind of glory?"

Aunt Claire looked at her nephew, a blank expression still on his face.

"It's hard to digest, I know," she offered, "but the point is this: one does not become heavenly by simply entering heaven's doors. A violinist cannot play a concerto in Carnegie Hall simply by picking up a violin. She must dedicate herself to practice and incremental improvement before she can ever enjoy that kind of experience. That is the fundamental nature of heaven, Jonas—you do not become something you are not by entering its gates. Rather, you prepare yourself to become one who can dwell there."

Jonas looked at Karen, trying his best to figure out how this all worked together.

"Are you trying to say you were serious about Karen's legs?" he asked, looking for a connection.

"Yes, I am," Aunt Claire confirmed. "Karen was brought to us because of a condition she suffered from since birth that cost her the use of her legs. The complication perpetuated even after she made her journey here, which isn't all that uncommon in situations like hers. It's taken some time to help her heal, but evidently she's found the hope necessary to take her first steps. It's just another 'impossible' thing made possible because of what we know here."

Jonas watched Karen spin under the arm of the tall brunette near her side, trying to put the pieces of the puzzle together.

"To tell you the truth, a lot of children are brought to this hospital under similar circumstances," Aunt Claire continued, "children who have come to believe that their future progression will forever be restricted because of their former limitations. Many of them haven't been helped by a world so full of indifference, either. Words like 'crippled,' 'retarded,' or even 'worthless' were words many of these children heard on a daily basis. But that does not change the fact that in order to heal from such negative conditioning, they must learn to counter its destructive effects. Here, their mind has much more control over their body, allowing them to heal as soon as they believe it's possible. But if they choose to hold on to their limitations, then their body will naturally fulfill that command."

Jonas noticed a small boy being helped about in a wheelchair.

"You mean they won't be able to walk?" he asked.

"Yes, but simply walking is rarely the issue," Aunt Claire replied, noticing the little boy as well. "Seeing oneself in a whole new light is the real challenge. It's sad, but many of these little ones have been treated like second-class citizens for so long, it's not easy for them to believe that they deserve the kind of freedom you and I take for granted. But in order for them to heal, they must choose to face their fears, to give up the life that was once familiar, for a future of something more. It's not an easy task, even terrifying for some, but it doesn't take long until everyone who passes through that door comes to understand one very simple thing . . ."

Jonas looked back at his aunt, seeing her staring intently into his eyes.

"Heaven isn't a place you can go to escape your fears—it is a place for those who have already faced them."

Jonas looked at Karen again, as the beautiful woman at her side lifted her in a ballerina-like twirl.

71

"So the people like you and her," he began to ask, "you're the doctors in this hospital who help them?"

Aunt Claire paused for a moment as she looked at the person Jonas was referring to.

"You mean Millie?" she asked. "That tall woman dancing with Karen?"

Jonas nodded.

"Oh, Millie is just a child," Aunt Claire said, holding back an overt smile. "She came to us just a few weeks before Karen arrived—she's her younger sister."

Jonas did a double take. There was no way a woman of perhaps twenty could possibly be younger than a girl of perhaps seven, even in a strange place like this.

"You're kidding, right?" he said aloud, wondering if they were talking about the same person.

"I know it's hard to see," Aunt Claire mentioned, "but when you listen to her speak, it's much more apparent. She might look like a beautiful adult, but she's still a five-year-old at heart."

Jonas glanced back at his aunt, and then at Millie, wondering once more just what kind of place this really was.

"Don't worry, though," Aunt Claire reassured, "one day Karen may choose to look like that as well—tall, beautiful, and able to reach books she wants to read off the top shelf. It's simply another ability made possible here, and one of the reasons you won't often see children anywhere else other than in places like this. Most of them like the freedom a larger body affords, and so they make the transition when they learn they can."

"Wait—" Jonas said, "did you just say there are other places like this?"

"Of course, Jonas," Aunt Claire replied. "There's a whole new world out there just waiting for you to explore."

Having just been introduced to the Reading Room, it hadn't yet dawned on Jonas that there might be other places hidden around the world similar to the one in which he now sat.

"Would you like to see more of it?" Aunt Claire offered. "I'd love to take you farther into the hospital if you'd like."

Fully intrigued by the invitation, Jonas turned to look in the direction of the two giant double brass doors at the end of the nave.

"Yeah, of course," he said enthusiastically.

"Wonderful," his aunt said. "But unless I'm mistaken, you may want to put something else on before we go too far."

Glancing down at himself, Jonas suddenly realized he was the only one in the room without a shirt on.

"Thanks. That would be great," he chuckled.

Aunt Claire laughed.

"I thought you'd say as much. Come on, let's go."

7

JONAS WAS AT A LOSS FOR WORDS.

As he and his aunt walked out of the Reading Room through the large brass double doors, he was amazed at the magnificence of the hallway he was led into. Its architecture was similar to the room he had just exited, with luminescent walls and recessed pillars, but these pillars were made out of stone instead of wood and were much larger in diameter. Shafts of light streamed down from above, illuminating a space even more majestic and beautiful than the Reading Room he was leaving.

As he looked to his right and his left, he saw that the hallway, which felt very much like a street because of its width, had a massive door at either end, each one appearing to be made of solid gold. Between these two doors was an entire world bustling with excitement. As he and his aunt moved to the right, down the length of the hallway, Jonas noticed that some of the children were happily skipping along while holding the hand of their adult supervisor, while others were being escorted about in wheelchairs or carried in the arms or on the backs of their companions. As Jonas took it all in, he noticed there was a wonderful feeling in the air, a sense of optimism and joy that could be seen in the eyes of everyone as they greeted each other.

But that was not all. As Jonas walked farther and became more aware of his surroundings, he noticed that every few feet there was a door on either side of the hallway. He would have expected to see uniform doors along each side, but instead he saw different, unique doors unevenly spaced along the corridor. Some were quite large, matching the style of the hall's architecture. Others were small and ordinary, almost as if they belonged in a different building altogether.

As the two walked farther, Jonas noticed that some of the doors they were passing were open, offering him a glimpse inside.

The first of these rooms was so unexpected, that Jonas felt the urge to stop walking and simply stare. From his vantage point, he could see that there were children in the room, each accompanied by an adult as seemed usual for this place; but what really caught his attention was that the whole space was filled with bubbles. There were thousands of bubbles inside the room. Big ones. Little ones. Medium-sized too. But these bubbles didn't seem to pop, even when the children touched them with their fingers. Rather, these bubbles stayed intact as they floated in the air, bouncing around, moving in every conceivable direction. Jonas saw how the children jumped to touch the larger bubbles, while running through walls of smaller bubbles, creating the most brilliant display. This effect was enhanced by the fact that each bubble reflected bits of color off their round surfaces, making the whole room look as if it were dancing.

"Did you see that?" Jonas asked, amazed, as he caught up to his aunt, who had not stopped walking.

"Yes, that's the Bubble Room," she replied. "It's beautiful, isn't it? And fantastic for teaching rudimentary motor skills like running, skipping, and jumping."

The thought of the room having a fundamental purpose had never crossed Jonas's mind, but before he could ask more, he found his attention drawn to another space just a few doors down.

As they approached, he saw that this space had no doors at all, as he had expected, but was rather an impressive open archway. The interior of the room didn't look like what he would have imagined either. It actually looked more like an exterior, because of the presence of a variety of trees and colorful birds chirping and singing as they flew from branch to branch.

"That's Karen's favorite room," Aunt Claire said.

Jonas turned to glance at his aunt and then back at the room. While his attention was drawn to the colorful birds above, he soon noticed the presence of children below, holding out their hands to offer a place for the birds to perch. And each time a bird did, Jonas watched as the respective child giggled with innocent glee and then begin to converse with the bird as if it were an old familiar friend.

"What's that place for?" Jonas asked as he quickened his stride to keep up with his aunt.

"Trust," she replied. "The birds won't stay on your finger long if you don't behave in a way that shows that they can trust you. It's also the first real interaction with nature for some."

Passing the doorway by, Jonas glanced back once more, seeing a younger girl whispering to a small emerald-colored bird with flecks of Prussian blue on its wings. But just when the small animal began to coo back, his aunt turned his attention to a door on the opposite wall that looked extremely familiar.

"Here it is," she said, motioning with her hands as if to present the small wooden door to Jonas. "Your room."

Jonas turned and looked at it carefully, wondering exactly what his aunt meant by "your room." It was hard to guess what could be behind the door after what he had just seen. Nevertheless, he looked at the simple white door, so simple in its design that it seemed a blight on the magnificent hallway. Realizing that this door looked slightly familiar, he decided to ask about its contents before entering.

"What's in there?"

"It's your room, Jonas," his aunt said again. "I'm sure you will find everything just as you left it."

Aunt Claire then reached for the knob and turned it.

Jonas instantly recognized the space. He had just passed a room full of bubbles, and an aviary of sorts, but he never thought he would actually see *his* room.

"It's impossible," he said, mouth agape.

"Remember what I told you about that word," his aunt cautioned as she motioned for him to enter. "Mind you, it's not actually your room, but a duplicate of sorts. We have the ability to create some pretty incredible things here, and reproducing familiar places is just one of the tools we often find useful."

Jonas was overwhelmed at the attention to detail this room had been given. If he had been brought here blindfolded, he wouldn't have known the difference between this place and the apartment he called home back in New York City.

"I imagine you'll be able to find something to wear in your closet," she added. "I made sure all your shirts were pressed so you would look more presentable."

Jonas looked back at his aunt.

"Presentable?"

"Yes," she replied. "We have an event to go to soon, and I think it's best if you wear something fitting for the occasion."

"Where are we going?"

Aunt Claire looked at him for a moment.

"I'll tell you soon enough, but for now, I think it's best that you get dressed. There's someone waiting to see you."

Jonas glanced from his aunt to the crowd of patrons walking in the streetlike hallway.

"Me?" he asked, aware that he couldn't possibly know anyone besides his aunt here.

"Yes," Aunt Claire replied. "She's a very good friend of your mother's actually, but we don't have much time to waste, so you may want to pick out something quickly to help move things along. In case you haven't noticed, there's a lot of work to do here, and time is a luxury we don't like to waste."

Wondering just who this mysterious woman might be that his aunt made reference to, Jonas entered the room that seemed in every way a carbon copy of the one back home.

Closing the door behind him, he couldn't help but take a moment to look around. There wasn't a single detail out of place. To his right, he saw closets, a flat-screen TV, and the shelf that housed the books he read each night before going to bed. On the left was his leather couch, a large wooden coffee table, and the floor lamp that gave light to the space. In front of him was his bed, low to the ground, with a white goose-down duvet and large fluffy pillows.

Walking over to the closet, he opened the thin wooden door and saw his clean pressed shirts set neatly in a row. This small detail must have been his aunt's doing, as he had never seen his closet looking so tidy.

Smiling at her attention to such things, Jonas quickly picked out a blue button-down shirt and a comfortable pair of pants. As he had no idea what type of event he was about to attend, he thought it best to dress somewhat conservatively, so as not to stand out. He put on a belt that matched the outfit and a comfortable pair of shoes, and then gave himself a quick glance in the full-length mirror at the foot of his bed.

Confident that he looked sufficiently respectable for wherever his aunt was about to take him, Jonas took one last look at his room when something inside of him went very still. It was a kind of a sadness—a yearning for the familiar. It was an odd emotion to experience, he thought, as he was surrounded by nothing but the familiar in this replica of his apartment. But shaking off the thought, he quickly donned a watch and made his way back through the door.

"Wonderful!" his aunt greeted him as he emerged into the grand hallway. "I always thought you looked handsome in blue."

Smiling in appreciation, Jonas looked down the hall in anticipation of where his aunt was going to take him.

"Does the woman want to see me now?" he asked, wondering again who this friend of his mother's could be.

"Yes, she does," Aunt Claire replied. "She works here in this hospital just a few doors down, so we won't need to go very far."

Interested in meeting this mysterious woman, Jonas followed his aunt down the hallway until they reached a very peculiar door. With its thick wood and bolted steel, it looked more like the entrance to a fortress—the kind of door one would expect to see on the front of a medieval castle, not a door gracing an elegant hallway such as the one in which they were standing.

Jonas noticed that this door also had an ancient inscription engraved with gold on its façade, and he couldn't help himself from asking his aunt what it said.

Aunt Claire paused for a moment and looked at the writing, a melancholy expression on her face.

THE CHOICE: DEATH IS JUST THE BEGINNING

"This is a very special door, Jonas," she began, "one not very many people are ever allowed to pass through. If you don't mind, I would ask that you carry yourself with the utmost reverence inside."

Jonas's former excitement turned into a kind of apprehension. He began to wonder just where his aunt was taking him.

"What do you have to keep locked up here?" he asked.

"Nothing," his aunt replied. "The bolts on this door are for the ones inside. It helps them feel safer."

She took a step closer.

"You see, Jonas," she continued, "this is a special wing of the hospital where we take care of the most severe cases, ones that need our particular attention."

Looking back at the door, Jonas began to wonder just what those types of cases might be.

"Would you like to know?" his aunt asked, picking up on his non-verbal thoughts.

For a moment Jonas questioned whether he really did want to know, but his curiosity won out.

"If you wouldn't mind," he said politely.

Aunt Claire took another step toward the door.

"Inside here," she began to explain, "we keep the abused—those children who have been brought to us after having endured a lifetime of anguish and pain. In here you will find the effects of mental, emotional, physical, even sexual abuse—the most serious cases we have. It is one of the reasons not many people are allowed through, as what they are confronted with is often difficult to take in."

She turned to look in his direction.

"It's not easy to witness such traumatic things without being affected yourself. What you will see behind this door is simply a reflection of the most terrible crimes that humankind is capable of."

Glancing back at the door again, Aunt Claire seemed to almost tremble as she spoke.

"There is a punishment far worse than death awaiting those responsible for what's in here. And they will learn how heavy a responsibility they have to bear once they leave their short, mortal lives."

Jonas glanced from his aunt to the door, feeling increasingly uneasy as he took in her words.

"Please forgive me," Aunt Claire said after a moment or two, noticing Jonas's apprehension. "I don't mean to make you feel uncomfortable. I just want to impress on you the importance of this place so that you may better understand the message written on this door."

Pointing toward the golden inscription, Aunt Claire read the translation aloud.

"THERE IS NO PLACE SO DARK THAT LIGHT CANNOT LEAD THE WAY," she said. "Remember that, will you?"

Nodding to show that he would, Jonas heard the scraping of metal on wood as the bolted door seemed to open of its own accord.

———

Initially Jonas noticed that the lights were dimmer in here, making the hallway they left behind blindingly bright in comparison. As the door closed behind them, his eyes began to adjust to the darker surroundings, and he was soon able to see more of the details before him. He noticed that they had entered a small foyer made of stone and detailed wood, and facing them, were three doors set neatly in a row. The sound of a man's whispering voice suddenly filled the echoing chamber.

"Jonas," the voice said, calling him by name. "We've been expecting you."

Looking around to see where the voice came from, Jonas heard another sound, like that of a blowing wind, when all of a sudden a man materialized before their very eyes.

"What the . . . ," Jonas said aloud.

While the sudden appearance of a man from nowhere should have caused Jonas to reel in bewilderment or perhaps run for his life back through the bolted door—oddly, he felt no inclination to flee. He was more than a little surprised to see the occupants of the room increase by one in such a fashion, but having his aunt beside him while it happened seemed to calm him. Aunt Claire had said that there was something unique about the way people traveled here.

This must have been what she was talking about.

"Michael," Aunt Claire said with a smile. "So good of you to come."

The man smiled in return, reaching out to grasp her hand in a way that made Jonas think they must have been the best of friends.

"I'm glad I could make it, Claire" he replied.

Turning to Jonas, Aunt Claire made the introductions.

"Jonas, this is Michael," she said. "He is the husband of the woman we've come here to meet."

Michael, Jonas noticed, was a pleasant-looking man, perhaps in his midforties, who had a unique aura about him. There was a look in his eyes that seemed to express something distinctive about his character—as if he had experienced many of the trials life had to offer, yet had emerged a more refined being because of them. There was also a kindness about the way he smiled that conveyed genuine goodwill, which made Jonas trust him almost instantly, even though he had no idea who this man really was. And then there was a tranquil serenity about the way the man carried himself, a peaceful confidence that Jonas found intriguing. It made Jonas imagine what it might feel like shaking hands with a president or a dignitary: someone with great command or incredible responsibility.

"Hello," Jonas said as he shook Michael's hand, wondering for a moment how he was being perceived himself.

"Hello, Jonas," Michael replied with an eager smile. "It's so good to meet you. I can't tell you how much we've been looking forward to your arrival."

Jonas was somewhat taken aback by the man's kind words, but more puzzled by the fact that his own presence had indeed been expected.

"I realize you have a schedule to keep, though," Michael said as he took a step back and looked at the two of them, "so, please, let me help you on your way."

He gestured toward one of the doors.

"Jonas, I believe your aunt has told you a little about this wing of the building?"

Jonas nodded.

"A little."

"Good," Michael said, "then I trust you will be able to keep your voice to a whisper while I escort you to where you need to go."

The door on the left of the foyer opened itself without making a sound and Michael beckoned them to accompany him through it.

Walking through the doorway, Jonas was taken into an area that stood at the front of an extremely long hallway which initially opened to his left, where an average-sized, and rather plain-looking living room could be seen. Three adults and three children occupied the space, sitting on the floor between two small couches and a coffee table. Each child sat close to his or her adult companion, intrigued by a board game they were all playing together.

At the very moment the adults noticed Jonas's presence, they quickly pulled the children they were next to closer while whispering in their ears. The children turned to look at Jonas with anxious stares, making him feel that he had intruded on their privacy. The adults smiled at Jonas, waving to him in a manner that showed he was no threat, and the small ones soon relaxed and turned their attention back to the game.

"This way." Michael pointed toward the hallway in front.

Following his lead, Jonas and Aunt Claire walked into the corridor together.

Having come from the well-lit and rather grand hallway, Jonas felt that this space was extremely dark and cramped by comparison. But there was a detail about this hallway that was somewhat similar to the one outside. Doors. Every ten or fifteen feet there was another door, spaced at uneven intervals along the dark passageway, each one unique.

Walking farther into the space, Jonas noticed there were hallways everywhere—hundreds of them in fact. As he followed Michael to the end of one hallway, another one split off in a different direction, revealing a new set of doors and a new set of hallways. Hallway after hallway, door after door. It was like a maze, a myriad of passageways and doors, which made it seem increasingly impossible for anyone to navigate unless they had been here before.

At first Jonas was curious about what was behind these doors, as the great majority of them were shut. But soon, he connected the thought of each door with the existence of a small child—a child who had experienced the kind of abuse his aunt had described. This realization made Jonas want to turn around and ask if Michael's wife could speak with him outside. He didn't feel comfortable in here, and judging by the faces of the children he had seen in the front room, he was sure they weren't comfortable with his presence either. But just as he was about to whisper the request to his aunt, he saw a few doors open just ahead.

Overcome by curiosity, Jonas quickly glanced in as they walked by the first one.

In the room he saw a small girl, not much older than four or five, sitting on a bed in what looked like a very small bedroom and talking to a woman near her side. Jonas couldn't understand their conversation as the little girl was speaking in such a muffled tone, but he could tell it was a struggle for her to articulate her thoughts, and she had to stop every few words to sniff back tears.

Jonas then heard another child speaking to an attentive adult as he passed by the next open door. When he took a quick look, he noticed that the room was actually the backside of a staircase, which revealed a small crawlspace. The adult was sitting to the side of the staircase looking into where the child was hiding, speaking to him in hushed tones.

Just a few feet farther along, Jonas saw that the space inside the third open room was pitch black; this caught him quite off guard. He couldn't see if there was anything at all in there, but suddenly a small child's voice rang out, followed swiftly by fearful sobs.

"No! He's going to find me!"

"I'm here, Joseph," Jonas heard a woman say somewhere in the darkness. "I'm not going to leave you. You're safe now. He can't hurt you anymore . . ."

Feeling like an intruder on an extremely private moment, Jonas sped up to keep pace with his aunt.

Walking silently at her side, he eventually mustered the courage to speak.

"What are these rooms?" he asked quietly, feeling even more anxious than before.

His aunt moved closer to him so she could speak more privately.

"Each of these rooms," she whispered so faintly that Jonas had to lean in to hear, "are places that have been prepared for the children to make them more comfortable during their stay here at the hospital."

Looking at his aunt, Jonas had a hard time believing what he was being told.

"Are you serious?" he whispered, trying to keep his voice low, pointing back in the direction of the massive hallway. "There must be a hundred other places they would rather stay."

Aunt Claire nudged Michael, motioning for them to pause for a moment. Upon doing so, Jonas felt embarrassed, as if he had been out of turn in saying what he had. But seeing a look of empathy in his aunt's eyes, he realized he wasn't about to be reprimanded; rather, he was about to be given more information about this unusual place.

"I know what you mean, Jonas," his aunt sighed, "I thought the same things when I first came. It's dark here, dismal, full of things one would hope not to find. But that's why not many people are allowed in here. To see so much pain, so much sorrow—it seems contrary to what these little ones should have to endure."

Jonas glanced at Michael and saw him nod in agreement.

"I know it's not easy to understand," she continued, "but you need to take into consideration the enormity of what these children have been through. What you and I take for granted—the trust of a loved one, the belief that people can be good, the knowledge that we are more than objects—these are all things these little ones have been conditioned not to believe. That is why we do not take them out into that vast hallway with all those people, forcing them to associate with strangers they do not know. Doing so would cause them more anxiety and pain with an intensity most people could barely

THE CHOICE: DEATH IS JUST THE BEGINNING

understand. So instead, we offer them a place they can feel safe, a space that is familiar, something like the one they would run to when things became too much to bear. And while it may not look like the conditions you or I would choose, it is the closest thing to heaven they've ever had."

Jonas lowered his gaze slightly, feeling sorry for what little these children had to hold on to.

"Are all the rooms like these?" he said, pointing toward the open doors they had just passed.

"Each room is different," Aunt Claire replied, as she motioned for the group to continue walking again. "Some of the children feel most safe in a room not unlike your own, an exact replica of the bedroom they used to know. Others want to get as far away from a place like that as possible. Some children find safety in a closet or a cupboard. But whatever it is, each personal space holds special meaning for the child who inhabits it."

Jonas walked quietly for a moment.

"Do they ever get to leave?"

"Yes, of course," Aunt Claire said with hope in her voice. "That is one of our purposes here. As they learn of the love we have for them, and understand that we can be trusted, they gain the confidence they need to leave their personal spaces, to venture out into the rest of what this place has to offer."

Jonas thought about the children he had seen when first entering this section of the hospital, wondering if, perhaps, they had just left their private rooms for the very first time.

"What do you do to help them?" Jonas asked. "I mean, what do you say to get them out of their rooms?"

"At first, we say very little," she answered. "It's better to listen. Each one of these children has a story all their own, so we listen intently to what they have to say."

Thinking for a moment about the types of things these little children would have to talk about, Jonas replied, "You don't mean they actually want to tell you about . . ."

But he stopped himself short.

"Actually, they do," Aunt Claire said sincerely. "Seeing that most of these children have been threatened into silence, or ignored by those who could have helped them, that's exactly what they want to talk about. Far too often, society shrugs aside the pain of these little ones. But problems cannot be solved by ignoring them, and healing cannot occur by refusing to listen to the truth, unsettling as it may be. So, yes, we sit and we listen to the stories of their lives. And as their burdens are lifted in the telling of such things, and they learn they are not responsible for what has happened to them, they begin to hope for a new kind of life and find the courage necessary to leave their personal spaces."

Listening intently to what his aunt had to say, Jonas noticed Michael stop near a purple door.

"Jonas, Claire," he said politely, "if you would be so kind as to wait a moment."

Pausing near the door, Jonas heard the faint sound of a children's lullaby being sung, which grew in volume as Michael opened the door and deftly slipped inside.

After a few moments, he reemerged.

"Jonas, I want to thank you for taking the time to meet with Gwen. You have no idea what this means to us."

Thinking of when he had ever heard the name Gwen spoken in connection to his mother, Jonas soon saw Michael gesture for them both to enter.

"I must be about my other work though," Michael added, "so I'll leave you here for now. But don't worry, I will see you again, Jonas, very soon."

Pausing one last moment to take in this man's kind presence, Jonas said a word of thanks before following his aunt inside the room.

———

The space Jonas entered was a nursery, complete with colored wallpaper, soft carpet, and a crib set off to one side. At the far corner of the room he saw the woman he was there to meet, Gwen, sitting in a rocking chair and holding a small child who was resting in her arms.

"Jonas?" the woman asked with an eager smile on her face.

"Yes . . . ," Jonas answered, still taking in his surroundings.

"Jonas," his aunt stepped in, "this is Gwen."

Jonas took a step forward to shake her hand but held himself back as he noticed that both her hands were occupied with the child in her arms.

"Hold on a minute," Gwen said as she looked over his shoulder at the door he had just walked through.

Turning in that direction as well, Jonas saw a breathtakingly beautiful young woman with long blond hair walk into the room. She had an oval face and bright eyes and moved with a sense of weightless grace. Initially, Jonas wasn't sure if he was looking at another five-year-old who had grown into an adult body like Millie, but when she spoke, she didn't sound at all like a child.

"Pardon my intrusion," the young woman interjected with a trace of an English accent. "Gwen, may I take the child for you?"

As she spoke, Jonas noticed how soft her voice was, as if she had grown accustomed to speaking in a whisper. As she glided past him, Jonas also noticed that she smelled like honeysuckle, the aroma that had drawn him into this place when his aunt had first opened the doors to the hospital.

"Thank you, Elle," Gwen said as she shifted in her seat to hand the small child over. "Have you met Jonas yet?"

Elle turned around and looked at Jonas for a curiously long moment.

"Sir," she said with a curtsy. "How lovely to make your acquaintance."

Jonas was caught off guard. For a girl as young as she looked, she didn't sound at all like any of the girls he had ever met. She was proper and polite, but in an exceptionally old-fashioned way.

"Jonas is pleased to meet you as well, I'm sure," his aunt said for him, breaking the odd silence Jonas had created by not responding.

"Yes, of course, I'm pleased to meet you too," Jonas said quickly, in the most proper way he knew how.

"Jonas just arrived not too long ago," Gwen remarked with a

smile. "Remember those days, Elle?"

"Of course," Elle said, still looking into Jonas's eyes.

Curtsying once more, the young woman turned and leaned over to pick up the small child in Gwen's arms.

"Thank you, Elle, we shouldn't be long," Gwen said appreciatively.

Elle nodded in recognition and then glided past Jonas once more, giving him another intriguingly long stare before exiting the room.

"Elle and I work together," Gwen said, looking back now at Jonas. "When she first arrived, she took to the work quickly."

"She came to work with you?" Jonas asked, trying to make small talk.

Gwen paused to glance at Aunt Claire for a moment before replying.

"No," she said, hesitating a bit, "I was the one who came to work with her. Elle may seem young, but she's been here quite a long time."

Observing the strange exchange of looks between the women, Jonas furrowed his brow.

"How long?" he asked.

Gwen looked back in his direction.

"Longer than perhaps is necessary for this conversation," she said, as she worked to change her expression. "But enough of that; it's you I want to talk about."

Since Jonas wasn't exactly sure why he had been brought here, he decided to wait for Gwen to initiate the exchange.

"You've grown up so well," Gwen observed, before turning to look at Aunt Claire again, who was also apparently having a hard time holding back the pride she felt for her nephew.

Jonas raised his eyebrows and gave a fake smile. He felt like a five-year-old all over again, on display at the kind of family reunion where his cheeks would inevitably be pinched.

"Forgive me," Gwen said, realizing that their doting had begun to make him feel uncomfortable. "It's not very often one gets the opportunity to see people they have thought about for so long."

"Aunt Claire told me you're a friend of my mother's?" Jonas

began to inquire.

"Yes," she replied, "a very good friend actually."

"I don't remember seeing you around," he said somewhat instinctively, before shifting his tone to sound more polite. "I mean, I never saw you come over for dinner or anything."

Gwen looked from Jonas to Aunt Claire, taking in a deep breath as she did so. Jonas noticed that there seemed to be another transfer of silent information between the two.

"Jonas," Gwen began as she looked back at him, "I know your mother from back in art school. I was her best friend, actually. We were roommates."

Jonas looked at her, more confused than before.

"My mom didn't go to art school," he said, wondering now who this woman in front of him really was.

Gwen paused, giving one more glance in Aunt Claire's direction.

"Yes, the mother who raised you never went to art school," she replied, looking back at him. "But the mother I knew is the one you've never met."

Jonas suddenly became very still.

"The woman I would like to tell you about, Jonas," she said, "is the one who gave you those beautiful blue eyes."

8

JONAS DIDN'T KNOW WHAT TO THINK OR HOW TO REACT.
He stood still as a statue, stunned by what Gwen had just told him.

All his life, he had wondered about his parents—his biological
parents. Noticing the difference between himself and the rest of his
siblings, Jonas couldn't help but wonder where he really came from.
His eyes were blue and his hair was dark brown. Everyone else in his
family had blond hair and brown eyes. And as he grew, and began to
take note of even more differences, he began to feel a dark, sickening
sensation that he didn't quite belong.

It was this impression he felt each time he looked into the mirror
and saw those blue eyes staring back at him—eyes that seemed to
scream out a truth he wanted so desperately to deny. He was different from them, from those he called his family. In his youth he
prayed for his eyes to change color or his hair to look like everyone
else's, but he realized praying would not be enough. No amount of
time on his knees would change who he was.

This feeling of not belonging was sharpest when he met people
for the first time while in close proximity to a member of his family.
Jonas hated that most. He knew he stood out like a sore thumb, a
sensation that was only accentuated by the inevitable pause created
when people would look back and forth between him and his siblings. Jonas would usually mention something about a great-grand-
father or a long lost cousin who shared his genetics, but every time
he tried to lie his way out of it, he ended up feeling hollow and
embarrassed. While his brothers and sisters never felt it appropriate
to correct him, he knew their silence only confirmed the truth.

His parents tried to talk to him many times about the fact that
he was adopted, but each time they did, Jonas would become cold

and defensive or particularly aloof. And he would hold on to that disposition for days, shutting out his family at the dinner table, finding excuses why he had to work overtime on some school project or needed to spend the night at a friend's house. This behavior didn't stem from any sort of ill will he silently harbored toward his family, though. On the contrary, he acted this way because of the deep affection he had for all of them. But there was something inside of Jonas that made him believe that the moment he acknowledged the existence of another mother and father, another family somewhere, he would automatically remove himself from the only family he had ever loved. And that thought—that thought of separation—cut so deep that distancing himself became the only way he knew to cope. If he had less to give up, there would be less pain to feel when the truth caught up with him.

Jonas's parents tried time and time again to reassure him of their love. And while this was temporarily comforting, Jonas still found it hard to accept. In his mind, if he was as loved as they said he was, then why did the two people who should have loved him the most— the two people whose blood ran through his veins—give him away? He was adopted, which meant that the mother and father who were obligated to love and care for him seemed instead to want nothing to do with him at all. And while he wished to feel like a part of his adoptive family, every time they brought up the reality of his past, it only accentuated the differences he saw in himself. In moments like that, it was hard not to think of his siblings as smarter, more talented, and all around more capable people because of their parents. It was quite a temptation for Jonas to pit their strengths against his weaknesses, making him wonder if there was something wrong with him, something broken inside. No one in his family would ever say such a thing, but Jonas didn't feel they had to. The evidence of his dark past was as plain as the nose on his face.

"You knew my mother?" Jonas asked softly, a lump growing in his throat.

"Yes," Gwen said, empathy in her eyes, "I knew her very well. She was an exceptional woman."

As Gwen described his mother, it filled Jonas with powerful, conflicting emotions. Part of him had hoped he would hear good things about her, as it might be some sort of reflection on his own self-worth. But if she was such a wonderful woman, how could she give up the child she was supposed to love? If she had such remarkable attributes, wasn't that simply evidence pointing toward the fact that Jonas lacked such characteristics himself? Why else would his mother give him away—unless she realized life would somehow be much better without him?

Jonas knew he was reaching with such thoughts, but he didn't care. The animosity that he had built up over the years for his biological mother wasn't something he was going to part with just because some woman whom he had never met was paying her a few compliments.

"What else do you know about her?" Jonas asked, a slight trace of aggression now in his tone.

Gwen looked at him, concern in her expression.

"Oh, Jonas," she said, "I'm so sorry. I know this must be so difficult for you to hear . . ."

"You don't need to apologize," he said flatly. "You didn't do anything wrong."

But she had. In Jonas's mind, being a friend of the woman who had done such a terrible thing to him was just as bad as having done it herself. She was an accomplice. He was sure Gwen had reassured his mother that giving him up was the right thing to do.

"Please, Jonas," Gwen tried to comfort him, "I know you didn't come here expecting me to tell you this . . ."

"Tell me what?" he said abruptly. "That she abandoned me?"

Focusing on the cruelness of his mother's gesture, Jonas couldn't help but picture the act in the most painful light. It was something he had done many times before: he would imagine what his mother might be like, a mother who was intelligent and beautiful, as thoughtful as she was kind. He would invent the kind of mother every child would want, one who would lovingly attend to every need. He imagined a child falling from a bike and scraping his knee, a small girl needing help with her homework, a little boy sick at home, wanting nothing more than to be reassured that he is loved. But as he saw his make-believe mother taking care of each child, Jonas would remind himself that she had never done any of those things for him. Where had she been when he fell off his bicycle for the first time? Where was she when he needed help with his schoolwork? And where was his mother when all he wanted to hear were the words "I love you"?

He knew that conjuring such images would only cause him pain, but in a strange way that is exactly what he wanted to feel. In some kind of self-debasing way, Jonas wanted to feel this pain, with the hope that one day his mother would be made aware of what she had done to him. It was a dark, loathsome feeling Jonas didn't even know existed within him. But it was there nonetheless—the desire to have his mother brought before him, asking for forgiveness, pleading for mercy for the pain she had caused him all these years, for the life she had so freely given away. All her beauty, all her charm, her goodness, her kindness, or whatever she seemed to possess would then be put on trial for what it really was—a mask to hide the truth of her selfish act. That would put things right. That would heal the wounds she had inflicted on him with her coldhearted absence.

Recognizing his anger, Aunt Claire touched Jonas's shoulder and turned to look at him. He saw her searching for something deep in his resentful stare. He could feel her looking into his soul, trying to find the small boy inside of him, the small boy who had recognized for the first time what having blue eyes in his family really meant. Jonas was only six when that took place, a terrified little boy teetering on a stool in order to get a better look at his reflection in the mirror above the bathroom sink. Earlier that day, someone at school had told him that Jonas's parents were liars, that they couldn't possibly be his real parents. Little Jonas didn't know what to do when his schoolmate pointed at his blue eyes, telling everyone around them that Jonas's "real parents" must have thrown him away because they didn't love him. "You don't look anything like your fake parents," the little boy accused. "You're just a garbage baby."

Even now, the memory of being called "garbage baby" was something that burned inside of Jonas. It was an experience that had cut so deep he had never told his adoptive parents about it. Though they had remained ignorant of what had happened to him that day, Jonas couldn't help but feel that his aunt somehow knew. He had never told her either, but as she stared into his eyes, he could almost feel her reading his thoughts, reliving the experience with him. He tried to shut her out, but he felt she could see much more than he was willing to let on. And as she began to speak, Jonas could tell it was not to him that she directed her words; no—it was a smaller, younger, much more vulnerable child with whom she wanted to communicate. Cutting through the darkness, Jonas could feel his aunt's words searching for that small boy who remained forever in front of the bathroom mirror, terrified by what his reflection was revealing.

"Jonas, I know how hard this is for you," she began. "You've carried this burden with you your entire life."

Jonas looked back at her, clenching his jaw.

"But it doesn't have to be that way, not if you don't want it to," his aunt said, her eyes still searching.

"She abandoned me," Jonas said sternly, "that's all there is to it."

"I know it feels that way," Aunt Claire continued, "but there's more to her story than that. She really did love you."

"Love me?" Jonas countered quickly. "Where I come from you don't abandon the ones you love. You don't leave them to fend for themselves."

"Exactly, Jonas," Aunt Claire replied. "She didn't leave you alone. She gave you a family, a wonderful family that gave you everything she couldn't."

Jonas fell silent, his thoughts turning suddenly to the mother who had raised him his entire life.

"Back when you were younger, I used to talk to your mother quite often about it," Aunt Claire remembered. "She would come to me with tears in her eyes, wondering how she could help you understand how being adopted didn't stop her from loving you. She wanted you to know that you were her son, even if she didn't give birth to you, and that nothing would ever change the feelings she had for you in her heart."

Jonas had to glance away as he grappled with the image his aunt's story began to paint in his mind.

"She wanted you to know," Aunt Claire said, "that nothing could break the bond you both shared. But like you, she was afraid—not that you would want to leave her when you found out who your biological mother was, but that you would live your entire life never really feeling like you were her son."

Jonas felt himself suddenly at a loss for words.

"I need to go," he said instinctively, searching for the door at his back.

Pulling on his sleeve, Aunt Claire drew him close, staring into his conflicted eyes.

"Jonas, I promise I'll take you to Chris and your family when we're done here," she said, "but Gwen has something to tell you, a story of sorts; something your mother would want you to know. And I think, given Gwen's unique relationship to your biological mother, she's probably the best one to relate it."

Looking back at Gwen as she stood up from her chair, Jonas began to feel a subtle sense of sorrow emanating from her being for having caused him so much pain. Somewhat similar to what he had experienced in the Reading Room with his aunt, Jonas could somehow feel Gwen's true emotions, helping him to understand the honest nature of her intentions. She was kind, he could tell, and truly giving. There wasn't a selfish bone in her body that he could perceive. But that didn't change the fact that he didn't want to hear what she had to say, especially in light of how he had been completely blindsided by the topic.

But as he stared at her, contemplating his options, Jonas realized he didn't know his way out. Even if he did storm out of the room, as he felt the urge to do, he would have no idea how to navigate his way back to the main hall. He was, quite literally, trapped. In addition, he began to feel a bit uncomfortable at how quick he had been to react. Surely Gwen must have been able to feel the strong resentment he had toward her, especially since this hospital seemed to accentuate such feelings. There was a part of him that wondered too, if she had picked up on his accusation of her as an "accomplice"—a thought that must have cut to some degree. But in the end, it was Gwen's relationship to Aunt Claire that gave Jonas pause. His aunt had never done anything other than look out for him his entire life, which made him want to know why she had brought him to this wing of the hospital in the first place. And if his mother would want him to listen to what Gwen had to say, there must be something important for him to hear.

Taking a moment to calculate his alternatives, Jonas realized that any hope of returning to normal life would most likely be expedited if he allowed Gwen to speak. Once she had done so, as his aunt had just promised, he would be taken back to Chris and his family, back to where life was as it should be. Chris was probably beginning to wonder where he had gone off to by now anyway—and worse, Sarah would soon be wondering if he had forgotten about her altogether. Since Jonas knew he was supposed to pick her up at the airport, he definitely didn't want to start off on the wrong foot by appearing forgetful about the time of her arrival.

Pausing in thought to remind himself where he had hidden the engagement ring inside his suitcase, Jonas turned his attention back to Gwen, feeling something of an apology was in order.

"I'm sorry, Gwen," he began, "I didn't expect this to come up."

"Please Jonas, don't," Gwen said with compassion in her voice.

Feeling his emotions beginning to resurface at the prospect of talking about his biological mother, Jonas took a deep breath and tried his best to regain his composure.

"I just don't understand," he confessed. "I don't understand how a mother could do that to her child, how she could just give me away like she did."

"That's exactly what I would like to explain to you, Jonas," Gwen said. "But perhaps, it might be a bit easier if we have a seat while I tell you her story."

Watching Gwen gesture at something behind his back, Jonas

THE CHOICE: DEATH IS JUST THE BEGINNING

turned to look, and saw two white wooden chairs placed neatly together. Having already seen the contents of the room earlier, he knew there had been no chairs there before; they seemed to have simply appeared, much like Michael, out of thin air.

Jonas sat down on the chair nearest him as he tried to gather his thoughts. Aunt Claire sat in the chair next to him, while Gwen pulled hers closer to create a more intimate space.

"Jonas," Gwen began, after a moment or two, "I'm not sure if your aunt has told you, but here in this hospital, we talk a lot about families. Do you have any idea why that might be?"

Jonas shrugged his shoulders. "Because they raise us?"

"Indeed," Gwen replied, pleasantly surprised with his response. "To a great extent, they help form us into who we are, how we perceive the world, and how we experience life."

Jonas glanced over at Aunt Claire as she gave him an encouraging smile.

"There is a bond," Gwen continued, "a bond that stretches generations. A chain, if you will, that links you to your parents, your parents to theirs, and so on. We discuss this family chain openly here, as it has a great effect on the minds of those around us. This chain, however, can be both good and bad. Seeing that it links you to the lessons your parents have handed down, it can teach you much about the value of love and respect. Conversely, it can also bind you to incorrect traditions and false beliefs that can corrupt the mind and introduce darkness."

Gwen gestured to the door behind Jonas's back.

"Many of the children in this place are here because of such chains, Jonas. They have been brought to us because those who should have loved and protected them have used and abused them instead. Half of what we do here is to teach these children the lessons they should have learned early on but were never given the opportunity. Love, peace, and joy are things you and I think everyone should want for themselves, but some people have been held in darkness so long, they don't even know what those things are."

Acknowledging the difficult circumstances of those around him,

Jonas felt his anger ease a bit.

"It's hard to understand," Gwen continued, "but there are people—men and women alike—who would do anything to control the will of others. Whether it be for pleasure or for spite, there are many who would seek to bind the ones who fall under their influence with those dark chains—chains we refer to here as the Chains of Hell."

Gwen paused a moment as a feeling of tension entered the room.

"Your mother was one who suffered at the hands of such people," she continued. "She was born into a difficult household, one in which she found herself abused, alienated, and alone."

Jonas felt his pulse begin to quicken as his mother's story, a story he had never heard but always wondered about, began to unfold.

"Her father had once been a brilliant businessman—but she never knew that version of him. In her only memories of him, he came home late at night, the smell of alcohol on his breath, sometimes with the strange aroma of perfumes she knew her mother didn't wear. He was a closet alcoholic, which eventually took his life, but not before he bankrupted his own business, leaving his family with little to live on after his death.

"Her mother wasn't exactly without vice either. She was an aristocratic type, quick to anger and capable of using any means necessary to whip her children into shape. She knew of her husband's infidelities, but she was willing to overlook them because of the comfortable lifestyle he initially provided. She was a cold, distant woman who cared more about the approval of her affluent neighbors than she cared for her own family—which she reiterated time and again to her children with the buckle of a leather belt. I was shocked the first time I saw it myself, but a good deal of your mother's body is covered with scars from when she was only five years old."

Jonas shifted in his seat.

"By the time your mother was almost fifteen, she had been sent to a correctional boarding school for girls. She didn't mind though. She enjoyed the change. It was the first time she was able to make friends, the first time anyone ever showed a personal interest in her. Having been neglected by her father most of her life, and physically abused by her mother, she welcomed the attention of the teachers and students.

"But like many girls her age who have been through similar experiences, she soon found that her life was somewhat hollow and incomplete. She enjoyed her newfound freedom, but she still felt something was missing, something she had never really experienced before."

Jonas found himself silent, listening.

"Love," Gwen explained. "She wanted more than anything to feel love. Having never experienced it while growing up, she began to wonder what it actually felt like. Although she was enrolled at a school for girls considered 'troubled,' she had seen more than one family come to visit her classmates—mothers and fathers who were truly concerned for their children. During the holidays, when all of the children were allowed to return home, she was one of the few always left behind. Her mother punished her this way, for being what she deemed 'an unruly child.' But solitude like that can only exist for so long before the one suffering finds herself looking for relief."

"What do you mean, looking for relief?" Jonas cut in abruptly, feeling, for the very first time in his life, a semblance of concern for the woman he had grown to resent.

"Well, many of the girls at that school became defensive and violent—understandably, of course—but your mother was different. She was a quiet, contemplative child, one who often lost herself in books. She read voraciously, especially novels about finding true love after a long period of waiting. The love of a parent. The love of a sibling. And over time, the love of someone with whom you can share the most intimate part of yourself."

Gwen paused.

"Sadly, it was at that time of yearning that she happened to meet him."

"Him?" Jonas asked. "Who?"

"The man who eventually led her down a terribly dark road."

Jonas glanced over at his aunt, feeling something stir inside.

"There was a man," Gwen continued, but in grave tone, "a local salesman who worked at a small publishing house that provided many of the textbooks used by schools in that area. As a part of his sales strategy, he donated his time at a few of the larger schools, tutoring students in mathematics as a way of ingratiating himself with the faculty and staff. When it came time for the schools to order new textbooks, they would naturally think of him.

"This man scheduled one-on-one sessions with the students during the evenings, after his day job at the publishing house. At your mother's school, he was given a small, private classroom to use where he would tutor young girls for a few hours every other day.

"Your mother excelled in nearly all her subjects, except geometry. For some reason that subject was especially difficult for her. She was a diligent student: she even asked her math teacher for extra homework so she could have more practice. But when he saw that her aptitude for mathematics was not up to par with the rest of the class, he suggested that she work with a tutor."

Jonas felt his aunt move closer to him in her seat.

"Your mother worked very hard on learning geometry with her tutor's help. But as time went by, she began to notice how their conversations slowly turned from mathematics to her. For the first time in her life, she found someone who seemed to be genuinely interested in her—interested in what she had to say and how she saw the world. Over time, the lessons became more frequent too, although the amount of time actually studying declined substantially. But your mother didn't care. She thought that she had finally met the person she had longed for all those years, the one she had read about in so many books. And after a time, she became convinced that she was in love, and that he truly loved her."

"How old did you say she was?" Jonas asked.

"At this point, fifteen," Gwen replied.

"It may seem difficult to believe," she continued, "but your mother had longed for a connection with someone who could be a father figure, a genuine friend, and, yes, someone she could share her most intimate thoughts with. Age seemed to hold no meaning for her within that kind of relationship, which is why she believed what the man told her. He was cunning and clever, always saying what she wanted to hear."

"What was his name?" Jonas asked.

"William—William Graves."

Jonas took a moment, then nodded for her to continue.

"Understand, this man had done this before. Having taught at many schools like this, he had more than enough experience doing what he did to your mother."

"Did?" Jonas cut in again. "What did he do?"

Gwen looked at him uneasily for a moment.

"During the course of those evenings," she said, "your mother began to feel things she had never felt before. Academics soon held little interest for her. She was interested only in William. He was handsome, charismatic, yet enigmatic: many of the attributes she had read about in her books. And with him, she felt special, beautiful, even desired . . ."

"But you said she was only fifteen," Jonas interrupted.

"Yes, but that didn't stop William Graves from using her age and innocence to his advantage, poisoning her mind. He began to whisper things to her, things he thought she wanted to hear. At first it was subtle. Fatherly compliments any schoolgirl would want to hear. But those paternal sentiments turned slowly suggestive—so subtly your mother didn't even see it coming.

"It didn't take much, as vulnerable as she was, but feeling his words to be genuine, thinking that she had finally found true love— it was short work for him to coerce her into giving him everything. The only innocence she had managed to cling to as a child was taken from her by someone who was supposed to be responsible for her care."

Jonas watched as the look in Gwen's eyes became even more severe.

"Believe it or not," she continued, "your mother came to think that she had finally found what she had been looking for her whole life, but within a few months, she learned her hopes were in vain."

"A few *months*?" Jonas asked incredulously. "It went on that long?"

"Yes, it continued until she became aware that she was pregnant. It was only then that she discovered the true intentions of this horrible man."

Jonas shook his head, disgusted by what he heard.

"As any fifteen-year-old would be, your mother was terrified when she found out about her condition. Initially, she thought of what her mother and father would say, what her new friends would think, and what the school would do to her. But feeling that she was not alone, she went and told her tutor about the pregnancy, hoping he could help her somehow.

"But the minute she spoke to him about it, William became enraged. To her surprise, he began to accuse her of being an unruly and irresponsible child, saying that her parents had been right to send her to a school for troubled girls. He continued to belittle her, telling her that he had only helped her with her studies because he saw how slow she was. He accused her of seducing him and making him do things he claimed he did not want to do. Then, he pressured her—telling her that she could tell no one about it until he figured out what to do. And as the minutes passed with your mother standing there in shocked silence, he began to tell her how she had ruined his life, how he would be sent to prison if anyone found out, and how she alone was responsible for what had happened."

In his mind's eye, Jonas saw the image of a frightened teenager, listening to the railing accusations of a man well beyond her years.

"Afraid that what she was hearing was true," Gwen continued, "your mother fell to her knees and begged for forgiveness, asking him to stay with her in return for her silence. But the only response William gave her was to turn and walk away."

Jonas looked at Gwen, astonishment in his expression.

"It was a dark, dark time for your mother. Everything that she had hoped for, had dreamed of, was taken away from her in that instant. Her mother had been cold and cruel, her father had neglected her, and now this man had taken everything she had left, including her innocence. And as she knelt there crying in that classroom, she began

THE CHOICE: DEATH IS JUST THE BEGINNING

to think there was no reason to keep going anymore. If that is what life was going to be like for her, she would have gladly ended it."

Jonas lowered his head, feeling somewhat ashamed for the quick judgment he had handed out to this fifteen-year-old girl.

"But in that moment of despair," Gwen said, "your mother realized she wasn't alone. She had you. Though you were no larger than a peanut at the time, you were enough of a reason for her not to end it all. Suicide had seemed like the only answer just moments before, but as she looked down, holding herself as if to wrap you in a tender embrace, she realized she had something to live for."

Jonas looked up.

"It was love, Jonas—the love she had for you, the love she had wanted for so long to feel," Gwen said. "But as a girl who would be turning sixteen just a short time after your birth, your mother knew she couldn't raise you alone. She knew that if she was going to keep you, she would have to bring you home, back to a place that had been so cruel to her, back to a life she wanted so desperately to escape. As a young, helpless, teenage mother, she knew the limitations of what she could provide for you. The home she hated would become a prison in which she would have to raise you. The love she knew she had to offer would be stifled by the cold influence of her mother and father. She knew she couldn't change who her parents were, but she had the ability to change who your parents could be. And realizing that her only hope of experiencing real love would be in the giving of it, she decided to let that love live on in you. It was in the moment of that decision—that terribly painful decision—that she experienced love, true love, for the first time in her life."

Jonas sat silently as he watched Gwen's eyes fill with tears, evidence of the bond she shared with this woman he had never met.

"You're mother is a good woman, Jonas," she said, "I promise you that. She sacrificed everything for you. And while I know it may not have been what you wanted to hear, I hope it can at least give you a little peace—knowing that she really did love you. She didn't give you up because she didn't want you. She gave you up so you would have the life she never could."

Jonas looked down at the floor, pondering what had become of this teenage girl.

"What happened?" he said in a low whisper, "what happened to her after he—" Jonas paused for a moment, making the connection in his mind as to who *he* really was. "What happened after *he* walked out?"

Gwen glanced at Aunt Claire, hesitating for a moment before explaining.

"William Graves disappeared, never to return to that school again," she said. "But your mother held on to the secret of what he had done to her, until she could no longer keep it hidden."

"She didn't tell anyone?" Jonas said, somewhat in disbelief.

"She was too scared," Gwen replied. "You need to understand—things of this nature are extremely delicate. While it's easy for people to think that victims of such tragedies should simply come out with the truth, actually doing so is far more difficult. Feelings of guilt and pain—even perplexing pleasure—can all combine to confuse an individual so much so that they may begin to question what they should reveal. Sometimes sheer embarrassment is enough to silence someone for a lifetime. And, as happened to your mother, some people even question whether they are a victim and not a willing accomplice. But that does not change the fact that they will suffer from those horrific experiences until they can come forth with the truth and properly heal."

Jonas saw his aunt turn toward him.

"Your mother did the right thing in the end," Aunt Claire said, looking at Jonas with compassionate eyes. "She came forth with the truth, as difficult as it was. And because of her, three more girls were able to testify to what William Graves had done to them."

"William Graves?" Jonas said, a new, more complicated, emotion beginning to take shape within him. "You mean, *my father* . . ."

Gwen leaned forward, placing her hand gently on his.

"The eyes that I see before me now are not the eyes of William Graves," she said softly. "While he may have been a part of your past, the connection you share does not have to impede your future. You are the noble son of a noble woman, and if there is something of her that I see in you, it is her goodness and her compassion, reflected in those blue eyes."

Jonas held her gaze, trying his best to process it all.

"She may not be much more than a story to you right now," Gwen said, "but I want you to know she was someone special—you are someone special, and every moment that has transpired since has been a testament to your shared goodness."

Jonas watched as Gwen's eyes filled with tears again.

"If she could only see you now—she would be so proud."

Taking a moment to internalize her words, Jonas turned to his aunt.

"What happened to him," he said, pausing again before saying the words, "to *my father?*"

"That's one of the reasons I brought you here, Jonas," she said cautiously with a concerned look in her eyes. "He's never been held accountable for what he did to your mother. We are hoping you could help us with that."

Jonas's eyes grew wide.

"Me?" he said, pointing to himself.

"We've had people watching him for some time now," his aunt replied, glancing briefly at Gwen, "but we've come to realize that there's only one person who can truly bring him to justice."

Jonas stared at his aunt, a blank expression on his face.

"The relationship you share with William is a unique one," she said, with slight hesitation. "It's put you in a position where you can actually do something about the devastation he's left in his wake. But it's also a relationship that will be exploited by others if we wait too long."

"Others? Who?"

Aunt Claire looked at Gwen for quite a long moment before answering.

"Don't worry, you will meet them very soon," she said. "Suffice it to say, the relationship you have with William Graves is far more important than you realize. If you decide to take on the responsibility of making him answer for his crimes, you may just save more than one life along the way."

Feeling his confusion mounting, Jonas looked at his aunt with even wider eyes.

"Save someone's life?"

"Yes. But if you feel the task is too great . . ." Aunt Claire added, noticing his reaction. "It is, after all, quite a lot to ask of someone who knows so little about our world."

His hesitation morphing into even greater confusion, Jonas took a while to respond.

"What are you talking about, *our world*?"

Aunt Claire placed her hand on his.

"Jonas," she said, slowly, carefully, "you can't tell me that you haven't wondered what's happened to you since I came to pick you up at the beach."

Jonas glanced down at his aunt's hand, feeling the unusual stream of electricity flowing between them again.

"You told me you came to help," he said.

"I did," Aunt Claire replied. "But don't you find it a little strange that I showed up just now, after all these years?"

Jonas pulled his hand back, shaking his head.

"Don't you think it was a little out of place that I just happened to appear in the back of someone's car, only to reappear behind your back?" she added. "Don't you find it odd that we can talk with our thoughts, heal incurable diseases, or simply cause things to appear out of thin air like the chair you're now sitting on?"

Jonas rose to his feet, turning toward the door at his back.

"You told me it was because of truth," he said, feeling suddenly betrayed.

"Of course it is, Jonas," his aunt said, standing up as well. "But the truth works both ways. You can't learn what it has to teach you when you try to ignore what it's already shown you."

Turning back around, Jonas stared at his aunt with resentment in his gaze.

"You never let me say it," he blurted out.

Understanding, Aunt Claire nodded.

"You never let me say what I wanted to say before you left us," he repeated, pain trembling in his voice.

"How could you have left, without even letting me say good-bye?" he accused, his voice breaking. "It's not fair—it's not fair what happened."

Aunt Claire paused, and took in a breath. She looked her nephew in the eyes, recognizing the young teenager who had come to the surface.

"I know, Jonas," she said with compassion in her voice. "I'm so sorry it had to happen that way."

Walking over to him, she reached out to take his hand.

"Just like you, I was called before I thought it was time. I still had so much life left to live . . . but it wasn't to be."

Looking down at her hand as she reached for him again, Jonas felt deep sadness begin to overwhelm him. It seemed to envelope him, reaching far into his soul, touching the young man who had reserved so much pain inside for this very conversation.

"What . . . ," he began to say, attempting to articulate what he had been too terrified all along to acknowledge. "What's happening to me, Aunt Claire?"

Looking toward her, Jonas waited for her to tell him, but fearing what she would have to say, he began to plead for the impossible.

"Please," he began to beg, "please, let me go home. Please, take me back to the beach . . ."

Aunt Claire shook her head.

"I can't take you back there, Jonas, I'm sorry," she said with a sadness matching his own. "If I took you back to the beach, no one would be there."

Tears mixing with his confusion, Jonas looked at his aunt, trying to understand.

"Jonas, time works differently in this hospital," she said slowly. "It may seem like you've just arrived, but you've been gone for over a week."

Jonas staggered backward.

"But you said . . . ," he said, grasping at straws, "you said you were going to take me to my family."

Aunt Claire nodded as she gripped his hand tightly in hers to steady him.

"I am, Jonas," she said in reply, "which is why we need to get you to your funeral."

9

NEW YORK CITY WAS MUCH COLDER THAN USUAL AS the young man made his way out of his apartment and onto the sidewalk. The morning sky was gray and overcast, with dying leaves falling from above.

But the weather was not what was bothering the young man. This preholiday cold snap would have been easily tolerable if, for the past two weeks, he had not been met with one horrific dream after another every time he went to sleep. Each dream was more graphic and more disturbing than the last. They were dark, violent, often sexually explicit dreams that felt more real than any dream he had ever had before. Sometimes he would wake up in a cold sweat screaming; other times he would wake feeling so overwhelmingly depressed that he couldn't move for hours.

Over the previous five days, he had noticed something even more disturbing than the dreams. He was beginning to hear voices—disturbing voices from inside his own head during his waking hours. These voices were not his own, and each one sounded distinct in tone and temperament. And, as if hearing voices wasn't unsettling enough, the more he tried to ignore them, the louder and more incessant they grew.

"You want to know how to make that idiot shut up?" a sarcastic voice said.

The young man glanced up from his path on the sidewalk and noticed a disheveled-looking old man holding a bible above his head.

"I love you! I love you! I love you!" said the old man to an imaginary congregation.

The young man saw this individual almost every day on his way to work. An apocalyptic evangelist, he thought, who looked more like a homeless man than a preacher.

"You want me to tell you how to get him to shut up?" said the voice again. "I can get rid of that piece of shi . . ."

No! the young man thought in his mind. He had realized that while he couldn't stop the voices in his head, he could try and crowd them out with his own.

"All you have to do," the voice said, "is take a knife and jab it into his throat . . ."

Damnit, I said no! the young man thought even louder as an image of himself holding a bloody knife, standing next to a body lying on the sidewalk flickered into his mind.

He shook the thought from his head and tried to find something else to focus on as he walked toward the subway entrance.

"Why would you think those kinds of things?" came another voice, which sounded younger, like a child.

"I'm not . . . ," the young man thought as if to defend himself.

Feeling anxious about starting an internal dialogue with the voices, he decided to concentrate on the subway stairs that would lead him down to the train.

"Why would you say such awful things about someone? You want to kill that man? That's evil. You're pure evil," came the young voice again.

"No!" the man shouted in his mind as he ran down the steps. "I don't want to hurt anyone. Just . . . please . . . *stop!*"

"He gets to talk, but I don't," replied the small, offended voice. "I never told you to murder anybody. I'm a good boy, and this is how you treat me, you stupid son of a bitch!"

The young man pulled out his subway card with trembling fingers, trying desperately to focus on anything but the conversation taking place in his head.

"He doesn't want to listen to you," came another voice, this one sounding like a rebellious teenager. "He's too damn self-interested to think about any of us. Isn't that right, you self-righteous prick?"

The young man made it through the turnstile and walked down the second set of stairs to the subway platform, where he joined a warmly dressed crowd waiting for the train.

What's happening to me? he questioned in desperation, muttering the words silently under his breath. An older gentleman a shoulder-width away from him peered at him over his morning paper.

Nervous, the young man looked down and noticed his hands were still trembling. Placing them in his pockets, he cautiously glanced over at the man who had looked at him, noticing that the gentleman had hidden himself behind his paper again as the sound of an oncoming train blared in the distance.

"It's okay," he heard yet another voice say with a soothing intonation, "you don't have to keep listening to all these voices. I can show how you can shut them all up."

The young man suddenly had a flash of stabbing himself in his windpipe, blood gushing all over the subway platform as the strangers around him screamed in horror. Even though the image lasted only a fraction of a second before he could stop it, the young man noticed how the feeling of stabbing himself in the neck brought a strange sense of relief: an escape from this living nightmare he had been experiencing.

The train slowed to a stop at the platform and everyone began jostling for position through the open doors. As the young man worked on quieting his thoughts, he found he was one of the last ones on the train, standing with his back toward the exit.

"Bing-bong" came the familiar sound of the closing doors. A voice came over the intercom. "Next stop, Forty-Second Street."

"You can't even understand what the hell they're saying," came the first voice back into the young man's head. "And did you hear the way he said it? Goddamn foreign . . ."

Stop it! the young man shouted in his mind. *Damnit . . . shut up . . . please!*

It was getting harder and harder with each day to control the voices that came into his head. Each voice was growing louder and more persistent.

"Who the hell do you think you are, anyway?" came a different, angrier voice. "You think you're in control?"

The young man began to panic. The crowded train was making him claustrophobic.

"I'll get them to shut up for you," came yet another voice, "but you're going to have to do something for me. You see that little girl over there . . ."

The young man looked around and noticed a small child sitting on her mother's lap.

Suddenly, a violent, grotesque sexual image flashed into his mind with such vividness that the young man had to look away from the child. He closed his eyes tightly in an effort to block it out. But as he tried to shut out the world around him, the images in his mind became even more disturbing, so awful that his body reacted with disgust, as if he were experiencing the wrenching spasms of a vicious stomach flu. Feeling the urge to vomit as he was almost doubled over by a sudden rush of guilt, he fought hard with what he saw in his mind. Although he knew the thoughts were imaginary, they felt real, almost as if he were reliving a memory of something that had taken place before.

Grabbing hold of a subway bar to keep from passing out, the young man opened his eyes, hoping there was something else he could focus on that would keep his mind from the repulsive images flashing before him. Everyone on the train was oblivious to what he was experiencing—everyone except the little girl. She was staring into his eyes with a piercing gaze. And with that connection came a feeling, a terrifying feeling that something inside of him was urging him to take a step forward, to lean in toward the little girl, to reach out his hand and . . .

"No! Stop!" the young man shouted out loud. The little girl flinched, struck with sudden fear at the sight of a stranger reaching for her with an outstretched hand.

Hundreds of eyes suddenly turned to look at him as the little girl burst into tears. Quickly, he put his hand into his pocket and looked down at his feet as whispers began to fill the subway car. He could sense the fingers pointing in his direction, the uneasy voices accusing him from afar.

"What did he say to that little girl?" said one passenger to another. "Is she okay?"

"What the hell does he think he's doing?" said another.

"He's probably crazy," came the reply.

The young man felt his heart pounding in his chest. The images that had once raced though his mind had vanished only to be replaced by the sound of adrenaline pumping in his ears. Beads of sweat began to form on his forehead as he felt the weight of everyone's gaze crushing him.

"Did he touch her?" said a man at the back of the train.

"Don't look at him," a mother scolded her child.

The young man closed his eyes, praying for the train to let him off. He knew he wasn't insane, or dangerous like everyone on the train probably thought. But as his mind raced back to what he had just done, he realized that the reason he had raised his hand was not to hurt the little girl, but to push her away from the force that was moving him toward her. It made no sense, but he didn't know how else to stop what he felt was about to happen. And as confusion about his intentions began to flood his mind, he began to think that everyone on the train might actually be right. Maybe he was losing it. Maybe there was something happening to him that was going to make him snap, changing him into something violent and threatening.

The young man counted off the seconds, each one seeming like an eternity, as he waited for the train to come to a stop.

"Forty-Second Street," said the overhead announcement, interrupting everyone's hushed conversations about the little girl still crying on her mother's lap and the strange man who had tried to do something to her.

The subway arrived at its destination and the young man got off. He didn't dare look up as he walked out of the train and toward the exit of the subway station. Most of the passengers quickly shifted their attention to the drudgery of fighting the morning crowd, yet the young man still noticed a few concerned passengers staring at him from the corner of their eyes.

But as he walked up the subway stairs and onto the sidewalk where he could make himself invisible in the sea of people that always crowded Times Square, the young man had an unexpected thought that actually brought him a sense of relief from everything he had just experienced.

The voices in his head were silent. At least, for now.

10

"WE'RE HERE, JONAS."

Opening his eyes as he released his aunt's hand, Jonas looked around to see where he had been taken. Having never traveled as a spirit, he was told to close his eyes and hold tightly to his aunt's hand. The entire trip had taken only an instant. While his aunt had yet to explain the physics of how travel like this was possible, she had mentioned that if one wanted to travel with a spirit who knew how to transport themselves in this manner, all one needed to do was hold on for the ride. It seemed, in a way, a kind of metaphysical piggyback ride, but the details of the trip quickly took a backseat as Jonas tried to figure out just where he was.

He seemed to be standing in an old Victorian home, at the entrance of a large foyer. Taking in the details of the home's construction, Jonas saw dark hardwood floors, white plaster walls, and a hanging stained glass light that resembled an upside down plant. To the right and left were large archways that opened into the rest of the house.

"Where are we?" he asked.

"A funeral home," Aunt Claire replied.

Since Jonas had never been to anyone's funeral except his aunt's, he had little experience in these situations. Realizing this, he followed his aunt's lead without a word as she walked through the archway on the left, entering what appeared to be a reception area for guests. Walking through this room, toward the rear, Jonas's interest was soon pulled in the direction of an open doorway at the back.

"They've already begun," Aunt Claire mentioned as an organ played quietly in the distance.

Jonas's heart began to quicken as he moved closer to the doorway. Seeing the room where he was being led, he stopped for a moment to take it all in. The space was filled to capacity with people seated neatly in benches, though their identity was somewhat hidden from view as they were all facing the front of the room. Looking around, Jonas saw that the space appeared very much like a chapel, with semi-opaque stained-glass windows flanking each wall. Three chandeliers hung overhead, and there was a small platform toward the front decorated with a variety of soft, glowing candles. In front of these candles was a large, wooden casket, surrounded with bouquets of white lilies. The lid of the casket had been opened.

"Jonas, this way," his aunt gestured, as she prompted him to walk with her down the center aisle.

Stepping across the threshold after an uneasy glance in her direction, Jonas soon found himself looking across at a few of the benches as he walked down the center aisle. He saw guests sitting close to one another, whispering quietly while the music played. Many of them held a piece of paper in their hands, a program offering a review of the events about to take place.

Looking around, Jonas recognized his neighbors sitting in the back of the room: Albert and Sheryl Blanchworth, an elderly couple who had lived next door to Jonas almost his entire life. Jonas had come to think of them as another set of grandparents because of their kind and genuine natures. He had been invited over for dinner on more than one occasion, as well as for after-school treats of milk and cookies. He still thought Mrs. Blanchworth's cookies were the best he'd ever had.

Sitting a few rows down from them, Jonas saw Mrs. Stout, his former piano teacher. Everyone in the neighborhood knew how to play Pachelbel's Canon in D because of her. She was a thin, gaunt woman who had a peculiarly shaped nose that often made a high-pitched whistle whenever her student's finger placement needed correcting.

Walking a few rows farther, Jonas saw more faces from his childhood, like Annie Sullivan—the first girl he had ever kissed—and David Findley, the friend he had first told afterward. But before he could take in more of the faces around him, Aunt Claire motioned toward the front row.

"Jonas," she said, "your family . . ."

Jonas hadn't yet taken the time to think of where she was leading him. Recognizing so many familiar faces, he had been caught up in recalling his experiences and memories of all those present. But when he turned to look in the direction his aunt gestured, his breath was suddenly taken from him.

"Mom . . . ," Jonas said, the word coming involuntarily from his lips.

There was no reply.

Glancing nervously at his aunt, Jonas approached the bench where his mother and family sat, somewhat confused at how his presence went completely unheeded. Everyone seemed oblivious to the fact that he was only a few feet away, even though he could see them all in perfect detail. The flickering light from the candles illuminated their faces, reflecting the magnitude of their grief and sorrow. Jonas wanted to reach out to them all, to tell them he was there and let them know he was okay. But as he attempted to do so, he quickly realized that it was impossible. They couldn't hear his voice, not even when he yelled. There was simply nothing he could do to make them aware of his presence.

"Jonas," Aunt Claire said in a quiet voice, "they can't hear or see you, but if you get near enough, they may be able to *feel* you."

Growing increasingly frightened and confused, Jonas took a few steps toward his family in an attempt to get their attention. He wasn't sure what to do exactly, but he soon found himself lost in the idea of how strange it was to see them all like this, with no one having even the slightest reaction to his presence. It made him feel removed, distant, and even a little angry at the fact that he couldn't somehow make them see him. It was like standing at the front of a movie theater with patrons staring at the screen, each one unaware of anything other than what was flickering before their eyes. There was so much more Jonas had seen, so many things he wanted to tell them, but none of it seemed of any value now that he couldn't get them to even look in his direction.

"Aunt Claire," Jonas said anxiously, staring back at her with fear in his eyes.

"I know, Jonas, it's not like before," she consoled him, glancing momentarily at a gentleman across the room.

Looking in that direction as well, Jonas recognized Aunt Claire's husband, with their two daughters sitting by his side. The girls had grown up. They were now beautiful young women.

"No . . . ," Jonas began to say, recognizing how long it had been since they had actually seen their mother, and thinking for a moment about the implications for himself.

Jonas turned back toward his aunt as he saw her gesture toward his own family.

It took him a moment, but following her instructions, he walked slowly, timidly, toward his mother. She sat with a motionless stare, unresponsive to anything around her. In all his life, Jonas had never seen her like this, not even when she had helped break the news of Aunt Claire's condition to the family. But there she was, unresponsive and all but empty, even when Jonas waved a hand in front of her eyes in a futile attempt to get her attention. There wasn't a blink, or a whisper, or a movement of any kind. There was nothing in her world other than the body of her son, set inside a casket of lacquered wood.

"Mom . . . ," Jonas attempted once more.

It was difficult for him to see her like this—open, vulnerable, so full of grief. She had always been the one in the family to draw her children near in times of trouble—holding them close while singing to them or stroking their hair while whispering reassuring words. But watching her now, Jonas could almost hear her heart break—feel a part of her dying—as she clung tightly to the hand of her husband, who sat quietly at her side.

Taking a step to the left, Jonas looked at his father, seeing him hold to the hand of his high school sweetheart with all the intensity of a soldier clinging to a dying comrade in battle. He looked tired and forlorn, no doubt from a succession of sleepless nights and endless prayers. And as Jonas walked in front of him, he began to feel the depth of his father's sorrow. Like many grieving fathers, it seemed he was doing the best he could to remain composed for everyone else in the family. But Jonas could still see the burden in his eyes as his dark pupils swam in a sea of sorrow. No parent, Jonas knew, wished to attend his own child's funeral.

"Dad . . ."

Next to his father, were Jonas's brothers and sisters, sitting close to one another, clinging to each other in a moment of disbelief. Their brother had been taken from them, and now they were left to ponder the reality of what an existence without him would be like. Thinking perhaps for the first time in their lives on the fragile nature of human existence, there was visible fear in their eyes as they wondered what the future would have left to offer them. There would be no more evenings where they could get together, playing board games or watching movies into the late hours of the night. Those times were gone now, and as much as they may have wished for just one more moment like that, there were no more to be had.

Looking at each member of his family, Jonas wanted to bow his head and weep. But seeing his best friend sitting just a few feet away, he couldn't help but walk toward him, if even for a brief moment.

Chris, terrified, grief-stricken, and nearly writhing in pain appeared far worse than Jonas could have ever imagined. Struggling to bring such emotions under control, Chris barely had the courage to look up, choosing instead to face any direction other than that of the casket at the front of the room. Survivor's guilt—Jonas could see his friend was feeling the worst of it. But there was something else, something in the way Chris trembled every so often when he glanced nervously at the guests in the room. It was almost as if he was waiting for the moment when everyone would turn on him with accusing fingers. Jonas knew he was in no way responsible for any of what was going on. His friend had simply been cheering him on when the accident had happened. But Chris didn't seem to see it that way.

Instead, Chris sat there, his eyes darting every so often in the direction of Jonas's parents, his features overwhelmed by terror every time he did so. For someone who had always had such enthusiasm for life, Jonas thought, it seemed now as if his friend wished for nothing more than to have it all taken from him.

As much as Jonas felt for Chris, or for his brothers and sisters, and even his own parents, the person he saw seated next to his friend nearly dropped him to his knees. He loved each and every individual he had seen—unbelievably so—but the sight of the girl with long red hair nearly took all he had out of him. Jonas found himself at last giving over to the pain as he took a step in her direction, looking into her eyes, feeling a dam of emotion burst with a sudden rush of grief and sorrow. Sarah, he knew, was the one person who made him complete, the one person who could truly touch his soul. But as he tried to do just that—touch her with his mere soul—he came to realize the impossibility of it all. They were separated by an invisible gulf, made more evident by what he saw in her eyes: the reflection of everyone in the room—everyone but him. He was invisible to her now, and although they were together, they had never been further apart—a terrible acknowledgment that caused Jonas to cry aloud as he fell down to the floor, unable to bear any more.

"Please, God, oh, please," he said, weeping tears upon tears for the life he once had. "Please—anything but this . . ."

But there was no reply. Only silence as he knelt in pain, too terrified to look up at what he had lost. The girl he was going to marry, the friend he loved, the family he couldn't live without—not a single one of them even flinched as his cries met their deafened ears. They had no idea that the very person they had come to remember was kneeling right before their feet, dying all over again, weeping into the darkness of his open hands.

"It's not fair," he sobbed, like a child. "I'm not supposed to be here . . . it's not supposed to be like this . . ."

But the music played on, and the candles burned, and everyone who had gathered to remember him bowed their heads in reverence. Their grief had filled the room with silence, but his—it rent the air. They all had a life left to live, but Jonas—he would have to watch it all from a distance, cursed with the ability to see every detail, but unable to be a part of it all as he had once been.

———

Quietly, a man approached the front of the room, clearing his throat while looking at each of the guests.

"My dear friends," he said softly, "we are gathered here today to remember our friend and brother Jonas, who has made his journey back home to heaven."

The journey, however, had just begun.

11

ON.

Off.

On.

Off.

The young man held the light switch to an empty office bathroom, gritting his teeth each time he flipped it.

On.

Off.

On.

Off.

"Please, can I stop now?" he pleaded.

"You can, when you get to fifty," the voice inside came back.

On.

Off.

On.

Off.

"But why?"

"It doesn't matter why. Just go to fifty and then we'll leave you alone."

On.

Off.

On.

Off.

On.

Off.

A knock came from outside the door.

"Is anyone in there?" a man's voice said aloud.

The young man tried his best to bring his own voice under control. "Yes . . . hold on a minute. I . . . I'm almost done."

The young man in the bathroom closed his eyes tight, trying again to focus on speaking to the voice inside his mind.

"How many have I done so far?" he asked.

"You haven't been counting?" the voice said in reply. "Well . . . tough shit. Start again."

The young man took a long, deep breath and began flipping the switch again.

On.

Off.

On.

Off.

On.

Off.

"Please, can I stop? This doesn't make any sense . . ."

"Like I said, count to fifty, then we'll talk about what's next."

———

Alone, in the only bathroom on the office floor, the young man whispered to himself as a line of impatient colleagues grew just outside the door.

On.

Off.

"One."

On.

Off.

"Two."

On.

Off.

"Three."

"That's more like it," the voice inside whispered. "Now you're getting the idea."

12

JONAS SAT ALL ALONE ON THE FLOOR, STARING AT THE casket that had been closed nearly half an hour before. The service had ended and all of the guests had walked to the reception area, but Jonas hadn't followed. Not even when his aunt came to him, urging him to come. Instead, he sat there, staring at the closed casket, wondering how it had all happened so fast.

It seemed only moments before he was still alive and happy, walking on black sand with his best friend at his side. But now he felt destitute, all but isolated in this empty chapel, and in this new life, frightened by what the future held in store for him.

After a few minutes, a sound came from the back of the chapel. It didn't sound like Jonas's aunt though, as she moved far too quietly. This sound was that of footsteps clacking against the hardwood floor, echoing off the walls in the empty room. Jonas didn't think much of it, though, being as lost in his own thoughts as he was. *If he could just have swum a bit faster . . . if Chris's leash hadn't got caught . . . if they had just gone out when the waves weren't so big . . . if they hadn't gone out at all . . .*

The steps grew louder. If it was his Aunt Claire or someone else who had come to get him, Jonas knew he would not follow. He needed more time to figure out what to do next in this new world. He had entered a completely new reality, one with its own rules and laws, none of which he understood very well. And while contemplating the cruelness of this newfound discovery, Jonas marveled at how he had once treated the idea of an afterlife with such flippant carelessness, as if it were simply a curious idea used to pacify children or, worse, a belief in a fairy tale where puffy clouds and golden harps would be found. But there were no clouds or harps where

Jonas had been. The afterlife, as far as he could tell, was a complex world, one patterned after the old, but with a set of physics and consequences all its own. People spoke with their thoughts, but could read yours as well. They traveled at the speed of light—but used that ability to take you to terrible places like this one. And they could perform miracles, though Jonas wondered what good it was to walk when the ones you wanted to walk with were in a world completely set apart from yours. Understanding now that he could travel in the mortal realm, Jonas assumed he could probably visit the places he once knew, to seek the familiar. But the very thought of doing so only depressed him—as if all he could look forward to was to become a wandering ghost, lingering in the hope of hearing his name mentioned. But time, he knew, would inevitably erase the memory of what he had once been. All the places where he had left his mark would change. All of the people he had once loved would slowly begin to reminisce about him less and less. And over time, he would be forced to watch a world actively working to forget he ever existed.

Hearing the footsteps near where he knelt, Jonas looked up, only to see a man he didn't recognize. He was older, perhaps in his midsixties. He wore a pinstriped suit with a white shirt and red tie. He had thick salt-and-pepper hair and dark brown eyes.

The man glanced over his shoulder, as if he were about to do something he shouldn't, just before walking up to the casket and lifting its lid in order to peer inside to see the contents.

Somewhat irritated by this audacious act, Jonas rose to his feet and walked over to the man, wondering again if this was someone he knew. As he drew near, Jonas couldn't help but look inside the casket himself, shocked by what he saw. Seeing oneself in a mirror, he thought, is something rather ordinary; a two-dimensional representation of the real thing. But this—seeing oneself from another's point of view—this is something altogether different. It took Jonas a moment to recognize the contours of his own face, the lines, and even the tone of his skin. The color of his hair, the shape of his lips— each seemed recognizable, yet simultaneously foreign all the same. It felt almost as if he were staring at a rock or a piece of driftwood—an inanimate object that held little purpose or meaning. But the reality couldn't have been further from the truth. What Jonas would have given to put that body back on like a glove, to walk around, to be seen, to be heard, and, perhaps, to ask this man what he was doing opening his casket after it had been closed.

But as Jonas watched him, the stranger did something even more disturbing, even more angering: he began to smile. It was as if the thing the man was looking at brought him a great sense of pleasure. There was a wicked gleam in his eye that made Jonas feel as if the man were relieved somehow—and not only relieved but enthralled that this body before him would never again lift a finger. In fact, as Jonas's angered curiosity grew into mounting frustration, he thought he just might give this man a piece of his mind, though he knew he wouldn't be heard.

"Excuse me," a voice came. It was Jonas's father, speaking from the back of the room.

The look on the stranger's face suddenly froze, startled at having been caught. But after only a second or two, the man cleared his throat and closed the casket, before turning slowly around to acknowledge the interruption.

Jonas saw his father approach, confusion in his eyes.

"I'm sorry," the stranger began, "I came late to the service, and I didn't think anyone would mind."

Jonas's father walked down the center aisle as his look of puzzlement slowly changed into one of interest.

"I didn't catch your name," he said, in a genuinely polite tone.

"I'm David," the stranger said confidently as he held out his hand. "David Levenson. I was a visiting professor of your son's back in college. I just wanted to come and pay my respects."

Jonas watched his father's serious expression turn into one of welcome as he held out his hand. The men shook hands cordially.

"Apologies, I'm Steven, Jonas's father," he said in reply. "I'm sorry you weren't able to make the service, but we would love for you to join us in the reception area if you could. I'm sure there are more than a few people who would enjoy hearing anything you might have to share about Jonas."

"Jonas was really one of a kind, you know," the man said quickly. "He's not the type of boy you tend to forget."

Steven nodded in agreement, smiling longingly as he glanced at the casket.

"But if you'll forgive me," the man continued, "I really should be going. I have an appointment and I'm already running a bit late."

Offering his understanding, Steven shook the man's hand again before looking him in the eye.

"You said you were a professor of Jonas's?" he reiterated.

"Visiting professor," he corrected. "I'm not even sure if your son would have remembered me," he added, feigning a smile.

Steven held on to the man's hand for a moment.

"I really only had a short time with him," the stranger said hastily, before breaking the grip. "But he left quite an impression on me, which is why I wanted to come and pay my respects."

Taking the comment as a compliment, Steven nodded before gesturing toward the guests in the reception area.

"Well, if you change your mind," he said politely, "we should be here for the next little while. It was very kind of you to have traveled all this way just to come to our boy's funer . . ."

But just then, Jonas's father suddenly choked up, unable to finish his own thought as he glanced at the casket partially hidden behind the man's back.

"Of course," the man interjected for him, "I consider it an honor. And thank you again for the invitation, though, I regret to say, I really should be going."

Offering a smile of genuine gratitude, Jonas's father turned around and made his way back to the guests, reaching for a handkerchief as he went.

After Steven had cleared the room, the stranger closed his eyes and let out a sigh of relief, a wicked grin forming across his lips.

"Well, Jonas," he whispered, turning to place a hand back on the casket, stroking the lacquered wood, "I couldn't have planned this any better."

The man gave a slight chuckle, rapping his knuckles thoughtlessly on the casket door.

"Too bad, really. I was almost looking forward to doing it myself."

The man placed an open hand once more on the fine-grain wood and stroked it with suspicious delight. Then, walking toward a door at the front of the chapel, he exited the building.

All alone in the room, Jonas had no idea how to react to what he had just seen. But before he could mumble even a word to himself, Aunt Claire appeared with Michael, the man from the children's hospital, at her side.

"Oh, Jonas," she said as she rushed toward him. "Are you okay?"

Feeling her hands steady his shaky frame, Jonas looked back at her with an expression of bewilderment. He paused, trying to think of what to say, but all that came out was, "Who?"

Aunt Claire nodded as she glanced back toward the door through which the stranger had exited.

"He came," she said aloud. "I knew he would . . ."

"*He?*" Jonas suddenly found himself saying. "Who is that guy— I've never seen him in my life!"

Aunt Claire studied Jonas carefully for a moment.

"Who did he say he was?" she asked.

"He said his name was David Levenson," Jonas quickly reiterated, "a visiting professor of mine from back in college. But I swear to you, I've never seen that man before—"

Aunt Claire nodded, glancing briefly at Michael while doing so.

"Jonas," she said, looking back at him, "that man you just saw—his name isn't David Levenson . . ."

"Then who is he?" Jonas asked, incensed. "And why did he open my casket to look at my body?"

Aunt Claire placed a careful hand on his shoulder.

"That man," she said slowly, "is William Graves, you're biological father."

Jonas staggered backward.

"He came here today because he's been trying to figure out what to do about you," she added.

Jonas glanced at the door through which the man had exited.
"*Do? Do what?*"

Aunt Claire looked around the room for a moment as she tried
to explain.

"Jonas, William Graves has known of your whereabouts for quite
some time now," she said. "After he learned that your mother gave
you up for adoption, he's been tracking you down, to ensure a safe
distance."

"Safe distance?" Jonas repeated. "From me?"

"Yes," Aunt Claire stated matter-of-factly. "You're the only evidence that could link William to his crimes. Even he knows what
would happen if you went looking for him . . ."

"But I only learned about him five minutes ago—"

"That may be true," Aunt Claire cut in, "but if you were ever able
to find him, it would be short work to link him to what he did to
your mother, and many of the other crimes he's committed since.
He's been tracking you down to make sure you would never find
out, because if you ever decided to turn him in . . ."

Aunt Claire looked over at the casket.

"Well, he was going to make sure you never got that far."

Jonas felt an anger beginning to burn from within as he looked
back again at the door through which the criminal had escaped.

"You mean to say, he was going to murder me?" Jonas said, trembling now with anger.

"William is a dangerous man," Aunt Claire replied, glancing at
the door as well, "one we've been working on for quite some time."

"So he's still out there, still doing stuff?" Jonas asked.

"Yes," his aunt replied, "but you weren't the only one in danger.
There are others." She glanced quickly in Michael's direction. "Others who are at risk because of him."

Jonas glanced at Michael as well.

"Jonas, there is still a lot you need to know before you can do
anything about William Graves," Aunt Claire quickly said. "Now that
you're one of us"—she gestured to herself and Michael—"someone
in the World of Spirits, you need to learn more about William's kind.

Only then will you be able to do anything about his crimes."

Jonas turned back toward his aunt.

"What do you mean, I need to learn more about *his kind?*" he asked.

"There are those in our world," she began to explain, "much like William Graves, who spend all their time spreading the work of darkness. They are good at what they do, but in order to stop them, one must know how they operate."

Jonas stared at his aunt as he listened to her explain.

"The reality of evil is something often lost on mortals," she said, "but now that you are one of us, you need to be educated in the principles of dark influences if there is any hope in countering their effects."

Aunt Claire pointed toward Michael, who had remained silent all this time.

"Michael has agreed to show you some of this," she offered, "which is fortunate, seeing as he has been the one following Graves. He has offered to be your companion for the next while, in order to help you fulfill your calling."

"*Calling?*" Jonas asked.

"We all have a calling in this life, Jonas," she replied, "at least those who are willing to shoulder the load. Mine is back at the hospital, but yours is now with Michael. You must bring William Graves to justice, as dangerous as he is. Time is running out though, and if you can't stop him soon, others will suffer."

Jonas watched as Aunt Claire motioned toward the reception area, just as Sarah walked into view.

"You don't mean . . . ," Jonas began to say in disbelief.

"Jonas, one of the responsibilities we have to those we leave behind is to do all we can to keep them safe," his aunt cautioned. "Even though they may not know it, there is an entire world just beyond their view waiting for the opportunity to strike."

Jonas looked fearfully into the distance as a guest of the party walked over to Sarah, offering her his condolences.

"Those who can see more clearly—people like us, Jonas—have

THE CHOICE: DEATH IS JUST THE BEGINNING

an obligation to help when danger is lurking just around the corner."

Jonas watched as Sarah reached out to shake the man's hand, while at that very moment her drink fell with a shattering crash to the floor.

Aunt Claire turned Jonas's head back in her own direction with a touch of her hand.

"If you want to help those you hold most dear, you will need to follow Michael to learn more about the reality of evil—and most importantly, what you can do about it."

Thinking for a moment on just what was at stake—with the idea of a potential murderer on the loose—Jonas looked once more at the girl he loved, the one he would have done anything for, but who evidently needed help in a way that only he could provide. And with that recognition—with the understanding that he needed to follow Michael in order to keep his loved ones safe—he turned to face his new companion, summoning the courage to do whatever was necessary.

"My companion?" Jonas asked, trying to figure out just what his place was in this strange new world.

"Yes, Jonas," Michael said, his kind demeanor turning momentarily a shade more severe. "But I need to warn you, this kind of work isn't easy."

Glancing once more at the room full of guests, seeing Sarah, Chris, and the members of his family all together—he turned his head and nodded.

"That's okay, I'm ready," he said.

Michael reached out to take Jonas's hand.

Feeling an electric surge flowing from his new companion, one even more powerful than his aunt's, Jonas looked Michael in the eyes.

"Were are we going?" he asked.

Michael smiled.

"To one of my favorite places, actually," he replied.

And with that, Jonas and Michael vanished in the blink of an eye.

13

SUDDENLY EVERYTHING AROUND THEM CHANGED.
Where once candles had glowed, and stained-glass windows had illuminated the casket in which his body lay, Jonas now saw hundreds
of people walking in every direction, chattering and pointing around
them as they went.

At first, Jonas thought Michael had taken him to another place in
the spirit world, as the architecture was unlike anything he had ever
seen. He could tell that he was in an enormous underground room,
with a glass ceiling opening to the sky above. Instead of being flat,
though, this ceiling looked like the interior of a massive glass pyramid. At first glance, Jonas felt as if he were in some sort of modern
Egyptian tomb, but that thought soon fled when he noticed a spiral
staircase leading from the floor on which he stood to an exit in the
pyramid above.

While his surroundings were indeed beautiful, he knew that he
had not been taken to the spirit world. For one thing, the colors of
everything around him seemed almost dim and muddy in comparison to the vibrant shades he had seen at the children's hospital. He
also had a feeling that everything around him was rather plain and
dirty. Not that the interior of the glass pyramid building was un-
kempt, just that in contrast to the Reading Room, this place seemed
to lack life. It didn't breathe.

Nonetheless, Jonas was impressed. True, he had been to a world
where the simplest of details overshadowed the beauty of anything
found in the mortal realm, but the glass pyramid was magnificent
in its own right, and it gave him the feeling that he was somewhere
special.

"Where are we?" Jonas asked.

"You've never been here before, I take it?" Michael replied.

Looking around him once more to see if anything in the space would spark a memory, he confirmed that he had not. But he could tell that, wherever he was, it must be a multicultural setting, since there was a cacophony of languages being spoken around him. Everywhere he looked, he saw people carrying backpacks, purses, small children, and pointing in so many different directions that Jonas began to wonder if they might be as lost as he was.

"Are we in a museum?" Jonas asked as he noticed a booth labeled INFORMATION.

"Not just a museum," Michael replied. "The Louvre. One of the world's greatest monuments to the past."

Jonas looked to his companion.

"The Louvre?" he asked. "You mean in France?"

"Paris, to be exact," Michael clarified. "The building we are standing in is the glass pyramid designed by I. M. Pei. It's situated in the center of the Cour Napoléon. The Louvre Palace is the older building you can see through the glass up there—"

Jonas looked up.

"But I'm guessing you're probably more interested in why we're here," Michael said.

Taking a second to gather himself, Jonas nodded.

"I brought you here because there is something I want to show you, Jonas," Michael said, "something that will help explain an event that you need to understand." He began walking toward one of the corridors. "It's a history lesson of sorts, but one that will help put things into perspective."

Jonas walked quickly to keep up with Michael as they approached a marble staircase that led toward a stone archway labeled DENON.

"And, please, Jonas," Michael added thoughtfully, his gentle gaze turning in Jonas's direction, "as we go along, remember that I am here to help you. If there is anything you need, anything at all, please don't hesitate to ask."

Given the circumstances, this was the first piece of good news Jonas had heard in a while. It almost made him think of Michael as a friend, even though he knew they had just barely met.

"Sure," Jonas replied. "Thanks."

Michael smiled.

Walking side by side, the two started up the staircase. Suddenly Jonas noticed a large man walking down the stairs toward them. He was holding a map of the museum and paying no attention to where he was going or who might be in his way. Jonas instinctively moved to the right to allow the gentlemen to pass, but as he did so, a young teenager came bounding down the steps from behind the large man, running toward—or rather *through*—Jonas's left arm.

"Whoa . . . ," Jonas said reactively, preparing for the impact that never happened.

"Sorry," Michael excused the young teenager, "it's quite crowded in here, and, well . . . they can't exactly see us."

Looking back, Jonas saw the teenager run happily to greet a group of friends.

"He just . . ." Jonas searched for the right words. "He just ran right *through* me . . . right through my left arm."

"Yes," Michael said with an understanding grin, "that does take some time to get used to. Just be glad it wasn't a car. I saw someone scream for three whole minutes after a bus drove straight through him on the street."

Jonas glanced at his mentor, not sure if he was joking.

Michael chuckled.

"You'll get used to it, I promise," he said reassuringly, patting Jonas lightly on the back. "But feel free to walk around them if you need to for now. It took me quite a while to get accustomed to everything too. Our instincts from the old life have a habit of getting in the way sometimes."

Jonas checked his left arm to make sure everything was intact.

"But as I was saying," Michael continued, "there is something I need to tell you. Something that will be very important for you to learn if you are to better understand what you are dealing with."

"You mean, my father?" Jonas asked.

"In part, yes," Michael agreed. "But I'd like to discuss more about the fundamental nature of what drives people like him."

Jonas looked warily around him for a moment, trying his best to dodge patrons as he listened.

"You mean like, pure evil?" he said, unable to think of a better word to describe someone like William Graves.

"Exactly," Michael replied.

Listening to his mentor, Jonas stepped to one side quickly enough to let a young mother and her toddler go by.

"Tell me, Jonas," Michael began, "have you ever stopped to wonder where evil comes from?"

Jonas found himself at a loss for words at the rather odd question.

"I don't know . . . the Devil?" he guessed awkwardly.

"That's a good start," Michael replied. "But why is the Devil so evil? What is it that drives him?"

"Wait—you mean he's real?" Jonas asked, somewhat unnerved.

"Of course," Michael said. "As real as you and I—though, there are some who might try and debate that fact."

Seeing his mentor gesture to a few of the museum patrons in the crowded room, Jonas took the subtle acknowledgment. Deciding to focus more seriously on the conversation at hand, he looked back at Michael.

"Well, if he's real, hasn't he just always been evil?" Jonas said, closing his eyes momentarily and flinching as he passed through the clasped hands of a young couple.

Opening his eyes again, Jonas noticed a small spiral staircase ahead of them that was packed with people ascending and descending.

"Are you okay walking up here?" Michael asked, noting Jonas's apprehension. "I can get you up there the other way if you'd prefer."

Jonas shook his head.

"It's okay," he said, deciding to take on the challenge. "I can handle it."

Nodding, Michael walked quickly up the stairs with Jonas close behind. In an attempt to ease his way into this new physical reality, Jonas tried looking at the wall as he made his way up the steps, instead of staring directly into the faces of the people he found himself walking through. He had somewhat anticipated a push or a shove because of the sheer number of people coming at him, but nothing of the sort happened.

"Good job," Michael said as they reached the top of the staircase, passing through an opening that led into a large arching hallway.

Slowing his pace, Jonas took a moment to look around while attempting to shake off the anxiety at what he had just experienced.

"What are these statues?" he asked, trying to buy some time in order to regain his composure.

"Hellenistic antiquities," Michael noted. "Beautiful, aren't they?"

Jonas nodded appreciatively, still feeling somewhat overwhelmed.

"If you would rather," Michael asked politely after a long pause, "I can take you straight there. But I thought you might want to walk for a few minutes while I explain some of this to you."

Relieved that his companion was aware of his trepidation, Jonas accepted the offer to walk as he listened to what Michael wanted to tell him.

"Thanks," he said gratefully. "We were talking about the Devil . . ."

"Yes, and the origin of his dark nature," Michael resumed. "It's a question very few stop to think about."

"So, isn't he just evil? I mean, that's why they call him Satan, right?" Jonas said, picking up where they had left off.

"Oh, he is evil," Michael replied thoughtfully, "but he was not always called Satan. There was once a time, long ago, when he was called Lucifer."

Jonas looked confused.

"Isn't that just another name for Satan?"

"Satan," Michael explained, "is a Semitic derivative meaning 'the Accuser.' But Lucifer is a Latin name meaning 'Light Bringer,' which is a translation of the original Hebrew name, 'Morning Star.' There's reference to it in many places, but the one you'd probably recognize is in the Christian translation of the Hebrew Bible, in the book of Isaiah, chapter fourteen." He quoted from memory: "How art thou fallen from heaven, O Lucifer, son of the morning!"

Jonas scanned his memory for the verse.

"Lucifer," Michael elaborated, "the Light Bringer, the angelic Son of the Morning, fell from heaven, becoming Satan, the Accuser, because of his rebellion in our life before mortality."

"Wait—" Jonas said. "Did you just say our life *before* mortality?"

"Yes," Michael continued, "Just as your life didn't end with your death, it didn't begin with your mortal birth."

Jonas was doing his best to listen to what he was being told, but it was a lot to take in with everything else going on around him. He tried hard to focus.

"Your spirit body," Michael said, "has existed much longer than your physical body. Mortality was but a temporary state, a necessary step in your progression."

"So I was alive *before* I was alive?" Jonas asked.

"Exactly," Michael replied. "I know it may sound like a new concept to you, but the reality of our pre-mortal life is a truth humankind has known about since the beginning."

Jonas gave him a questioning look.

"*Praeexistentia*, as it is called in Latin," Michael continued without hesitation, "or 'the preexistence,' is a common belief for many around the world. You can find evidence of it in religions, myths, philosophies, and art. Rabbis, imams, priests, and even some of the world's greatest scientists have spoken about it at length. Kabbalah, for instance, one of the most ancient disciplines within Judaism, references it. Written there, you will find stories of heavenly councils; of a time when all the souls of men and women were created, waiting for their turn to be sent to Earth. In fact, Jewish tradition even has a name for the place each spirit waits before receiving a mortal body. It's called the Guf, the Treasury of Souls."

Jonas stepped to the side as a museum docent walked quickly by.

"I've never heard of that before."

"Not many have," Michael replied. "But even in traditions stemming from the Talmud, one of Judaism's most sacred texts, you will find reference to the idea of humankind's journey into mortality; of an angel they say who helped you in the process of your birth. Your philtrum—that teardrop shape just below your nose—that is said to be the indentation left behind by the angel who pressed a finger on your infant lips in an attempt to calm you down before placing you inside your mother's womb, asking you to forget all you had once known."

Jonas touched the soft groove just above his lip.

"I've definitely never heard of that before," he said aloud.

"Perhaps—but Judaism isn't alone in its teaching of praeexistentia," he continued. "The Qur'an also teaches that the spirits of men and women were created before they were sent to Earth."

"And they forgot too?" Jonas asked, his finger still on the soft groove of his upper lip.

"Precisely," Michael affirmed. "Upon entering the mortal realm, the memory of their heavenly estate was removed, so they could search for the truth themselves."

"And there are others?" Jonas asked, suddenly interested.

"As early as the written word, humanity has documented these kinds of beliefs. In accounts written in Akkadian, one of the most ancient languages—there are stories of Mesopotamian gods conferring with each other as to the nature and existence of pre-mortal humankind. Some of the oldest creation myths ever to be discovered explain how the human soul originated in a heavenly sphere before being mixed with a body of earthly clay. It's everywhere—Chaldeans, Persians, Egyptians—"

Jonas quickly found himself lost in Michael's words as they walked into another section of the museum where frescoes flanked each wall. Hearing his companion speak, he couldn't help but imagine himself on an exciting archaeological expedition, unearthing tablets of stone beneath deserts of sand, discovering some of the world's greatest intellectual treasures.

"But the concept of our preexistence is not just to be found in religion and epic myth," Michael added. "One of the greatest philosophers of all time espoused the idea."

"Who?" Jonas asked, genuinely interested.

"Plato," Michael replied. "The Greek philosopher and mathematician, founder of the Academy in Athens, the first university in the western world."

"He believed in it?"

"Some would say he was the greatest contributor to its dissemination," Michael noted. "Although certain Jewish philosophers argued that his concepts of the preexistence were taken from Moses, a life before mortality and its residue on our memories were at the very core of Plato's teachings. Platonism, as it would later be called, spread across the western world, influencing some of the most brilliant minds over the next two millennia."

Jonas soon found himself in another room, this one with a high vaulted ceiling, early Christian art hanging along each wall. Intrigued as he was by everything around him, he still couldn't understand why what Michael was telling him sounded so foreign.

"So why don't I know about this kind of stuff?" Jonas asked. "I've never heard of the preexistence before?"

Michael gave his younger companion a quick glance.

"You have," he said, "recently, in fact. If you remember, at the beginning of your funeral service, the officiator offering your eulogy made mention of the idea that your soul had returned home to heaven."

Jonas thought about it, still puzzled.

"Think about it," Michael replied. "Returned home to heaven? How do you *return* to a place you've never been before?"

Jonas began to reply, but quickly found he had no answer.

"It's not your fault," Michael quickly interjected. "Christianity has had a long and difficult history with the concept of the preexistence. It's troubling how truths so important could become lost so quickly."

"Lost?" Jonas said. "You mean Christians knew about this kind of stuff?"

"Knew about it?" Michael remarked with surprising vigor. "The concept of the preexistence was discussed in the early Christian church for nearly five hundred years."

Jonas raised an eyebrow.

"The first converts to the Christian church were those who already knew and believed in the reality of a pre-mortal life," Michael began to affirm. "Since the time of Alexander the Great—Jews, Greeks, Egyptians, and, eventually, Romans all discussed their beliefs on the subject. Semitic doctrine and Platonic philosophy thrived so much back then that an understanding of the preexistence became almost secondhand in that part of the world—especially among Christians. It was an idea that was more of a theological assumption than a questionable theory."

Jonas didn't know what to say. It may have been true that all these people had known about the concept of a life before, but that still didn't seem to change the fact that this was his first time hearing about it.

"But the reason it may sound unfamiliar to you," Michael said, picking up on his companion's confusion, "has to do with the fact that it was purged from the doctrine of the early Christian church nearly five hundred years after it was preached from the pulpit. There were some who felt the concept of the preexistence was too closely related to pagan ideology."

"Pagans?"

"The Greeks were pagans," Michael explained, "and paganism happened to be a religious philosophy very threatening to Christianity at the time. Even though many of the early Christian fathers were students of Platonism themselves, there were some that began to suppress specific teachings that they felt were endangering the unique aspects of Christian doctrine. You need to understand that Christianity was once a relatively small and obscure sect. Differentiating itself was a prime concern for many within the church, which is why they often went to great lengths to eliminate doctrines that could be seen as originating elsewhere. Interestingly, though, it was a political figure that found the concept of the preexistence most threatening—a Byzantine emperor named Justinian the Great.

"By the way," Michael mentioned with a wave as they continued to walk, "this is the Italian wing. Some of the greatest works of the Renaissance are in this hallway."

Jonas found himself momentarily drawn to the art that surrounded him as they entered another section of the museum. There were paintings he recognized along each wall, depictions of various biblical stories that he had learned as a boy. Others, he recognized from pictures in his old college textbooks.

Michael allowed Jonas a moment to look around before resuming their conversation.

"As I was saying, Justinian wasn't just any ordinary emperor; he was one of the most famous Christian emperors of antiquity, and he found himself struggling to reclaim many of the lands his predecessors had lost to usurpers and foreign invaders. But in the midst of his military conquests, he began to feel it was necessary to purge his empire of paganism and the sacred traditions of the Jews. The religious and spiritual hegemony of his subjects was, he felt, necessary if he was to establish a unified empire. And so, with that as his goal, he massacred thousands of his own people in an effort to convert the masses to Christianity while simultaneously 'purifying' the church of any problematic doctrines by anathema. The concept of a pre-mortal life is just one of the many doctrines he purged in this manner."

"Did you say anathema?"

"Yes, it's Greek," Michael explained. "It means to denounce something as heretical and to excommunicate anyone who professes otherwise."

"Sounds drastic," Jonas commented.

"Building an empire isn't generally for the faint of heart," Michael replied.

Doing his best to keep up, Jonas again began to feel a little overwhelmed.

"So an emperor eliminates a doctrine that's been around for centuries," Jonas reiterated.

"For millennia," Michael corrected.

"Right," Jonas took the correction, "for a really long time—and all this affects us how?"

But before Michael could answer his question, Jonas noticed a sizable group of people gathering around an open doorway to their right. Craning his neck to catch a glimpse of what was drawing all the attention, he could see hundreds of people snapping pictures and talking excitedly about one relatively small painting hanging on the far wall.

"The *Mona Lisa*," Michael explained.

"Really?" Jonas remarked, notably impressed, though his companion didn't seem to want to slow their pace.

Glancing at Michael, and then back at the crowd, Jonas began to wonder what his companion could possibly want to show him that would necessitate passing one of the greatest works of art in the world without much more than a glance. It didn't take long for Jonas to find out just what that was.

"The reason the concept of the preexistence is so important to understand," Michael said as they moved toward an object in the hallway, "is because of that."

He pointed to a painting about twenty feet away. It was large, about nine feet tall, and set neatly between two pillars.

"What is it?" Jonas asked.

"A Raphael," Michael replied.

Looking at the painting as they came to its base, Jonas noticed that two figures dominated the scene. The figure toward the top was of a man in the form of an angel—or at least someone who had wings, which made Jonas think the figure was an angel. He wore a flowing robe of bluish gray, giving the illusion of motion, as if he were flying down from above. This figure also wore a protective covering of feathered gold around his torso, and a skirt of royal orange, a sword tied to his waist.

Jonas then noticed that the man was in the act of doing something violent: holding a spear in thrusting position, pinning down the second character in the painting, who lay with his face to the ground, struggling against a heap of fiery boulders.

This second figure looked demonic, Jonas thought. Horns grew from his thick brown hair, and reptilian wings emerged from his back. A long tail grew from where his tailbone should have been, and it curled like a snake ready to squeeze its prey. Where fingernails and toenails should have been, Jonas saw claws, long and sharp. One of the demon's hands was clinging to a weapon, a double-pronged iron fork of sorts. And his expression was one of pure hate. The whites of his eyes had been replaced by a dark and menacing shade of red. But by the looks of the picture, his burning animosity seemed to be of no avail, as he had obviously lost whatever battle this was.

Jonas looked at the small plaque next to the painting to learn more, but quickly found it was written in French.

"*Saint Michael Vanquishing Satan,*" Michael translated for him. "It was a gift from Pope Leo X to François I, the King of France, depicting a war that happened a long time ago."

"What war?" Jonas asked, intrigued.

"An ancient war recorded in various texts," Michael paused to explain, "a version of which you may have read in the Book of Revelation."

Jonas glanced once more at the painting as his mentor continued.

"It is a depiction of when Lucifer rebelled in our pre-mortal existence, igniting the war in which he, and those who followed after him, were cast out of heaven."

Jonas listened carefully as he focused on the figures in the scene.

"And there was war in heaven," Michael quoted, "Michael and his angels fought against the dragon; and the dragon fought and his angels, and prevailed not; neither was their place found anymore in heaven. And the great dragon was cast out, that old serpent, called the Devil, and Satan, which deceiveth the whole world: he was cast out into the earth, and his angels were cast out with him."

Jonas understood now where the artist had gained his inspiration for the reptilian wings and serpentine tail.

"The one called Morning Star, or Lucifer," Michael explained, "was cast out of heaven, becoming Satan, or the Devil. And, as was also recorded, he took with him his angels—one-third of the hosts of heaven."

Jonas paused to think about that for a moment.

"One-third?"

"Yes, but in order to understand all this, you need to put it into perspective," Michael cautioned. "Because we lived in a heavenly pre-mortal realm, those angels who followed after Lucifer weren't just strangers—they were our brothers and sisters, spiritual siblings we had associated with since the beginning of time. But because of their rebellion, they have become the dark beings we now call demons, whose only desire is to fight against light and truth."

Jonas stood silently as he turned to stare at the painting, contemplating this strange new idea.

"I know it might sound far removed to you right now," Michael noted, "but those spirits spoken of were cast from their home in heaven by the archangel Michael, and all of us who fought with him."

"*Us?*" Jonas said rather reactively. "You mean to say *we* were there?" he gestured toward the painting.

Although his companion had explained the fact that they had lived in a heavenly, pre-mortal realm, Jonas nevertheless had a hard time imagining himself as part of an angelic army in a battle of such epic proportions.

"You are not so far removed from eternity that you can ignore your place in it," Michael cautioned. "The events you participated in during your life before mortality have impacted your life now more than you even know."

Jonas looked uneasily at his companion.

"Come," Michael said, holding out his hand again, "let me show you."

Jonas took the hand of his companion and again found everything around him change in an instant. The skylight above, the people in the hallway, and all the paintings that surrounded him disappeared from view while another room materialized before him.

Looking around, Jonas found himself in a similar place where paintings hung and artifacts sat protected behind glass enclosures.

"What part of the Louvre are we in now?" he asked.

"We're not in the Louvre anymore," Michael replied. "We're in the Tate Britain."

"London?" Jonas asked, shaking his head, still surprised at how quickly spirits could travel.

"The Tate has put together a special exhibit from an artist that attempted to paint the world beyond the mortal realm. What you see before you is the work of a man named William Blake, one of England's most notable artists."

Jonas's eyes rested on a dark, rather obscure-looking painting in front of him. Taking a few steps closer, he recognized the heavy strokes on the canvas to be rocks and what looked like small caves. Amid the barren landscape, Jonas saw nude people, in fearful, agonizing pain. Above all this was a prominent figure—a man, also nude, but holding his hands up as if he were calling out to those around him.

"*Satan Calling Up His Legions*," Jonas read the plaque next to the painting.

"I show you this painting," Michael said, "because in order for you to understand Lucifer's story, you need to imagine him as he really is. Artists have depicted him over time as some sort of monstrous creature with horns and scales, but he is just like you and me—a spirit in the form of a man. And he speaks like a man, using logic and persuasion to win adherents to his cause."

Jonas listened, taking in the unsettling image of the painting.

"As one of us in the pre-mortal realm, we used to call him Lucifer because of his elevated status, but he only became the entity he is now because of his tragic fall. He was a Son of the Morning, a noble spirit created at the beginning of our family's organization. We may call him Satan now—but the origin of his power still rests in what he once was, the glorious Bringer of Light. Some may wonder how someone so evil could have once been so angelic, but what power does evil have other than the manipulation of that which is good? Darkness is nothing without the existence of light. Satan possesses no innate power, only intelligence gained through obedience in his heavenly home. And understanding the history behind his celestial origin, you can begin to appreciate that he is no mythical beast, no species set apart from you and me. He was our brother, our sibling, as were those who followed him."

Jonas held himself in silence.

"The difference in our potential as angels or demons is the effect of time on the decisions we make," Michael summarized with austere gravity. "That is why our pre-mortal life is so important to understand."

Remembering the question he had raised about the significance of a pre-mortal life, Jonas thought about what he had been told. Looking at the painting in front of him, he saw no demons as he had assumed demons would look—no beings with bat-like wings or serpentine tails. Every notion of the supernatural had been removed from this depiction. But as Jonas stood there, staring at the baleful figures suffering in pain, he realized that he too, was now a part of the world artists tried to recreate—a spirit inhabiting the realm beyond the veil of death. And with that thought, Jonas began to wonder if, in fact, this painting before him was actually more true to form than the one he had just seen hanging in the Louvre.

"I do not tell you these things to frighten you," Michael said, placing a careful hand on his student's shoulder, "but you must be made aware of the reality you now face."

Michael took a step in Jonas's direction.

"Lucifer waged a war," he reiterated, "with our siblings at his command. And because we were forced to cast them from their home in heaven, they seek now to take the hope of heaven from us."

"You mean the war is still going on?" Jonas asked as he took a step back, his eyes fastened on the painting before him.

"We've waited as long as we could to tell you this, Jonas," Michael said, "but you're in far more danger than you know."

14

WILLIAM GRAVES' CELL PHONE RANG IN THE CENTER console as he was driving in his Cadillac DeVille.

"Hi, honey," he answered.

Flipping the turn signal near the steering wheel, he held the phone with his shoulder to his ear, using both hands to steer the vehicle.

"Yes, yes, I know . . . I had some work issues come up . . . I'm going to be late for dinner tonight though . . . I'll give you a call when I'm headed home from the office . . . I know, it's a big project, but you understand . . . I'll see you at home . . . okay . . . bye."

Pressing the red button on his phone to hang up, he quickly dialed a number from memory.

"Brad," he said, "I'll be there at eight. I'm bringing a camera with me this time."

Holding the phone from his ear as a string of loud expletives came across, William Graves waited for the man to calm down.

"Don't worry," William said in a commanding tone. "It's just for me. No one else will see them."

Hearing the man slowly acquiesce, he grinned.

"Just make sure no one's there," he added, "and have her wear that outfit I bought."

Turning into an empty parking lot as he listened to the man grumble in submission, William quickly ended the conversation.

"Just make it happen. I've got to go. I'll see you later tonight."

Pressing the red button on his cell phone once more, William

Graves pulled his car neatly into one of the empty stalls before turning off the ignition. Looking into the rearview mirror, he stroked his fingers through his peppery, well-groomed hair.

"Perfect."

15

STILL STARING INTO THE EYES OF HIS COMPANION, Jonas saw the background behind Michael change once more. The small room where they had just been discussing the nature of evil was replaced by a massive entrance hall.

As Jonas looked around, he saw hundreds of people filling the space, making it look somewhat similar to the entrance of the Louvre. There was even a uniquely shaped glass ceiling above, illuminating everything below. But unlike the one in the Louvre, this ceiling was doughnut-shaped, with a circular stone structure reaching from the ground up into its center. Wrapping around each side of this massive stone edifice were two elegant stairways, each one wide enough for many people to pass.

Michael checked his watch and began walking toward the staircase on the right.

Jonas followed and began to climb the same stone semicircular staircase, wondering where he had been taken this time. There was a sign at the top with a map of the building; the answer to his question was simple enough to read.

"The British Museum?" he read aloud, looking back at his mentor.

"Yes," Michael replied. "There's one last thing you need to see before I can take you to where they are."

"They?" Jonas repeated. "Who?"

"The ones we have been talking about," Michael reiterated as they both came to a stop in front of the museum map. "The one-third who followed Lucifer."

"We're going to see *them*?" Jonas asked, wondering what such a meeting would be like.

"We must," Michael replied. "It's far better to do so for the first time on our terms than on theirs."

Jonas glanced at the map again as he felt his heart race.

"What do you need to show me?" he asked.

Seeing his mentor gesture toward room number sixty-three, Jonas quickly referenced the corresponding description on the map: Egyptian Death and Afterlife.

Jonas paused tentatively, but suddenly Michael turned to the right and walked in the direction of room sixty-three. Startled by the pace at which his companion was moving, he sped up.

"One thing you need to keep in mind, Jonas," Michael explained, as they moved swiftly through the museum, "is that The Dead have never had their memories of our former life removed."

"The dead?" Jonas began to comment. "You mean people who have died, like us?"

"No," Michael explained, "I mean The Dead, with a capital *D*. While you and I may be dead, we don't think of ourselves that way in this life. The Dead I'm talking about are those who fell with Satan without ever having received a mortal body—the ones who hold spirits like you and me responsible for what happened to them in the life before."

"They haven't forgotten?" Jonas stammered.

"Nor are they likely to," Michael replied. "Even though the memory of our preexistence may seem vague to you, The Dead can recall everything in perfect detail from the time we cast them from our home in heaven."

Jonas walked into room sixty-three but stopped short in his tracks, somewhat overcome by the brilliant display of ancient artifacts that surrounded them.

"Here we are," Michael indicated.

Looking around the room, Jonas saw the remnants of Egypt set neatly behind protective glass enclosures: there were coffins; golden sarcophagi painted with the faces of the deceased; small containers with animal heads, canopic jars, prepared to receive the brains and intestines of the dead. He saw statues of Egyptian gods, some standing with weapons in their hands, others sitting like royalty on thrones. On the far side of the room, Jonas could see scrolls of papyrus; copies of *The Book of the Dead* laid out flat for visitors to read.

Impressed by the display, Jonas saw a body encased behind glass: an unwrapped mummy that had been skillfully preserved against the effects of time. Staring at the corpse, Jonas began to see the details of death, as bones gave shape to hard and leathery skin. Where fleshy legs had once been, he saw thin, hardened sinews, made more grotesque by the bulbous size of the kneecaps and anklebones. The lips of the corpse had dried and shrunk, pulling back to reveal a row of blackened teeth. And the eyes were shut, with small wisps of eyelashes still visible.

Shifting his attention from these gruesome details, Jonas noticed Michael looking at a small piece of material that had been partially eaten away by time.

Walking to his companion's side, Jonas saw Michael gesture toward the artifact written in Egyptian characters, and the descriptive plaque nearby.

Hieratic papyrus referring to the warding off of hostile dead persons (*mutu*)
Ptolemaic Period, 305–30 BC.
Provenance unknown.
This papyrus was part of an archive of magical-mythological texts in the tomb of a man named Pawerem for his use in the afterlife. It includes a spell for driving away the *mutu*, i.e., the dead who have not reached the exalted status of *akhu*, but who oppose the sungod and threaten the blessed dead with harm.

Moving his lips as he read silently, Jonas suddenly heard his companion speak.

"I brought you here to impress upon your mind the unique situation of the *mutu*."

"*Mutu?*" Jonas asked, looking up from the plaque.

"Spirits like your father," Michael clarified. "Those whom The

Dead have persuaded to join their side."

Jonas glanced at the ancient papyrus once more.

"Persuaded—how?"

"Since the beginning," Michael began, "The Dead have roamed Earth, using any means at their disposal to lead their enemies astray. Because they have a recollection that spans millennia, they are patient, working generation by generation to ensnare the wills of men and women. They stay mostly silent and invisible to mortals, whispering in their ears, pushing them toward specific natural inclinations that lead toward darkness. They plant seeds of contempt and greed that corrupt the soul and damn progression. Their influence puts kings on thrones and brings nations to prominence. They infiltrate religions, philosophies, schools, and even the most humble homes. And there is no tool they are unwilling to use. They promulgate pornography on the Internet, use financial institutions to bring down economies; they steer mass media to sway opinion, and even turn to scripture in an effort to spread the disease of bigotry. They have been here from the very beginning, which makes them incredibly intelligent. There is no language they do not know, no culture they have not touched, no realm they do not wish to overthrow. Anything that reminds them of what they have lost is a target for their voracious scorn.

"And, as you can see," Michael continued, gesturing to the translation next to the decaying document, "they teach those within their grasp to do the same."

Reading the translation again, Jonas recited aloud the words that caused his heart to skip a beat: *"Hostile dead persons . . . mutu . . . threaten the blessed dead with harm."*

"Satan and his followers are after us, Jonas," Michael explained. "They are building an army even larger than the one they had before. But for those of us who will not join their side, they go after the ones we love in the mortal realm, in order to make us suffer."

Feeling the hand of his companion on his shoulder again, Jonas turned to see Michael staring at him.

"They are death and hell, pain and suffering," he said. "But in their darkness, they are wise, and in their chaos they are cunning, which is why they should not be meddled with unless absolutely necessary."

Jonas saw his companion take a step closer.

"And this is one of those rare occasions when such a necessity exists, Jonas," Michael said, nearly whispering now. "If you want to bring William Graves to justice, you will need to visit the place where spirits like him reside. Only then will you be able to comprehend his dark nature and those he obeys."

The memory of why Jonas had been brought here in the first place came rushing into his mind once more. The man named William Graves. The one who got away. His biological father. Having lost himself in a world of tourists and museums, angels and demons, Jonas had almost lost focus on the calling he had just been given.

Remembering Graves' evil grin when he peered over the casket at the funeral home, Jonas found himself standing a little taller and swallowing his fear. His fingers trembled with the thought of where he was about to be taken. But if bringing his biological father to justice meant visiting a place full of dark spirits, then so be it.

"Are you ready?" Michael asked in an ominous tone.

Nodding, Jonas felt his companion's hand tighten around his shoulder.

"Okay, then—let's go."

The two suddenly vanished from sight, leaving a crowd of meandering tourists to fill the space they had once occupied.

16

AT FIRST, JONAS SAW NOTHING. ALL AROUND HIM WAS black, midnight black. A black so thick it made him want to gasp for air.

Michael's voice pierced the darkness.

"Look at me."

Turning to look in the direction of the voice, Jonas's eyes began to adjust until he saw his companion's face appear. It took a few moments, but soon he could make out the shape of Michael's eyes, then his cheekbones, followed by his mouth.

"We will wait here for a moment, until we can see clearly enough to move," Michael said.

The next thing Jonas noticed as they stood there was sound, a faint but terrible rumbling in the distance. It was unnerving, as if everything around him was in chaos. As he listened, he began to pick up subtle tones that he felt more than heard. There was a deep, penetrating vibration that shook his core, making him feel as if his insides were churning. And then he heard a bellowing, ripping sound that permeated the darkness around him. But the sound itself was so low and so faint that Jonas had to concentrate on it in order to pick it up.

While everything felt as if it were building toward the brink of utter chaos and cataclysmic destruction, Jonas noticed that the area immediately around him was actually quite still. Deadly still, in fact. While his chest felt as if it was in constant upheaval, the ground beneath his feet was absolutely motionless. The air as well. But more than the absence of movement in the ground, Jonas felt as if everything around him was dead. It was like a vast expanse of nothingness so palpable that he could very well have been standing on the dark side of the moon.

"Can you see yet?"

Turning once more toward Michael, Jonas realized that his eyes had acclimatized to the surroundings. Where before he had had a difficult time differentiating his companion's facial features, he could now see him with clarity. But as Jonas looked around to see the source of light that made them visible, he realized that Michael was glowing. Taking a moment to look at his own hands, Jonas noticed that he, too, was glowing. Like the soft, subtle luminance of a light bulb or a firefly, their presence made the ground around them visible.

"Can you see that rock ahead?" Michael asked, pointing in the distance.

Jonas squinted into the darkness. Still unsure, he looked back at his feet where he could see the ground, and then followed what was visible to his eye until he could see a shape of something ten or fifteen feet from where they stood.

As he did this, Jonas became aware of what he was standing on. Black stone rubble. It looked a lot like crushed volcanic rock; the kind of rough, coarse debris purged of any form of life through intense pressure and extreme temperature. Yet the thought of hot volcanic lava seemed out of place, as the darkness all around him felt teeth-chatteringly cold. There was enough of a chill that he knew he couldn't stay in this place for very long.

"Do you mean that rock?" he asked, pointing, while looking back at his companion.

Michael gave him a nod.

"Walk with me, but stay by my side. And don't call attention to yourself. We are not welcome here."

Jonas was determined to follow Michael as closely as possible. Anything could exist out in this darkness, and he didn't want to take the chance of finding out what that was alone.

Taking the first step in unison with his mentor, Jonas heard a shrill, echoing scream off to his right, only a few hundred feet away. Far enough away to make Jonas feel as if he was out of immediate danger but close enough to let panic take hold of his imagination.

"What was that?" Jonas asked.

"It's okay," Michael said in a low tone. "Just keep walking."

"Where are we going?" Jonas asked in a whisper as they continued on.

"Going?" Michael replied. "Nowhere. There is no place to go here. It's all the same no matter what direction you move in."

With darkness looming all around, Jonas could see that his companion was right. In every direction the scene was exactly the same: a vast, barren landscape of coarse rubble and small rocks that receded into nothingness. The echoing scream caused Jonas to look up. He expected to see a cave-like ceiling above, but instead saw only blackness. He realized that the borders of this space were immeasurable by any of the senses he possessed. And with that thought, Jonas suddenly felt trapped. There were no doors, no windows, no means of escape. Just darkness, and the not so subtle feeling of someone or something close by.

"dddaaaAAAMMMNNNYYYOOOUUU!!!"

Jonas stopped in his tracks as he heard another raspy, angry scream echo in his ears. Instinctively looking in the direction from which the scream had come, he saw nothing but darkness. He heard the creature, whatever it was, begin to moan and grit its teeth with such fury that Jonas felt as if he could actually taste bitterness in the air.

Looking to his companion, Jonas silently pleaded with him to go no farther. He didn't say the words out loud, but fear filled his thoughts as he began to visualize what could be out there.

"It's okay, Jonas," Michael reassured. "They are not here for us."

Jonas heard the confidence in Michael's voice, but he felt weak in comparison. He pleaded even more in his thoughts to be taken away from this awful place.

"I know it's difficult to be here," Michael reassured him, picking up on Jonas's unspoken thoughts, "but the sooner you understand what goes on, the sooner we can leave."

"But can they hurt us?" Jonas asked.

"As I said," Michael answered, "they are not here for us. But we should keep moving nevertheless. It is not wise to linger."

Jonas looked behind him, and then ahead. He felt as if he had nowhere safe to turn. His senses had become more attuned to his surroundings with every passing minute, and he could now hear the faint sound of more voices in the darkness. Whispers, moans, noises that didn't even sound human. And as he and Michael walked in the impenetrable void, Jonas began to feel that the voices had something to do with their presence in this dark realm.

"Can they see us?" Jonas asked in a whisper, walking almost shoulder to shoulder with his companion.

"Yes," Michael replied. "It seems opaque to you and me, but those who dwell in this place have adapted their senses to it."

Hearing this, Jonas felt even more uneasy, knowing that he could see nothing out there but they could all see him.

"But even though they can see us, most of them don't," Michael added. "Like him, for instance."

Michael pointed to something in the distance; a massive black rock, three times as tall as it was wide.

"That?" Jonas whispered, seeing only a boulder.

"That's the back," Michael said. "Keep your eye on it."

Doing as his companion had told him, Jonas walked and kept his eyes on the faint, glistening surface of the tall boulder. But instead of walking straight toward it, Michael led Jonas around the object, revealing a figure standing on the other side.

It took a few moments for Jonas to realize what he was looking at, but there in the darkness stood a naked emaciated man, transfixed, staring at something on the other side of the rock.

"What's it staring at?" Jonas whispered, feeling as if the grotesque figure could hardly be considered human.

Taking a few more steps, Jonas saw that the thing was actually looking at itself. The rock it stood in front of was a mirror of sorts, having been cut in half and polished on one side. The figure's ghastly reflection was visible in the rock's façade. It was horrifically thin and sickly looking, as if it had been starving for months or even years. Its face was gaunt. Sunken cheeks and dark circles around its abnormally huge eyes gave shape to a face that resembled a skull with skin stretched tightly over its surface. There was no way a person like this could have ever lived in the mortal realm. Someone so withered and weak would have died long before they were brought to this point. But as Jonas looked at the figure, he thought its oddest characteristic was that it had no light. The only reason its horrid frame was at all visible was because its thin, bluish skin reflected the light that apparently came from Jonas himself and from Michael.

"What's it doing?" Jonas asked.

"*He*," Michael replied, "is suffering because he no longer has a mortal body. He's slowly beginning to understand just how complicated life as a spirit can be."

Jonas took a step closer.

"It's easier to understand when you take into consideration how our spirit bodies differ from our mortal ones," Michael continued to explain. "Back in the old life, if we experienced something uncomfortable, there were a number of ways in which we could cope. Drugs, alcohol—any number of stimulants were at our fingertips that could quickly alter our situation. Our bodies' natural reaction toward guilt, fear, even sorrow could be chemically overridden in a matter of minutes.

"But as spirits, we do not share those limitations. Composed of a more refined physical matter, our spirits cannot be dominated so easily. Unlike mortal bodies that can be swayed or thrown into shock by an overabundance of pleasure or pain, our spirit bodies carry no such protective restrictions. Our capacity for physical and emotional sensation is nearly limitless."

Michael took a step forward.

"The Dead use such knowledge to their advantage, placing their victims in front of these makeshift mirrors to accentuate the latent effects of mortality. Given the horrific surroundings, their victims quickly gravitate toward staring at their own reflection in an effort to seek comfort in the familiar. It is then that they begin to yearn for an escape—a substance or experience to dull their senses—anything to lessen the frightful intensity they feel here. But unable to obtain such relief, they eventually turn to their memories of a time when they once had access to them.

"But each time they seek out a memory of that sort from their previous lives, they find themselves tortured—forced to relive the very deeds that ultimately shackled them to an existence here. Cursed with a perfect memory of mortality, they can't help but make the connections between their desire for escape and the pull it had toward vice, which when fueled by their appetites, eventually led toward a life of darkness. It is at that point of recognition that they usually seek out another memory, another distraction, in hopes of finding relief. But making the same connections all over again, they ultimately find themselves clinging to these mirrors, reliving every regret they've ever had, every crime they've ever committed, over and over again."

Jonas watched as his companion gave the man in the mirror a glance that contained both empathy and disgust.

"It's a miserable existence," Michael added. "Having never learned to control their limited, mortal bodies, they fall prey to the sheer intensity of what they can feel now. Death is not an option for them as they suffer in this place. But as long as they stand in front of these mirrors, they will be doomed to view the effects of everything terrible they have ever done. In such a state, they become famished— literally starving for their bodies that have long since moldered in the grave. They crave the ability to feel less, to subdue, but more importantly, to forget. But that is no longer an option for them in this world."

Turning his attention from the man's anxious, pain-ridden expression, Jonas looked at the figure's full appearance. Thin, bluish, monstrously misshapen.

"Why is he naked?" Jonas asked.

"He took his clothes off a long time ago," Michael replied. "You wouldn't know it by looking at him now, but he was a handsome young man like you when he first arrived here."

Jonas took a step toward the mirror in an effort to see the man more fully, causing both of their reflections to come into view. The second he did so, he suddenly felt Michael grab his arm and pull him back with surprising force.

"Stay still," Michael whispered.

Jonas looked from his companion back to the man in the mirror, only to find that the figure was no longer staring at his own reflection. Instead of searching for memories of times gone by, the starving man had turned his face, just enough to look him in the eyes.

"Hello . . . ," Jonas heard the emaciated spirit whisper in a tone so feeble and so airy that it was hardly audible above the other noises around them. "Step out of the light, let me see you."

Jonas felt Michael's hand tighten on his shoulder. "Look away," he said.

Jonas was too terrified to obey. He was captivated by the figure he saw before him. It was repulsive and hideous, but it drew him in nonetheless. And, as his gaze fixed on the man's face, Jonas soon felt a darkness—a hatred that flowed from the man's bloodshot eyes, piercing him to his core. It was like facing a vacuum, a desert-like famine that fed on anything around it. Then, as he felt the darkness trying to pull him in, he heard thoughts of unspeakable acts. Disgusting and violent images filled his mind with repugnant horror as the skeletal form began to move slowly toward him.

The spirit suddenly stopped short.

"I know who you are!" the gaunt figure abruptly accused with bitter rancor in his voice, a terrible stench coming from his mouth. "You've come to take my memories! You've come to read my mind again! Damn you! *Damn you all for trying to take my thoughts!*"

"Look away," Michael said.

Jonas stared at his shoes as he heard the man fall to the ground, only to pound on the rubble beneath him.

"Goddamn you for coming here!" the spirit screamed. "Goddamn you for staring at me and reading my thoughts! They're mine! You can't have them! Leave me alone! *Stop torturing me!!!*"

The starving figure quickly fell into hyperventilating gasps. Jonas could hear the spirit wheezing and spitting as he angrily clawed at the ground in frustration.

"Wait," Michael said.

"Please . . . ," yearned the spirit in a tortured tone. "Please give me something . . . something to stop the pain . . . anything . . ."

Jonas covered his eyes with his hands to make sure he wouldn't be tempted to open them again. But after a few more moments of listening to the spirit beg himself into submission, Jonas heard his tone suddenly change again.

"What's this . . . ," he heard the figure whisper to himself in surprise. "What's this doing here? . . . Ah yes, there you are. . . . Where have you been? . . . It's been so long . . . you can't imagine what I've been through."

"It's okay," Michael said after waiting for the creature to stop speaking. "You can look now."

Jonas slowly took his hand from his face.

"It's all right," Michael repeated. "He won't bother you any more."

Looking back to where he had seen the spirit ranting, Jonas saw something he did not expect. Instead of a skeleton writhing on the ground in anger and pain, he saw the man kneeling in front of the mirror, transfixed again by his own reflection. He was as motionless as the lifeless air around him, except for his lips, which quivered in soundless conversation.

"We should leave him alone now," Michael said.

"I'm sorry," Jonas whispered. "I didn't know . . ."

"It's okay," Michael replied. "But be cautious. There are many strange things here—things that our presence can make worse if we aren't careful."

Jonas swore to himself that he wouldn't take so much as a step out of line again as he walked in the darkness with his companion once more. Hearing sounds of weeping, lamenting, and screaming all around him, he wondered what else was out there in the black unknown.

"Can I ask you something?" Jonas whispered quietly after a time, hesitant to bring more attention to himself.

Michael nodded.

"You said the spirits here are like my father," Jonas asked.

"Yes, I did," Michael replied.

"In what way?"

Michael walked a few more steps before explaining.

"This place," he said, "holds the spirits of those who take pleasure in darkness—the kinds of pleasures that come at the cost of others. And there are some, like your father, who have learned to love darkness so much that others become the very means by which they fulfill their most base desires."

Jonas heard another scream in the distance.

"People who choose such a course in life end up here," Michael said as he turned to look in another direction. "Much like that woman up there."

Looking in the direction Michael gestured, Jonas saw something floating in the distance.

"Stop here," Michael said, after taking a few more steps. "This is close enough."

Moving in and out of the light they gave off, Jonas saw an object in midair. It took him a moment to realize what it was, but soon he saw that it was a woman, spinning and twisting in the most contorted manner, her arms and legs flailing helplessly at her sides. She writhed in such pain as to make Jonas feel that she must have been unable to control what was happening to her.

"What's going on?" Jonas whispered.

Watching the woman being thrown about in the air, Jonas noticed another person nearby. A man was standing beneath her, doing nothing more than staring in her direction. Jonas heard the woman struggle as she emitted a sound like that of a person being strangled by the throat. But as her body contorted and thrashed about in the most violent manner, Jonas could see no hands around her neck. In fact, there was no one around except the man beneath her, staring into her bulging eyes.

"What's happening?" Jonas said, while looking for the cause of her pain.

Before Michael could answer, Jonas saw the woman tear at her own neck as she screamed at the top of her lungs. The sound was so high and earsplitting, it almost caused him to reel in shock. He had never seen such violence before, and the entire scene made him so uncomfortable that all he wanted to do was shut his eyes and block out what was happening. But unable to take his eyes off the spectacle unfolding before him, he watched in horror as the woman was thrown against an invisible wall, only to fall to the ground and then be lifted up by her neck again.

"She is reliving memories," Michael said.

Jonas turned to his companion, horrified at what was happening, but even more unnerved at how calm Michael was.

"What did you say?"

"This woman," Michael repeated in measured tone, "is reliving memories. But not her own. Instead, she relives the memories of those she hurt in her previous life."

Staring at his companion, Jonas thought through what this meant.

"Other people's memories?" he said. "You mean *she* did this to other people?"

Michael nodded.

"But how?" Jonas quickly asked next. "How is it happening?"

"She was too quick to anger in her former life," Michael said, "someone who rarely exercised self-restraint. Being so reactive, she never learned how to control herself, making it easy for the man below her to feed images into her mind."

Looking back at the woman, Jonas saw her pinned up against another invisible barrier, her face hit by something with incredible force. He couldn't help but notice how ordinary she looked. She didn't look at all like the man in the mirror; she looked like someone who could have lived down the street in Jonas's own neighborhood. She wore a floral patterned dress and had short, curly hair. But just as Jonas started to think of her as someone he could relate to, he watched as something invisible tore at her dress, revealing a soiled pair of underwear.

Protecting her face with upraised hands, the woman cried out, "Please, Mommy . . . Stop! *Please* . . ."

But the voice that rang out was not the voice of a middle-aged woman. It sounded more like that of a little girl.

"Her mind has been weakened by a lifetime of giving in to the impulses of anger and rage," Michael continued. "Now she finds herself helpless as that man below her uses such weaknesses to his advantage—forcing her to relive memory after memory from her victims' point of view."

"But why?" Jonas asked, wishing there was something that could be done.

"Because, in life," Michael replied, "she felt nothing. Not in the end, at least. Having given in to her awful temper, the light that was once in her became extinguished. The conscience that most of us take for granted was no longer her companion. She didn't feel the sting of guilt or regret as she committed her crimes. She became dead to all that was good. Dead among the living. A person without feeling or remorse. Rage and indifference were her only companions, but here, she is made to understand what the fruits of such actions really are."

Jonas looked back to the scene before them.

"Who's he?" he said, pointing toward the man below her.

"He is one of those . . . ," Michael began to explain, "one of the spirits who rebelled in the beginning—one of The Dead."

Feeling anxious all of the sudden, Jonas turned to look at his companion.

"He won't bother us," Michael reassured Jonas. "He's keeping eye contact with that woman in the air to ensure she does not think of anything except what he puts into her mind."

"But why is he doing it?" Jonas asked after a moment of contemplation. "Is it her punishment?"

"No," Michael replied, shaking his head. "The Dead do not believe in the punishment of sin. They only believe in the punishment of those whose wills are not one with their own."

Jonas looked at his mentor, still anxious.

"This isn't a punishment?"

"It was not the wish of heaven that one-third of our brothers and sisters become demons only to torture the rest of us," Michael explained. "The wish of heaven is that everyone partake of the blessings it has to offer, but only if it is what we truly desire. Having been endowed with free will, the man in the mirror and this woman before you now still retain the right to choose their destiny. But they have decided instead to love darkness more than light, which is how they arrived in this terrible place. But this woman who felt nothing in her mortal life because of a seared conscience will be of little use to The Dead here unless they can get her to comprehend the gravity of every crime she has ever committed. They must make her cognizant of how far she has truly fallen through her own choices. Only then will she be convinced that those who choose light over darkness are her enemies, as the evidence of their joy works to accentuate the depth of her pain. In that state of mind she will then look upon anything of truth and godliness as that which burns within her now. She will become miserable, wretched, murderously vengeful, and overflowing with wrath. But that is the state of The Dead here—their pain emboldens their position in hell."

Looking back at the woman, Jonas tried to imagine how much more of this she would have to endure before her spirit would finally break.

"The Dead cannot tempt us beyond that which we can bear," Michael said, "and there will always be a way prepared for our escape—but those who dwell here have turned from such help, and suffer the consequences of despising that which gives life. They have come to detest the purity and reason of truth, as it works now to shed light on the evidence of their crimes. As a result, each one would rather waste away here in darkness than associate with anyone in our realm. They are The Dead in infant form—B'nai Gehinnom, the Children of Hell as we call them. And soon, they too will join forces with their captors."

"The Children of Hell," Jonas repeated in ominous tone.

"As I said before," Michael replied, "Satan is building an army, and this is one of the places he has set aside to prepare the spirits that will fight for him. But because they used their free will to oppose him in their pre-mortal life, they must feel the pain of what it means to sacrifice that self-same gift here in order to join his side."

Glancing once more at the woman floating in midair, Jonas heard a gurgling sound that seemed to be caused by some sort of invisible liquid being forced down her throat.

"But enough of this," Michael said. "We must keep moving."

Turning to walk with his companion, Jonas fell silent at the thought of the real reason all of this was going on around him. When once he had imagined the purpose of hell to be a punishment for those who had done wrong, he was now beginning to see it for what it was: a kingdom where darkness reigned.

While contemplating the terrible reality of this place, Jonas heard its inhabitants as he walked with his companion. Shrills and shrieks. Wailing and the gnashing of teeth. All of the sounds working together to make Jonas feel as if he were in the midst of a host of wild and ferocious beasts caged against their will. But he knew now that these were no animals, but the souls of men and women living out the natural consequences of their actions.

But just when Jonas was about to ask to be taken away from it all, he saw something that was out of place, something that should not be there. No matter what the laws of justice demanded, he felt this place was too dark, and too terrible for what he found himself staring at.

"A child," Jonas said, pointing in the direction of the small figure.

Having remembered his aunt telling him that not very many children were usually seen outside the hospital in which she worked, Jonas began to wonder how someone so small and so innocent could be brought to a place as horrifying as this. But there he was, a tiny child of only five or six, standing with his back to them.

"That's no child," Michael replied.

Even more confused than before, Jonas looked at his companion, sure that one of them must be hallucinating. But before Jonas could ask further, he heard a small voice pierce the darkness.

"Why, Daddy?" the small boy said in innocent tone. "Why would you do that to us? Why did you leave us like that? Where's Mommy?"

But the child was not speaking to Jonas or to his companion. Instead, he was speaking to a man cowering at his feet, who was pleading silently for mercy as he rocked back and forth with his hands covering his face. The man struggled fiercely, tightening himself into a ball as he knelt, trembling.

Jonas felt Michael's hand squeeze his shoulder once again.

"This is not a place we should be anymore," Michael said in a whisper.

But before Jonas could even look at his companion, the small child turned, revealing tear-stained cheeks made wet by two beautiful green eyes. His appearance made Jonas think that he must have been down here for quite some time, pleading with his father and asking questions to which there were no answers.

"But he's just a boy," Jonas said, holding out his hand as if to take the small child with them.

Suddenly, a grin began to form on the child's face as he slowly walked toward them.

"We are only here to observe!" Michael said in a commanding tone.

Looking at his companion, Jonas was confused as to what was actually happening.

Making eye contact with his tutor, Jonas heard Michael's voice come into his mind. "He is not a child, Jonas," the voice in his head whispered. "He's one of The Dead."

But before Jonas could register the meaning of his companion's words, a sound like rushing wind came into his ears, and a terrible crackle of thunder exploded beneath his feet, shaking the ground on which he stood. As he looked toward the sound, he saw a thick, black cloud enshroud the small figure until the child disappeared altogether. Jonas then saw the full frame of a man walk from the dark veil in terrible majesty, his bright green eyes slicing through the darkness.

"We are only here to observe!" Michael said again in a louder and even more authoritative tone.

The man walked toward them, stopping only a few feet from where they stood. As Jonas began to take in his presence, he quickly saw that this man did not look like a monstrous demon. Instead, Jonas saw a man, tall and strong, staring at them with a commanding presence. There was an air of restrained power about him, a feeling of overwhelming intelligence. He looked well built and healthy, and he wore a perfectly tailored suit. He was confident and distinguished, handsome and debonair. But there was something about him that made Jonas want to run.

"Welcome, brethren," the man began, a shade of intellectual superiority in his tone. "To what do we owe this pleasure?"

Jonas stood paralyzed by fear while Michael stared in restrained anger, neither one verbalizing a response.

"Well," the man continued, "so much for decorum. I see you've come from your kingdom of light and glory to visit us, to observe the difference between yourselves and those you detest. But unless I am mistaken, there is no reason for you to be here. There are no souls for you to gather today. Tell us, then—what is your business?"

"As I said," Michael reiterated with confidence, "we are only here to observe."

The man turned to match eyes with Jonas, causing Jonas to look away. There was something about this man that he had never felt before. It was not a feeling of famine, like he felt toward the man in the mirror, or disgust like he felt toward the woman being tortured by her invisible self. Rather it was a feeling of connection, as if the man with green eyes knew Jonas intimately and could reiterate everything unpleasant he had ever done in his previous life.

"Oh, I see," the man said, as he looked back at the both of them. "You've come to observe what we have to deal with here? Wonderful. Perhaps you can give us a sermon. I suppose you could talk about the virtue of charity or how you wish to wrap us in the arms of your everlasting love?"

The man took a step in their direction.

"Please, I haven't been to church since—*yesterday*," he continued ironically. "I would love to hear about the pity you have for all that you see around you. Or perhaps you could tell us of your world, of the gayeties and frivolities you enjoy there. I'm sure everyone here would love to be enlightened. . . ."

"Be about your business," Michael said. "We have not come here for you."

"Of course not!" the man retorted, a sudden venomous surge in his tone. "You come down here to gloat over that which you have had no hand in earning! Your burdens are light because you have cast them on the backs of these who have been committed into our care. You come to offer life to those less fortunate than you, but wherever you go, you sow the seeds of discontent. We know your kind—offering forgiveness for sins, yet your very definition of sin consists of nothing more than that which stands in opposition to your privilege and power. You speak of redemption from a world of corruption, yet you have created the corruptible through your laws, which are neither merciful nor just. You come to offer these damned souls hope, but your speech elevates them little beyond the idea of how vastly superior you are to them! Is it not enough that you have cast us from our heavenly home? Why do you feel compelled to come down and remind us of what we have lost, when it was you who stole it from us?"

The man moved closer to them.

"But of course, you go here and there," he continued, "telling fables of redemption and mercy, which only remind those who think they need redeeming of how far they have fallen. You speak of happiness in glory and perfection, a conscience free from regret and pain, yet you create the divide with which you measure guilt and take away the simplest of pleasures from those who can enjoy but little else."

Suddenly, Jonas noticed the wrathful gaze of the green-eyed man focus on him.

"Like you, boy—no doubt you led a life of pleasure and ease, offered by privilege you had no hand in creating. You had influence, friends, merriment; yet how oft did you think about how all this came to be?"

Jonas fell silent, too afraid to speak.

"Far be it from you to understand the history behind your own salvation!" the man spat. "You had the courage to face your own reflection in the mirror as a child, to wonder about the origin of those blue eyes, but you learned as an adult to cast the thought aside when the truth became too much to bear."

"How—" Jonas stumbled.

"Are you much better than those you come to denounce? Had they not hopes and dreams? Had they not friends and acquaintances?" the man seethed. "Yes, but theirs were taken from them as they were sent into a world to see if they would choose the prospect of heaven for themselves. The limited sensations they were expected to control became nothing more than a curse. The ripened fruit they partook of to ease their human suffering turned quickly to ash in their mouths as your kind pronounced it forbidden. Your prudence in mortality may have withheld you from certain condemnations, boy—but to what end? You may think yourself different from the damned in this place, but you are one of them. You are a miserable, corruptible thing. Your heritage speaks to that fact."

"That is enough!" Michael replied.

"Oh, don't let me trouble his mind with the truth he has been evading his whole life," the man replied without taking his eyes from Jonas. "You are nothing more than the sum of what has come before you, little boy—like that of your mother—a simple whore who brought the lusts of a practiced pedophile upon herself to give you life."

Jonas suddenly felt a surge of anger.

"Quite a heritage, really," the green-eyed man deduced. "No surprise that your mother did not even have enough love to keep you near. A common prostitute tossing the by-product of her vice aside. You may think you are special—a chosen spirit destined for heaven, but I've seen refuse in this place of more value than you."

"It is time to go, Jonas," Michael said.

"But of course, don't set your mind on such troubling thoughts," the man replied. "The truth is hard and best be cast from your view so that you may enjoy the comfort of a higher realm. Think not upon these lowly souls, those of whom your kind have made liars, murderers, whoremongers, and the like. Go! Return from whence you came and leave the work of the damned to those more capable of carrying the burden."

Jonas felt Michael's hand squeeze his shoulder—but he suddenly felt no desire to leave. All he wanted to do was stay and confront this man about his string of accusations.

"You may have won your own souls," the man cautioned, "but remember, your peace has been bought with a price, the cost of which you see here."

"Jonas . . . ," Michael repeated.

Pulling his resentful gaze from the man's glowing green eyes, Jonas reluctantly looked back at his companion.

"Do as your master bids you, boy," the man said maliciously. "There is nothing for you here. You have no good thing to offer. Be gone from our presence before we decide to visit those you hold dear with the plagues you have thrust upon us."

Jonas looked back and forth between his companion and the dark spirit. He still felt the urge to confront this man before him, especially after what he had said about his mother, but seeing the earnestness in Michael's gaze, Jonas decided to obey his mentor's instruction.

Giving Michael a reluctant nod, the two quickly disappeared from the darkness, leaving behind the man with green eyes.

———

The figure stood in the darkness, his visage burning even more.

"Don't worry, Jonas," he said to himself, his mouth changing slowly into a grin. "This is not the last time we shall meet."

Turning toward his prey, the man with green eyes transformed once more into the form of a doleful child, making his way back to where his victim knelt.

"Daddy . . . ," he said in a small, hushed voice, "Daddy . . . I love you . . ."

17

ALL OF A SUDDEN, JONAS FOUND HIMSELF IN THE backseat of a car.

"Why did we leave?" he asked, still incensed.

"I'm sorry, Jonas," Michael began to apologize, "that's how The Dead operate. They find a weakness easy to exploit and use it to keep you near them."

Jonas glanced momentarily at the driver of the car before looking back at his mentor.

"But did you hear what he said about me?" he asked quickly. "And my mother?"

"I heard, Jonas," Michael said in an empathetic tone, "and I'm sorry for that. I should have known that's what he would have brought up. But again, you must understand—if you didn't have the wits to leave when you did, you might very well have stayed there forever debating yourself into insanity. Nothing good can come from confronting The Dead on their terms. All they want to do is drag you to hell. But if you're not careful, you may find yourself leading the way."

Doing what he could to control his emotions, Jonas took a deep breath and looked around. Glancing out a window to his right, he noticed they were driving down a dimly lit neighborhood road at night.

"Where are we?" he asked.

Michael gestured toward the driver of the car.

It took Jonas a moment to recognize who it was. From the back, he could see that the driver was an older man of medium build. He had dark peppery hair, and from the placement of his hands on the steering wheel, Jonas could see a gold wedding band with a peculiar-shaped diamond inlay. But it wasn't until Jonas glanced into the rearview mirror that he actually knew who it was.

"William Graves."

Michael nodded.

"Where are we going?" Jonas asked next, his anger replaced by a sudden intense anxiety.

Pointing out the window, Jonas saw Michael motion toward a home on the left, not too far from where they were. Lit from the inside, it had a sizable front porch, and two large bay windows with white trim. It looked much like the other homes in this tree-lined neighborhood: comfortable and charming.

But looking back at the driver, Jonas wondered what his father was doing there. Knowing his devious nature, he quickly grew afraid for every family in the area. And as he looked into the windows of the homes around him, he saw children, families, mothers and fathers, people watching television or having dinner together. It was all so wonderful but so wrong. None of them had any idea about the criminal driving up their lane.

As they pulled in front of the house Michael had pointed out, Jonas noticed that the shades of all the windows had been drawn. Unable to see anything inside, he wondered if there was a family in there, and what their reaction would be when William Graves arrived on their doorstep.

"Is he going in there?" Jonas asked as William parked the car and leaned over to grab something from the passenger's seat.

Michael nodded in the affirmative.

Jonas watched William lift a brown paper bag as he checked his appearance in the rearview mirror. Seeing his father do this, Jonas actually found himself matching eyes with his father in the small mirror, making him feel for a moment as if they were staring right at each other. It was unnerving, but he relaxed when he remembered that he was invisible to mortals.

"What are we going to do?" Jonas asked.

"We're going to follow him," Michael replied.

With that, his companion walked through the car without opening his door. Still uneasy with his metaphysical abilities, it took Jonas a few moments to attempt to walk through his own door, but with everything happening so fast, he didn't have much time to waste. Closing his eyes, he quickly went through the barrier and turned around to catch up with Michael as he made his way toward the front of the house, right behind William Graves.

Ding-dong, the doorbell rang as William placed his finger on the small glowing button, glancing quickly over his shoulder to see if there was anyone watching.

"Hello," a dark-haired man said in a hushed tone after the door had opened. He glanced nervously over his guest's shoulder. "Come in."

Jonas was surprised to hear the cordial greeting. He had half expected a scene, like a woman screaming at the sight of a sex offender standing on her doorstep or a man resorting to physical violence just to keep this stranger out of his home. Disturbingly, this man had not only welcomed William quickly into his home; he acted as if he were expecting him.

Adrenaline rushing through him now, Jonas tried to quiet his feelings by focusing his attention on the interior of the home as they followed Graves inside. It was a stylish place, with dark cedar hardwood floors and muted blue and grayish purple walls. To his left, there was a sitting area with a chocolate leather couch and a fireplace. To his right, a dining area, dimly lit by a wrought iron chandelier. In front, Jonas could see a stairwell leading up to a second floor.

On the mantel and hanging on a few of the walls were framed photographs of the man who had let them in—or who had let William Graves in, at least—and a light-haired woman whom Jonas assumed was the man's wife. Two young teenage girls were in some of the photos as well. The most prominent picture was hanging on the wall adjacent to the fireplace; it showed the entire family. This picture included another girl, much younger than the two in the other photos, probably only three or four years of age with sandy blond hair. She looked different than the rest of her family, which is what caused Jonas to take particular note of her. And he saw that she was absent from all of the other photographs.

"Jonas, I need you to listen to me," Michael said, pulling him from his silent observations.

Jonas turned to look at his mentor.

"Something is about to happen, and I need you to stand close by me unless I tell you otherwise," Michael cautioned. "But whatever you do, don't say anything—no matter what happens. Do you understand?"

Nodding his acquiescence, Jonas felt nervous apprehension thumping in his chest.

"When are they coming back?" William Graves suddenly said from the direction of the dining area.

He took a seat in one of the dining chairs, placing his brown paper bag on the surface of the polished table. The man he had come to see stood nearby, checking his watch.

"We've got two hours," the man said. "She took them to her mother's."

Glancing at his watch as well, William Graves looked toward the empty staircase.

"We need to hurry then," he said hastily. "I want to leave at least a half an hour before they get back."

The stranger lifted a cupped hand to the side of his mouth to yell. "Holly, get down here!"

Jonas was confused as to who Holly was, and what she had to do with his biological father. But before he could put the clues together, out of the corner of his eye he suddenly saw five grown men appear out of nowhere. It was a sight that caught him off guard, as he was still getting used to the way spirits traveled.

Looking at the men closely, Jonas saw that he did not recognize any of them. Three of them wore button-down shirts with neckties slightly loosened, and pants that still had a bit of a crease left in them. But the other two spirits looked much more out of place and disheveled than the rest: one was wearing a thin greasy T-shirt, while the other was wearing no shirt at all.

But it was their demeanor, not their clothing, that put Jonas on guard. They were angry—extremely angry, nearly hyperventilating with agitation, and they looked around the room as if searching for something to devour. They were like ferocious beasts on a hunt, and Jonas felt as if he and Michael would soon become their prey.

"Michael," one of the properly dressed spirits said in a vicious tone that was more breath than voice, "I see you've brought a friend."

Michael stared back at the man, suppressed anger visible on his face.

"Isn't that going to be awkward when your companion has to watch you cry like a little girl," the spirit seethed through a wry smile before another spirit spoke up behind him.

"You come here every time, disrupting the one thing we enjoy— why don't you just leave us to our work and stay where you belong?"

Motionless as a statue, Michael said nothing.

"He likes it," the spirit wearing a greasy T-shirt sneered as the others began to jeer in response. "He gets off on it."

Out of the corner of his eye, Jonas noticed something beginning to move. Looking down, he noticed Michael's hands trembling in anger.

Laughing, the first man held up a hand to quiet the others.

"No—this one is here because he has to be," the spirit said, narrowing his eyes. "Isn't that right, Michael?"

Looking up at his companion, Jonas saw Michael's expression harden even more.

"But that's okay," the spirit said. "I rather enjoy an audience, don't you all?"

The other four spirits began to laugh.

"Who's the boy?" the spirit asked next, glancing at Jonas.

Keeping his lips pursed in his vow of silence, Jonas waited for his companion to speak for him. But seeing that Michael wasn't interested in conversing with the men, Jonas simply stared back, following his lead.

"Ah, so silent after all these years," the spirit said as he looked back at Michael. "Too bad, really. I'm sure the boy would like to learn why he's here."

The spirit smiled before looking back at Jonas.

"Did you know, boy, that he's responsible for all this? Has he told you that?"

Jonas hardened his gaze, feeling suddenly protective of his companion.

"Hmmm," the spirit muttered under his breath. "I didn't think so."

The spirit narrowed his eyes on Michael once again.

"You see," he continued, "Michael's greatest weakness is that he tries to do so much good. But you can't be everywhere at once—isn't that right, Michael?"

The spirit shook his head with feigned emotion.

"I'm sure he was planning on telling you," he continued sardonically, "but a long time ago, distracted with matters he felt more important, Michael neglected to tend to the more pertinent duties of his position, namely, the protection of those under his care. But now that the innocent suffer because of his thoughtless neglect, he tries to quell his conscience by fruitlessly attempting to fix what he has allowed to happen. But you cannot change the past with deeds of the present, can you, Michael? Neither can you stop what will happen tonight—"

The spirit took a step closer.

"How does it feel?" he continued, staring straight into Michael's eyes. "How does it feel knowing you're the reason we're all here?"

Jonas could sense the tension growing in the room.

"That's why you come, isn't it?" the spirit accused. "You come to watch because you want to feel the pain. You want to punish yourself because you know you're responsible."

Fire growing in his eyes, the spirit leaned in even more.

"You haven't even begun to feel pain!" he fumed, his face becoming more distorted by the second. "We've suffered at the hands of your kind for far too long—it's time you share in our agony and realize what hell we can bring!"

Jonas felt a darkness beginning to overwhelm him as he watched the ferocious spirit prepare to attack his companion. But just then, a voice rang out in a commanding tone.

"*Silence!*"

The spirit suddenly looked behind him, to find that another spirit had appeared in the room. He was dressed in a dark suit, with a reserved yet menacing look in his gaze. His hair was white, bone white. But the feeling he gave off was exactly the opposite. Dark. Vicious.

The ominous spirit raised his left hand without much of an effort, causing the other spirit in front of Michael to suddenly fly backward, clearing the length of the room. Stopping his victim just short of smashing into the wall, the man with white hair held him in suspension for a second before sending him crashing to the floor.

The man locked eyes with Michael.

"Michael," the spirit said in a disturbingly polite tone as he bowed slightly without breaking eye contact.

Michael's eyes narrowed.

The man in the black suit turned and made his way to the dining area; the other four spirits followed in line while the fifth one picked himself up from off the floor. They situated themselves around the two mortals in their midst. The man in black stood nearest William Graves.

"Michael . . . ," Jonas whispered carefully. But his mentor quickly turned in his direction and shook his head.

"Holly, I said get down here!" the man of the house yelled again.

Standing right up next to William Graves, the man with white hair leaned over his shoulder, as if to whisper in his ear. But he didn't whisper. In fact, he didn't even move his lips. All he did was close his eyes and concentrate on something in his mind.

"We're running out of time!" William suddenly blurted out angrily as he reached for his brown paper bag, pulling it toward his lap.

"Damnit, Holly!" the man yelled toward the top of the staircase. "You get down here right now, or I'm going to come up there and get you myself!"

It took a few seconds, but soon, two little feet appeared at the top of the landing, making their way down the steps, slowly, timidly, so as not to slip on the slick hardwood surface.

Turning to look, seeing her sandy blond hair falling past her shoulders, Jonas instantly recognized the small figure as the little girl in the photo on the wall. She seemed to be only a couple of years older than when she had sat for the portrait. She was petite, with large hazel-green eyes, and she moved slowly and steadily, biting down on her lip in nervous concentration, clinging to the staircase banister with a small, deliberate hand.

Glancing at Michael, Jonas noticed that his companion was looking at the little girl as well. But there was fear and longing in his countenance. A deep and poignant sadness. It seemed as if his mentor was struggling somehow, struggling with the conflicting emotions of tender fondness and extreme pain. Jonas wasn't sure what it was exactly, but Michael seemed to be suffering at the sight of the child making her way down the steps.

"Hurry up, honey," the man of the house said.

As she made her way down far enough to see the two men in the dining room, she stopped suddenly, her eyes filling with fear.

"Don't be silly," the man said, annoyed. "Come down here."

The little girl looked away.

"You remember Uncle Willie?" the man said, referencing his guest. "He's come to see you again."

"Yes," William said in a high-pitched tone. "You know me. We have such a good time together."

William opened the brown paper bag on his lap.

"Look," he said, holding the open bag out in front of him. "I've brought something for you."

The little girl turned to look as he pulled out an old-fashioned Polaroid camera.

"I've come to take some pictures of that new nightgown I bought you," he said, holding up the camera to his eyes as if to snap a photo.

"If you come and sit on my lap, I'll show you how it works."

Jonas looked back to his companion, unsure of what was really going on.

"Michael," he whispered again, "please . . . what's happening?"

But watching his mentor shake his head to quiet him again, Jonas looked back at the scene before him.

William began to shift awkwardly in his seat, reaching in between his legs to maneuver something. It was an odd motion, causing even the man at his side to take particular note of it. But angling his body slightly with apparent discomfort, William revealed something that made Jonas recoil in disgust. Where there should have been an even crease toward the top of his suit pants inseam, there was instead a bulge, grotesque in size where there had been none before. He stroked it a few times.

Jonas felt himself stagger backward, shaking his head in disbelief.

"No . . . ," he whispered to himself.

But there was no way to deny what William had come here to do. Despite his crimes back at the girls' school decades ago, Jonas had not imagined him capable of doing something as disgusting as this. It was a revolting, loathsome thought, and it caused Jonas to double over with a stomach-churning lurch.

William cringed with excitement as the little girl made her way farther down the hardwood steps. She seemed scared, but interested in the object she had been offered.

"Michael," Jonas said, turning with eyes that seemed electrified with shock. "Michael we have to stop this—"

Michael made no reply, he simply stood, staring at the little girl, melancholy in his eyes, a tear running down his cheek.

"Michael," Jonas said again, pulling on his companion's shirt, "Michael we have to do something."

But Michael didn't seem to hear him.

"Michael, *please* . . ."

The room remained silent, but for subtle whisperings that began to grow as the five spirits in the dining room began to speak to each other, growing more excited as the little girl made her way toward William Graves. Feeling suddenly alone, Jonas pleaded in his mind for Michael to acknowledge him, to somehow stop this horrific scene from unfolding.

"Jonas, I'm sorry," Michael suddenly whispered with great

despondency in his voice, a look of hopelessness on his face. "It's too late."

"Too late!" Jonas exclaimed. "Why?"

Michael shook his head in defeat, looking back in the direction of the dining room.

"William has already made his choice," he explained.

Jonas turned back to his companion, unwilling to let it go. Michael seemed to be giving up without a fight, but Jonas decided he wasn't going to be pushed around so easily. After all, he had been given the job of stopping his biological father from perpetrating crimes of this very sort.

"Do what you want, Michael, but this isn't happening tonight."

"Jonas, *no!*"

Michael's hand grasped at his sleeve, but Jonas broke free and walked forcefully toward the men in the dining room.

"Come here, you sons of bitches!" he exclaimed, fists raised.

But before Jonas could get in another word, he felt his body suddenly overcome. He was unable to speak, as if his tongue had swelled up in his mouth. His feet lifted off the ground, and he found himself suspended in midair. While floating there, he felt his body contort with spasms; every muscle tightening in a vice-like grip. His eyes bulged from his skull as he heard what sounded like vertebrae exploding up and down his back. His entire frame began to shudder and vibrate so violently that he could hardly hear anything other than the chaos that seemed to be tearing his body apart.

Turning slowly upside down, Jonas could see the penetrating eyes of the white-haired man staring at him. It filled him with a cold, dark sensation. But as he felt the ferocity of the man's gaze controlling the sound of popping cartilage and tearing tendons—Jonas suddenly felt the touch of Michael's hand on his shoulder, relieving him instantly of the unbearable agony.

Dropping to the floor with a sudden smack, Jonas looked above him in confusion. Michael began to quiver and shake against the very same force that had only seconds before held Jonas in its grip. He staggered and fell to his knees, spasming under the weight of the unseen power. Clenching his teeth, the veins in his face and neck began to swell. Jonas was unable to do anything more than watch his companion shudder as bones began to visibly break beneath the skin of his arms.

Horrified, Jonas watched for what seemed like an eternity as he screamed at the white-haired man to release his merciless grasp. But when he noticed the bones in Michael's arms mending themselves, he realized his mentor was slowly gaining control. He didn't know how, but Michael began to purge his body of the unseen force, as violent throbs diminished into twitching spasms, and then into small and sudden jerks. It took some time for him to expel the invisible venom, but soon Michael was able to take a deep breath, fully in control of his body again.

Relieved to see his mentor healed, Jonas nevertheless felt the sharp sting of guilt as he realized it was his own disobedience that had caused him to suffer in the first place.

"You would do well to control your inferior," the white-haired man cautioned Michael from across the room. "You know the laws by which we operate."

"Michael, I'm sorry—"

"No, Jonas. It should be me asking for your forgiveness. I was too preoccupied to listen when you asked for my help."

Seeing his mentor begin to rise to his feet, Jonas rose quickly too, offering what little assistance he could.

"Thank you, Jonas," Michael said as he stood, turning to look at the little girl.

Glancing in that direction as well, Jonas saw the small child take a step toward William, staring curiously at the camera in his hands.

"Jonas," Michael spoke aloud. "I need you to wait outside."

A sudden feeling of panic returned, and Jonas looked at his mentor with fear in his eyes.

"I need you to go now, Jonas," Michael said firmly. "You are not prepared for what is about to happen."

Turning to look at the little girl once more, Jonas saw her take another timid step in William's direction, causing the old man to smile with devious anticipation.

"Please, Jonas, I don't have much time."

"But what are you going to do?" Jonas asked, wishing there was still some way to stop this.

Michael took a deep breath.

"I'm going to stay here and watch over her," he replied.

Jonas noticed a look of trepidation in his mentor's eyes.

"You need to understand," Michael said solemnly, "with what they are going to do to her—I can't let her go through that alone. I can't just walk away and let her suffer something like that by herself.

"Please, Jonas," he pleaded, "I don't have much time before they begin. Please wait outside. You have enough to worry about without this."

Staring into the fear-stricken eyes of his companion, Jonas could scarcely comprehend the grief that was staring back at him, like that of a father pleading on behalf of his daughter. Jonas watched as tears streamed down Michael's face. But he already knew he had stayed too long. His companion was right. He wasn't prepared. And as Jonas turned to watch the little girl move close enough to touch the camera in William Graves' hand, he forced himself to close his eyes and walk away.

"Thank you, Jonas."

———

Slowly, quietly, making his way through the door he had previously entered, Jonas left Michael and the little girl to face the horror that awaited them both.

18

WALKING BACK AND FORTH IN FRONT OF THE HOUSE, Jonas tried his best to block out what was happening inside. But he kept seeing the flash of a camera illuminate an upstairs window every few minutes. He didn't know the little girl in there, but tears soon came to his eyes as the pain of his imagination forced him to his knees. And feeling that life shouldn't have to be this way, he began to cry, knowing of nothing else he could possibly do.

19

BUSINESS SEEMED SLOW AT THE CONVENIENCE STORE as Chris placed the bottles of alcohol on the counter, avoiding eye contact with the employee on the other side.

"Having a party tonight, huh?" the young man said as he began to punch numbers into the cash register.

"Something like that," Chris muttered.

"Your ID, sir?"

Looking up, Chris threw the employee an annoyed glance.

"Just doing my job, sir," the young man stated with a smile.

Fumbling with his wallet, Chris took out his driver's license and held it up closer than necessary in front of the clerk's face.

"Thank you," the young man said, leaning back awkwardly to glance at the card.

Chris placed the card back inside his wallet.

"That'll be sixty-eight fifty," the cheerful clerk said.

Swiping his credit card, Chris quickly signed the small computer screen with the plastic pen before grabbing the bag on the counter and making his way toward the exit.

20

"JONAS . . ."

A voice from behind him broke the silence.

Kneeling on the grass on the opposite side of the street, Jonas felt the soft touch of someone's hand on his shoulder.

Turning to look, he saw Michael.

"Jonas, it's over."

Glancing back at the house where he had left Michael and the little girl, Jonas saw an upstairs light turn off.

"How are you?" Michael asked.

Looking at his mentor, Jonas didn't say anything. He just stared at Michael with heavy eyes as he noticed the sound of a woman's voice singing a child's lullaby. It must have been another spirit, he thought, as he had seen no one enter the house since stepping outside. But it was still a strange sensation, being able to hear something at such a great distance. He had heard a lot more than that though, over the previous hour. With the newfound aural abilities he seemed to possess, he had heard things through brick walls no mortal would have been able to detect—things he now wished he could forget.

"Come," Michael said, "let's walk."

Rising to his feet, Jonas began to walk with his companion down the dark neighborhood street. They walked silently, side by side, going nowhere in particular as they both contemplated the events that had just occurred. After a while, Jonas couldn't help but ask about the one they were leaving behind.

"The little girl," he began, "what's going to happen to her?"

Michael looked up at hearing the question.

"She'll fall asleep," he said, taking in a deep breath. "By morning, she'll have forgotten this ever happened."

"Forgotten?"

Michael nodded.

"But how . . . ?" Jonas stammered.

Michael glanced at his younger companion.

"Things of this nature," he said slowly, "aren't easy to understand. What happened to that girl back there—"

His voice broke, and he looked away.

Giving his mentor a moment, Jonas looked away too as they both walked in silence.

"It shouldn't have happened," Jonas said after a while.

Wiping a tear from his eye, Michael took a few steps before replying.

"You're right, Jonas. It shouldn't."

Both continued to walk as the wind began to blow in the trees, shaking leaves from rustling branches silhouetted against the night sky.

"But she'll really forget?" Jonas asked, picking up their conversation.

"She'll have to, if she's going to survive," Michael replied. "It might sound odd, but the mortal body has its own way of dealing with things like this."

"How do you mean?"

"You're probably already familiar with it," Michael began, "but there is a term called PTSD."

"Post-traumatic stress disorder."

"Yes," Michael replied, "a complex condition that can occur when people experience exceptionally traumatic events."

Jonas listened quietly as Michael explained.

"PTSD has a way of causing the body to shut down certain functions when in the midst of trauma," he described. "It's an automatic reaction that can bring about a number of symptoms, one of which is temporary memory loss."

"Amnesia?"

"A type of amnesia, yes," Michael replied. "Dissociative amnesia—a serious condition that can cause someone to forget the particular details of an exceptionally traumatic event for long periods of time."

"How long?" Jonas asked.

"For some, weeks or months; for others, a lifetime," Michael answered. "But while the memories are forgotten, they never actually disappear. They're always there, hidden deep in the subconscious."

Jonas continued walking as he thought about the concept.

"And her?" he gestured back in the direction of the house. "She'll really forget?"

"Yes," Michael said with a slight pause. "By tomorrow morning, she'll have forgotten everything that happened tonight, until of course, it happens again."

They walked for a few more moments in silence as Jonas gave his companion some time to regain his composure.

"Why couldn't we do anything?" Jonas asked after a while, an image of the little girl still bright in his mind's eye.

"There was nothing we could do, Jonas," Michael said. "We're spirits now—it's not like the old life anymore."

"Then, why did it have to happen?" Jonas said.

Michael looked ahead.

"It didn't," he replied. "It didn't *have* to happen. Someone *chose* for it to be that way."

Michael suddenly stopped, causing Jonas to do the same.

"I want you to understand, though," he said, a look of seriousness on his face. "Even though your father was the one who did that to her, his actions in no way reflect on you."

Jonas looked back with a blank stare.

"Do you understand?" Michael asked.

Jonas nodded his head.

"Just because your father has become a tool of darkness, that's no reason to think that you are somehow bound to the same end."

Jonas glanced at the house behind his mentor's back.

"A tool of darkness?"

"Yes," Michael replied. "Your father has become a tool in the hands of The Dead."

"What do you mean?"

"While The Dead are extremely powerful spirits, there are a few limitations they have to face when attempting to control the will of men—one being how they can affect children."

Michael gestured for them to continue walking.

"Because The Dead can't directly influence the spirits of children, they have to solicit the help of people like William Graves to do it for them."

"How?" Jonas asked.

"With adults," Michael explained, "The Dead work by persuasion, convincing the spirits of mortal men and women to focus on the instincts of their earthly bodies. In that way, the spirit's influence is diminished, as it bends to the more animalistic impulses of the flesh. Heavenly light and intelligence is quickly suppressed, replaced by the more primitive triggers of arousal and fear. The body then transforms into a kind of self-imposed prison, which The Dead can use to their advantage."

"To make them do bad things?" Jonas added.

"Precisely," Michael agreed. "But while The Dead can control the spirit of a man or woman in such a way, they cannot directly influence the spirit of a child."

"Why not?"

"Because they are too full of light," Michael replied. "That doesn't stop The Dead from trying to influence their bodies though—their mortal bodies are still vulnerable."

Jonas listened as they walked side by side.

"A child's body is just like that of an adult's, terrestrial matter under the influence of terrestrial laws. But in order for The Dead to control a child's mortal body, they need the assistance of someone who lives in the mortal realm—someone older and much more susceptible to corruption."

Taking a moment to put the pieces of the puzzle together, Jonas finally understood.

"Like my father."

Michael nodded.

"It's one of the reasons The Dead work so hard to control people like him," he agreed.

Jonas focused his gaze in the distance, remembering what his father's dark eyes looked like when he saw them in the rearview mirror of the car just a short time ago.

"So he is a tool of darkness . . ."

"Yes," Michael replied slowly, picking up on Jonas's thoughts. "People like William who have given themselves completely over to darkness are used as tools to spread more darkness in places naturally outside the influence of The Dead. By terrorizing, eroticizing, and abusing the bodies of little children, they can create some of the same conditions The Dead try to produce themselves. Addiction, obsession, compulsion, and fear can all plague the spirits of little children if someone like William can find a way in."

Michael paused slightly before continuing.

"But to rob the free will of a child's spirit by forcing him or her to inhabit a body that has been abused," he said, emotion rising in his voice, "a body with such debilitating disadvantages . . . that is the epitome of evil, which is why child abuse comes with such severe consequences. And those who engage in it will one day come to understand the gravity of their crimes—how they have literally been doing the work of the Devil."

Jonas fell silent again as he looked down at the pavement, imagining what the little girl back at the house had experienced.

"Your father has become a tool in the hands of The Dead," Michael reiterated. "And unless we can stop him, there will be more than just that little girl who will suffer."

"There are others?" Jonas asked.

Michael nodded.

"But how can we stop him?" Jonas asked, somewhat in desperation. "You saw—there's nothing we can do."

Michael studied him for a moment.

"We can't do it alone as spirits, you and I," he agreed, "which is why we're going to need the help of someone in the mortal realm in order to expose him for the man he really is."

Jonas looked up at him.

Suddenly, the sound of a car engine roared to life in the distance—the car belonging to William Graves. He was escaping again. Jonas was reminded of how his father had fled the scene in similar fashion after leaving a terrified, helpless, pregnant teenager to fend for herself. Thinking on this, he knew he couldn't let it happen again.

"Where do we need to go?" Jonas asked, urgency in his voice.

Michael reached out a hand.

"Come, let me show you."

21

LYING ON HER BED ALONE IN HER APARTMENT, SARAH
picked up the phone, dialing the number with trembling fingers.

It rang.

Once.

Twice.

Three times . . .

"Hello?" came a voice at the other end.

"Mom?" she said, her voice shaking.

"Sarah?"

She couldn't say anything. Sitting in the silence, she clung tightly
to the phone, her eyes filling with tears.

"Sarah, darling . . ."

But Sarah couldn't speak. She just sobbed as her mother listened
helplessly on the other end.

"Oh, Sarah, I'm sorry, I'm so sorry . . ."

22

JONAS LOOKED AROUND TO SEE WHERE HE HAD BEEN taken. It was a small apartment, old and cramped. But as he looked outside a window to his right, seeing the lights of Manhattan glowing in the distance, he realized the size of the space was actually quite average for New York City. There was a couch, a desk, a bookshelf, and a few pairs of shoes set neatly in rows along one wall.

Suddenly, he heard a sound coming from the room to his left.

"One thousand one, one thousand two, one thousand three," a voice whispered amid the sound of running water.

After a moment, Jonas heard it again.

"One thousand one, one thousand two, one thousand three."

"What is that?" he asked.

Seeing his companion point in the direction of an open doorway, Jonas took a few steps toward it, discovering a small kitchen.

"One thousand one, one thousand two, one thousand three," a young man inside the kitchen said. He appeared to be only a few years younger than Jonas. He rocked back and forth while rubbing soapy hands together, rinsing them under a faucet of steaming hot water.

"Who is that?" Jonas asked, perplexed by the strange, repetitious behavior.

"Someone who can help," Michael answered.

Jonas glanced at his mentor in bewilderment.

"What's he doing?"

"He's beginning to remember."

"One thousand one, one thousand two, one thousand three," the young man continued, squirting more liquid soap into his swollen hands.

"Remember what?"

"He's beginning to remember his past," Michael said. "Like the little girl, he too was abused as a child by William, but he's since forgotten what's happened to him."

Jonas watched as the young man placed his hands back under the water.

"It's been years since the last occurrence," Michael added, "but the horror of his past is just now coming to the surface."

"One thousand one, one thousand two, one thousand three," the young man repeated, trembling.

"Keep in mind," Michael continued, "if we can't stop what's happening to the little girl soon, this is what her future will hold."

"But who is he?" Jonas asked, pointing at the young man. "I mean, who is he, really?"

Michael took another step in Jonas's direction.

"You don't see a resemblance?"

Puzzled, Jonas looked back at the young man. He wasn't sure what he was supposed to notice, but he searched the young man's face to see if something familiar might appear. Squinting through the steam, he looked closer. Then, in a moment of unexpected recognition, he saw it: a likeness too similar to refute, an appearance reminiscent of his own. Like looking into a mirror that slightly changes the shape of things, Jonas saw himself, only with vaguely different dimensions.

Michael put a hand on Jonas's shoulder.

"That's William Graves' other son."

Jonas glanced at Michael for a long moment, and then back at the young man.

Time seemed to stand still as he took in this strange figure, this young man who appeared familiar yet distant all at the same time. Like meeting an old classmate from elementary school after decades, Jonas saw facial features that appeared recognizable, yet difficult to place.

First, there was the young man's hair. It was dark, the same color as Jonas's, but thicker. His face, Jonas could see, was also similar, with

THE CHOICE: DEATH IS JUST THE BEGINNING

contours that reminded Jonas of what he had seen in the mirror every morning since the last stages of adolescence. He was about the same height as Jonas too, but with broader shoulders. They looked to be almost the same age, though Jonas guessed the young man must have been at least a couple of years his junior. But when he looked at the young man's eyes, he saw a striking difference. While Jonas's own eyes were deep blue, this young man's eyes were dark brown, like the color of wet tree bark.

Aside from that one substantial difference, Jonas felt as if he were looking at an alternative version of himself. Not exactly a twin, but something almost as close.

"He's my brother?" Jonas whispered, taking in every detail.

"Half-brother to be exact," Michael clarified. "And he's one of the few people around who's beginning to see William Graves for the man he truly is."

Jonas looked again at the dark hue of the young man's eyes.

"What's his name?"

"Charlie," Michael replied.

Jonas whispered the name to himself as he watched his younger brother scrub his hands yet again.

"One thousand one, one thousand two, one thousand three."

Jonas couldn't help but think how strange his brother's behavior was—washing his hands over and over in burning water, unable to stop. It made him feel sorry for him. It was obvious that the activity was something Charlie did not wish to do, but he seemed to be under an influence that entirely overwhelmed him.

"One thousand one, one thousand two, one thousand three."

"Why is he counting?" Jonas asked.

"He hears voices in his head," Michael replied. "He feels compelled to do what they say."

Jonas found himself leaning in to see if he could pick up on any of the voices. There was the sound of running water, the sound of Charlie's voice counting the seconds, and the subtle sound of soap being rubbed between frothy fingers, but he could not hear voices.

"You can't hear the voices," Michael said, "because they're the voices of his mind. You're still new to our world, so you haven't yet learned how to read the minds of mortals."

"Why is he hearing them?" Jonas asked. "Is he . . . crazy?"

"No, he isn't crazy," Michael replied. "His body is reacting in a very natural way to extremely unnatural circumstances. Similar to what I told you about PTSD: there are people who suffer such extreme trauma, that their mind hides the reality of their past as a coping mechanism."

"Dissociative amnesia," Jonas remembered.

"Yes," Michael replied. "But for those who suffer repeated trauma, especially as children, their condition can be compounded by the fact that they have so much more to bury."

"More memories?"

Michael nodded.

"The more trauma one is made to endure, the more memories there will be to store away, much like a file cabinet with each drawer holding the particular details of a specific moment in time. But when these memories are shelved away into the subconscious, to be locked under key until a later date, the brain stores each memory in a particular way in order to isolate that part of the mind from further trauma."

Watching Charlie wash his hands, Jonas began to wonder what something like that might look like—filing away memories in such a fashion. He wasn't sure what a memory looked like exactly, but he imagined dropping something white and wispy into a drawer, locking it up with a small metallic key.

Noticing Charlie's feverish repetition increase in speed, Jonas began to visualize not just one file cabinet, but a room full of file cabinets. He was almost certain someone like his younger brother must have had to endure quite a bit to cause this kind of reaction.

"One thousand one, one thousand two, one thousand three," Charlie counted on.

"But each compartmentalized memory is much more than a simple recollection," Michael continued. "Each memory is linked to a person's consciousness at a particular moment in time. When the brain seals off access to those types of memories, a person's personality, natural inclinations, perceptions, and everything else that makes up that individual get locked up too—kept safe from further abuse. So if someone at the age of five is abused severely enough to cause that kind of reaction, the brain will lock up the memory of that painful event, as well as the five-year-old self that had to endure it. And when the memory comes back, usually at a much later date—the five-year-old part of the brain will come back too, thinking and feeling the same thoughts and sensations it originally did."

Michael's words began to paint a different picture in Jonas's mind. Instead of a room of tall gray drawers, Jonas instead saw children, each one looking at him with despondent eyes, reminiscent of the little ones he had seen at the children's hospital.

"When trauma that intense happens," Michael continued, "the brain begins to create dissociative states, or states of the mind where an individual can experience more than one personality."

Still looking at the children in his imaginary room, wondering what each one had to share, Jonas felt suddenly unsettled at hearing the phrase "more than one personality."

"You mean like schizophrenia?" he asked.

"No," Michael replied, shaking his head slightly. "Schizophrenia is something entirely different."

"But you're talking about split personalities, aren't you?"

Michael turned to explain.

"Schizophrenia is a psychotic disorder," he said. "It causes delusions and hallucinations, making the imaginary world of the mind seem terribly real to the one suffering from it. But this kind of disorder," he said pointing to Charlie, "is very different. It's the mind's way of coping with actual traumatic events of the past."

Turning to look inside the kitchen, Jonas again saw his brother's pain-ridden expression.

"Does it have a name?"

"Yes, it does," Michael said. "It's called a dissociative disorder, or dissociative identity disorder. It's closely related to PTSD, and it can affect anyone, regardless of age or genetic background. It's simply the body's way of dealing with the shock of an extremely harrowing event."

"And him?" Jonas asked, pointing toward his younger brother.

"Charlie suffers from it. The voices he hears in his head are the younger versions of himself—the parts of his mind that have been sealed and isolated, restricted from developing normally into adulthood. They are quite literally children who have been compartmentalized at varying stages in his life, awakening to the reality that they have long been forgotten. But while the conscious adult Charlie remembers very little of their experiences, the younger versions of himself are now just beginning to come out. Their stories need to be heard in order for them to heal, but for that to happen, they have to get his attention first."

"And so they make him wash his hands?" Jonas asked, confused.

"Not exactly," Michael replied. "Some of them have experienced horrific things, things that have made them feel disgusting and dirty. So they ask for Charlie to wash his hands even though it makes no sense to him. It may seem like a strange thing to do, but not if you think like a child. It's one of the ways they know how to get clean."

"But that doesn't look like he's getting clean," Jonas gestured. "It looks like he's being tortured."

"One thousand one, one thousand two, one thousand three."

"True," Michael said. "What's happening to him now is painful and exhausting, but it's not unlike what he has suffered before."

"This isn't his first time?"

"As a child," Michael explained, "Charlie was abused in a number of ways, not that uncommon to victims his age. His hands were held under burning water in an effort to punish him. He was stabbed with pins in his arms and legs, a torture that leaves little evidence behind. His head was submerged in the bathtub. He was locked in dark closets for hours at a time and told that he would be killed or beaten if he ever divulged who was abusing him. He was forced to endure many, many things, but perhaps the worst torment of all was when they made him do things to other children, tricking him into feeling that he was the perpetrator. It's awful what he went through at such a young age, but people like William Graves do not get away with what they do by simply asking their victims to be quiet. They force them to do so, using fear, guilt, and any other means at their disposal in order to guarantee their victim's silence."

Michael glanced at Jonas.

"Sadly, people like William know that the more horrific they can make the abuse, the more afraid of revealing the truth the child will be. Many adults are not ignorant of dissociative states either, and abuse the phenomenon to erase the evidence of the crimes they commit."

Charlie began to strain under the pressure, letting out a soft, whimpering cry.

"It's awful," Michael said, looking back at the young man. "And to make things worse, people like Charlie usually have no idea what's happening to them when they first react this way. One minute, they seem to lead apparently normal, productive lives, and the next— they find themselves at the mercy of something like this."

Both Michael and Jonas watched as Charlie trembled.

"One thousand one, one thousand two, one thousand three," he said, his voice quivering under the pain.

"But this is exactly what The Dead want—a confused, anxious, terrified adult, suffering because of the crimes of another."

"Please, God," Charlie suddenly cried out, lifting his eyes to the ceiling, "please, please make it stop!"

He paused—but it didn't stop.

"One thousand one, one thousand two, one thousand three," Charlie cried, unable to prevent the awful torture.

All of the sudden, Michael moved into the kitchen, walking right up next to Charlie. He leaned over his shoulder and closed his eyes as if to concentrate. Almost immediately, Charlie began to calm down, lowering his hands from the running water.

In seeing this, Jonas thought that Michael would perhaps open his eyes again, having stopped Charlie's strange behavior. But he didn't. He kept his eyes closed and whispered something into Charlie's ear.

Charlie's eyelids soon grew heavy and he began to sway—first to the right and then to the left, as if he was drunk or so exhausted that he might collapse. And after a few seconds, that's exactly what he did. His eyes rolled back in his head and his legs gave way. He fell slowly at first, but then landed with a loud thud on the kitchen floor. Soapy bubbles flitted in the air, knocked loose when his hands hit the edge of the kitchen counter. He lay motionless on the ground, his eyes closed, unconscious of anything around him.

"Is he okay?" Jonas asked, having instinctively taken a leap toward Charlie to help.

"He's okay," Michael said reassuringly. "I made sure the rug was under his head."

Looking down, Jonas noticed a blue kitchen rug beneath his brother's body.

"Are you sure?"

"He'll have a bruise on his forehead when he wakes up," Michael said. "But at least he'll be able to rest."

Jonas leaned over to get a better look at Charlie's head.

"Besides," Michael added, "Charlie's not the only one you should be concerned about tonight."

An image of the little girl suddenly flashed into Jonas's mind.

"Is she okay?" Jonas replied, suddenly worried that someone else might be coming to hurt her.

"I'm not talking about Holly," Michael said. "I'm talking about your friend Chris."

"Chris?!"

"He's in a lot more trouble than he knows."

Michael turned and walked toward him, leaving Charlie unconscious on the floor. Jonas was still concerned about his brother, but even though Charlie was out cold on the kitchen floor, he was taking deep, even breaths. At least he was resting instead of counting numbers to infinity.

Jonas prepared himself for another journey. And, feeling the hand of his companion on his shoulder again, he knew that's exactly what Michael had planned.

"I'm ready," Jonas said.

Less than a split second later, Jonas and Michael transported themselves to Chris's apartment halfway across the city. Once they arrived, Jonas could tell that there was something terribly wrong. Looking around, he thought at first that Chris had been robbed, as everything in the place looked like it had been ransacked. Chairs, tables, and shelves had been flipped over and thrown to the ground. Mirrors were shattered. Pictures that once hung neatly on walls were strewn across the floor. Books, magazines, clothes, and even pieces of a broken guitar could be seen everywhere.

Something moved in the corner. Jonas saw his friend slumped in the only unturned chair, a bottle in his hand.

"What happened?"

Michael took his hand from Jonas's shoulder.

"He's been drinking."

Jonas stopped short.

"But Chris doesn't drink. At least not this much," he said.

Michael was right, though: the bottle in Chris's hand was half empty, and not only that—there were more bottles of various sizes and colors all around him. It was a strange sight for Jonas to behold, seeing alcohol in such close proximity to his friend. He knew Chris usually avoided the stuff.

Without warning, Chris scrambled for a garbage can near his feet as vomit came spewing from his mouth. Bile covered his face. Waiting only a second or two, he lifted the bottle in his hand and, wiping his mouth with his sleeve, took another drink.

"I don't get it," Jonas said, bewildered. "He's never done this before. Not as long as I've known him."

Michael nodded.

"You're right. This isn't like him."

But just when Jonas was about to take a step toward his friend to see how he could help, two more figures suddenly appeared in the room. Turning instinctively to look, Jonas felt his heart in his throat as he saw who they were.

"Hello," the one on the right whispered in a raspy tone.

It wasn't that Jonas knew who these two men were exactly, but he could tell their kind—*mutu* or B'nai Gehinnom, as Michael had called them, the Children of Hell. And much like the five other spirits back at the little girl's house, these two seemed crazed, their eyes wide, nearly hyperventilating as they looked around the room.

"We've got company," said the one on the left. "You've come to join our little party?"

Michael straightened himself to full stature and took a step forward, causing the spirit who just spoke to take a cowering step back.

"We're not leaving," he said in a hushed but commanding tone.

"Fine, then," the first one spat. "Stay and watch if you want!"

"Not tonight," Michael said. "You will leave him alone."

The spirit on the left trembled, looking away. But the one on the right made a sound like an animal growling through gritted teeth, his anger flaring like the flash of fire in a heated pan.

"You can't stop us!" he said, his eyes growing wide. "You see what he's done to himself. He's practically invited us here!"

Michael shook his head again.

"Be that as it may," he said, "we will not leave him alone with you."

Jonas stepped in front of his friend, blocking the two spirits' view of him from across the room.

"You have no right!" the spirit spat back, hatred quivering in his voice.

But Michael said nothing. He just stood there like a sentinel.

"He can't do this!" the other spirit muttered under his breath. "He has no authority!"

But no one in the room moved an inch.

"Damn you!" the first spirit finally said, after a long pause. "Damn you and your little friend!"

Jonas stood his ground.

"We'll be back, you know," he threatened, staring right at Michael. "You can't protect him forever."

But Michael stood his ground as well.

Lashing out like a wild animal again, the spirit opened his mouth and let out the most foul sound—like a roar strangled by a scream—

his jaw opening so wide it looked nearly unhinged. But the two menacing spirits soon disappeared as a sudden crack of thunder exploded through the air.

All was silent once again, until the sound of a garbage can could be heard scraping across the floor.

"Whhhoooaaa!" came a nauseating sound.

Chris dropped the can to the floor while shoving himself awkwardly off the chair. On his hands and knees, he made his way over to his bed.

"Is he going to be okay?" Jonas asked without looking at Michael.

"Tonight perhaps," Michael said. "But that's not what I'm worried about."

They both watched as Chris stumbled over shards of glass and open books until he came close enough to flop himself onto the mattress, blood dripping from cuts on his knees.

"Can we stay with him tonight?" Jonas implored, looking back at Michael with an anxious expression. "They said they might come back."

Michael nodded.

"We can stay till morning," he replied, turning to look back at Jonas. "It's been a long day anyway. You should take some time for yourself."

Jonas looked back at his friend lying on the bed.

Chris . . . what are you doing?

23

WILLIAM GRAVES PULLED INTO HIS DRIVEWAY AND PUT the car in park. Leaning over, he reached inside the brown paper bag resting on the passenger's seat and pulled out a small handful of photographs that he quickly placed in his coat pocket. Wedging the bag and its contents under the driver's seat, he turned off the engine, opened his door, and walked toward the house.

Entering through the side door that led into the kitchen, he was greeted by his wife, who was busy setting a table for two.

"Hello, dear," she said with a smile, making sure the spoon she had just laid down was evenly spaced with the knife at its side.

"Long day, Carol," William commented, trying his best to look slumped and tired as he made his way toward the staircase.

"Here, let me help you with your coat," she offered.

"That's all right," William replied with an upraised hand. "You look busy enough."

He walked up the stairs and down the hallway, eventually making his way to the master bedroom on the second floor. Before taking off his coat, he went over to the bathroom sink and looked into the mirror at both sides of his face. Seeing something on the edge of his mouth, he grabbed a tissue from the vanity and wiped a glistening pink substance from his lips. Then, walking passed a garbage can, he flushed the tissue down the toilet.

Making his way toward the walk-in closet near the entrance to the bedroom, William took a quick glance down the hallway that led to the top of the stairs. He waited a moment or two until he could hear the clinking and clanging of pots and pans, and then he took off his coat. Placing it on one of the hangers, he reached inside the left pocket and pulled out the photos he had put there before.

He looked through them, one by one, his eyes narrowing and then growing wide with each successive image. He did this three times over before squaring them in his hands and reaching for a small footstool that was situated behind the row of clothes in front of him. He placed the three-tiered footstool in the center of the closet, and stepped on the top if it with the photographs in one hand. Reaching with the other, he lifted a panel in the ceiling above, revealing a small crawl space. He pulled down a sizable black shoebox, one large enough to fit a hefty pair of boots. Carefully opening the lid, he looked at the three rows of Polaroid photographs that were inside. They were neatly stacked and arranged by date.

He searched rapidly for a spot in the most recent row to place his new photographs. Sliding them in place, he took one more moment to look over the contents of the box. The collection brought a wry smile to his face. There were hundreds of photographs. Each one had its own story to tell—stories William liked to relive when his wife was away.

Trembling with the anticipation of looking at them all again, he heard a noise from the hallway. He quickly put the lid back on the box and shoved it inside the small crawl space before sliding the panel back into place.

"William?" came a voice from somewhere in the bedroom.

Stumbling, William turned around just as Carol walked by the doorway.

"Dinner's ready," she said as she turned to look inside the closet.

Balancing precariously on the edge of the stool, William grabbed one of the taller closet shelves to keep himself from falling.

"What do you think you're doing!" he said loudly as he shot an annoyed look her way. "You almost made me fall!"

"I'm so sorry," she said nervously, taking a step toward him. "I didn't mean to . . ."

"It's fine," William retorted, as he pushed her away.

"I didn't mean to startle you," she apologized again.

"I said it's fine!" William said sternly.

Using the pause to his advantage, William looked around, trying to find something that could explain his situation.

"I was just getting this down," he said, reaching for a flat white box that was only a few inches from his hand on the shelf. Leaning over, he pulled down the white box while his wife came quickly to help from below.

"Please, let me get it for you," she said anxiously as she took the box from his hands.

"Careful," he said, as he handed it down to her, making sure she could hear the tension in his voice.

"I'm so sorry," she apologized yet again, as she took a step back with the box safely in her hands.

"It's okay, just be more careful next time. You don't want to kill me, do you?" he said, before changing the demeanor of his voice. "The only reason I was up here was because I wanted to get this down for you."

Pointing at the box in her hands, William lifted the lid to show what was inside, a cream-colored photo album engraved with the words "Our Wedding." Seeing the contents, Carol relaxed a bit, her anxious look transforming slowly into something more like a smile.

"I was hoping we could look at it over dinner," he said. "That is, if I make it down there alive."

Carol looked up at him with bright eyes.

"You never cease to surprise me, William Ernest Graves," she said with a genuine smile. "What would I do without you?"

"You couldn't live a day without me," William said, grinning, while taking a moment to sniff the air, "just like I couldn't live a day without your wonderful cooking—what did you make tonight anyway?"

"Chicken casserole with buttered green beans," she replied, eager to please him.

"Mmmm, my favorite," William said, escorting her carefully from the closet.

———

Walking with his wife hand in hand down the hallway, William had been too hasty to realize that he had not quite closed the ceiling panel completely, leaving behind a small crack in the ceiling where there had been none before.

24

THE LITTLE BOY IN THE BATHROOM KEPT HIS EYES ON THE *older man as his hair was tussled under the white cotton towel.*

"Now, remember what I told you," the older man said.

The little boy nodded his head under the weight of the moving towel and the heavy hand on top.

"Nobody can know about what we did in there, okay?"

The small boy nodded again as he watched the older man place the towel around his frail little waist.

"Not even Mommy," the older man continued, adjusting the towel.

Looking back up, the little boy noticed something resting on top of the toilet seat, behind the man in front of him.

"Listen to me," the older man said, seizing the small boy's face in his hands, forcing his gaze.

"You and me, we're buddies, right?"

The little boy nodded.

"And buddies like you and me can keep secrets."

The little boy glanced at the ground, knowing what was to come.

"So if we want to stay buddies, we need to make sure we can keep our secrets."

Looking back up again, the little boy glanced at the man and then again at the thing resting on the toilet seat.

The older man turned to look as well.

"That's not a toy," he said, turning around. "I know you want to play with it, but it's part of our secret too. You can take pictures with it later, but only I can take pictures of us together."

The little boy stood, staring.

"Do you understand?"

The small boy remained motionless, his eyes frozen.

"Do you understand!" the man said, this time forcefully.

But the little boy did not respond. He just stood there, staring at the camera resting on the toilet seat.

"Goddamnit, Charlie, listen to your father!" the older man said, grabbing the arm of the child. "If you don't want to end up head-first in that bathtub again, you're going to promise me you won't tell anyone!"

The little boy looked up.

"I promise, Daddy."

"Good," the older man said with finality as he let go of the boy's arm, leaving behind white fingerprints that quickly turned to the color of flesh. "Now go get dressed before Mommy gets home."

Turning to leave, the young boy felt a sudden tug on the towel around his waist.

"Hey," a voice from behind said. "I love you. You know that, right?"

Turning around, the little boy looked back into the eyes of his father. They seemed kind all of the sudden—kind and loving. He had seen these eyes before, but he knew from experience they would only last for a moment. But it was moments like these that the boy lived for. Moments that made him want to believe. Moments that he felt something other than hurt. That's why he stayed quiet. That's why he told himself no matter how bad things got, he would never tell. If this is what it meant to love somebody, then he would do so willingly, if only to hear those words again.

"I love you," the man said, "and I want you to know that."

Staring in silence, the little boy took a picture in his mind, hoping it would be enough when things got bad again.

"Now go get dressed," the man said, his countenance changing instantly as he pushed the little boy away. "And make sure you bring back that towel. I don't want to explain to Mommy again why they keep turning up in your room."

The little boy nodded. He wanted to say the words "I love you too," but he didn't. He was too afraid. While saying those words meant something significant to him, they meant something completely different to his father.

Because that's sometimes how it started.
At least, that's how it had started today.

———

With darkness clouding over—the bathroom, the man, and the boy were suddenly all gone.

Charlie lay with his face to the floor, a new reality beginning to take shape in his mind.

25

A LIGHT WAS COMING IN THROUGH THE WINDOW AT Michael's back. It was morning, which meant their conversations had taken up the better part of the night.

"It's time to go, Jonas."

"Where are we going?"

"It's breakfast time."

"For us?"

Michael shook his head with a smile.

"No, not for us," he replied. "But for a lot of other people, yes."

Jonas felt a smile wash over his own face. This wasn't the first time he had come to a new realization while watching over his best friend during the night. In fact, over the course of the evening, while watching over Chris, he began to ask Michael questions about the World of Spirits: questions he had thought about silently to himself, but had not had the time to ask.

The first question he asked Michael had to do with his new spirit body. From what he had so far experienced, it seemed to have all the physical sensations his old body did, but with far greater intensity. When he was in the children's hospital for example, he could see, touch, smell, and hear things around him like never before. Of course, while attempting to interact with the mortal realm, some of those functions were limited, but all this is what he thought to be so strange. Ghosts weren't supposed to be able to do any of those things, no matter where they were. They were supposed to be like wisps of smoke, floating through the air, numb to all around them. Or at least that's what he had thought until he became one.

"I thought that kind of stuff was only possible because of a physical body," he said. "Things like spirits and ghosts just seemed so immaterial."

"That's just it," Michael said, "your current body is still very physical, it just exists on a level of energy and mass outside the realm of what is observable in the terrestrial sphere. Only five percent of the universe can be seen by mortals. Besides, when most people think of life after death, more often than not they either imagine some sort of blissfully happy state or one steeped in pain and sorrow—neither of which would be possible without the enhanced physical sensations we now possess."

"The Children of Hell—" Jonas began to form his next question, "why do they look the way they do? They're not like The Dead; it's like they're crazy or something—like they're out of control."

"Quite often, they are," Michael replied. "Keep in mind, though, The Dead have had a lot more time to work on their self-control. They have spent eons as spirits, exercising the discipline necessary to bring others under their influence. But the Children of Hell haven't. They're just like you and me—spirits exiled from mortality, finding themselves in a new and unexpected reality. But because life as a spirit is the only reality The Dead have ever known, their longevity has given them power over those less formidable than themselves. Time has offered them precious knowledge in how to manipulate the laws that govern our world to their advantage."

"And do they always wear black suits?" Jonas asked next. "The Dead, I mean?"

"No," Michael explained. "As you saw earlier, The Dead can take on any form they wish. A child, an animal, an inanimate object. They have the ability to look like anything they want."

"But what about the breathing?" Jonas asked, remembering the disturbing detail that suddenly put him on guard back at the little girl's house. "Why do the Children of Hell always look like they're hyperventilating?"

"That's actually one of the easiest ways to differentiate them from their captors," Michael replied. "In case you haven't noticed, The Dead don't breathe."

Jonas gave him a confused look.

"It's true," Michael said. "As spirits, we don't need to breathe either, but we do so out of habit. Our mortal instincts still have a pretty good hold on us. Even now, when we get nervous or anxious, our eyes dilate, and we begin to breathe more rapidly. But the reason the Children of Hell appear to hyperventilate is because of the pain they bear. They do the best they can to conceal the burdens they carry, but it's usually too overwhelming to control completely.

"The Dead, on the other hand, don't have the instinct to breathe. They've never had a mortal body, so they would have to consciously mimic the action if they wanted to create that kind of deception."

Jonas spoke with his mentor on these subjects for the better part of the night. Every once in a while, when Chris stirred in his sleep, or an unexpected sound came from somewhere in the room, Jonas would stop in midsentence and look around. Michael seemed much more at ease; he would wait for Jonas to calm down or offer a word of comfort before resuming his explanations of the spirit world. But the time passed quickly and morning came with the rising of the sun.

"Are you ready?" Michael asked, holding out his hand.

Turning from the light coming through the window, Jonas took his mentor's hand and looked back at Chris lying on the bed.

There his friend lay, stirring as the first rays of sunlight began to warm his skin. But just when Jonas thought he might see Chris wake up, everything around them changed. It wasn't altogether unexpected, as Jonas was beginning to anticipate how he and Michael traveled now, but the speed at which it took place was still a shock. The bed, shelves, books—all of it instantly disappeared. In its place, a restaurant table full of pancakes, muffins, scrambled eggs, and glasses of juice materialized.

"Looks delicious," Michael said.

Michael turned around and nudged his younger companion to do the same, pointing at something across the room.

Looking in that direction, Jonas realized they were in a café not too far from his old apartment. He had been here many times before. This was where he and Sarah would go every Sunday morning for brunch. It was their place, and as Jonas looked across the room, he saw that at least one thing hadn't changed.

"Sarah," he whispered, holding up his hand as if to get her attention. But he lowered it slowly, realizing there was nothing he could do to make her see him. He didn't know why he had been brought here, but it tore him apart being in her presence like this.

Michael gestured for him to spend some time alone with her.

Looking back at her, Jonas began to feel the instinct to breathe more rapidly. He knew now it wasn't necessary, but he couldn't help himself, as anxious as he was. Seeing her so close and all alone, he just wanted to run toward her and tell her everything he had been experiencing—everything he had seen. He wanted to talk to her, listen to her voice, hear her thoughts and sorrows. But unable to do so, he walked slowly over to her table, noticing an untouched cup of hot chocolate with whipped cream, ordered for him just the way he liked it.

The seat across from Sarah was only pulled out partway, but Jonas didn't care. He walked right through it and sat down anyway. Looking at her from across the table, as he had done so many times before, Jonas could see that her eyes were red and puffy. There was no doubt she had been crying. It didn't matter though. She looked beautiful.

Jonas sat for a while, just staring at the girl he loved, taking in every detail of her appearance. Like her freckles—the little golden brown spots that he jokingly tried to scrub off one day until she pushed him away and said in a very serious tone, "They're angel kisses, Jonas, and you'd do well to think about how few you have!" And then there were her lips, round and supple, sipping a cup of elderberry tea. It reminded him of when she first introduced him to herbal tea, which Jonas thought tasted more like watered-down weeds. But he drank it just the same, hoping that one day he would pick up on the joy and comfort it brought her. And then there were her striking green eyes. Eyes that spoke to a life of goodness and beauty. But today they were different. As beautiful as they were, they weren't smiling.

"Sarah," Jonas said, looking into those eyes.

But nothing happened. She just looked down at her tea.

"Sarah—" Jonas tried again but stopped short.

She couldn't hear him, and he didn't want to waste the precious time he had been given. No doubt, Michael had other places to take him, but all he wanted to do was be with her. Sitting. Watching. Taking in her every move. Time, he knew, was limited, and he didn't want to throw it away on trying to get her attention. So he watched and he remembered.

As Jonas looked at the girl in front of him, something suddenly made Sarah's expression change to one of shock and fear. Something behind him had alarmed her. Jonas turned around to see what it was.

There, waiting for a table, he saw his half-brother Charlie.

Sarah began to stare at Charlie, making Jonas wonder if they had met before. But watching her closely, he could tell that she had no idea who he really was.

Looking back at his brother, Jonas saw Charlie sit down at a table just a few feet away, placing a book to his right while ordering a cup of coffee from the waitress. Seeing this, Jonas began to sense an odd feeling, a feeling he couldn't altogether explain. On the one hand, he was happy to see that Charlie was doing much better—he wasn't counting, or mumbling, or rocking back and forth. On the other hand, this normalcy caused Jonas more than a little apprehension, especially when he caught his half-brother glancing in Sarah's direction.

Looking back at Sarah, the feeling only grew worse. Moments ago, Jonas had been looking into her eyes, knowing that while she couldn't see him, she was most likely thinking of him, or at least of his absence. But now she was distracted, looking at the handsome newcomer. And in that moment, Jonas began to realize that the feelings he was having for Sarah were quickly being replaced by an entirely new sensation.

"Here's your coffee, sir," the young waitress said to Charlie.

As Charlie took the cup and saucer, his hands began to shake. He dropped the cup, spilling coffee over the table and splashing some of it on the waitress's clothing.

"I'm so sorry—" Charlie exclaimed.

Invisible all the while, Jonas stifled a grin.

"That's okay," the waitress replied, as politely as she could.

Sarah rose from her seat to offer her assistance.

"Are you okay?" she asked, stopping just a few feet in front of Charlie's table, a wad of napkins in her hand.

Looking up from the dark liquid that was dribbling down onto the floor, Charlie nodded.

"Yeah, I'm okay," he said, just as he noticed his book lying in a pool of coffee.

He tried to rescue it, but more than half the pages were already soaked through.

"Here, let me help you," Sarah offered, as she took the wad of napkins in her hand and began to wipe up the mess.

Jonas shifted slightly in his seat upon seeing this.

"No—really, you don't have to," Charlie protested.

But Sarah quickly went to work, placing the napkins over the liquid to soak it up, just as the waitress began to make her way back with a small towel.

"I'm really sorry," Charlie apologized to the waitress as she helped to wipe up the mess.

She didn't say anything in reply.

The three went to work, and as they did so, Sarah tried to catch a glimpse of Charlie every so often. After a few minutes the mess was cleaned up. The waitress left to get another cup of coffee.

Charlie looked up at the beautiful girl who had come to help him.

"Thank you," he said again as he took a step toward her, wiping his hand on his shirt before holding it out for her to shake.

"It's okay," Sarah replied, taking his hand timidly.

As she shook his hand, Sarah began to stare at Charlie openly. She hadn't planned on doing so, but there she was—staring into his eyes, taking in his every feature.

Jonas leaned in from afar, waiting to see Charlie's response.

"Are you all right?" Charlie asked.

Instead of answering Charlie's question, Sarah asked him a question of her own.

"Do I know you?"

"I don't think so—"

"Have we ever met?"

"I . . . I'm pretty sure we haven't."

"Are you sure?"

There was a pause.

"We could have," Charlie admitted, "but I think I'd have remembered if we had."

Jonas's eyes narrowed slightly.

Breaking her grip with Charlie, Sarah continued to study him openly.

"Have you ever come in here before?" she pushed.

"A . . . a few times, I guess," he stuttered. "I'm sorry—what was your name again?"

Realizing at last how strangely she was coming across, Sarah suddenly flushed red.

"I'm sorry. You just . . . ," she began apologetically. "It's just . . ."

Glancing at the floor and then back up at the stranger in front of her, she gave up in the midst of her embarrassment.

"Sarah," she finally said. "My name's Sarah."

Charlie smiled kindly.

"Good to meet you, Sarah. My name's Charlie."

Jonas glanced over his shoulder at Michael for a moment, wondering what was going on.

"You just . . . ," Sarah began again, stuttering as she did so, "you just look like someone I know, that's all."

Hearing this, Jonas turned back around, listening more attentively than before.

"I hope that's okay," Charlie said, trying to lighten the mood.

Sarah suddenly turned to look in Jonas's direction, staring at the cup of hot chocolate on the table in front of him.

"Are you waiting for someone?" Charlie asked, noticing the cup too.

Taking a moment to reply, Sarah shook her head.

Jonas sank slowly in his chair.

"You can have breakfast with me if you'd like," Charlie offered, pointing to the empty seat at his table.

But Sarah didn't reply. She just bit her lip and looked nervously at the floor.

"I mean . . . you don't have to," Charlie began, "I just thought . . ."

Cutting in on their awkward conversation, the waitress appeared, holding a new cup of coffee in her hands.

"Ahem," she cleared her throat to get Charlie's attention. "Where do you want it?"

Seeing the cup in the waitress's hands, Charlie quickly looked around, pointing to a spot on his table that was easily within her reach.

"Right there's fine," he said, taking a step to the side so as not to get in her way.

Without so much as a nod, the waitress placed the cup of coffee on the table, and then pulled out a pen and a small pad of paper. Writing on it for a moment, she soon ripped off the top sheet and placed it on the table near the coffee.

"Your check," she said, matter-of-factly.

Charlie glanced at the check and then at Sarah's table, seeing no slip of paper there.

"Um . . . please," he said, grabbing the waitress's attention just as she was turning around. "Could you put her order on my check too?"

Sarah looked a little stunned as she saw him pointing toward her.

"No," she protested, "don't—"

"Yeah, don't," Jonas agreed.

But the waitress pulled out her pen and pad once again. She looked at what was on Sarah's table, scribbled something quickly, and ripped off another sheet placing it next to the first one. "I'll let you both figure that out," she said, turning on her heel and walking back to the kitchen.

Jonas shot her a glare as she walked by.

"Please," Charlie implored, looking at Sarah, "you didn't have to clean up my mess."

Still not sure what to think, Sarah took a moment for herself, but in the end, decided to let it go. Looking over at the empty chair she had been offered, though, she realized Charlie was probably still waiting for an answer.

"I . . . I can't," she said, pointing to the chair across from his. "I can't sit with you, it's just that . . ."

Jonas looked back in Sarah's direction, holding his breath as he waited to hear what she would say.

"No, it's me . . . ," Charlie began to apologize. "I wasn't trying to—you know. I just thought that since you were alone . . ."

Hearing himself stammer, Charlie decided to just hold out his hand and end the awkwardness.

"It was good to meet you, Sarah," he said with an uncomfortable smile, shaking her hand once more before turning around to sit back in his chair.

Jonas watched him sit down while Sarah began to make her way back over to her chair. Pleased that they would be alone again, Jonas faced forward in his seat once more. But just when he thought Sarah would sit down, he saw her glance back over her shoulder to stare at Charlie. She stood there, looking at the handsome young man who had just begun to pour cream into his coffee with a trembling hand. Then, without so much as a word, she leaned over and picked up her teacup and saucer and walked back over to the seat she had been offered.

"Is it still okay?" she asked sheepishly.

Surprised, Charlie gestured toward the chair.

"Yeah . . . sure—of course."

Sarah placed her cup of tea on the table, then pulled out a chair and sat down. Jonas's heart sank.

"You've got a book," Sarah said after a moment or two.

"Yeah," Charlie replied, glancing at it briefly. "Works great as a sponge."

Sarah looked back up, feeling a little more at ease thanks to Charlie's subtle humor.

"What's it about?" she asked, smiling politely.

"Nothing really," Charlie replied. "Just an old book of poems."

"Poems?" she asked, studying him again.

"I know—sounds a little weird. It's just something I read back in college," he explained.

"Oh . . . ," was all Sarah said in reply.

"It's ruined now, of course," Charlie said, lifting the book to look at the sodden contents while shrugging his shoulders. "But there were only a couple of poems I liked anyway."

Having spoken, they each took a sip from their cups as the busy background of the café filled the silence between them.

"I really am sorry for the way I came across back there," Charlie said after a while, glancing up at Sarah. "I wasn't trying to pick you up or anything."

Sarah looked up from her tea.

"Not that you don't get picked up a lot, I'm sure," Charlie added, so as not to sound rude. "I mean—you probably get that all the time . . ."

Sarah smiled.

"It's okay, don't worry about it," she said.

Charlie and Sarah sat silently once more, sipping their beverages, neither one really making eye contact with the other.

After a while, Sarah glanced up, a nervous expression growing on her face.

"I have to tell you something," she began to say, looking over at Charlie. "I . . . I lied—"

Charlie looked up from his coffee, his eyes just visible over the rim of his cup.

"Huh?" he said.

Sarah took in a deep breath.

"I lied back there," she confessed, glancing toward the table she had been sitting at. "I *was* waiting for someone."

Jonas sat up tall in his seat.

"Oh . . . ," Charlie said, breaking eye contact with her.

Seeing Charlie's reaction, Jonas looked back at Sarah, waiting for her response.

"I lied about waiting," Sarah began to say, "because . . ."

She shifted in her seat as she began to choke on her own words.

"Because he's not going to show up."

Listening, Jonas became very still.

"How do you know?" Charlie asked.

Sarah's eyes began to fill with tears. She lowered her head, trying as best she could to hide her face.

"I just know."

Jonas watched as she looked down at the floor, his own eyes beginning to fill with emotion.

Charlie leaned over the table toward Sarah. He wanted to help, but he wasn't exactly sure what to do.

"But he might . . . ," he tried to console her, not sure what to say. "I mean, there's always a chance he *might* show up—right?"

Sarah looked up suddenly in confusion, but understanding what Charlie meant, she looked back down.

"He's not going to show up," she tried to explain, "because he can't . . ."

She choked on her words.

"He died last week."

Jonas watched from afar as Sarah lowered her head, falling into silent sobs.

Charlie looked down at the table, upset with himself for not having figured it out sooner.

"I . . . ," Charlie began to apologize, "I'm so sorry. I didn't—I didn't know."

"How could you?" Sarah said with her head down. "It's my fault. You had no idea."

Sitting in silence, Charlie watched as the girl in front of him began to wipe her eyes, trying as best she could to regain her composure. She looked so fragile and alone. He took a napkin from the table and offered it to her.

"Who was he?" Charlie asked.

Jonas looked up at hearing this and watched Sarah take the napkin from Charlie's hand.

"His name was Jonas," she began. "He was my best friend."

Jonas watched her wipe her eyes.

"This was our place," she explained, while glancing briefly around. "It's where we met."

Charlie held his silence, offering her a moment to speak.

"We came here every Sunday morning, just to have brunch," she said, "We loved it here. We never missed a week."

Charlie smiled briefly at the thought. Jonas did the same.

Sarah smiled too, but only for a moment. Looking back at her table, she caught a glimpse of the untouched cup of hot chocolate she had ordered.

Jonas's heart skipped a beat.

"So I came here, just like we used to," she said, looking back down at her lap. "I don't know what I was expecting, really, but when I saw you walk in the door . . ."

Sarah looked up at Charlie, staring at his eyes.

"I thought," she stuttered, her voice quivering, "I thought you were him. It's just . . . you look so much like him. It scared me."

Charlie froze for a moment, mesmerized by the striking green hue of her eyes.

"Oh," he said, glancing away, touching the ceramic edge of his coffee mug with a fingertip.

Wondering what Charlie would do in an effort to comfort Sarah, Jonas watched as his half-brother reached for his ruined book of poetry, opening it up and flipping through the pages.

Tugging on a page he had picked out with a gentle pull, Charlie removed the paper from its binding and handed it over to Sarah.

"You don't have to read this right now," he said, looking a little embarrassed, "but you know, maybe later when . . ."

But before Charlie could finish his thought, Sarah's cell phone rang, interrupting their conversation.

Reaching instinctively inside her pocket, Sarah pulled out a thin black phone and looked at the name that appeared on the screen.

"I'm sorry," she said, looking more embarrassed now than Charlie. "I have to go."

Glancing from her to the page in his hand, Charlie paused a moment, thinking.

"Hold on a second," he said, turning to get a small shoulder bag that was hanging around the arm of his chair. Rummaging through it, Charlie pulled out a pen from inside. Taking the cap off with his teeth, he scribbled something on the backside of the page he had torn from the book.

Jonas leaned in to see what he was doing.

"Here—please," Charlie said, folding the piece of paper in half and offering it once more to Sarah.

Looking at the writing on the page, Sarah saw that Charlie had written down his number.

"I . . . ," she began, hesitation in her eyes, "I shouldn't . . ."

Jonas looked at Charlie. Charlie hesitated.

"I'm sorry," he said, staring down at the page in his hand. "It's just . . . it's just I've learned a little bit lately of what it means to feel alone too."

Pulling his hand back, Charlie slid the torn page back inside the leather-bound volume.

"It was good to meet you though, Sarah," he said, "even if it was only for today."

As Charlie rose from his chair politely, Sarah took a deep breath and glanced from him to the page sticking out of the book. She closed her eyes for a second—thinking, deciding. Then, opening her eyes again, she quickly reached for the slip of paper and pocketed it.

Making her way toward the exit, she turned to look at the expression on Charlie's face. He looked surprised.

"Thank you, Charlie," she said with a gentle voice. "It was good to meet you too."

Then she was gone.

It took a few moments for Charlie to react, but soon he found his seat again and began to drink his coffee. He glanced at the empty seat across from him, and smiled.

Invisible all the while, Jonas sat, his face blank, attempting to understand just what had happened. He looked out the window, and saw Sarah hop into the back of an empty cab. How he longed for her to know he was there. But looking back at Charlie, he began to feel a dark, unsettling sensation. Heat flushed in his face, forcing him to look away.

"We have to go," Jonas heard Michael say, as a hand touched his arm.

Jonas felt the urge to ask his mentor why—why had he been taken here—why had he been brought to see all this? He had just witnessed the thing that terrified him most: the possibility of losing the one person he feared to let go of. It was as if his heart had been ripped from his chest when he realized what little he could do to stop it from happening.

Suddenly all of the tables and chairs disappeared. The waitress, the crowds of hungry patrons, and the food transformed almost instantly into a long carpeted hallway. The light that once streamed in from large storefront windows overlooking the streets of New York City was replaced with artificial track lighting.

Michael began to walk while Jonas took a few hurried steps to keep pace as they made their way silently toward a door at the far end of the corridor.

"Where are we?" Jonas asked, focusing his mind on his new surroundings.

Michael glanced over his shoulder.

"William's house."

Halting suddenly, Jonas gave his companion a sobering look.

"Why?"

But just as Michael opened his mouth to answer, two more spirits emerged from nowhere, appearing suddenly at Jonas's side.

At first, Jonas wondered if more dark spirits had shown up to cause trouble, but as he took a closer look, his apprehension eased considerably. These spirits were women, young and quite amiable looking. But they seemed to be in even more of a hurry than Michael.

"Sylvia, Ester," Michael greeted the two spirits before gesturing toward his younger companion, "this is Jonas."

The two young women smiled briefly in his direction, but a noise from behind the door at the end of the hallway grabbed their attention.

"We have some time before he'll be home," the one named Sylvia said.

"But we need to hurry nonetheless," Ester quickly added. "She's almost there."

Following swiftly behind the group, Jonas found himself entering a roomy master bedroom where a woman was busy tidying up. Singing a cheerful tune to herself, she moved laundry from the bed to a hamper.

"Jonas, that woman's name is Carol," Michael commented quietly. "She's William Graves' wife."

Taking a step from behind the other two female spirits to get a better look, Jonas noticed the woman pick up a large white box that lay resting on a side table near the bed and make her way over to a spacious walk-in closet.

Without hesitation, the two female spirits followed quickly behind. As the woman pulled out a small footstool from behind a row of clothes, the spirits moved in as close as they could, whispering something in her ears. In fact, as the woman placed the footstool in the center of the small room and stepped up on it, the two spirits at her side levitated off the floor, maintaining as close a proximity to her as they could.

Jonas looked back at Michael, wondering what was taking place.

"Watch," Michael instructed before Jonas could speak, pointing back toward the women.

Looking back into the closet, Jonas saw the woman place the white box on a shelf. While she was doing this, the two spirits pointed to something above her head, whispering all the while. It took a few moments for the woman to react, but slowly, she looked in the direction where the spirits gestured, noticing a small crack in the ceiling. Jonas didn't think much of the crack himself, but it seemed to be of enough interest for her to lift a hand and reach for the ceiling panel that was just above her head. Standing on her toes, she lifted the white square.

Taking a step toward the closet, Jonas looked up and saw that something had been hidden inside the ceiling. He watched as the woman shifted her weight and reached into the crawl space with her free hand. Slipping a bit, the woman worked to pull down what looked like a large black shoebox. Placing the ceiling panel back in its place, she looked down to study the front of the box, searching for any signs of what it might be. Seeing no obvious markers, she stepped down to the ground before lifting the lid.

When she removed the top, Jonas thought the contents of the box didn't look like much—just a few organized rows of small white paper squares. An old collection of family photographs, perhaps.

"Do you remember that Polaroid camera William had?" Michael asked.

Jonas nodded.

"That's where he keeps his pictures."

Jonas looked back at the woman as she slowly pulled out a little white square. Though he was unable to see what she was looking at from his perspective, he realized he didn't need to—not with the look of horror that suddenly appeared on her face.

"Come, Jonas," Michael said while grabbing his shoulder. "We've seen enough."

Unable to take his eyes from the woman's ghastly expression, Jonas found it difficult to move.

"Jonas," Michael said, tightening his grip, "please—"

Frozen to the spot, Jonas just stood there in silence as the woman dropped the box of photographs, scattering the contents across the floor.

"Jonas, walk," Michael insisted, this time pulling on his younger companion's arm as he began to make his way toward the door through which they had entered.

Jonas followed. They walked swiftly together down the small

corridor, just as the thought to look back entered his mind.

And then he heard it.

Racing down the hallway as if to catch up with them, Jonas heard a terrified scream echoing off the walls. But the dreadful sound lasted only for a second before everything around him vanished.

26

WAITING IN LINE AS CROWDS OF AIRPORT PASSENGERS bustled in the distance, Chris approached the counter.

"Hello, sir," an attractive young woman said with a smile.

"When's your first flight to Maui?" Chris asked tensely, glancing briefly at her name tag.

Looking down at the computer in front of her, the young woman began to type on her keyboard. "It looks like we've got one leaving in about two hours . . ."

Chris waited impatiently, tapping his fingers on the counter.

"But with the connection, you would be landing in Kahului airport around three a.m."

Chris checked his watch, his hand trembling.

"I'll take it," he said, reaching for his wallet.

Looking back up at her customer, the young woman noticed the absence of any luggage.

"Will you be checking any bags, sir?"

Pulling out his wallet, Chris shook his head.

"No, nothing, thank you," he replied hastily, while taking out his credit card and picture ID.

"What date shall I put for your return?" she asked, somewhat hesitant to book a one-way flight for someone with no luggage.

Noticing her hesitation, Chris glanced at her name tag again.

"Just one way, Avery," he said coolly. "I'm going to . . . surprise an old girlfriend of mine, and I'm not sure how things will go."

Relaxing a bit, Avery took the credit card from Chris's hand and swiped it.

"I guess I should wish you good luck then," she smiled.

Nodding, Chris did his best to smile too.

"Here you go," Avery said after a few more moments, handing Chris his ticket along with his credit card and picture ID. "You leave from gate twenty-three."

"Thanks."

Just as Chris turned to walk toward the security gate, he heard the young woman suddenly call out his name.

"Chris—"

Chris saw that she had stepped from behind her post and was holding something in her hand. Walking back to her, he saw that the item was a business card.

She smiled sheepishly as she handed it to him.

"In case things don't work out," she said, blushing, "you can call this number and I can book your return flight."

Taking the card, Chris saw that she had written her cell phone number on the back.

"Thanks," he said, looking uneasily at her for a moment.

"I hope that's okay?" she asked, seeing the reaction in his eyes.

"Yes—sorry, it's great," he replied. "Thank you."

Matching eyes, the two stared at each other for a moment until the awkwardness caused them both to part with a simple good-bye. But turning to walk back toward the gate with what he felt was the weight of the world resting on his shoulders, Chris glanced once more in her direction, before he disappeared into the crowd.

27

"SO, WHAT DO YOU SAY?" THE TANNED BUSINESSMAN said, putting his small white ball on the green.

Watching it roll across the grass, all three men held still until it disappeared into the hole.

"Two under par, Richard," a stocky man commented. "Not bad."

Richard picked up where he left off.

"We'd like to meet this family you talk about so much, William. I always say you can learn a lot about a man by the way he manages his household."

Preparing to putt himself, William Graves tried to hide his intense concentration.

"Consider it done then," he said coolly, taking in a breath just before hitting the ball.

All three watched as William's ball rolled along, stopping just short of the hole.

"I hope your wife's cooking is better than your short game," the stockier man joked.

William forced a chuckle and walked toward his ball, tapping it in.

"How about tonight?"

"Dinner?" Richard cut in.

"Of course," William replied.

"Don't you need to call your wife?"

"Don't worry about that. I'll make all the arrangements. You just get ready to sign the contract."

"You don't mess around, do you, William?" the stockier man asked.

William leaned over to pick up his ball. "I see opportunities and make things happen. You don't succeed in business for as long as I have by sitting around and waiting for things to come to you."

Looking from his business partner back toward William, Richard smiled.

"That's the kind of initiative Mitch and I are looking for."

"Well, then," William said, "let me make a call."

Walking back toward his golf bag, William pulled out his cell phone and speed-dialed a number.

"Hello?" came a weak voice on the other end.

"Carol?" William asked. "Are you okay?"

Hearing no response, William glanced at his cell phone to make sure he was getting reception.

"Carol, can you hear me?"

Again, there was no reply.

"Hello, are you there?"

Finally, a muffled voice spoke out. "Yes . . . yes I can hear you."

"You sound awful—are you sick?"

"No . . . I'm . . . I'm all right."

"Good, because I need you to get to the store. I've got potential clients coming over for dinner this evening and you need to set the table for five."

"Five?"

"Yes. You, me, Richard, Mitch, and Charlie."

"Richard . . . ? Mitch . . . ?"

"Look, I can't explain everything to you. Just make sure dinner is on the table at seven o'clock and Charlie is there to eat with us."

"But Charlie is at his apartment in the city . . ."

"I'm working on the biggest deal of my career here," William cut in. "All I want you to do is whip up a little something and make sure Charlie is there—is that too much to ask?"

There was a long pause.

"Carol?" William asked impatiently.

"No . . . I . . . I can do it."

"Make sure that you do," William added. "I can't have you messing this one up."

Hearing no reply other than halted breathing, William changed his tone. "I told Richard and Mitch all about your cooking. I said they haven't tasted anything nearly as good as your tiramisu."

There was another pause.

"Thank you," Carol said, hushed.

"I love you, honey, you know that," he said. "I'm just under a lot of pressure right now, you understand. I can count on you though, right?"

Again, there was another long pause.

"Yes . . . of course."

"That's the love of my life talking now," William said as he turned back around and slid the putter inside his golf bag. "Tonight. Seven o' clock. Don't let me down."

William hung up the phone with his wife still on the line and walked toward the two men who were now sitting lazily in a golf cart.

"So," he shouted from across the green, "lunch, anyone?"

28

"WE'VE GOT HIM!" JONAS SAID, LOOKING AROUND
only to find that he had been taken to an airport terminal. He looked
at his mentor, wondering why Michael wasn't as excited as he was.

"Didn't you hear what I said?" Jonas asked. "We've got him! We've
got William Graves. His wife has the pictures—she can prove it!"

Seeing that a particular person in the distance had made eye
contact with him, Jonas's attention was thrown. No one else in this
terminal seemed to be aware of his and Michael's presence, but this
person had looked right at him.

"I know what you mean, Jonas," Michael began, pulling his younger companion's gaze back toward him, "but I don't think it's going
to be that easy."

"What do you mean it's not going to be that easy?" Jonas replied.
"She's got proof. All she has to do is show someone the pictures."

"It's not that simple, Jonas," Michael replied.

"Why not?"

"Because," Michael explained, "not everyone sees the truth for
what it is. Some people see what they want to see, no matter what
the truth is."

The man Jonas had seen from afar suddenly approached and
broke in on their conversation.

"Excuse me," the man said. "Were you looking at me back there?"

Jonas glanced at the stranger, a little taken aback. "Me?" he asked.

"Yes you," the stranger said. "I couldn't help but notice you were
looking at me."

Jonas glanced nervously at Michael.

"I only ask," the gentleman said, "because it's been difficult to get
anyone's help around here."

Jonas looked back at the man, who suddenly began to glare at the people around him as if suddenly annoyed.

"It's these New Yorkers," he said. "They won't look at you—let alone stop to give you the time of day."

The man interrogating Jonas was slightly heavyset, he wore blue jeans with white tennis shoes, and a collared athletic shirt, tucked in with a black leather belt. His hair was mostly white, with a bushy moustache beneath square-rimmed glasses. But the feature Jonas noticed most about the man's appearance was his complexion, which seemed to turn a deep shade of purple as he grew more frustrated with the people around him.

"It's just that I'm looking for my wife," the man said irritably. "You haven't seen her, have you?"

Jonas shook his head.

"She's a little over five feet tall," the man said. "Doesn't talk a whole lot, kind of overweight—she's wearing a brown sweater."

Looking around at the crowd of people, Jonas tried to see if he could find anyone matching that vague description.

"Sorry," he said, shrugging his shoulders.

Visibly upset with the response, the man shook his head, and began calling out the woman's name.

"Nancy!" he yelled. *"Nancy!"*

There was no response. Not a single passenger in the terminal even turned to look in the man's direction as he continued to yell angrily.

"You tell somebody to wait," the man said, his anger rising, "they should be there—right? She thinks she can do these things, but we're in New York City. She can't just go wandering around, getting herself lost."

Michael cut into the conversation.

"Can I help you, Thomas?" he asked kindly.

The man looked at him coldly.

"Not from you."

"You've been looking for Nancy for quite some time now," Michael continued.

The man grew aggravated at hearing Michael speak. "So what's it to you?" he goaded.

"How long has it been?" Michael asked, taking a step toward the man. "Almost a year?"

The stranger suddenly turned from speaking to Michael to staring directly at Jonas. "Are you with him?" he asked sharply.

Jonas nodded to show that he was.

"You've known him for long?" the man asked next.

Thinking about it for a moment, Jonas had to shake his head no.

"Well," the man cautioned, "I wouldn't hang around him any longer if I were you."

The man turned to Michael.

"I thought I told you I didn't want to talk to you anymore," he said.

"I remember," Michael replied.

"So why don't you just leave me alone while I try and find my wife?"

"Because you don't have a wife," Michael replied. "Not anymore."

The man suddenly rounded on Michael in a flash of anger.

"Don't—you—dare!" he threatened under heavy breath.

"I don't want to cause you any more pain, Thomas," Michael said calmly, "but you can't keep this up forever. You know what happened after your plane tried to land—they came and picked her up. She's not here anymore."

"Picked her up!" the man said incredulously. "*Picked her up!* Nancy wouldn't move an inch without my saying so."

Pointing into the distance, the man gestured toward an empty chair.

"I told her to sit and wait until I came back," he said with resentment. "I went to get some help, but when I returned . . ."

The man suddenly glared at Michael.

"You know where she is, don't you?" he whispered menacingly.

Michael said nothing as the man took a step slowly toward him.

"You're hiding her from me, aren't you?"

Michael shook his head. "No."

"I swear—" the man began to threaten, "if I find out you've been keeping her from me . . ."

"You're not going to find her," Michael interjected calmly, "not in this airport at least. She's in a better place now, starting a new life."

The man narrowed his eyes. "I don't believe you," he said incredulously.

Michael stared back at the man for a moment before replying.

"You know I'm not lying, Thomas," he said. "She didn't want to be with you anymore—she'd had enough."

Shaking with rage, the man's face turned red. "Show me where my wife is, you goddamned son of a bitch!"

"You have no claim on her anymore," Michael said firmly. "Her vow to you ended when that plane went down."

Suddenly lunging toward Michael, the man lifted his hand as if to throw a punch. But instead he held his fist back and stared into Michael's eyes. Unnerved by Michael's calm demeanor, he slowly lowered his hand.

"We walked away from that the plane crash *together*!" he said, his lips white. "I don't care what you say."

Michael shook his head in silence.

"What are you looking at?" the man suddenly barked at Jonas.

Jonas took a step back.

The man made a derisive, snorting noise and then turned around and walked back into the crowd of passengers. After a moment, he was gone.

"What was that?" Jonas asked.

"I'm sorry you had to see that," Michael replied.

"Is that guy nuts?"

"No, just a little lost."

"He doesn't know, does he?"

"Know what, Jonas?"

"He doesn't know he's dead."

Michael shook his head solemnly. "He knows—he just doesn't want to accept it yet. Like I said, sometimes people see what they want to see, no matter what the truth is."

———

It was some time before Jonas asked another question. He simply walked with his mentor through the terminals, watching a few other spirits glance in their direction as they made their way. None of these other spirits seemed to be members of The Dead though, or ones Jonas had learned to call the Children of Hell. Most seemed quite pleasant. He even saw spirits whispering in the ears of people who looked like they were afraid of flying. He wasn't sure what they said exactly, but he could tell it made a difference to the mortals they were trying to help.

Comforting as this should have been, Jonas couldn't help but wonder what they were doing there in the first place. He had been so preoccupied with what he had seen at William Graves' house, he hadn't stopped to think about why they had traveled to an airport when they had the ability to fly anywhere in the world at the speed of light.

"Why are we here?" he finally asked.

Michael searched for something in the distance where a bustling crowd of people could be seen walking down a long stretch of airport.

"We're here," he said, pointing over Jonas's shoulder, "because of him."

Turning to look in the direction his mentor gestured, Jonas saw Chris.

"Chris?" Jonas said aloud. "What's he doing here?"

"Nothing good," Michael replied with sad expression. "Nothing good."

29

HER HAND TREMBLED AS THE PHONE RANG.

Ring . . .

Ring . . .

Ring . . .

"Hello," came a voice.

"Charlie?"

"Yes—Mom?"

"Yes, it's me, dear."

"Is everything okay?"

"Yes, of course."

"What is it?"

"I just wanted to invite you over for dinner tonight."

"Oh . . . I . . ."

"Your father has some important people coming over, and he's asked that I make something very special. And seeing as how we don't get to see you like we used to . . ."

"About that . . . Mom?"

"Yes, dear?"

"Can I ask you a question?"

Carol paused for a moment, her hand trembling again.

"Of course, you can ask me anything."

A stillness hung in the air, as each one listened to the other's breathing.

"How . . . how well do you know Dad?"

"Your father? I've known him for years."

"I know, but . . . how much do you know about him?"

"I don't understand. What do you mean, Charlie?"

"I don't know, I've just . . . these *things* have been happening to me and I—I just wanted to know . . ."

"Things? What kind of things?"

"It's hard to explain . . ."

"Well, I can't very well help if you won't explain what's happening to you."

"I know. It's just that . . . I don't feel like myself anymore. I feel different somehow."

"Have you been eating all right? Is it your job? I know work can be stressful."

"No, it's not that. It's Dad. I think it has something to do with Dad."

There was another long pause before Carol spoke again.

"I'm sorry, what did you say?"

"I mean, like when I was a kid, Mom. Do you remember Dad ever spending a lot of time with me—alone? You know, away from you?"

"Not any more than any other father might have, I'm sure."

"Did you ever find him doing . . . unusual things? Anything out of the ordinary?"

"Not . . . not that I can remember," Carol stuttered.

"You don't remember anything, at all?"

"No Charlie—I'm sorry . . ."

"I just . . . " Charlie struggled on the other end of the phone. "I have these memories, and I can't tell if they're real or not."

Without warning, Carol suddenly changed her tone.

"Listen to me, Charlie—and I want you to listen very carefully. I know your father, and I know that he loves you. He might have his weaknesses just like anybody else, but that doesn't mean he's a bad person. Do you understand?"

"I know, but . . ."

"No matter what you think you remember, you're doing well now, and your father and I couldn't be more proud."

"Yeah, I know, but . . ."

"But nothing. You shouldn't worry about these kinds of things, Charlie. They'll only make you upset."

"But I want to know . . ."

"Charlie, we want you to come home for dinner tonight at seven. I'm making your favorite—chicken cordon bleu with asparagus. It's the least you can do."

"Yes, but—"

"You need to put these thoughts from your mind, Charlie. I don't know what they are, but I can tell they're upsetting you."

"But I'm not thinking, I'm *remembering.*"

"Well, I can't tell you what to do with your life, but I can vouch for your father—and he's never been anything but kind to you and me. And if you'd like to see him this evening, I know he'd love to see you. It's been too long, Charlie. You don't visit us like you used to. You should come home more often."

"I know. I just . . ."

Neither one said a word as Charlie thought of what to do.

"Okay," he finally conceded.

"Good. Seven o'clock. Make sure to wear something nice."

"Sure."

"And keep a stiff upper lip. You can't let little things like this get you down."

There was no reply.

"See you then?" Carol asked with forceful reassurance.

Charlie swallowed as he worked to stifle his emotions.

"Yeah . . . okay, Mom. I'll see you then."

30

IT HAD BEEN A VERY LONG DAY, JONAS THOUGHT, EVEN for a spirit.

Jonas and Michael trailed behind Chris as he made his way onto the plane. There, Jonas saw excited tourists looking for an experience of a lifetime, locals waiting to reunite with loved ones, and business-men lucky enough to be traveling to the islands for work. Finding himself in an empty seat next to his friend, Jonas sat quietly for the better part of the long flight.

While sitting there, Jonas was left to ponder everything he had experienced since entering the World of Spirits. He could barely be-lieve his eyes when his aunt had first ushered him into the Reading Room. The colors, the magnificent building, it all seemed so peace-ful, so wonderful. But he had also been shown the darker side of his new world, and he was left to contemplate his place in it all.

To begin with, there was his biological mother, whom he had re-sented every day since learning of his adoption. Her story was a hard one to hear, but finding the courage to do so, Jonas began to see her in a whole new light; a young girl who had sacrificed so much in or-der to give him a real chance. And then there was William, the man who had taken that life from his mother. William. The man who had come to his funeral just to stare at his body. And that poor little girl, Holly. William Graves had to be stopped, but as Jonas thought about how to do that, he felt anxiety stirring inside him as he realized he had no idea how. Mortality seemed so simple: if you learned some-thing was going on back in the old life, all it took was a phone call to the authorities to end it. Or so Jonas had thought.

Which led Jonas to think about Carol, William's wife. She had a box of photographs in her possession that was enough evidence to put her husband away for years, if not for good. But as Michael had suggested, a future of that sort might be more than she was willing to handle. As much as she must have been disgusted by those images, sometimes it's just easier, Jonas thought, for a person to turn a blind eye and hope to eventually forget.

Then, lastly, there was Charlie, William's son, Jonas's half-brother. He, too, had evidence that could help bring his father to justice. But remembering when he gave that slip of paper with his phone number to Sarah, it almost made Jonas want to punch the seat in front of him. Sure, it was a childish instinct to harbor, especially taking into consideration everything Charlie had been through. But his brother had proved to be handsome and charming—and above all, mortal.

Looking at Chris, Jonas didn't know what to do or how to help. His friend was silent. Silent and angry. Angry at the world perhaps, or his situation, or fate. There was something dark in his eyes. Pain? Yes, there was an overwhelming sense of pain. But regret? A feeling of inadequacy? The inability to stop the inevitable from having happened?

He couldn't get over it, Jonas knew—the guilt. It still racked Chris's soul. Chris felt responsible for something completely out of his hands. He had lost his best friend in an instant, but his bitterness wasn't likely to pass away so quickly. He was lost. Lost in his own thoughts. Lost in his own darkness. Lost to such an extent that not even Michael could get his attention—though not for lack of trying. Michael had stood by his side, calling out his name, even whispering closely in his ear. But he couldn't reach Chris, and he soon stopped trying. So Chris just sat there, his jaw clenched, fists taut, staring vacantly at the small television screen in the seatback in front of him.

"Jonas . . ."

Jonas turned to look in the direction of the voice.

"Jonas, we have to go," Michael said. "Chris will be all right for now. He'll be safe until we get back."

Still worried that members of The Dead might show up, Jonas didn't want to leave his friend behind.

"Do we have to?" he asked.

Michael nodded.

"But where?"

"William's wife is throwing a dinner party for her husband and a few guests," Michael explained. "Charlie is going to be there."

A dinner party? Jonas thought, unnerved at the idea that William's wife could put together a soiree after finding evidence of her husband's disgusting crimes.

"Exactly," Michael concurred, hearing Jonas's thought. "It's not a good sign, but I think it's wise to see what we're up against."

Feeling uneasy at having to face the situation so suddenly, Jonas looked out the window where an amber sunset was melting into the horizon. He felt a tinge of frustration with the speed at which everything was moving, and annoyed at the fact that they seemed to be making little to no progress. Was this the life of spirits in the mortal realm—traveling to and fro at the speed of light, unable really to do anything about the devastation they continually witnessed?

"We're coming back though, right?" he asked for reassurance.

"Yes," Michael agreed. "We won't be gone too long."

Jonas gave Michael his hand, but before everything around them disappeared, he noticed a look in his mentor's eyes, a look that held a glimmer of hope. He wasn't sure if Michael had a plan, or if having lived as a spirit for so long just gave him the ability to keep moving even though nothing seemed to be getting any better. But looking into those kind eyes, Jonas couldn't help but feel there was something to hold on to. Even if it was just someone else's hand.

Before he could think any more on the subject, Jonas was suddenly transported across the continent, arriving in the well-lit dining room of William Graves' home, with a table full of meticulously prepared food nearby.

"Could you pass the asparagus please," a voice called out.

The man reached for a bowl of green vegetables being handed to him by a woman sitting from across the table.

"These look delectable, Carol," the man appraised.

William sat at the head of the table, Carol to his right, with Charlie next to her. Across from these familiar faces were two men Jonas had never seen before.

"Who are they?" Jonas whispered.

"They are potential clients of William's," Michael replied. "Their names are Richard Morgan and Mitchell Summons. They own a large private equity firm, and William has been trying to get them to invest in a project of his."

"Are they good guys?" Jonas asked next.

"Depends on what you mean by good," Michael replied. "They're not like William, if that's what you mean. But they've done their fair share of shady deals that have left more than a few people out on the street."

"So, Carol, tell us, how you became such a good cook?" Richard said.

"Oh, goodness—I don't know what my husband has been feeding you . . ."

"Nothing as delicious as this, that's for sure," Mitchell said with a wry grin.

"She's just being modest," William interjected, placing a hand on his wife's shoulder.

Seeing Carol give William an enamored smile, Jonas felt his stomach churn.

She's smiling? he thought, remembering how she had looked earlier that morning.

Michael nodded sadly.

"But how can she act like that—with him, sitting right there?" Jonas asked.

"She's compartmentalized it," Michael said with a sullen voice. "I was afraid this might happen."

"Compartmentalized it?"

But Jonas didn't need it explained to him. He hadn't forgotten the man in the airport with an angry red face, searching for a woman who was nowhere to be found. Compartmentalizing can make people do strange things, he thought, but Jonas had yet to understand just how strange those things could be.

"So, Charlie," Richard began, pointing with his fork, "your father tells us you've been promoted. Congratulations. How's that going?"

Charlie forced a grin, but it fell from his face rather quickly when he saw his father looking at him.

"It's good," he said, distracted. "It's a . . . it's new, so that's good."

Hiding his annoyance, William spoke up. "Charlie's just being modest. He's been working for this promotion for quite some time, and it came with a substantial raise."

Charlie nodded, and tried to smile graciously.

"Charlie knows—right?" Jonas asked Michael in a hushed voice. "About his father?"

"He's remembering," Michael concurred. "But he's still not sure what to believe yet. It's not easy viewing someone in a whole new light like that. Especially your father."

"Charlie's just like his dad," William began to say. "Everything he touches turns to gold. But he's a bit more tight-lipped about it than I am."

"So we hear," Richard said, reaching for a bottle of wine on the table. "Which is why I thought it best to ask the lady who knows. Tell us, Carol, do you think your husband has what it takes to run this project?"

Carol glanced at William, smiling brightly.

But before she could respond, Richard noticed there was no wine left in the bottle.

Seeing his guest's disappointment, William snapped his fingers. "Charlie, kitchen," he said forcefully. "Get Richard another bottle of wine."

A little bewildered, Charlie looked up at his father.

"Charlie," William pointed, "go to the kitchen and open a new bottle."

Seeing the reaction on Charlie's face, Richard protested.

"No, it's fine, I'm—I'm okay."

"It's no problem," William said, forcing a smile. Then, looking back around at Charlie, he spoke, this time slower, but much more forcefully. "Charlie, would-you-please-get-our-guests-something-to-drink?"

"Right . . . yes," Charlie stuttered as he began to gather his bearings. "I'm sorry, I'll just . . ."

"It's fine," William said, trying to suppress his irritation, "just go to the kitchen and get a new bottle from the rack. Make sure to get a good one from the second row."

William then turned to look at his wife, trying to pick up where they left off. "You were saying, dear . . . ?"

Glancing at the guests in front of her, Carol began to describe all the attributes she found so admirable about her husband.

"I can't listen to this," Jonas began, looking up at Michael. "I can't stand here while she's saying all those things."

"I know it's difficult to hear," Michael said, "but that's the sound of a victim. It's not often they speak poorly of their abusers."

"A *victim*?" Jonas said, pointing toward Carol. "Her?"

Michael looked back at the woman who was now genuinely smiling at her guests.

"William may not have done to her what he has done to Charlie, but the way he treats her is another form of abuse. He's deprived her of her self-esteem and warped her notions of human emotion. When once she thought she knew what love was, he has conditioned her to believe it is nothing more than the absence of fear. When you think about it, she's been reduced to a life of isolated servitude. A slave within the walls of her own home."

Jonas thought about that for a moment, feeling somewhat hasty in his conclusions.

"But she still has Charlie," he offered.

"For now," Michael replied. "If she doesn't find the courage to wake up to reality, though, she may lose him as well."

Having mentioned Charlie, Jonas glanced toward the kitchen, wondering what was taking his brother so long. There had been plenty of time for him to open a bottle of wine and bring it back to the table, yet he was nowhere to be seen. Jonas seemed to be the only one aware of this, as the other diners chatted away. In fact, it wasn't until Richard lifted his empty glass to take a drink that William remarked on his son's absence.

"I'm so sorry," he began to apologize. "I can't imagine what would be taking Charlie so long."

"Please, excuse me," Carol said politely. "I'll go and see what's keeping him. These business things are way over my head anyhow."

Smiling graciously, the two guests stood for a moment as Carol turned to leave, then sat back down at the table to look over at William.

"You've caught a winner," Richard said.

William smiled back. "It takes some time to train them right, but in the end, it's a worthy investment."

All three men laughed.

Just as they were beginning to discuss the details of the deal they hoped to put together, a scream came from the other room, followed by the sound of glass shattering.

William turned in his chair to see what was the matter. Unable to view the doorway that led into the kitchen from where he was seated, he looked quickly back at his guests, giving them a smile as if to show that he had everything under control.

"I'm sure it's nothing," he began to explain. "I'll be right back."

Grinning confidently, William folded the napkin that was in his lap and placed it neatly next to his plate. Calmly, he walked toward the kitchen, with Jonas and Michael following silently behind him. He opened the kitchen door and walked in, but suddenly stopped short—shocked by what he saw before him.

There, on the floor, was Charlie—kneeling in a pool of red wine with shards of glass all around. He was staring at his mother with a look on his face as if she had just woken him from a dream. But upon seeing his father enter the room, fear flickered from deep within him, causing him to tremble.

Glancing down as if noticing for the first time where he was, Charlie lifted his hands and tried to explain. "I'm sorry, I don't know what . . ."

On top of counters, tabletops, shelves, and even the floor, were dozens of glass containers, each with a few tablespoons of red wine in them. Glasses, vases, bowls, and cups were everywhere. Numerous drained bottles of red wine were stacked neatly in rows right next to where Charlie knelt. His mother stood nearby with a hand over her mouth, too terrified to speak.

"I'm sorry . . . I . . . " Charlie mumbled again.

William turned on his wife.

"What the hell is going on here?" he said venomously, but in a tone low enough so as not to be heard by his guests in the dining room.

"I don't know, I just . . . ," Carol stammered.

"Goddammit, woman—open your mouth when you talk!"

"I don't know, I . . . I just walked through the door, and Charlie was right there . . ."

Carol pointed to where Charlie was kneeling on the floor.

"And he was counting," she continued, "and pouring some wine into that . . . that . . ."

She pointed down, in the direction of a large chunk of glass on the floor.

Furious, William took a step toward Charlie.

"Do you think this is funny?" he said, shoving a finger in his son's direction. "Do you think tonight is some sort of a joke?"

Too terrified to speak, Charlie shook his head.

Spinning back around, William laid into his wife.

"Dammit, Carol! I ask you to do one thing—*one thing!* And you can't even keep your son from screwing it up."

Both Carol and Charlie trembled as William stared at them with rage in his eyes.

"You two better get this cleaned up—and I mean *now!*" William said, positioning himself so that each of them could feel the full force of his wrath.

"I said now!" William shouted through gritted teeth, causing both his son and his wife to recoil in fright.

Looking down at the liquid beneath his knees, Charlie reached for a large shard of glass, cutting himself unexpectedly on the edge of it.

Seeing the blood run down his son's finger, William took a step once more toward his wife, his face only inches from hers.

"Would you please clean up your pathetic excuse for a son, and wipe up this mess?" he hissed, spit flying from his lips.

Watching her turn and stumble toward Charlie, William shook his head in disgust before turning around himself. He walked back in the direction of the dining room, slowly, controlled—preparing himself for the explanation he would soon have to give.

Making it around the corner, William was pleased to see that the two gentlemen were pleasantly discussing some minute business detail together, apparently unaware of the confrontation that had taken place.

"As I said," William began to jeer with a voice loud enough that everyone in the house could hear, "no big deal. Just a little spill in the kitchen. But that's what wives are for—right?"

———

Hearing William and his guests laugh together, Jonas felt a burning anger rise from within.

31

STANDING ALONE IN HER BEDROOM, SARAH HEARD THE phone go directly to voicemail just before she spoke.

"Chris, I know it's been a while, but . . ."

She looked down at the floor, not sure what to say.

"I . . . I hope you're all right . . ."

She clung to a wet tissue in her hand.

"I wanted to call because . . . I just . . . I just needed someone to talk to . . ."

She held still.

"Please—when you get this, will you call me?"

Taking the phone from her ear and ending the call, she walked over to her bed, glancing at a picture of Jonas on her nightstand. She reached for a small folded piece of paper near the picture and turned the page over, looking at the phone number scribbled on it.

She slowly unfolded the page, seeing the title of a poem near the top.

On Another's Sorrow
William Blake (1757–1827)

Looking down, she slowly read.

> *Can I see another's woe,*
> *And not be in sorrow too?*
> *Can I see another's grief,*
> *And not seek for kind relief?*

Can I see a falling tear,
And not feel my sorrow's share?
Can a father see his child
Weep, nor be with sorrow fill'd?

Can a mother sit and hear
An infant groan, an infant fear—
No, no! never can it be!
Never, never can it be!

And can He who smiles on all
Hear the wren with sorrows small,
Hear the small bird's grief and care,
Hear the woes that infants bear—

And not sit beside the nest,
Pouring pity in their breast;
And not sit the cradle near,
Weeping tear on infant's tear;

And not sit both night and day,
Wiping all our tears away?
O, no! never can it be!
Never, never can it be!

Sarah looked back at the photograph in front of her. She lifted the frame from her nightstand before slowly lowering her head. And then she cried.

32

JONAS HADN'T SAID A WORD SINCE LEAVING WILLIAM Graves' house, and that didn't change as he and Michael followed Chris from the airplane, through the arrivals terminal, to a rental car depot where Chris got a small compact automobile.

Thinking about everything that had happened, Jonas wondered if anything could actually be done. The only two people who knew about William Graves' crimes were too terrified to speak. Charlie was still trying to figure out to what extent his father had abused him, and William's wife was too afraid to come out with the evidence she had in her possession.

Sitting in Chris's car, wondering what could be done to stop Graves, Jonas barely even noticed they had begun the nearly two-hour drive to the other side of the island. Riding in the backseat, with his companion in front, Jonas looked out the window. Trees flew past his view alongside towering cliffs. This was the road to Hana, he knew; a road famous for its six hundred hairpin turns and fifty-nine narrow bridges. The last time Jonas drove this road with Chris, he had nearly thrown up. His friend had to pull over to the side of the road to let him catch his breath so they wouldn't have to drive with the stench of vomit in the car.

But instead of feeling carsick now, Jonas was consumed by thoughts of William Graves and the fear of not being able to stop him. What good was it to be a spirit with supernatural abilities if he couldn't fix anything? It was infuriating to watch so much pain and suffering without the means to prevent it.

A voice came from up front.

"Jonas, we're getting close."

Having been so lost in his thoughts, Jonas hadn't even realized how much time had passed. Looking out the window again, he saw how the midnight sky had begun to give way to a subtle hue of golden blue on the horizon. Turning to the driver's seat, Jonas looked at Chris. He could tell his friend wasn't interested in the natural beauty that surrounded them. He seemed to be completely overwhelmed with his own thoughts.

Looking ahead, Jonas realized where they were headed; he could see the all too familiar spot in the distance. He was back at the same strip of sand he had walked away from when he entered a completely new world.

As the car came to a stop, Jonas looked over at Chris, noticing something troubling in his expression: dread mingled with rage. Chris was fighting some sort of internal battle as he sat quietly behind the wheel, staring out into the distance.

For nearly half an hour, Jonas and Michael stared at Chris, while Chris stared at the waves—waves that were much larger than before.

"Can't you say something?" Jonas asked, looking toward Michael. Michael shook his head.

"I tried already," he replied. "He's too obsessed with his own thoughts right now. And my voice isn't familiar to him."

Jonas looked back at Chris.

"There's a storm raging inside his mind," Michael added. "Everything around him is beginning to cloud over."

Feeling all the more helpless, Jonas stared at his friend, whose hands gripped the steering wheel with whitened knuckles. Then, without any warning, Chris opened his door and got out of the car.

Startled, Jonas watched as Michael quickly exited the car as well. Doing the same, Jonas caught up with his mentor as they made their way behind Chris down to the black sand beach. The waves crashed against tall dark cliffs, geysers of white spray shooting high into the air.

As Chris walked out onto the sand, Jonas took a moment to notice the small detail of his friend's footprints against the soft black surface. Last time they were here, there had been two sets of footprints. Now there was only one.

Stopping momentarily, Chris reached into his pocket and pulled out a cell phone. He glanced at it.

Taking a step closer, Jonas looked at it as well. There, lit up on the screen, was a voicemail from Sarah. But rather than listen to the message, Chris threw his phone down on the black sand and took off his shirt and shoes. He turned around momentarily, glancing over his shoulder, right in Jonas's direction. He stood there, staring for a while, searching for something that he couldn't see. Shaking his head, he looked back around and began walking toward the water's edge.

Turning to his mentor for some sort of direction, Jonas saw two more spirits suddenly appear in their midst—one, a youthful-looking woman, and the other, a man equal to her age.

"Oh, Garrison! He's going to do it!" the woman gasped. "He's going to try to . . ."

"Wait—" Jonas suddenly said aloud, studying their faces. "I've seen you before."

Michael cut in.

"Jonas, these are Chris's great-grandparents."

Amazed at how young they looked, Jonas took a step forward to study them a bit closer.

"You're the ones who were kneeling with him on the beach after the accident," he observed, somewhat in shock.

Nodding in recognition, the man looked back at Jonas with pleading eyes.

"Jonas," Michael said, pulling his younger companion's attention toward him once more. "I think you know why I've brought you here."

Jonas glanced from Michael to Chris's great-grandparents.

"We need you to do something we don't have the ability to do ourselves," Michael said, slowly, tentatively. "We need you to go down there and give him a reason not to do this."

Jonas stared back at his mentor, his eyes wide in disbelief. Out of the four of them, surely he was the least qualified to stop Chris from drowning himself.

"Emma and I have tried to help him," Garrison said, moving closer toward Jonas, his wife still clinging to his arm. "But he won't listen to us. He can't hear us. We've tried so many times . . ."

"Jonas," Michael added in a low whisper. "Your death is the reason he's here. He won't listen to anybody but you."

Jonas saw Chris walking determinedly out into the black ocean, the boom of exploding waves reverberating all around.

"But how?" he said anxiously. "He doesn't even know I'm here. He can't even hear me."

"Don't worry. If you get close enough, he'll listen," Michael said.

Jonas looked back at his mentor, visibly shaken by the impossibility of the task.

Letting go of his wife's hand, Garrison took a step toward Michael and Jonas. His eyes were wet with tears, but his voice was calm.

"Only Chris can make the decision to listen to you," he said. "But as his friend, Jonas—as his best friend—I can't imagine there would be anyone he would rather hear from more than you."

Jonas watched as the man's lips began to tremble.

"Please," he entreated, with all the intensity he could muster, "please, will you help him—give him a reason not to end his life today."

Jonas looked into the eyes of the man in front of him. He could see his sadness and feel his desperation. Yet the man stood tall, reminding Jonas of his own father and how he had tried to be strong at Jonas's funeral.

Glancing back at Chris, watching him walk out into the dark, foreboding ocean, Jonas knew he couldn't let this happen. He knew he couldn't go to his friend's funeral knowing that there was something he could have done to prevent it. Chris wasn't prepared. This wasn't his time. But if he didn't learn to let go of his guilt, Jonas knew there was a possibility that it would follow him to the other side. If Chris couldn't shed the heavy weight he insisted on carrying, it might very well drag him down into the depths of something much deeper than the bottom of an ocean.

Jonas made his decision.

Making his way down to the frothy shore, Jonas thought about how he could get Chris's attention. He wanted to yell, but he suppressed the action, knowing that even if he were still mortal, the crashing waves would easily drown out the sound of his voice. Fighting against his nerves as he approached the ink-black ocean, Jonas took a few steps into the water. Looking down at his feet, he saw how the water ran right *through* his body. It was strange, watching the turbulent liquid make no movement against his ankles. Taking little time to contemplate these metaphysical details, Jonas walked faster until he found himself chest deep in the water.

Looking back toward shore, Jonas could see the faces of his mentor and Chris's great-grandparents hoping that whatever he had to say would be enough to keep his friend alive. Looking ahead, Jonas saw Chris wading out into the deep, yelling angrily at the pounding ocean, a fist raised above his head.

"C'mon you son of a bitch!" he yelled. "Come and get me!"

Jonas was making his way out to his friend as fast as he knew how, when he saw a massive wall of water beginning to form in the distance.

"That's right!" he heard his friend yell. "You want me! I'm right here!"

Jonas saw a peak begin to form, a translucent edge near the top. And then, like a ton of bricks being thrown from the top of a building, Jonas watched as the wave came down, landing right on top of Chris's head.

"Chris!"

An explosion rang in Jonas's ears as a wall of white came rushing toward him. It moved fast. He closed his eyes and held his breath in preparation for the impact.

But nothing hit him. He heard the thundering noise envelope him, but when he opened his eyes back up, he was still in the same place he had been before. Looking back, he saw the white barrier rumble toward the shore like a stampede of frothy wild horses, causing him to realize that while he was in the midst of the open ocean, none of it seemed to be touching him at all.

Jonas heard a gasping noise from behind him. Turning to look, he saw Chris's head bobbing in the distance.

"Damn you!" Chris yelled, trying to tread above the white foam in the water. "You can do better than that!"

Jonas made his way in Chris's direction, while another wave grew quickly in the distance. Going as fast as he could, Jonas gained only a few yards on Chris before he watched the wave peak and crash down on his friend's head again.

WOOSH—

The wave's frothy aftermath rushed through Jonas again, but not before pulling Chris down below. Looking around him in alarm, Jonas saw Chris's head pop back up, but this time there was red blood dribbling down his forehead.

"Goddamn you!" Chris screamed, his eyes filling with the blood streaming down his face. "Is that it!"

But the sea wasn't done with him yet. Rising in the distance, slowly but surely, was another wave beginning to form—this one much larger than the last. It rose like a sea monster waking from its sleep.

"Take me!" Chris yelled angrily. "Take me!"

As if it wished to follow the command, the wave rose high in the air, far above either of their heads. Jonas looked up in awe as it emerged from the depths, climbing higher, ever higher, blocking out the stars above.

"Chris!"

Jonas and Chris craned their necks to look straight up at the wall about to come crashing down upon them. Though he knew his friend to be the only one in jeopardy, Jonas couldn't help but panic. Every remnant of mortal instinct screamed for him to dive down, to swim away from the wave that was about to collapse on top of them. But watching the wall peak, and begin to curl in on itself, there was nothing Jonas could do other than close his eyes and wait for it to pass right through him.

KABOOM!

Like a thunderous clap of lightning, Jonas heard the force of nature exploding all around. With his eyes still closed, he heard a dampening of sound, an echoing reverberation shuddering through the dark liquid. Opening his eyes, he saw that he was entirely under water, bubbles everywhere, swarming in all sorts of forceful directions as the washing machine began to take hold. Watching it all occur right in front of him without the slightest sensation of it pulling him one way or the other, Jonas saw a hand fly past his view, before it disappeared quickly into the depths below.

Instinctively reaching in that direction, Jonas moved as fast as he knew how in hopes of pulling his friend back up to the surface. Gliding quickly with the flow of water as his guide, he descended to the dark bottom below.

Jonas went farther, deeper, until the bubbles cleared from his view. As they did, he saw the bottom of the ocean with an astonishing clarity. With some kind of newfound ability, Jonas could see everything around him in perfect detail. No longer did his eyes sting and his vision blur; he saw the underwater world as he saw the one above. Everything became clear to him. But when he saw the limp body in the distance, he suddenly lost interest in all those astounding capabilities.

There, pinned between the crack of a rock and a massive mound of brain coral, was Chris, his head swaying in the water, his eyes barely open. Red liquid was spewing from his head. His legs and arms swayed helplessly in the drifting currents. It seemed as if he had found his place—the place where he could wait it out until the last breath escaped his burning lungs.

Moving quickly toward his friend, Jonas felt panicked, unsure what he could do. Instinctively, he reached for Chris's arm in an attempt to pull him free, but seeing his own hands pass straight through, he realized there was nothing physical that he could do.

Looking around him, he hoped to see Michael or Chris's great-grandparents somewhere in the depths, rushing to his aid. But there was no one there. Just him and Chris, imprisoned at the bottom of the sea.

Jonas felt panic surge through his system, wondering if anything could actually be done. They were so far underwater now, there was nothing Jonas could do to talk his friend out of this. He would have to be above water for his friend to hear him.

But then Jonas remembered that he was a spirit—and as a spirit he might just be able to do the impossible. Gliding closer to his friend, Jonas looked at Chris's blank expression, hoping with all his might that it would work.

He slowly opened his mouth, expecting to feel the cold dark liquid pouring in; instead, he felt as if air surrounded him now, in place of a shadowy thick mass of water. Recognizing this, Jonas attempted to speak to Chris, hoping to find the words his friend so desperately needed to hear.

"Chris," he said, hearing the sound of his own voice as crisp and clear as ever. "Chris . . ."

Jonas could have sworn he saw Chris look in his direction, his eyes still half shut under the weight of a slurry consciousness.

Jonas wasn't sure if it was the simple force of a current turning Chris's head to the side, but he didn't think about it for long. His friend was in his last moments, and if Jonas didn't say something to move him into action, to get him to change his mind, he would soon have to watch Chris wake to the reality of his own spirit separating from his body.

"Chris, you need to listen to me," Jonas spoke again, trying to match eyes with his friend. "You're not supposed to do this. It isn't your time . . ."

Chris's face turned in the opposite direction.

An overwhelming rush of panic flowed through his system. Jonas tried to grab Chris's face to turn it back around. But seeing that he couldn't, he moved his entire body to face Chris once more.

"Chris," he began, "Chris—"

But there was no response. Just a floating body stuck in the crag of a rock waiting to die. And as Jonas saw this, he suddenly wondered if it was already too late.

But he knew he had to say something—anything. Chris's

great-grandparents were still waiting on the shore, and he knew he couldn't face them without his friend—alive—at his side. But as he opened his mouth again to speak to Chris, nothing came out. He didn't know why, but he felt as if the words he had to share weren't the ones Chris needed to hear.

Looking at his friend lying on the bottom of the ocean, Jonas tried to think of what to tell him. He wanted to say "Get up!" "Snap out of it!" "Swim to the top!" but looking at Chris pinned between the rock and the coral, he realized his friend didn't want to do any of those things. Chris didn't want to rise to the surface and take another breath. He wanted to be down here in the dark, waiting to bring an end to his pain.

But if there was something Jonas had learned from his short experience as a spirit, it was that life didn't end after death. It continued on, like it or not, and so did the pain.

Realizing this, Jonas knew his friend didn't need to hear things like "Snap out of it!" Instead, he needed to know why he should want to do any of those things in the first place. If Chris was going to keep himself alive, Jonas knew he had to give him a real reason not to end it all. He had to help Chris understand there was still something worth saving in himself.

Watching his friend hold on to the breath in his lungs, Jonas moved a little closer to him. But instead of talking loudly as he had done before, he looked at his friend and simply whispered.

"Chris," he began, "you've gotten yourself into a mess."

Jonas found himself surprisingly calm as he watched Chris's head bob and sway in the current.

"You've only got a few seconds left, so I need you to pay attention—I need you to listen to me."

Whether or not it was the influence of the water, Chris's head stilled.

"In all the years I've known you, I've only seen goodness," Jonas whispered, "how you've treated people, how you've treated me— you've been the best friend I've ever had."

Suddenly, in the midst of Jonas's words, Chris began to spasm as his eyes grew wide with fear, the lack of oxygen beginning to take hold.

Jonas wondered if these were the last throes of pain before his friend would be forced to take in a breath, but he didn't stop talking.

"I want you to think about this, Chris. Because when I went out to save you that day, I went out to save the person that had always been there for me."

Jonas saw Chris's wide eyes begin to roll back in his head, his lids begin to close.

"I saved you that day because I saw there was something worth saving . . . something inside you so brilliant and good. But if you can't understand that there's something worth saving in yourself, then there's nothing I can do. But please, Chris, please try to see . . ."

Jonas lifted a hand to his friend's face, his fingers hovering over Chris's cheek.

"See the good that is in you . . . believe in the friendships you have . . . believe in the family that still loves you . . . but most of all Chris, believe that you are someone worth saving."

Jonas choked on his own words.

"You're my friend, Chris. I don't want you to die. I want you to live the life that you deserve, and I'm telling you now, you don't deserve this."

Jonas felt himself holding his own breath as he looked into the white slits of his friend's eyes. He wasn't sure if it was over yet, but he pleaded in his heart for it not to be too late.

"Please, God," Jonas cried within himself, "he's my best friend. Please don't let him go like this."

Looking at the lifeless face of his friend, Jonas began to wonder if it was over, if Chris's spirit would soon separate from his body to enter a world he was not ready for. But then, suddenly, and without warning, Chris's eyes opened wide, and looked straight at him. And then there was a sound, a sound of screaming as Jonas watched bubbles blast out of Chris's mouth, enveloping his view.

Drawing back instinctively, Jonas was surprised to find that his friend wasn't about to go limp and let the dark water overcome him. No—Chris was thrashing about, struggling for his life, trying to break free of the rock and the coral that pinned him down.

Even knowing that he couldn't help, Jonas didn't care. He rushed to his friend's aid and thrashed relentlessly at Chris's arms and legs, trying to do something to help him get free. And in the midst of flailing limbs and swarming bubbles, Jonas saw Chris break free, push off the rock, and kick with everything he had toward the surface, a dark stream of red blood trailing behind him.

Jonas instinctively tried to push the body of his friend upward, though his hands kept going straight through. But that didn't matter, he pushed anyway, rising with Chris toward the surface.

And then, as the darkness below began to subside, replaced with the light from above, Jonas looked up and saw the ocean ceiling. He watched Chris grope upward for air, fighting against the spasms that rocked his body.

Reaching the top, Chris's head broke the surface, and he took in a breath that sounded more like a scream. Jonas had come up as well, and he watched his friend suck in oxygen. Blood seemed to burst forth from broken capillaries visible in the whites around Chris's pupils, but he was alive, and conscious, shuddering for breath as he did his best to stay above water.

His friend was alive! Chris was alive! He had made the right decision, to fight for another day.

Turning to look back at the beach, Jonas was somewhat stunned to see Michael and Chris's great-grandparents making their way to his side. Already in the water, they moved swiftly to offer help, surrounding Jonas and his friend who was still gasping for breath.

"Jonas, stay close to him," Michael instructed as the three positioned themselves around Chris.

Turning to look at his friend, Jonas saw that Chris had begun flailing in the water, just as another wave was coming their way.

"Chris, look behind you," Emma said aloud as she drew close to her great-grandson's side.

Still fighting to keep control, Chris seemed to automatically react to her words, slowly turning around with the look of terror in his eyes.

"No," he said fearfully to himself.

"It's okay, Chris," Garrison reassured him. "Just take a breath and don't fight it."

Following the instructions, almost by instinct now, Chris took in a deep breath and closed his eyes, just as the wave crashed in on itself, the aftermath tumbling toward him at racing speed.

WOOSH—

The water tossed him violently around, but the wave's grasp only knocked him closer to shore. His head popped up in the thick white foam as he gasped once more for air.

"Swim," Garrison said, still at his side. "Swim!"

Without thinking, Chris began to grope toward shore, his heavy arms nearly useless.

In all the chaos, Michael quickly looked at Jonas.

"It's working, Jonas. Say something—he'll listen to you."

Staying near Chris's side, Jonas looked at his friend and spoke to him once more.

"You can do it, Chris! Just a little bit farther . . ."

But as Jonas spoke, Chris turned to glance in his direction, almost as if he expected to see something there.

"Don't look at me," Jonas blurted out, "look at the beach! You're not out of this yet!"

Turning back toward shore, Chris lifted his heavy arms in the frothy foam as another wave could be heard crashing in the distance behind him.

"Get ready for it!" Garrison shouted in Chris's direction. "Get ready to hold your breath . . ."

Emma spoke up.

"It's almost here, Chris," she said while watching the exploding wall coming their way. "Get ready . . . *now!*"

His eyes bulging with fear, Chris sucked in a breath as the wave broke over his back. It shoved his head forward with overwhelming force, but it continued to move him toward shore.

Chris's head soon broke the surface as he strained to reach land.

"Go, Chris, go!" Jonas shouted.

And so it went, with Chris struggling to reach safety, and the four spirits urging him on, helping him fight through the waves crashing in on him from behind. Soon Chris found himself in the safety of shallow water, and he began to crawl on the sand beneath his knees, until he was able to fall face-down, exhausted, on the beach.

Lying there, gasping for breath, Chris struggled to gain control over himself as Jonas, Michael, and his great-grandparents gave him words of comfort and reassurance. After a while, Chris found the strength to turn over on his side. Working against the pain, he maneuvered himself until he could sit down, taking in deep breaths as he tried to stop his body from shuddering.

"He heard you," Michael said, turning to look at Jonas.

"You saved his life!" Garrison added. "How can we ever thank you?"

Jonas glanced away, feeling undeserving of their gratitude.

"Jonas, you did it!" Emma exclaimed. "You said just what he needed to hear!"

Looking back up, Jonas noticed Michael pointing in Chris's direction.

"If you hurry, he may still be able to hear you."

Taking the opportunity, Jonas slowly knelt down in front of his friend. He thought of what he could say in a moment like this. All the times they had been together, the years spent at each other's side, suddenly came to mind. The movies, the double dates, the road trips to nowhere special; the nights when they stayed up eating junk food and dreaming about what the future held in store for them. On and on each memory went. But as Jonas thought about all this, wondering what he should say, he decided instead to sit down at his friend's side and look out over the open ocean, just like they had done the last time they were here.

Side by side, Jonas and Chris sat as the sun began to cast its rays over the vast expanse, transforming the once dark ocean into a shimmering sea of golden reflections. The three other spirits, if they were there at all, seemed to recede into nothingness as the two friends took in the moment together.

Jonas turned to look at his friend, remembering the very word Chris used to describe all this when they were here with their surfboards a little over a week ago. "Beautiful," he said, thinking of how far they'd come in such a short period of time.

Turning his head to one side slightly, watching a bird flying high in the air, Chris looked at the water again and nodded.

"Yes, it is."

33

IT WAS MIDMORNING WHEN A KNOCK CAME AT THE apartment door.

Surprised, Charlie went to open it.

"Mom?"

"Yes, dear. I hope I'm not bothering you."

"No, no. You're fine. Come on in."

Charlie stepped to the side to let his mother in.

"Can I take your bag?" Charlie asked.

Carol clutched it tightly. "No, that's okay. Thank you."

Charlie watched his mother look nervously around the apartment.

"Are you all right, Mom? Is there something I can get you?"

"No, thank you, Charlie. I just . . . I don't intend to stay long."

Charlie glanced at the floor, pricked by a feeling of guilt. "I really am sorry, Mom . . . for everything that happened last night."

Charlie felt his mother's hand suddenly on his wrist.

"No, Charlie, don't say that."

Charlie gave her a confused look.

"That's one of the reasons I came to talk to you this morning. That wasn't your fault."

Charlie tried apologizing again. "I really am sorry, though . . ."

"Please," she said, stopping him short. "I came to talk to you about something else—about the phone call. When you were telling me about your father."

Charlie looked up, unsure what to say.

"You said you've been feeling different—remembering things," she said.

He fell silent.

Carol reached for his other hand.

"Tell me, Charlie, do you really think your father has done something to you?"

His heart began to race. "I don't know," he said, doubt and panic in his voice. "I don't know what I'm remembering . . ."

"Please, Charlie," his mother pleaded.

"I don't know, Mom," he said, looking anywhere but in her eyes. "I don't know what's happening to me. I just think . . . I think, I'm going crazy or something."

Carol placed the bag on the floor. She knelt down and took out a large black shoebox.

"I don't think you're going crazy, Charlie," she said. Then she rose to her feet and handed him the black box. "But I need your help. I don't know what to do."

34

JONAS FELT AT EASE AS HE SAT NEXT TO CHRIS ON THE airplane back to New York. His friend had managed to salvage the business card he had been given by the attractive young woman at the check-in counter, and she had been able to help book him a flight home.

While en route to the airport, Chris had placed a quick call to Sarah to let her know that he was okay and to apologize for not having called sooner. Listening from the backseat of the car, Jonas heard Sarah ask where Chris was and what had happened to him. "I could tell you," Chris replied, "but I doubt you'd believe me."

He was probably right.

And, after fifteen stitches at a local hospital and two trips to fast-food restaurants along the way, Chris walked through airport security with his spirit entourage and boarded the plane they were all now on.

Sitting next to his friend, Jonas still felt Chris seemed a bit shaken. The painkillers for the gash on his head were taking their time to kick in, and Chris didn't seem quite as talkative as he usually was when the flight attendant came to offer him something to drink. But at least he wasn't staring angrily at the TV in front of him.

More than that, there was something different about him. Very different. Jonas sensed that, while his friend still had a lot to think about, Chris at least had a better handle now on how to process it all.

"He's doing quite well, given the circumstances," Jonas heard a voice say.

Seeing Garrison sitting next to his wife, Jonas smiled.

"Yeah, I think so," he agreed.

This wasn't the first time that he and Chris's great-grandparents had talked on this flight. For almost the entire trip, Jonas had been entertained by the young couple as they answered all his questions. Initially, Jonas's main concerns rested on Chris—how he would cope once he got back to the city, what could be done to help him once he got home. But as the time passed, Jonas began to ask about Garrison and Emma's lives together: what it was like when they were still mortal and how they felt when they crossed over to the other side.

Appreciative of his genuine interest, Garrison and Emma took turns describing where they had grown up, how they had met, and what it was like when each of them entered the World of Spirits. They seemed to enjoy relaying the details of their lives—the kind of life, Jonas could tell, they wished their own great-grandson to have one day.

Just as Jonas began to feel that everything was finally happening as he thought it should, there was a sound from the back of the plane that startled him.

"Michael!" a woman's panicked voice rang out. "He's going back tonight. He's already on his way there!"

Turning, Jonas was surprised to see Gwen, Michael's wife. She had appeared out of nowhere and seemed to be in an incredible hurry.

Michael stood up and nodded to show he understood. Then, turning around to face his younger companion, he held out his hand.

"Jonas, I'm sorry but we need to go."

"Now?"

Michael nodded.

"Why?"

Jonas glanced quickly at Garrison and Emma.

"He's right, you should go," Emma said with a reassuring look. "Don't worry, we can take care of Chris."

Jonas heard a sound like that of crackling thunder erupting near the front of the plane. Looking in that direction, he saw eight menacing spirits appear out of thin air.

"We told you we'd be back," one of them said.

"No," Michael whispered angrily to himself. He turned to look at Jonas again.

"Jonas, we have to go," he said, even more emphatically.

"But—Chris?"

Jonas looked at his friend. Chris seemed oblivious to all that was happening around him as he thumbed through the pages of his magazine.

"He's in capable hands," Michael replied.

Jonas looked at Michael again, then at Garrison and Emma. Garrison had already moved down the aisle to contend with the spirits and Emma followed closely behind him.

"It's okay, Jonas," she said. "We've got it from here. I promise."

Looking back at the eight malicious spirits, Jonas wasn't so sure. Garrison and Emma were easily outnumbered, but to make matters worse, they were also Chris's *great-grandparents*. While Jonas knew they looked young and healthy, he couldn't help but feel nervous for them as old as they really were. Sure, they looked cute together, but Jonas had to wonder if they could deal with the threat now moving toward them from the front of the plane.

"But . . ." Jonas began.

"Jonas," Michael persisted, "we don't have much time. Please."

"It's okay, Jonas, really," Emma assured him again. "We can handle it."

Jonas looked one last time at the spirits near the front of the plane. Seven of them were grinning, but the one in front seemed incensed and showed no signs of backing down.

"You've got to get out of here," Garrison said, glancing only long enough to convey the sincerity of his message.

Once again Jonas didn't understand what was happening around him, but he decided to follow the instructions he had been given. He reached out to hold Michael's hand. Looking one last time at his friend, he saw Chris turn a page in his magazine. But before that page landed on the opposite side, everything suddenly vanished from sight.

Ten spirits glared at each other from opposite ends of the airplane.

Walking to Garrison's side, Emma let her husband speak first.

"You shouldn't have come," he said sternly.

The eight spirits stared at their opponents with venomous disdain.

"You don't need to be here," the spirit in front said. "We've come for him," he pointed in Chris's direction.

Walking in front of her husband, Emma gave the spirit an intimidating glare.

"Not tonight," she said, blocking his path toward Chris.

"There's no reason for you to stay," the spirit said. "We'll take care of him just fine . . ."

"You have no claim on him tonight," Emma said with a command in her voice that caused two of the spirits in back to cower. "He's made his decision. We're here to protect him."

"Protect him!" the spirit in front seethed. "You dare stop us in our work!"

Taking another step forward, Emma stared the spirit down.

"*Try me.*"

The spirit began to gnash his teeth and tear at his chest, emitting a horrid cry that sounded more animal than human.

Garrison took a step toward his wife and stood shoulder to shoulder with her. "We'll let you decide," he said, a trace of a grin growing on his face. "You can go quietly, without any harm—or you can go the other way—with our help."

Incensed, the spirit in front suddenly lunged high into the air with hands outstretched. But less than second later, Emma raised her own hand in his direction.

SLAM!!

The lunging spirit was halted in midair and then thrown to the floor with a sudden crash. He seemed to be pinned down against his will and he struggled to look up at his foe. Angry at being controlled, the spirit glared at the woman, who slowly brought him to his knees with a mere flick of her finger.

Emma stared fiercely into his eyes. "Leave my great-grandson alone!" she hissed, as she sent him flying back down the length of the cabin, slamming him violently against one of the taller spirits.

Garrison took another step forward.

"I told you to leave when you still had a chance," he reminded the six other spirits.

Ignoring his warning, the remaining spirits gathered themselves together and walked determinedly toward the young couple.

"Very well, then," Garrison said as his wife raised her hand once more. "We warned you."

———

There was a sudden rumble of turbulence on the plane, making more than a few passengers reach for the armrests at their sides. Glasses fell from a number of tray tables, and the lights inside the cabin momentarily flickered on and off.

"Sorry about that, folks," the pilot said after a few seconds over the intercom. "Looks like we hit an air pocket. Should be no problem, though—just sit back and enjoy the ride."

35

STANDING IN THE DARK OUTSIDE THE LITTLE GIRL'S home again, Jonas looked at Michael.

"What are we doing here?"

His companion pointed to the left as a car came rolling to a stop in front of the house.

"William's back," Michael said.

Jonas felt anger burning inside him again.

"Holly?" he asked, looking back at his companion.

Michael nodded.

Jonas took a step toward the house, but then he felt a hand on his arm, pulling him back.

"Jonas, I need you to stay here," Michael said.

Remembering what had happened the last time they were here, Jonas took a moment before he slowly acquiesced.

"Isn't there anything I can do?"

Michael smiled sincerely, but for only a moment.

"You've done wonderfully," he said, looking into his young companion's eyes. "What you did back there—back at the beach—you've proved yourself capable beyond your years."

Michael glanced at the house.

"But this is my fight," he said. "You don't need to be burdened with what is going to happen in there. Out here is where I need you."

Michael pointed down the road toward a broken street lamp about a hundred feet away.

"Wait there for me," he said, "until I come to give you further instructions."

Jonas looked back, wondering why Michael wanted him to wait so far away. But instead of asking more questions, he nodded and let his companion go, knowing that time was of the essence.

"Thank you, Jonas," Michael said, and with those words, he disappeared from sight—just as William Graves walked up to the door and rang the bell.

"Come in," a familiar voice said after the door had been opened. "She's waiting upstairs . . ."

Jonas felt his temper burn as he watched William enter the home with a smirk. Jonas still wished there was something he could do to help. The little girl in there had no chance, and Michael would have to watch over her alone.

Shuddering at the thought, Jonas walked toward the lamppost in the darkness with his shoulders hanging low. He could hear the sounds of voices through the walls of the houses around him. When he came to a stop under the broken street lamp, he tried not to look at the little girl's house. He knew that if he did, he would be able to hear what was going on inside.

He did his best to wait patiently, but the minutes passed by like hours. He tried not to calculate the time passing, as each moment was another reminder of the torture the little girl was being made to endure. But after what seemed like an eternity, he suddenly heard the roar of an engine in the distance.

But this was not William Graves' car. William was still in the house, still taking pleasure in his evil deeds. This car came from further down the road, in the same direction Jonas had previously been walking. It started driving slowly toward him. And looking even closer at it, Jonas saw something he did not expect.

Charlie was in the driver's seat, steering cautiously and moving at a snail's pace. He crept toward the broken street lamp and parked right at the spot where Jonas stood. Then he turned off his lights.

Charlie stared at the house William had entered, looking anxious, almost scared, as if he were about to get caught doing something wrong. He checked his cell phone and placed it on the center console. Then he waited.

Slipping silently into the backseat, Jonas sat and waited, keeping an eye on his brother. Every so often, he heard muffled screams from the upstairs window. Charlie couldn't hear the little girl's voice, but then again, Charlie didn't share Jonas's sensory abilities—abilities Jonas silently wished he didn't have at the moment.

Sitting in the dark, Jonas began to wonder if this night would ever end and what would happen when Charlie saw his father stroll across the grass to get into his car. His brother had evidently remembered enough of what his father had done to him to decide to follow him under the cover of night. But how much did he actually know? And what, if anything, could he do about what was happening now?

Jonas suddenly felt a chill in the air; a cold like death that made even Charlie tighten his coat around his shoulders. Then Jonas saw something terrible appear: one of The Dead.

"Hello, Jonas," the well-dressed spirit said, turning around from the front passenger's seat to reveal menacing green eyes.

Jonas's throat closed up, choking with fear as he remembered seeing this spirit in the dark realm of the underworld.

"I see you've met your brother," the spirit said, glancing briefly at Charlie. "You've both come to observe the events of a very interesting night, I suspect?"

Jonas had nothing to say. He couldn't. He felt his tongue swell up in his mouth. No words could escape his lips. He couldn't even utter the simplest of words when the impulse to do so entered his mind.

Jonas looked back at the house, at the second-floor window, wondering if there was any way his companion could suddenly appear to help him.

"Ah, yes, the house," the spirit said, turning to look in the same direction. "You can hear it now, can't you. It's too bad, isn't it—your father, the things he does. It's enough to make one cringe . . ."

Jonas watched as the spirit shook his head with feigned disgust.

"But the apple never falls very far from the tree, does it, Jonas?" the spirit said, glaring. "We are who we are, like it or not."

Jonas wanted to reply, but his mouth was stiff.

"Take your brother, for example," the spirit continued, looking in Charlie's direction. "He's out here waiting, just like you—waiting for that pedophile of a father you both share to come wandering out on the lawn."

Jonas glanced at Charlie.

"Isn't that right, Charlie," the spirit now spoke in the other direction. "That's what you've come here for, is it not?"

Jonas watched as Charlie gripped the steering wheel tight.

"Yes . . . ," the spirit said with an airy rasp, "you can end it, you know. You can end all the pain and suffering tonight, Charlie . . ."

Jonas saw Charlie's jaw clench.

"You know who your father is," the spirit continued, leaning in closer to Charlie's ear, "you know what he's come here to do. You heard him when he called your mother earlier today, telling her that he would be working late. But why? Why would he *lie* like that?"

Jonas watched as he saw Charlie lean forward to get a better look at the house. Passing by in the lamplight above, the silhouette of a man could be seen grabbing the small arm of a child with long hair.

"Yes," the spirit whispered, "yes, that's it. You can see her up there, can't you?"

The smaller figure struggled to get away, just as the room went dark.

"He's doing it to her," the spirit seethed. "He's doing the same things to her that he used to do to you, Charlie . . ."

The spirit leaned in even more, hovering just a few inches from Charlie's ear. "You know what it feels like, Charlie. You know the pleasure he takes . . ."

Charlie began to tremble.

"Yes, you can remember how it feels, can't you? You can still feel his weight pressing in on you . . . the smell of his breath, his face so close to yours. But you can stop it, you know—you can stop him from ever hurting anyone again. He doesn't have to control you anymore, Charlie. All you have to do is reach for it. Just reach for it with your hand . . ."

Charlie suddenly reached toward the phone he had laid on the center console. For a split second, Jonas hoped he was going to pick it up and dial the police. Instead, he touched a lever near the front of the armrest and the center console opened with a click.

"That's right," the spirit continued, "just think about what you can do . . ."

Jonas saw Charlie reach into the center armrest, fidgeting with something hidden inside.

"Just think of who you can *save*," the spirit said. "He won't be able to hurt anyone anymore. He won't be able to hurt *you* anymore. It will be over, Charlie. You can end it. You can end all the suffering tonight . . ."

Charlie removed his hand from inside the console, holding a shiny metallic revolver.

"The voices you hear in your head," the spirit continued, "you can silence them. You can silence them forever."

Jonas saw the spirit glance at the window in the house.

"He's the reason you hear them," the spirit said with disdain. "Your father's the reason they keep you up at night . . . make you do bad things . . . make you feel sick inside . . ."

Jonas saw a glint of light shine off the revolver in Charlie's hand.

"All you have to do is squeeze. Point the gun and squeeze. No one will know. No one will care. You'll be a hero Charlie, saving the little girl in there . . ."

Jonas looked at the spirit, noticing the ease with which he told his lies.

"And you will be free," the spirit said with a trace of a smile, "free to live your life however you want. You deserve it, Charlie, you deserve a life free from your father, free from all this pain."

Jonas suddenly felt something within, something that gave him the courage to speak.

"That's a lie!" he said, glaring at the dark figure.

Slowly turning his head, the spirit looked Jonas up and down.

"I see your companion has taught you something of bravery since we last spoke," he said. "But has he taught you of sacrifice? Has he told you what you will be asked to give up in order to save your father's despicable life?"

Jonas fell silent, unsure of what to say.

"Of course not," the spirit said with a searing voice. "They never tell you what you have to give up. They just expect you to do it. But you need to think it through first. You need to contemplate the implications of saving the life of someone as revolting as your father."

Without warning, Jonas felt his consciousness beginning to unravel, his mind becoming unhinged. His vision was being taken over against his will. Everything clouded in around him, obscuring his view, just as the image of something else began to take shape.

Through the mists of his mind, he saw his father, William Graves, welcoming Charlie into his home with a pat on the back. And behind Charlie, Jonas saw Sarah, pregnant, with a little girl at her side.

A voice suddenly spoke out.

"William is a persuasive man," the voice of the spirit rang in Jonas's ears. "Facing the truth of your father's dark deeds is something not even Charlie wants to do. Like his weak, gullible mother, he too will choose over time to ignore what your father has done, giving in to his doubts of what he remembers instead of trying to heal from the pain."

In his mind he saw Sarah lean in to give William a hug.

"And her," the spirit's voice said, "you haven't thought about her. The girl Charlie met in the café will soon call him, wanting to ease the pain of her own suffering. She'll want companionship again, an escape from her memories of you, and she will find it—in Charlie."

Jonas trembled as he saw an image of Sarah in a wedding dress, smiling as she admired her reflection in a floor-length mirror.

"His relationship with your beloved will blossom and grow. Meeting her future father-in-law, she too will be reeled in by William's charm. And the love she will have for Charlie will cloud her vision, until she will no longer be able to see clearly . . ."

The original image of Sarah with the little girl at her side returned. He cringed as he saw William lean down with a grin to give the little girl a kiss on the cheek.

"And her," the spirit said more, "he will do the same things to Sarah's daughter that he is doing to Holly now."

Jonas's stomach tightened as he tried to suppress the picture being forced into his mind.

"Not even the love of a grandfather, if he had any, could stop him from that."

Jonas suddenly saw Sarah turn to him, holding out her hand as if to reach for his.

"This is not the life she deserves, Jonas," the voice in his mind said. "She will be led like a lamb to the slaughter, to face an existence of misery and pain. Is this what you want? Is this the sacrifice you are willing to make to save William Graves?"

Jonas felt control of his mind come back to him.

"The choice is yours," the dark figure said from the front passenger's seat. "Allow Charlie to put an end to the suffering your father has caused, or watch your brother answer the phone call that will inevitably come from Sarah."

Jonas felt the shock of it all overwhelming him.

"Either way, someone must pay for what your father has done," the spirit said. "So the question is, who do you want it to be?"

Hearing a sound, Jonas looked back toward the house to see William opening the front door.

"I'm confident you'll make the right decision," the spirit smiled, without taking his eyes off Jonas. "But you best hurry. Time waits for no man."

And with the sudden sound of a rushing wind, the spirit disappeared.

Panic surging through his system, Jonas watched his brother grip the gun, sweat beading on his forehead. Charlie was trembling, looking from the revolver in his hand to the man standing on the porch. Jonas wished with everything he had for Michael to appear at his side—and not a moment too soon, that's exactly what happened. But before Jonas could even open his mouth to explain what had occurred, Michael spoke.

"Jonas, listen to me," he said, urgency in his voice. "You need to stop this."

Jonas watched Michael glance at Charlie and the gun in his hand.

"You need to stop Charlie from hurting anyone tonight."

Jonas tried opening his mouth to speak, but Michael pressed his fingers against his lips.

"Do you understand, Jonas?" Michael said, an emphatic tone to his voice. "Do you understand what I'm asking you to do?"

Jonas understood, but he wondered if Michael did. He wanted to open his mouth to tell his companion what had just happened—what would take place if he stopped Charlie from doing this very thing.

"I can't stay," Michael said. "I have to go. But please, Jonas—for your own sake."

Seeing pain mingled with fear in the eyes of his companion, Jonas saw Michael suddenly disappear without even finishing his sentence.

Jonas could feel his heart thumping through his chest, his breathing nearing the point of hyperventilation. Charlie was right in front of him, gun in hand, trembling with the thought of ending his father's life—an end Jonas felt was more than deserved. Looking out the window at William Graves, Jonas could have sworn that he actually saw a smile on the man's face. He had abused the little girl in the upstairs room once more, and most likely, he would be back to do it again.

Looking back at his brother, Jonas thought about what would happen if he were to remain silent and let Charlie follow through with what he had come to do. Charlie would raise the gun in his hand and pull the trigger—not only ending his father's life but destroying his own as well. If Charlie were to kill that man, he would be a murderer. Even if William did deserve it, was it worth asking Charlie to sacrifice everything he had to look forward to—his entire life and all that lay beyond—just for this one moment?

But then he thought of Sarah. The love of his life. It pained him, but Jonas thought of how his brother might meet her again, and how Sarah might fall in love to numb the sting of Jonas's passing. He thought of Charlie's hand in hers, a simple kiss to join their union, and the life they would begin together after walking down the aisle. The memory of Jonas would inevitably be replaced by Charlie—and events would be set in motion to bring the cold hand of William

Graves into her life.

Trembling under the weight of his decision, Jonas looked back at Charlie. He could tell his brother was fighting with the voices in his head, wishing for the pain to end.

But as Jonas sat there and watched, wondering what to do, he knew it wouldn't end. It would never end. If Charlie gave in to his anger, the world would be less one criminal, but it would have gained another. And knowing that to say nothing, to watch his brother pull the trigger—even if it was with the hope of saving Sarah—the act would echo on both sides of death's door. Jonas would become an accomplice. And Sarah—whether on this side of mortality or the other—she would one day learn the truth of this evening, and Jonas would have to answer for his actions.

Sarah . . .

What happened at this very moment had consequences for them all. But taking a moment to think of what Sarah would tell him to do if she were here beside him, Jonas knew exactly what needed to be done.

"Charlie," he whispered, leaning toward his brother. "Charlie . . . don't."

Charlie didn't react—he just sat there, the gun in his hand, staring at his pedophile father.

Leaning in closer, Jonas continued.

"Charlie," he said, his eyes closing with the intensity he felt. "It will destroy you."

Jonas opened his eyes to see his brother shaking, quivering helplessly in his seat.

"He's not worth it, Charlie," Jonas said. "Do you really want to become like him?"

A whimper came from Charlie's lips.

Jonas looked up in the distance, seeing William Graves turn from the porch doorway as he began to walk to his car. In a matter of seconds, William would get in, turn on the engine, and drive away.

But Jonas wasn't the only one making that connection. With only seconds left to make a decision, Charlie began to muffle his sobs behind clenched teeth. He gripped the gun, unsure of what to do.

Jonas felt another surge of panic. He was supposed to stop Charlie, but as he saw William's smug face, the same face he had seen grinning over his casket just a short time ago, there was something inside of Jonas that wanted Charlie to pull that trigger—to step outside the car and end the terror this man had left in his wake.

But Jonas knew that couldn't be the answer: to give into one's fear as a mask for courage; to end another's life only to destroy your own; to do those things that would transform you into the one you hate. Revenge is a hollow victory. Revenge offers no hope of deliverance, no justice, no true healing. It only adds to the crimes already enacted until the one who wished to stop the injustice can no longer differentiate between his own actions and the ones he wanted to prevent.

Jonas whispered into the ear of his brother again, hoping that Charlie could somehow hear him.

"Charlie, listen to me, *please* . . ."

Charlie's hand trembled.

"If you do this, you can't turn back. If you pull that trigger, it's all over Charlie—your life, everything—it's all over . . ."

Charlie fought back a wave of emotion.

"And even if you do it, you need to know: you will not be free of him," Jonas begged for his brother to understand. "You cannot walk down the same road he has traveled and end up in a different place."

Trembling in the black of the night, clutching his gun, watching William walk to his car and open the door, Charlie let out a long pain-stricken wail.

"Please, Charlie," Jonas whispered, "haven't you suffered enough?"

Jonas heard William's car roar to life. He saw his father put the car in gear and slowly begin to drive down the dark street. He held his breath, wondering what his brother would do. But soon, William's car turned a corner and disappeared from sight.

Thinking he had escaped the worst, Jonas relaxed and let out his breath. But then he heard the click of the gun being cocked. He looked back at Charlie and watched as his brother pointed the gun on himself, holding it to his temple.

"*No!*" Jonas screamed, trying to take the gun from his brother's hand. But it was no use; he couldn't physically stop him.

Jonas listened in terror as Charlie whimpered, trembling under the weight of what he was about to do. He had had enough. He couldn't take it anymore. Looking out to where his father had disappeared in the distance, Charlie bit down on his lip and shut his eyes.

Listening for the crack of the gun—the explosion that would end his brother's life—Jonas saw a light suddenly shine in the darkness.

Ring!!

It was the cell phone on the center console.

Ring!!

Looking at the screen, Jonas instantly recognized the number. It was Sarah. She was calling Charlie—at the moment his world was about to come crashing to an end.

Ring!!

But as Jonas stared at the phone, he began to think of what it would mean if his brother answered it. Would all those things the spirit showed him come true? Would Charlie find companionship with Sarah, and she with him if he answered this call? Would his half-brother take his place in his one true love's life?

Perhaps. But sitting in the car, looking at the light coming from the phone as it rang, Jonas realized that was exactly what his brother needed. He needed hope. A belief in something better. A future brighter than the one he was about to end. And if Sarah was going to start a life with Charlie, or if she wanted to start a new life with someone else altogether, it would be her decision, and hers alone. As much as it pained Jonas to think about it, he had to face the reality that he wasn't going to be the one at her side anymore. He had crossed over. Everything was different now. But even though Sarah couldn't be with Jonas in his new life, he could still take comfort in what she had already given him in the old one.

Seeing the life they had shared together flash before his eyes, Jonas suddenly remembered everything Sarah had done for him. She had taught him about kindness, goodness, empathy, and love. She had smiled and given him reasons to do the same. She had shown him how to find the good in others, even when he could see no goodness there. She sang with him and danced with him. She had taught him to look at the stars, to stare at the sky and feel small. To glance at each other in moments of silence, where their eyes could say far more than words ever could. But most of all, Sarah taught him to live a life with more wonder and amazement than Jonas could have ever known.

In thinking about this, Jonas knew these were lessons Charlie needed to learn. Whether Sarah simply became his friend, or something more, Jonas knew his brother would need that kind of hope in order to stay alive, to fight and stand up to the man who haunted his darkest dreams.

Watching the phone ring again, Jonas took a breath and leaned over his brother's shoulder.

"Answer it, Charlie," he said in a whisper. "Please—answer it."

Trembling, with the revolver still pointed at himself, Charlie looked down at the center console. He slowly lowered the gun and reached for the phone with his other hand. Though he didn't recognize the number on the screen, he pressed the green button to answer the call anyway.

Lifting the phone slowly to his ear, his feeble voice broke through the darkness.

"Hello?"

A female voice came from the other end.

"Charlie?"

Charlie's hand still trembled.

"Yes?"

"Hi . . . it's Sarah," she said. "You know, from the café?"

"Sarah?"

"Yes, it's me," Sarah said, sounding a little nervous. "I don't know why, but I just had the feeling to call you . . ."

Charlie's lips quivered as he tried to speak, but not a word came out.

"I just wanted to thank you," she continued, trying to fill the silence, "you know, for that poem you gave me. It was beautiful."

Charlie nodded, still unable to talk.

"And . . ." Sarah stumbled, "I was wondering also if perhaps, you might want to join me and a friend on Saturday at the park. We're going to have lunch, and I thought—maybe, if you'd like to come . . ."

Looking down for a moment, Charlie saw the gun in his hand. His fingers trembled as he pressed them against the cold, shiny metal. A glint of light from a nearby street lamp reflected off its surface. But hearing Sarah wait patiently on the other end, having invited him to spend an afternoon with her and a friend, Charlie looked back up, a new feeling slowly beginning to take hold.

"Sarah," he said, tears welling up, "I would like that very much."

Jonas watched as his brother pursed his lips, trying to keep himself from crying aloud.

"Great—I guess I'll text you or something, let you know where we are?" Sarah said.

Taking a short breath, Charlie nodded again.

"That would be great," he choked.

"Okay, then," she said. "I guess I'll see you later."

"Yes," Charlie whispered. "I promise, I'll be there."

He hung up the phone.

———

Sitting in the front seat with the phone still in his hand, Charlie leaned his head against the steering wheel and began to cry. The gun he had gripped so tightly fell to the floor as he sobbed into the darkness of the night.

"It's okay," Jonas said, tears coming to his own eyes. "It's okay."

36

WIPING HIS EYES WITH HIS SLEEVE, CHARLIE LOOKED AT the phone in his hand and did his best to control his emotions. Slowly dialing a number with an uneasy finger, he waited for someone to pick up.

Ring . . .

Ring . . .

"Hello?"

"Hello, Mom."

"Charlie?"

Charlie sniffed back his tears.

"Yes, it's me."

"Are you all right?"

Charlie glanced back out into the distance, looking at the place where his father's car had disappeared around the bend.

"Mom, I need you to listen to me . . ."

There was silence on the other end.

"I need you to take those photographs and get out of the house."

37

RAIN BEGAN TO PELT DOWN AS WILLIAM CHECKED HIS cell phone. The lights in the distance on either side of his car were refracted through the raindrops dripping down his windows. As he turned on the windshield wipers, he suddenly felt the instinct to check his rearview mirror. He didn't know why, but there was something that bothered him. He looked at the backseat. There was no one there, but he couldn't help but feel as if someone were staring right at him.

Shaking off the thought, William drove for quite some time, working through heavy traffic on the highway before eventually making it to his own neighborhood. After glancing a time or two more at the seat behind him, he soon saw his house up ahead, lights glowing from within.

Pulling into his driveway, William turned off the windshield wipers and shut off the engine. Then, grabbing a newspaper on the seat beside him, he held it over his head as he opened his door and ran toward the side of the house. Rain poured down in heavy sheets as he made his way quickly through the side door. Closing it tightly behind him, he shook off the raindrops that clung to his clothes.

"Carol?"

But there was no reply, just the smell of something cooking in the kitchen to welcome him home.

Still shaking the rain from his jacket, William walked to the kitchen. The room was empty, but there was a roast cooking in the oven, the timer above it still ticking away.

"Honey? Hello?"

He made his way through the empty downstairs rooms to the staircase.

"Carol," he shouted. "Are you home?"

Still nothing. William shook his head impatiently as he walked up the stairs.

"Carol? I'm home! Where are you?"

With every step he took toward the bedroom, William grew more and more uneasy. His wife should have been there, if for no other reason than she always had been. He could see that she was obviously in the middle of cooking dinner, but the uneasy feeling remained, making him fidgety as he searched through the house for his wife.

"*Carol!*"

William was growing angrier about his wife's absence. There was no note, she hadn't called, and it was pouring far too much for her to have gone traipsing over to the neighbor's house to borrow a cup of sugar.

Becoming even more anxious, and unable to shake the strange feeling that he was being watched, William began to make his way through the bedroom door. His brow furrowed as he tugged on the tie around his neck. But turning the corner, he looked down at the floor and saw something that made his heart stop cold.

Lying on the ground with its cover tossed to the side was a box. A large black shoebox. Empty inside except for a note and one small square photograph. William instantly recognized the photograph as one he had taken just two nights ago, of a little girl with hazel-green eyes and long, sandy blond hair. Seeing the note right next to the photo, William bent down toward it, fear in his gaze as he read the two words written there.

I'm sorry.

Trepidation turned instantly into rage, and William let out a sound like that of an animal as he grabbed the note and the photo, clutching them both tightly in his trembling fist. Then, looking up with crazed ferocity in his eyes, he walked quickly over to the bed, bent down, and pulled something out from underneath.

He drew out a small metallic box and reached for a key taped to its side. His movements were quick but methodical. He pulled the key from the side of the box, the tape tearing with it, and placed it inside the keyhole, turning it one-quarter clockwise to the right.

Lifting the small gray lid, William let out a cry. There was nothing inside but a few empty boxes of bullets.

He threw the box to the floor, got up from his knees, and walked back in the direction of the hallway. Making it through the bedroom door and toward the top of the steps, he pulled out his cell phone, speed-dialing a number.

The phone rang and rang as he walked quickly down the stairs. The call went through to voicemail: "Hello, you've reached Carol, I'm sorry I can't . . ."

Hanging up quickly, William dialed another number as he turned a corner on the first floor and entered his study. Striding across the room and rounding on a large red oak desk, he held the phone to his ear as he reached for a drawer, throwing the photo in his hand to the floor.

Ring . . .

Ring . . .

Ring . . .

"Hello," came a voice on the other end.

It was Charlie.

"Hi, Charlie," he said in a forced, lighthearted tone as he began rummaging through the drawer.

"Yes . . ."

"Hey, you haven't heard anything from your mother, have you?"

There was only breathing on the other end.

"Charlie?" William asked again.

Silence.

"Charlie . . . ?"

"Why do you ask?"

William stood up behind his desk for a moment, still as a statue, detecting a peculiar tone in his son's voice.

"I . . . ," he began to say, "I just have something I need to tell her."

Again, there was silence on the other end of the phone.

"*Charlie?*" William said as he began to flush with anger.

Then, Charlie replied in a voice that was more composed and

collected than William had ever heard from his son before.

"She's safe from you, and that's all that matters right now."

William's face contorted in fiery rage. He bent down and shoved his hand into the very back of the open drawer, pulling out a box like the one underneath the bed. Working quickly, a look of bitterness on his face, he opened the small box.

"You have no idea who you're dealing with, you little shit!" he hissed, his lips trembling as he lifted a gun from the box.

"No, that's just it," came Charlie's voice in reply. "I finally *do* know—and now I can do something about it."

William paused for a moment before reaching for a handful of bullets from the small metallic container on the desk.

"You're going to turn your father in—is that it?" William said, loading his gun as fast as he could. "You're going to send your father to prison for the rest of his life?"

William closed the spinning compartment of the revolver with a loud click.

"No," Charlie said, trying his best to control his emotions. "You've done that to yourself already."

William gritted his teeth with a nasty sound.

"I swear to God, when I get my hands on you . . ."

But Charlie cut him short.

"You're not going to," he said, a bitter resentment in his voice now. "Not anymore. You're done hurting people."

Shuddering with anger, William took a few steps around his desk toward the door, the gun gripped tightly in his hand. But before he could get very far, the interior of the study was suddenly illuminated with blue and red flickering lights.

Spinning around instinctively toward the source of the lights, William saw no fewer than five police cars pulling up in front of his house.

"It's too late, Dad," William heard his son say over the phone. "It's time you face justice for what you've done."

As though in slow motion, William dropped the phone to the floor, his mouth agape as he watched the uniformed men rush the house.

"Police—open the door!" an officer shouted. "William Graves—we have a warrant for your arrest!"

Standing in silence, it took William a few moments to turn around and notice the crumpled photo of the little girl at his feet. He saw her eyes staring up at him, a piercing gaze that ignited a fire of panic in his chest. With his knees almost buckling, he tried to steady himself.

Looking up in the direction of his bedroom, he pictured the empty black shoebox with the lid lying near its side. His wife had left with more than enough evidence to put him away for life. His son had called the authorities, who were at this very moment trying to break down his door. William tried to think of a way he could escape—escape the nightmare he felt he didn't deserve. But looking around, the only option he could find was the one still gripped in his hand.

And so, closing his eyes as he trembled, William pointed the loaded gun underneath his chin—and squeezed the trigger.

38

AN ECHO RANG OUT INTO THE NIGHT AS THE CONTENTS of William's head blasted onto the ceiling. Dark red blood and clots and pinkish gray brain matter fell with a *slop* onto the floor. Still trembling uncontrollably, William found himself with the gun in his hand, squeezing the trigger again.

Click.

This time the gun didn't fire. It just rotated to the next bullet chamber. He tried once more.

Click.

Click.

Click, click, click.

Slowly opening his eyes, William looked up, startled at the sight of blood dripping down from above. Taking a step back, he glanced down at his feet, noticing a body lying crumpled on the floor.

Reacting with a sudden flush of panic, William staggered backward as he watched blood gush out onto the floorboards; a deep red lacquer pulsating from a hole in the head of the corpse. It came out in throbbing squirts, spreading its stain all around.

Looking around the room with fear in his eyes, William saw a menacing figure suddenly appear as if out of thin air in the doorway. It was a man with white hair dressed in a dark black suit—and he was staring straight at William.

"Hmmmm," the man observed as he looked from William's disbelieving gaze toward the corpse on the floor. "Not too bad. Quick, clean, effective."

Looking deep into William's eyes, the man continued.

"You probably didn't even feel a thing, did you?"

Too terrified to speak, William took another step backward.

"Yes, William," the man said, walking slowly toward him. "You finally did it, after all these years . . ."

William took another step, trembling.

"And now it's my turn," the man said, as he stopped only a few feet in front of William.

Still gripping the revolver tight in his hand, William pointed it at the man and squeezed the trigger a few more times.

Click.

Click.

Click.

The man laughed.

"Come now, William," he said incredulously, "there's no use for that."

With a wave of the man's finger, William saw the gun fly from his grip as if by magic.

Terrified, William staggered farther backward, crouching on the floor, the corpse twitching lifelessly in front of him.

"Please, William, cowering does not become you," the man said, raising William with a mere gesture of his hand. "It's not me you should be afraid of . . ."

Feeling an invisible power bringing him to his feet, William watched with terrified eyes as the man pointed to a dark corner of the room where two other men stood. One, an older-looking gentleman with sandy brown hair, and the other, a handsome young man with bright blue eyes.

"*They* are the ones you should fear."

William looked again in the young man's direction, recognizing the color of his penetrating eyes.

"I'm sure you remember your son," the white-haired man said to William, pointing at the youth. "He looks a bit more lifelike now that he's not in a coffin, wouldn't you say?"

William felt his body begin to shake again.

"And the other," the spirit said, pointing to the man standing next to the youth. "I believe you two have something in common."

Spasms took control of William's feeble frame, as the man from across the room stared at him with a burning gaze.

"I'm sure you remember that little girl you like to spend so much time with. In fact, I believe you were coming back from her house just a few minutes ago."

William saw the man with sandy brown hair clench his jaw.

"Well, let me introduce you to her father, William," the man said to him. "His name is Michael. He and your son have been following you all the way home."

Panic overwhelming him, William dropped to his knees.

"Please," he begged, trying not to be overheard. "Please help me."

The man leaned over, his eyes ablaze with a darkness deeper than death.

"I'm sorry. What did you say?"

Still trembling, William glanced at the two in the corner, feeling another tremor of terror shudder through his body.

"Get me out of here. *Please* . . ."

The man before him smiled with an evil grin.

"Are you saying that you want to come with me?"

Nodding his head, William confirmed his desire to be taken from that place. As he lowered his eyes for fear of looking directly into the man's penetrating gaze, he saw the body before him again, noticing for the very first time the remnants of a face with one eye staring straight at him. Seeing blood oozing out of it like tears, he was gripped by a terrible, sickening sensation.

"Yes," the spirit mused, leaning in over William's shoulder. "Looks different from this perspective, doesn't it?"

William watched in horror as the man laughed again while reaching for him with an outstretched hand.

"Say good-bye, William. There's someone you need to see who's been dying to meet you."

Feeling the ice-cold grip of the man's hand on his arm, William glanced at the two still staring at him before everything went black.

———

Still twitching lifelessly on the floor, the body pulsated gore near the very same spot where William and the white-haired man had just vanished. After a small moment of silence, the older man gave his younger companion a nod, and the two suddenly disappeared from sight.

39

THERE, IN THE VOID, WILLIAM SAW TWO GREEN EYES emerge from the darkness.

"William," a voice said. "So good of you to come."

William stood, trembling.

"Please," the voice continued, "have a seat."

Too frightened to move, William whimpered as the green eyes drew nearer. He could feel them staring at him, burning into his very center.

The man who had brought him here bowed in reverence.

"Master."

Dismissing his servant with a simple gesture, the man with green eyes glanced back at William Graves. "I offered you a seat, William. Did you not hear me?"

Looking all around him, William searched for something to sit on. But seeing nothing more than coarse, black rubble all around, he simply stared back at the man before him, feeling more confused and more terrified than ever.

"Hmmm," the voice said sternly, "not interested in formalities, are we?"

The man with green eyes took a step in William's direction, unveiling his full, terrible stature.

"Well, then—perhaps you'd rather kneel."

———

Screaming out into the darkness, William could be heard inciting a new wave of tortured responses from other beings hidden in the void. But the sound that came from his lips did not sound like that of a grown man. It sounded much more like the voice of a little girl, crying out for mercy, adding to the chorus of animals and humans and the gnashing of teeth that echoed all around.

40

JONAS LOOKED ABOVE HIM AT THE BRILLIANT DISPLAY
of colors. As they intermingled and changed their hues, he was captivated once again by everything around him. He had been taken back
to the children's hospital, back to the Reading Room where he had
begun his journey. But now, as he sat on one of the plush sofas near
his mentor, an entirely different emotion began to take hold.

"Michael?" he said tentatively.

"Yes?"

"Can I ask you something?"

"Of course."

Jonas shifted in his seat a little before gathering the courage to
speak.

"Why didn't you ever tell me that she was your daughter?"

Michael took a deep breath and exhaled slowly, pausing for a moment before looking at something in the distance. He held his stare
for a while but soon began to speak.

"I'm sorry about that, Jonas," he said, glancing back. "I really am.
But with all the responsibility you already had on your shoulders, I
just couldn't add that kind of weight to your load."

There was another pause between them, as Michael looked at
Jonas and Jonas looked back at him. But as they sat underneath the
shimmering colors of the rainbow reflecting off the walls above their
heads, there seemed to be a silent understanding between them both.

"How long have you known?" Jonas asked, still a bit tentative.

Michael gave his companion a reassuring look. "Three years ago
last week, Gwen and I saw our bodies pulled from a car wreck in the
middle of the night. I'm sure you can appreciate how difficult it is
to understand how everything changes in a moment like that. But as

we searched through the smoke and twisted metal for signs of survivors, we thought that there couldn't be anything more frightening than being confronted with the sight of our own bodies."

Michael glanced away for a moment.

"That is, until we were shown what was happening to our little girl as she was being babysat that very night," he said, pausing once again. "It was my sister's husband. Nobody knew."

He wiped away a tear that was slowly falling down his cheek.

"It was in that moment that we learned there is a pain far worse than death," he continued, "which is why we've fought ever since to do whatever was in our power to give her comfort and bring her to safety."

Jonas felt the impulse to say something reassuring, but sadly, there weren't any words that could take away the sting of something so terrible.

"But then you came, Jonas," Michael said, his demeanor changing considerably, a new hope returning to his tone. "You were the one we had been waiting for, the miracle we needed to save our daughter."

Jonas looked away, feeling undeserving of such praise.

"You need to understand," Michael continued, "you not only saved Charlie's life, you gave him the courage to turn his father in. If he hadn't done that, the connection between William and our daughter might very well have been lost, and with it, the truth that will ultimately set her free."

Michael took a few more moments before resuming.

"But now, with the evidence your brother has given to the authorities, it will only be a matter of time before our little girl will have the chance at the life she deserves."

Jonas cleared his throat, looking his mentor in the eyes again.

"And your sister's husband?" he asked.

Michael nodded.

"The police will be showing up on his doorstep any moment now," he replied. "That's why I had to bring you back here. My sister is going to need some help with everything that is about to happen, and I think it's best I do that alone."

Hearing the sound of someone approaching, Jonas looked up to see Gwen.

"But, Jonas," Michael added, "I need to ask you a question of my own."

Jonas gave Michael a blank stare, wondering what his mentor could possibly want to know that he didn't know already.

"The phone call from Sarah," Michael began to inquire, "what made you tell Charlie to answer it?"

Jonas looked out into the distance for a moment as he contemplated the question, remembering just what had happened before he told Charlie to pick up the phone.

"It was you, wasn't it?" he said.

Michael looked at him questioningly.

"The call," Jonas reiterated, "you had to leave so you could get to Sarah, to get her to call Charlie before it was too late."

Michael looked at him empathetically, then nodded.

"Yes. But what made you tell him to answer it?"

Jonas thought for a moment.

"The light," he said. "The light from the cell phone. It lit up the entire car."

Looking at his younger companion with an even more confused expression on his face, Michael leaned in as if to hear Jonas better.

"What?"

"It was the light," Jonas reiterated, this time with a trace of animation. "The entire car was dark before, but when Sarah called, I just knew . . ."

"Knew what?" Michael interjected.

"I knew what my aunt had told me was true."

Michael stared at his younger companion as he waited for the answer.

"There is no place so dark, that light cannot lead the way."

Michael smiled.

"You're aunt's one smart woman," he said.

Jonas smiled too.

"She is."

A woman's voice suddenly broke the silence.

"Oh, Jonas!"

Jonas had nearly forgotten that Gwen had been making her way over to them. She had tears in her eyes as she rushed up to him, embracing him in a fervent hug, saying thank you as she squeezed him tighter than he had ever been squeezed before.

"Thank you, Jonas—you have no idea what this means," she exclaimed. "You're an angel! Do you know that? An angel!"

Feeling rather shy, Jonas blushed. But soon, there was another voice in the Reading Room—and turning to look, Jonas saw Aunt Claire with someone else behind her.

"Jonas, you're back!" Aunt Claire said, holding her arms out, running quickly in his direction.

Jonas smiled as Gwen stepped to the side, giving a clear space for his aunt to sprint toward him for a hug of her own.

He held his arms open as she ran up to him—but just before she gave him a hug, he held her back, confused, noticing a different-looking aunt than the one he had seen before.

"Aunt Claire?" he asked, holding her at arm's length.

Smiling in front of him, Jonas saw not a forty-year-old woman with tears in her eyes, but a much younger version; a contemporary, someone his own age.

"You're . . . ," Jonas stuttered, "you're young."

Aunt Claire laughed and gave him a hug.

"This is how I usually am," Aunt Claire said, with an even larger smile. "I had to make sure when I came to pick you up that I looked like I did before, so you would recognize me."

"And you?" Jonas said, turning to look at Michael.

Holding hands with his wife, Michael chuckled, giving Jonas's aunt a quick wink.

"Would you have really listened to someone your own age, with everything we had to tell you?" he said, glancing back at Jonas with a smile.

Jonas shook his head, chuckling himself.

"I suppose not," he said appreciatively.

"Well, then," Michael said, with a grin, "Now you know."

Then, right before his eyes, Gwen changed to a much younger, more beautiful version of herself. It happened with a flash of light, causing Jonas to hold up his hand in front of his face—but there she was, looking not a day over twenty-five.

Looking at Michael, Jonas raised his eyebrows, as if to give his mentor permission to do the same. But Michael just laughed even louder.

"Don't worry, I will one day. But I have a feeling I'm not done lecturing you yet."

Jonas laughed as well.

"Jonas," his aunt said, pulling his attention toward her. "Jonas, there is still so much to see—so much more for you to learn."

Jonas smiled, looking for the first time at the woman by his aunt's side.

"Elle has agreed to show you some of it too," Aunt Claire said, holding back a smile. "But there are a few people I think you should visit before we take you further into our world."

Looking at Elle, Jonas remembered her as the person he had seen when he first met Gwen—the young woman with the soft voice and piercing gaze.

"We'll be back to see Michael and Gwen soon," Aunt Claire said to Jonas, offering him a moment to say a short good-bye.

Jonas turned and slowly took a step toward his mentor, holding out a hand that was quickly pulled in for a bear hug.

"Thank you," Michael whispered in Jonas's ear, true sincerity in his voice. His eyes were wet with tears. "Thank you so much."

Once released from his companion's firm grip, Jonas found himself in Gwen's arms, as she smiled through watery eyes. She spoke to him softly and cried on his neck, offering him words of appreciation.

But soon, Jonas found himself arm in arm with his aunt as she escorted him with Elle at their side toward the large double brass doors that led to the interior of the great hall. Taking a last look at the mentor he had been privileged to be with all this time, Jonas gave Michael one last smile and mouthed a thank-you of his own.

———

Jonas looked up and saw birds flying in the air as they walked down the massive hallway, soaring high above the crowd of people around them. He passed the familiar rooms—the one with floating bubbles and the one with all the trees. But there were new rooms that he could swear had not been there before—a room of exotic animals and another that looked like a suspended wall of water, bright blue and orange fishes swimming alongside the children.

As they made their way toward the end of the hall, Aunt Claire gestured to the bolted door with the gold-leaf inscription above.

"This is where Elle will meet you when you return."

As the young woman matched eyes with him, Jonas felt the strange instinct to look away. He felt butterflies in his stomach that he couldn't ignore.

"Okay," he said awkwardly as he looked her in the eye again.

Elle nodded kindly and smiled. Curtsying, she turned around and walked toward the door.

As she walked away, Jonas caught himself silently staring at the light reflecting off her soft blond hair, creating the effect as if she were glowing.

"You know, I think she's taken an interest in you," Aunt Claire whispered as they both watched her open the door with the simple wave of her hand.

Jonas glanced at his aunt with a slight look of confusion.

"What?"

"Well, I can't be sure," Aunt Claire admitted, "but whenever she's around you, her eyes change color."

Jonas looked back toward the door.

"What color are they normally?"

"Brown," his aunt replied with a slight smile. "But when she's around you, they turn blue."

Jonas shook his head.

"Keep in mind," she added, "if you want to make a good impression in the future, it would be wise to brush up on your eighteenth-century etiquette."

Jonas smiled awkwardly, trying to figure out exactly what she meant. But before he could, another young woman approached. She had curly hair that hung down to the middle of her back, and a countenance that seemed positively radiant.

"Hello," she said kindly, "you're Jonas—Charlie's brother, right?"

Jonas looked back at her, nodding.

"Yes?"

"When you see him next, would you mind delivering a message for me?"

Jonas looked her over.

"Sure . . ."

"Would you mind telling him that I'm okay, and it's not his fault?"

Confused, Jonas looked at her a bit closer.

"I'm sorry, who did you say you were?" he asked.

The young woman smiled again.

"My name's Lily—I was Charlie's best friend growing up. Don't worry, he'll know what you're talking about when you tell him."

Still confused as to who this young woman was, Jonas saw her smile once more, just before she turned around to walk with a little girl who had been waiting for her in the distance.

Seeing the two hold hands as they made their way back into the heart of the hospital, Jonas just shrugged his shoulders and looked at his aunt.

"Are you ready?" Aunt Claire asked as she looked from the young woman to Jonas. She gestured toward the large golden door that marked the end of the spacious corridor.

Eager for what she had in store for him, Jonas nodded his head. Walking together side by side, the grand façade opened of its own accord before them.

———

What lay on the other side of the door was not what Jonas had expected. Preparing himself to be taken to another breathtaking wing of the hospital, he was instead met with the sight of his childhood home back in the mortal realm. It was a lovely autumn day; the sun was shining and the autumn leaves were falling around him. Colorful foliage of golden yellow and pumpkin orange trickled down from above as he stared at the house where he had spent most of his former life.

Walking with his aunt by his side, Jonas made his way across the lawn, up onto the porch, and through the front door. Turning a corner, he walked into the kitchen, where his family was gathered, plating sliced fruit and the special orange rolls his mother made every Saturday morning for brunch.

His brothers and sisters were seated around the table; his father and mother were together at the head. They had set a place for him too, Jonas noticed, in front of an empty seat. But before digging in like they usually did, Jonas saw his father hold up a hand to get everyone's attention. And then he did something Jonas had never seen him do before.

Bowing his head, with everyone else in the family following suit, Jonas's father said a prayer, his voice full of emotion.

"Dear God," he began, his wife squeezing his hand gently, "we want to thank you for this lovely day, and for this wonderful food that is set before us."

Jonas drew near as his father spoke.

"And Father," he said, pausing, "we want to take this time to thank you for our son and brother, Jonas."

Jonas listened as his father's voice quivered. A few of his siblings attempted to hold back their tears.

"We want to thank you for his presence in our lives, Father, and we pray that you watch over him with you in heaven," his father said, his eyes now brimming over with tears. "And please let him know . . . let him know that we miss him, and we love him."

Jonas's mother began to cry, letting go of her husband's hand to sob silently at the table.

Jonas glanced at Aunt Claire, and she gave him a nod, gesturing toward his mother. Leaning over her shoulder, Jonas closed his eyes, thinking of what he could say to let his mother know he was okay, to let her know that he would be all right, but most of all, to let her know he was still—and would always be—her son.

Whispering the words into her ear, Jonas prayed she could hear him.

"I love you, *Mom*."

Jonas's mother glanced up from the table. She stopped crying for a moment and looked around.

Jonas said something similar to his father and siblings and then watched as silence held the room, everyone in it feeling something they had never felt before.

"They know," Aunt Claire said, taking his hand as he walked back toward her.

Jonas looked back at them all, but feeling a gentle squeeze from his aunt, he found himself instantly transported to the front yard of another home, a home he had never seen before.

The weather was very much the same as it had been near his home: bright, shining, with leaves all around. But there was a woman he did not recognize in front of him, not many years younger than his own mother. She knelt in a small garden near a bed of flowers, using a small hand shovel to turn up the soil around her knees.

"Who is that?" Jonas asked.

Aunt Claire turned to look at him with an understanding smile.

"Mary," she replied, "your biological mother."

Startled, Jonas looked back at the woman in the small garden, her long dark hair pulled up into a bun. She began to place a flower bulb into the ground, covering it up with earth.

Jonas found himself walking toward her.

There was nothing out of the ordinary about her appearance. She was just a woman working in her garden, humming a tune on a lovely day. But as Jonas drew near, she stopped humming and held still for a slight moment before looking straight ahead.

Seeing her beautiful blue eyes flash before him for the first time, Jonas was drawn to this woman whom he had only known through the words of others. Remembering all she had been through, he felt a lump in his throat as he watched her in silence.

She was grown now, probably with a family of her own. There

was nothing to confirm this idea, but Jonas could see a calm assurance in her eyes, a sign that life had been better since those dark days long ago. He saw a man open the front door of the home, give her a wave, and ask if there was anything he could do to help. He was a tall, slender man with a friendly smile. Glancing back at his mother, Jonas saw her eyes light up.

She gave the man a wave, letting him know that everything was okay and she'd be coming in soon. Hearing this, the man smiled once again and walked back into the house.

Jonas turned around and took a step closer toward his mother. She grew silent once again. He knelt down right in front of her, looking into her deep blue eyes that radiated with love. He paused, thinking of what to say. Then, leaning forward, he softly whispered just two words.

"Thank you."

A rushing wind blew across the yard and the leaves from the ground swooped high in the air and fell lightly all around them. Still staring at his mother, he hoped she could feel the truth of his words.

"Sarah's waiting, Jonas," he heard his aunt whisper from behind.

Jonas looked to his aunt and then back at his mother, who now had her face buried in her hands. He knew she was crying, though he hoped they were tears of peace—the kind of peace that comes after a lifetime of wondering whether you had done the right thing.

She had.

After a few more silent moments, Jonas followed his aunt once again. But this time, she didn't instantly transport them to their next destination. Instead, Jonas found himself flying, crossing over mountains and streams, tall buildings and small houses, watching the world beneath him whiz by in a beautiful blur. And soon, he felt himself slow down and descend like a soft feather from above.

Beneath him, everything was glowing gold because of the shimmering colors in the beautiful fall trees. Still descending, he saw a fountain set in a stone basin in the midst of a beautiful park. It took him a second to realize where he was, but upon being lowered farther, he saw that he had come to Bethesda Fountain, one of his favorite spots in all of New York's Central Park.

He noticed a girl alone in the distance.

"Sarah . . ."

She was there, sitting on the edge of the stone basin that surrounded the fountain, with the silhouette of a statue arching high over her head. Looking up, Jonas recognized the statue as that of an angel, holding lilies in one hand, pointing in Sarah's direction.

"I've seen this before," Jonas said to himself, feeling as if he were having a moment of déjà vu.

Gazing at the lifelike statue, Jonas saw the figure's flowing robe and angelic wings, bringing to mind the vision he had seen immediately after his surfing accident.

"It's the angel," he said in astonishment, gesturing toward the statue while turning to look at his aunt.

"You've been here before, I take it?" Aunt Claire said.

"No," Jonas said, shaking his head. "I didn't see her here—I saw her that day, when I was in the water . . ."

Aunt Claire looked at him with an inquisitive expression.

"When I blacked out, right before I died, I saw a vision," Jonas began. "I mean, I don't know what it was—a dream or something, but I saw her"—he pointed—"that angel. She was flying to the ground, and Sarah was right there below her."

Aunt Claire looked at Sarah with an expression of wonder.

Jonas took a moment to let it all sink in.

"There's something else, though," he said, glancing down at the ground beneath his feet. "There's something else I haven't told you."

Turning to look at her nephew, Aunt Claire lifted his sad gaze with a gentle touch of her hand.

"Yes?"

"It has to do with what you told me," he began to explain, "when you first brought me to the hospital."

Jonas saw his aunt nod, as if she understood already what he was about to say.

He looked back at Sarah for a moment.

"There was something you said, something I don't think I really understood until now . . ."

Aunt Claire nodded once more, urging him to continue.

"I don't know, maybe I just didn't want to understand it at the time, but when you told me about heaven, you mentioned that it isn't a place you go to escape your fears. It's a place for those who have already faced them."

Aunt Claire placed a gentle hand on his arm.

"And what are you afraid of exactly, Jonas?" she asked as she drew him close, embracing him with one of her arms.

"I don't want to let her go, Aunt Claire," Jonas tried to explain, "I just love her—I love her so much."

He hesitated, tears coming to his eyes.

"And now?" she asked.

Jonas paused.

"Now I know I need to love her more than I was willing to before."

He looked back at his aunt.

"I need to give her the chance at life that she deserves."

Aunt Claire looked back at him with compassion in her eyes as she took her arm from his shoulder.

"I have a feeling she would like to hear that from you."

Taking his eyes from his aunt's tender features, Jonas looked again at the love of his life sitting quietly in the distance, waiting unknowingly for her world to end, so another, much brighter one, could begin.

Feeling his own instincts pulling him back, Jonas nevertheless took a step forward, trying to think of what he would say. As he walked slowly, meditatively, toward Sarah, he pondered on the words that could possibly express the feelings he held for her in his heart. But pain was all he could feel inside as he prepared himself to tell her what he knew he must.

Drawing near, he once again felt the strange sensation of what it was like to be by her side yet feel so distant, so far away. The invisible gulf was between them again, and even as he came close, he knew that it couldn't be bridged. He thought she probably wondered if there was a life after death, and if there was, if Jonas was still Jonas. But there was a life after death, Jonas knew, and he was still who he had always been—but now he had to watch the entire world pass before his eyes, without being a part of it like he had once been before.

But he had seen how the veil could grow thin, how others like Chris and Charlie could hear his whisperings in their minds and hearts. Hoping that Sarah could feel the same thing now, he sat down next to her, as near to her as he could, and he spoke in no more than a whisper, to the girl he still loved with all his heart.

"Sarah," he began, placing his hand just above hers. "Sarah I'm here."

Sarah looked down. Her hand twitched.

Jonas looked into her eyes as he saw a trace of confusion in them.

"Sarah, it's me—Jonas. I'm here."

Her confusion turned slowly to a look of pain.

"Sarah, I've come to you today to tell you something—something you need to understand . . ."

Jonas watched as she pulled her hand back from his, retreating into the safety of her mind.

Leaning in closer, Jonas reached for her hand once more.

"I've come to tell you something important, Sarah, but before I do that, there's something else I would like to say first."

Jonas hesitated.

"It's something I never told you before—a question I never asked you when I was alive. I think I was just too scared."

Jonas paused again as he gathered his courage.

"I thought I had more time—you know—like life would some-how never end, that you'd always be at my side. I wanted to ask you, Sarah, if you would be my wife," he whispered, tears now coming to his eyes. "I wanted to know if you would spend eternity with me, watching the sun rise each and every morning, dancing together each and every night. I wanted to hold you in my arms and never let go. Kiss you on your cheek and watch you smile. I wanted to give you all that I am, with the hope that you'd feel the same in return."

Jonas's head hung low as he prepared himself for what he had to say next.

"But then it happened," he said with trembling lips. "I don't know why—but it happened. I made a decision that changed the course of our lives forever. But looking back, I can't see any other way . . ."

He felt a tear run down his cheek as he watched Sarah bite down on quivering lips.

"And now as I look toward a future without you as my wife, I want you to know I regret this one thing."

Jonas looked into her eyes, taking in the moment as best he could.

"I regret wasting so much time, wondering if we were meant for each other—wondering if I was your soul mate and you were mine. Looking back now, it seems so foolish to have wasted so much of my life in doubt and fear."

Sarah turned toward him, staring in his direction, but seeing nothing.

"I wish I could turn back time, but I can't, Sarah. I just can't . . ."

Jonas felt his voice shaking.

"But even though you are there and I am here," he said, grasping for some ray of hope, "there is one thing that stretches into eternity on both sides of death's veil."

Looking into her eyes again, Jonas wished for her to understand.

"It is the love we shared, Sarah. The moments we had. As brief as it was, it gave the life I led more purpose than I had ever thought possible. To have felt the miracle of being loved by someone like you, and loving you in return with all my heart . . ."

Jonas looked down, reaching for the right words to say.

"That's what it's all about," he said in a feeble whisper. "The love that we shared. That's the feeling you take with you, Sarah—the only thing that matters."

Just then, Sarah locked eyes with him, staring straight into the blue sea of his emotions.

"I love you," he said, feeling like there was nothing at all between them now. "I love you more than you could ever know."

A tear began to fall from her cheek.

"And if I could do it all over again, I would never waste another moment without letting you know just how special you are to me."

Jonas felt the words swell in his throat.

"But since I can't give you the kind of life you deserve anymore," he said, tears falling freely now, "I want you to know, I love you more than to take that life from you."

Sarah lifted a hand in his direction, her fingers shaking.

"I love you, Sarah, and I want you to have the life that can still be yours—the husband you should marry and the children that will carry your light one day."

Jonas watched her through glossy eyes.

"And when the sun falls down, and life grows cold, I want to be there when you cross over to this side. I want to be the one to greet you when you make your way home. And even though I know that you will have given your heart to someone else, I hope you will remember the gift I am trying to give you this day."

Another tear fell from Sarah's cheek as a look of fear and loss came into her eyes.

"I want you to be free, Sarah, free to live the life you deserve, free to love the man you will choose one day . . . free to let your heart become one with another."

Jonas couldn't take it any longer; he had to look away, but as he did, he heard her whisper.

"Jonas . . ."

He looked up, and there, in that moment, he saw her and she saw him. She glowed like an angel, and his light shone on her. The fear, the trepidation, and everything else she had been feeling washed away as she basked in the light of the boy she once knew.

"I love you, Sarah," Jonas said, looking into her eyes.

"I love you too, Jonas," she said, knowing that he was there with her.

And with that moment—a moment they would each remember forever, Sarah held her hand to her lips and began to cry.

———

That afternoon, Jonas sat with Sarah, reliving some of their best memories together. There were times when she heard him better than others, times when she grew still, listening. Jonas even heard her laugh when he retold the story of their second date, when he had misplaced his wallet after taking her to a fancy restaurant, having no alternative other than to allow her to pay for their decadent meal.

It was the small things like this that mattered most. The touch of each other's hair. The taste of a kiss on warm lips. The sound of their breathing in a tight embrace. These memories wove the tapestry of their lives together, giving the days their meaning and the years their strength.

But Jonas knew they couldn't reminisce forever. The afternoon was coming on, and with it, a new host of experiences for each of them to live. Sarah would be in her world, and Jonas in his. But there was something sweet about their parting, something that gave their loss a new kind of hope.

Even though their lives had never been joined in marriage, they were entwined through love. And on both sides of eternity, that was something they could look back on with fondness—knowing that they were who they were because of what they had shared together.

———

"Sarah!" a voice from the distance shouted.

Coming from underneath a bridge near the fountain was Chris, waving his hand, jogging in their direction.

Sarah looked down and took a deep breath. Then, looking back up, she smiled. She had had her moment with Jonas alone, but now it was time for life to turn another page.

"Chris," she said with a newfound hope in her voice. "I'm glad you made it."

"Yeah, sorry I'm so late," he said, slowing to a walk.

"Are you okay?" he asked, as he reached her. "You look . . . different."

Sarah fidgeted a bit. "Something just happened," she started to say, "but, it's kind of hard to believe . . ."

"I'll be the judge of that," Chris said, remembering what he had said to her back at the beach.

Sarah began to describe everything she had felt over the past few days, culminating in this overwhelming feeling that Jonas had some-how been nearby. Having felt similar sentiments, Chris explained where he had been, and that he felt Jonas had come to save him in his time of need.

Sitting there all along, right by their side, Jonas listened, and smiled, and shed a tear or two as he heard them retell the miracles that had taken place. They were finally all together, sharing in the beauty and wonder of life, and it wasn't until they heard another voice calling out from the distance that they all paused to look.

"Sarah?"

It was Charlie. He looked a little tired and worn, but happy to be in the park on such a beautiful fall day.

Sarah turned toward him and smiled, standing up to introduce him to her friend.

"Charlie, hi," she said, a little timidly. "This is my friend Chris— Chris, this is Charlie."

They shook hands, but Chris held on to Charlie's for a split sec-ond longer.

"I'm sorry—have we met before?"

With that, Sarah began to laugh, and after a second or two, so did Charlie.

"What?" Chris said, joining in the laughter but not knowing why.

"It's okay," Sarah said, smiling genuinely for the first time in a long while. "He gets that a lot."

Jonas felt a hand on his shoulder, and he turned to see his aunt by his side. She had been there all along, standing at a distance, watch-ing everything unfold.

"Jonas," she said, "would you like to stay for a bit?"

Glancing at his friends, and then back at her, he wished for nothing more.

"Could I?"

Smiling, Aunt Claire nodded and gave him a hug.

"This is your day," she said pulling him close with a squeeze. "I think you deserve to spend it however you'd like."

Looking back at his friends, Jonas felt the impulse to run toward them as they all began to walk away.

"It's really okay?" he asked, just to be sure.

"Yes," she said, urging him on. "Have a good time, and when you're ready to come home, just call for me."

Jonas looked at her, a little confused.

"Call?" he asked.

Smiling, Aunt Claire turned Jonas around to point him in the direction of the angelic statue atop the fountain of water.

"You should know by now, Jonas, angels are never more than a whisper away."

———

It was one of the best days of Jonas's life, listening to stories of times gone by as Chris and Sarah shared their favorite memories of him. They visited some of the places they all loved to go, strolling for hours through the beautiful streets of Manhattan. The fall foliage fell from above, trickling down with brilliant colors, painting a backdrop to a city teeming of life. But when the night drew near, it came time for Jonas to say his good-byes—good-byes that he knew now wouldn't really be forever.

"See you later," he whispered to his friends.

And indeed, he would, one day.

SHARE THE CHOICE
HELP US BRING BOOK TWO OF THE SERIES TO LIFE

SHARE THE CHOICE .COM

ACKNOWLEDGMENTS

To my wife Andrea, for teaching me to smile, encouraging me to work, and never letting me give up even when I wanted to.

To Lane Anderson, for taking the time to reply to an email entitled: "How do you write a book?"

To Catherine Edwards, who, from the very beginning said, "This story needs to be told."

To my editor Jesse Coleman, whose mastery of the written word still makes me envious. Thank you ever so much.

To Natasa Lekic, for the years of guidance and hour-long phone calls discussing the future of this novel. I am in your debt.

To Ivo Horvat, for lending his vision generally reserved for Hollywood blockbusters so the world of *The Choice* could be seen.

To Martha Cameron and David Coen, for their work and dedication in polishing the final manuscript.

To all my wonderful friends who lent their advice, expertise, love and support through all the ups and downs.

And to H.A. and L.V., who I believe, by now, must be the best of friends.

ABOUT THE AUTHOR

Slade Combs is a New York-based commercial director. About this novel, he says, "Creating an entirely new world on a blank sheet of paper has been a terrifying, yet inspirational process. It is this range of emotions that I hope readers of *The Choice* come to enjoy."

Slade lives with his wife and two young sons in New York City. This is his first book.

Made in the USA
Lexington, KY
13 October 2014